THE BALLAD
OF
BISHOP HILL

Julie McDonald

*For Pat & Harvey Fife
with the warm good wishes
of the author,
Julie McDonald*

Sutherland Publishing
Sutherland Printing Co., Inc.
Montezuma, Iowa 50171

First edition 1985

ISBN 0-930942-02-7
Library of Congress Catalog Card Number 85-90372
Manufactured in the United States of America
by Sutherland Printing Company, Inc.

Dedication:
"For Scott Pearson,
the Swedish-American I love best."

THE BALLAD OF BISHOP HILL
A Novel
By
Julie McDonald

The University of Uppsala, Sweden, May, 1839—

The professor of theology made a neat pile of his lecture notes, dismissed the class and watched his students rouse themselves from daydreams of God knew what indecencies to rush from the lecture hall.

His discourse on the variations of natural theology, mysticism and revealed theology was one of his best, and he resented the waste of it. What louts they were, these budding ministers of the Gospel!

The boys from the forests and the Kjölen mountains had a natural affinity for things of the spirit, but once they came to Uppsala, they lost the laudable thoughtfulness of their lonely home places and became like the others—half-dead from long nights with the whores, muddle-headed from too much brännvin, or, if their financial condition warranted no other dissipation, hollow-eyed and sallow from self-abuse.

The ringing words of Luther struck no fire in these carnal breasts so quick to misappropriate the words of Arndt. Hearing the word "love," the students came to life briefly and affected salacious leers when he quoted, "Love is such an ambiguous virtue that human beings may be more easily deceived by it than by any other means. Therefore, there is nothing which we should distrust so consistently as love."

Divine calling? They heard none. Scrambling like their elders for artificial honors and hollow rewards, they regarded the priesthood as a secular occupation.

They seldom crossed the threshold of the University Library, that rich pearl of wisdom that had been adding layers of lustre since 1620. They never stood in awe before the Codex Argenteus, the Sixth Century Gothic translation of the Gospels by Bishop Ulfilas called the Silver Bible, preferring to idle about the old gardens and the Conservatory of Linneaeus.

The young barbarians would think him daft if they knew how he savored the past, how he sometimes joined his mind and spirit with that of Archbishop Jakob Ulfson, who founded the University in 1477.

He shivered in the empty hall and hugged the wide sleeves of his gown. The Walpurgis Eve welcome to spring was several weeks past, but the buildings still retained the chill of winter. Collecting his books and papers, he put on his stovepipe hat and walked toward the sunshine outside the open door.

The mass of black-billed white student caps with blue and yellow buttons was a flock of gulls bobbing on the Baltic. He blinked and looked again, seeing unfinished heads of clay in which the molder had lost interest beneath those caps, and then they were gulls again—squalling, quarrelsome eaters of refuse.

His students would become parish pastors who owned distilleries, lived in parsonages dank with green mold, used the bodies of any likely females, and bored their parishioners to distraction of a Sunday morning. And no one would complain. The authority of the Church was absolute. He stopped and gazed up at the spires of Uppsala Cathedral, despairing of the gulf between the ideal and the real.

Students eddied about him, bowing to his tall hat, the symbol of his doctorate, but caring nothing for the head that supported it. He suspected himself of a taste for suffering, which he deplored, but nonetheless he chose a passing student of theology and mentally dressed the pimple-faced youth with shifty eyes in a pastor's ruff, a heavy silver cross, a dark waistcoat and breeches, and a flowing cape.

He saw this cleric in a farmer's cottage preparing to administer the yearly test on sacred matters to the household. The women had scrubbed the floors until the boards were white as bleached bone, polished the copper pots to mirror sheen, and burned spruce twigs to give the room forest freshness. They had prepared all manner of delicacies to tease the pastor's palate, and coffee cleared with a bit of fish skin simmered on the coals.

The pastor, smelling strongly of brännvin, allowed the nubile, sixteen-year-old daughter of the house to take his cape, peering down her bodice with appreciation. He wore several heavy, gold rings which he twisted out of sheer boredom as he waited for the girl to return. He ignored the farmer, his wife, a girl of about twelve, and two small, wriggling boys who stood in a line before him like respectful serfs, waiting for him to begin.

He sniffed the coffee with approval. The real thing, not the everyday roasted rye with chicory. Under the pretext of looking at the clock, he stole a glance at the table and was pleased to see herring, jellied eel, meat balls, several kinds of cheese, wheat bread, and sugar cakes. These people had offered him more than they could afford, but he reflected that the sacrifice would be good for their characters. He had eaten a great deal at the last cottage and idly considered the Roman expedient of vomiting before continuing his feast but rejected it as too unpleasant.

The girl returned and took her place in the line. The tight lacing of her bodice pushed the globes of Venus high, prompting a comparison to the disadvantage of the pastor's housekeeper. He consoled himself with a coarse proverb, "One woman in bed is worth two in the pew."

The family stood there, expectant and frightened, waiting

for the pastor to begin. His mind, dulled by a surfeit of food and spirits, could not fix upon the proper questions. They swam past like fish until he finally caught one.

"Who are our masters?" he asked with his chin tucked low and his eyes as fierce as he could make them.

In ragged chorus they answered, "Our masters are all those who by God's ordinance are placed over us in the home, in the state, at school, and at the place where we work."

They yearned for some sign that they had answered well. That yearning was a palpable presence in the room, but the pastor did not feel it. He had not heard their answer, and only when the Mora clock struck did he realize that another question was required.

The professor froze the scene in tableau, then blinked his eyes to dismiss it. He could bear no more. He walked, looking down at the River Fyris with its many footbridges and the shops of old Uppsala. Why occupy oneself with bitter imaginings on such a fine day?

He passed the impressive mansion that was the home of the Västgöta Nation. An officer of Gustavus Adolphus had built it for his son, a student at Uppsala, paying for it with plunder from military campaigns of the Seventeenth Century when Sweden was a formidable power.

And now? King Charles XIV John, that Catholic Bernadotte turned Lutheran, was crowning his long reign with reactionary irascibility that made his earlier conservatism seem wildly liberal. The Riksdag was powerless against his opposition to any kind of reform. The Queen must find him difficult to live with, the professor thought, then laughed at himself for the notion. What might be friction in a modest house would dissipate in the spaciousness of a palace. If the aging but still beautiful Désireé wished to avoid the King, she could put countless chambers between them.

Sweden was a pendulum stubbornly stuck at the low center

of its arc, but so was the rest of Europe. In Prussia, Frederick William III was suppressing student societies, supervising university professors, and muzzling the press. Louis Philippe's July Monarchy in France was a government fixed in amber, impervious to change. Czar Nicholas I of Russia was a frightful autocrat, enforcing his will with the Third Section, a mysterious and terrifying body of secret police. Austria was like an airless room, its people ennervated by the weak-willed Ferdinand I, and Britain was ruled by a mere girl, Queen Victoria. In Spain, the throne was being contested bloodily by Isabella II and her uncle, Don Carlos. Only in Italy could the professor see stirrings of the liberal spirit. There, a group of young intellectuals was agitating for a Roman republic, concerning itself with the rights of the common man.

He shivered suddenly in the bright sunlight, fearing that the pendulum would pull free, and in so many places at the same time that the world would shake. "God," he murmured, "Your creation is in a fine fix!"

Leaning against a building, he removed his hat and tilted his face to the sun. Like all northerners, he drank in the warming rays with ecstasy, and the weighty affairs of the world vanished from his mind. Instead, he thought of the brevity of Swedish summer with a pang, remembering long and dark days. *What fools we Swedes can be, wasting our pleasure by imagining its absence!*

He straightened abruptly like a man who has fallen asleep in church, arranged his academic garb and retraced his steps to the library, where every season was the same. Books were the only antidote for his strange malaise.

Domta, Osterunda parish, Västmanland, May, 1839—

Charlotta Lovisa Jansdotter bundled branches from one fallen pine tree as her father chopped at the trunk of another tree. She wished she could help, swinging another ax in turn, but Pappa would not allow it. He always said he was glad for the four daughters God gave him and had no intention of using them for sons.

The ax head flashed and bit deep into the raw, golden vee, showering wood chips, and Jan Andersson traded his ax for the bucksaw, a tool best used by two men.

Charlotta knew the story of the bucksaw all too well. The saw was a gift. When Pappa had fathered two daughters and Mamma was pregnant again, it came. "May it bring you a son!" Instead, there was Charlotta. The saw, oiled and wrapped in a length of old linen, lay on a shelf in the barn until Sabina's birth. No sons, not ever. Jan Andersson learned to push and pull the bucksaw alone.

The tree was ready to fall, and Charlotta turned her head, not wanting to see it go down. The saw rasped, the branches sighed through the air, and the impact of the trunk shot through her wooden clogs and tingled in her legs. The tree was dead forever. An oak might live again in fireplace flames, but pine blazed too quickly and spewed out dangerous explosions of pitch. Pine was suitable for making furniture and fenceposts, but there was no need. Generations of her father's family had made such things to last. This tree would be cut into dead rounds and rolled to the edge of the forest. Pappa would plant barley where it had stood.

Pappa chopped off some branches, and when Charlotta carried them to the burning pile, they bled pitch. They didn't yet know they were dead.

He mopped his brow and leaned on his ax handle. "That's enough for now, Lotta. Go and enjoy the sun for a little. We wait for it so long, and it runs away so fast!"

"Thank you, Pappa!"

He knew that she liked to be alone. That part of her was like him. Sometimes when the winter stretched long and the cottage was thick with the smell of sausage, smoked fish, strong soap, and wet wool, he clawed at the throat of his shirt and ran out into the cold to be alone. He loved the plowing season when he could be by himself, pushing the blade deep while he thought his own thoughts. When old Mayrose died, Mamma urged him to get another horse, but he said he didn't mind pushing the plow himself. Besides, if he didn't have a horse, he could not be forced to spend a day at the post house driving people wherever they wanted to go when his name came up on the province governor's list. Pappa hated to have anyone tell him what to do, and, she thought, *so do I!*

"Why are you standing there dreaming?" Pappa said with a laugh, "I know how you love to ramble!"

She quickly chose a direction and gathered up her red and black striped skirt to run, curling her toes to hold her wooden clogs in place. Tomorrow she would be fifteen and everyone would expect her to behave like a grown-up, but today she would run and skip like a child. She wondered if she would feel different inside when her parents and sisters, dressed in their best clothes, brought real coffee to her in bed and wished her another good year? Probably not until Pappa pulled her close to measure her height and said, "My *flicka* is fifteen years high!" Those words would make the added year real.

Running was lovely, but it made the trees and the sky jump up and down. She slowed to a walk to look around her with pleasure. At the edge of the pines, the birches sprouted shy, curled leaves. The ash trees had thousands of narrow, green fingers, and the beeches mixed their new leaves with the stubborn yellow ones of another spring. Those yellow leaves had seen her last birthday, and soon they would fall to the forest floor and be forgotten like the year she was leaving behind.

She moved on to the pines, enjoying the springy carpet of

needles underfoot, the light filtering through heavy branches, the silence. Some people were uneasy among the pines, but she found them patient and friendly. She laid her hand on a sticky trunk in silent apology for that murder at the edge of the barley field, breathing the pungent smell of resin. So little sunlight came through the pine branches that she soon felt cold and hurried toward a break in the trees.

An underground stream emerged in what some people called the Troll Clearing. They thought the lichen-covered boulders were trolls turned to stone, but Charlotta knew better. Her father's grandfather, Axel Pehrsson, had gouged the boulders from his field with an iron bar and brought them here in his cart. The tale of his great strength was still told.

She knelt beside the stream and gazed at her broken reflection in the fast-moving water. Why must she have braids as brown as dried walnut hulls? Her oldest sister, Carolina, had hair as bright as the flames of the Santa Lucia crown.

She gathered an apronful of blue hepaticas and tried to weave them into a garland. They were too small. The stems broke. Ready to brush the blooms from her lap, she thought of using a pine branch as a base. It twisted nicely into a circle, holding the tiny blue blossoms like set jewels, but it also pricked her scalp.

She knelt to look at the effect in the stream and confirm what she already knew. Crowning herself with a garland was like putting a necklace on a pig! The dark hair was bad enough, but her eyes were the real problem. They peaked in the center of the lid. Mamma said this was a Finnish characteristic. Someone far back in the family lived in Finland long before the Russians took it away from Sweden. Cousin Erik was the only one who liked her eyes. He called her "Little Pine Tree" because they reminded him of the tip of a young pine.

Charlotta sat back on her heels, thinking about Erik. If she felt different and ugly, what must *he* feel? His forehead was scarred from a fall from a wagon when he was little, his brother accidentally chopped off his finger with an ax, and his teeth stuck out until he could scarcely close his lips. What were brown hair and odd eyelids compared to all of that?

Of course Erik didn't care about such things, and why should he? God had spoken to him. It was five years ago, just before her tenth birthday. Erik had fits and rheumatism then, but one day when he was plowing, God said, "If ye shall ask anything in My name, I will do it." Erik asked God to forgive his lack of faith and give him good health, and he had been well ever since. No fits, no pain.

Erik had married his mother's housemaid, much to Aunt Sara's disgust, and they rented a farm at Vappeby. No one understood how a farmer who balanced a book on the handles of his plow could prosper, but Erik did, and soon he had enough money to buy Lötorp estate. God certainly was on his side.

A bold idea came to Charlotta as she thought about Erik. She pushed forward to a kneeling position, cleared her throat, and said diffidently, "God, do you have anything to say to me?"

A bird trilled. A calf's bawl came from a great distance. God said nothing.

"I *am* Erik's cousin," she said bitterly, "and there were things I wanted to ask You!"

The stream dashed against the rocks in its bed, mocking her. The slant of the sun was much lower than when she had left Pappa, and she felt guilty for staying away so long. She got to her feet and ran back through the pines.

When she reached the edge of the barley field, her father was nowhere in sight. He had felled two more trees while she was gone, and his ax lay beside another pine with a single cut in its trunk. Pappa would not leave the ax if he meant to be gone long. The ax was his pride, sharpened each night and hung on the wall. No doubt he had gone into the trees to relieve himself.

She bundled more branches and stacked them on the pyre. Some resisted her small knife, and she went for the ax, thinking Pappa wouldn't mind. As she stooped to grasp the handle, she saw the pinkish-brown film on the blade. The deep, cold fear that told her to hurl the ax from her struggled with the practicality that insisted that she carry it home. She could not throw it from her because it was Pappa's and he would need it. Her hands seemed frozen around the handle.

She ran, gasping for breath, and when she reached the doorstep, the ax fell from her grasp, knicking its blade on the stone. Her hands flew to her mouth in horror. She felt their stickiness and remembered the garland, snatching it from her hair and throwing it behind Pappa's neatly stacked woodpile.

I won't go in. If no one tells me, it won't be true.

But she had to go in. Herta Olsdotter, the healing woman, motioned her inside as she came to the door with a basin filled with bloody moss.

"If you have anything to say to your father, you'd better hurry!"

Charlotta felt cold. The core of her body had turned to ice. "What—what happened?"

"The ax slipped and hit his groin—where the blood flows fast. This moss is good for bleeding, but it isn't doing much for him!"

Charlotta looked at the door to her parents' bedroom, a small partitioned space just off the kitchen. She heard her mother's soft weeping and the wails of her sisters. She could not move.

The healing woman gave her a push, and she found herself wedged between Sabina and Anna-Maja staring down at the bed. Pappa's face was white and still. Even his calloused hands were pale—the color of coffee with a lot of cream.

"Oh Pappa!" she said weakly.

His eyes opened to a narrow, glinting line, and one hand moved slightly on the quilt. Charlotta placed her own hand in the upturned palm. Cold. Cold as a newly-caught fish.

"Oh Lotta," her mother wailed, "why didn't you stay with him?"

He struggled to speak. "I—I told her—she could go—what could she have—done—anyhow?"

Herta Olsdotter came in, holding the quilt over the wound as a screen while she worked with one hand to remove the sodden packing and replace it with fresh moss.

"Do you want to send for the priest?" she asked.

Jan Andersson moved his head from side to side on the bolster. "No—" he said with a faint smile, "I need—no one—to introduce me—to God—"

Charlotta's hand was pulled from Pappa's as her mother fell to her knees beside the bed, cradling his head in her arms and cried, "Jan, I have loved you!"

Charlotta tried to back away, but the wall of the small chamber held her where she stood. She thought it wrong to see or hear what passed between her parents now—Mamma's voice—her words—Pappa whispering, "Anna!" She closed her eyes and pressed her hands hard against her ears.

But she could not escape Mamma's anguished cry, "Oh God, no! Jan!"

Herta Olsdotter elbowed between Charlotta and Anna-Maja to hold a polished metal disc before Pappa's nostrils. It shone without a trace of clouding.

Charlotta stood against the wall a pillar of ice, while her sisters sobbed and shrieked. Mamma sat at the head of the bed holding Pappa's upper body, looking at the dead face, then staring at a corner of the ceiling in blank disbelief.

Charlotta had the strange feeling that she had seen all this before, but it couldn't be. No, she was remembering the Popish picture a long-dead sailor relative had brought home as a souvenir of his voyaging. Mamma kept the sad Mary and her dead Son in the painted chest in the *formak* in memory of her cousin Bertil. That picture always made Charlotta want to cry, but she could not cry now. Tears of ice would not flow.

She was a clock with a broken mainspring, a timepiece that forever records the time of its breakdown until other fingers move the hands.

Osterunda parish, spring and summer, 1839—

The funeral sermon was familiar. Pastor Nilsson said the same words and paused in the same places at every funeral. Charlotta thought Pappa should have special words, spoken for him alone. She pleated her yellow mourning apron with angry fingers until her sister Carolina captured her hands and forcibly folded them on her lap.

Shutting her mind to the sermon, she stared at the vaulting arches of the whitewashed ceiling. A crack in the whitewash revealed the barest touches of pink, blue and green. Long ago, Osterunda church had been painted with Popish images, people said, robed figures with rings of light above their heads, but that was before God spoke to Martin Luther.

The weathered, old crosses in the graveyard outside the church were from that time. They prayed for the dead then, she had heard, and she wished she could do it now, but Pastor Nilsson said it was too late. Could he be wrong? The thought was her first challenge of the Church, and it made her sit straighter to bolster her courage.

The service ended with a mumbled prayer, and Cousin Erik went to the altar with his three brothers, his father and the shoemaker from Torstuna to carry the tapered coffin to the graveyard. As they lifted the coffin from the trestle, Mamma gave a stifled gasp and Charlotta's sisters whimpered softly, but she could only stare, dry-eyed, at the smoothly-sanded lid that covered her father's face and feel cold, frozen. Pappa had made that coffin himself, carving and sanding in the long, winter days when he could not work outside. Every decent family had at least one coffin ready for eventual need.

She walked with Mamma and her sisters behind the pall-bearers out of the church, into the warm May sun she could not feel. To her, it was December.

Not wanting to see the coffin touch earth in the grave, Charlotta turned away. Her eyes fell on Maja-Stina, Erik's wife. Pregnant again. Two babies dead from breast fever and whooping cough. Another child would help Maja-Stina forget the two she had lost, but there was no such comfort in the loss of a husband and father.

"For dust thou art, and unto dust shalt thou return," said the pastor. His hand blurred as he threw earth to the coffin lid. The rasp of impact struck Charlotta's ear with the force of a gunshot. She winced. "Amen!" said the pastor.

Mamma and Aunt Sara wept in each others' arms and Charlotta's sisters sobbed aloud. She could not cry and felt she must get away before anyone noticed and thought her hard. How she wished she *could* cry!

She forced herself to walk slowly, moving toward the bell tower beside the church. Pappa had laughed when she told him the wooden frame looked "like a lady all laced tight." But he laughed in a pleasant way, seeing it as she did, not with the scorn that her fancies brought from others. Now there would be no one to share things with, no one to care what she saw or thought. She stroked the weathered timber of the bell tower sadly.

The funeral feast of black-dyed mourning foods was waiting at Domta, and there would be the ceremony of cutting a dozen small firs as a sign of respect to the dead. And when all that was done, what then? Who would plow the fields Pappa had planted? Who would cut up the trees he had felled? Women alone, how could the five of them live?

"Lotta?"

She caught her breath at the sound of Erik's voice and rubbed her eyes hard with her fists to redden them before she turned to face him.

He smiled at her, baring the outward thrust of his long, broad teeth. The hand with the mutilated finger grasped her arm. "You are not to worry, Lotta. I will be a guardian to your family. I'll register that intention with the parish officials tomorrow, and since God has prospered me, I'll send one of my hired men to do the field work at Domta."

"Do you read minds, Erik? I was just worrying about how we would manage."

"Of course I do! God has given me that gift. I'm glad to see that you are facing this loss with serenity, Lotta. Your behavior shows that you understand we are in the hands of God and must accept what He brings into our lives."

Charlotta opened her mouth to protest, to tell him that she was not serene, not ready to accept Pappa's death, but he was too busy talking to listen to her.

"I tell you, Lotta, Lutheranism is a stinking corpse, crawling with the maggots of a dead liturgy!"

He says he reads minds, but it cannot be so. If it were, he would know how it is with me.

"We must go back to the simplicity of the early Church to find a new and better faith. I'll teach you, Lotta!"

Charlotta resisted him inwardly, remembering how skeptical Pappa had been of Erik's revelations. "He wants to be a new saviour," Pappa had said, "and there is no need." She would allow Erik to help them in other ways gladly, but her soul was not his concern. She was, after all, a good Lutheran. She knew the catechism and could answer any question when the pastor paid his yearly examination visit and made away with a huge bowl of Mamma's *papilan hätävara*, a Finnish sweet of lingonberry preserves folded into whipped cream. She always wished the pastor would leave enough for their supper, but he never did. One *had* to be a good Lutheran in Sweden. No one could marry without taking communion first, and anyone who testified in court had to give proof of taking the sacrament within the year. Since no one could take communion who could not read, everyone learned. She and her sisters had been taught, first by their mother, and then by a spinster from Enkoping who came to the country for her health.

Erik was still talking, unaware that her thoughts were elsewhere, and when he paused for breath, she suggested that they start for Domta. The guests were there already.

She hurried to help with the platters of mourning food, moving quietly through the constrained gathering. After much scrubbing, only a faint shadow of Pappa's blood showed on the oak floor. No one else would notice, but Charlotta saw the bloody trail in all its freshness and stepped over the marks carefully.

The house had been cleaned as for a celebration, but like an embroidered flower, it had no life. Copper pots shone from their hooks on the wall, reflecting the serious faces of relatives and friends. Every chair and bench in the house was in use. Two people sat on Mamma's painted chest and others leaned against the loom that held a partially finished wool coverlet dyed with the expensive indigo that had been Pappa's Christmas gift. Charlotta thought she saw a speck of blood in the weave and wondered if Mamma ever would have the heart to finish the coverlet.

As the evening wore on, Erik's father brought out a jug of brännvin to pass among the men. Erik refused it, saying that he objected to contributing *riksdaler* to the distillery owned by the pastor.

"Come, come, Erik!" his father said, "You know that the distillery goes with the living, and where else can I buy brännvin?"

"That man allows his parishioners to put a whole crop into the bottle!" Erik said angrily, "They have nothing left to eat!"

"He pays them for their rye and potatoes."

"Not enough by half! He strikes his bargain when they are befuddled by drink, and their children suffer for it! Do you realize that Sweden consumes at least 40,000,000 gallons of brännvin a year?"

Talk, talk, talk. Charlotta left the room and stretched out on the bed where her father had died, the only place where she could be alone. They were still talking about brännvin out there, and she was reminded of the first time she tasted it. She begged and begged for a sip until Pappa said she could have it. He broke off a chunk of the hardtack round baked at her birth and strung on a pole near the fireplace between Anna-Maja's and Sabina's. Soaking the rock-hard fragment in brännvin, he gave it to her and watched gravely as she choked and spat it out. Then, as now, the house was full of relatives, and they all laughed, all but Pappa, who said, "Sometimes we find we do not like what we think we want, Lotta."

"Oh Pappa!" she whispered, clutching the bolster and finding no comfort in it. Then Sabina was shaking her arm.

"You have to come. We're carving the grave marker."

The ritual was performed in silence except for the scrape of the knife on the oak slab. Erik's father carved the first letter of Pappa's name. Then Aunt Sara took up the knife, followed by her children. Erik's sister cut the "e" too shallowly, and Erik deepened it. He did the same for Sabina, whose pudgy hands were not strong. When the knife was passed to Charlotta, she shook her head. "Let me be last."

"That is for your mother, Lotta," Erik said.

She sighed and took the knife. Her letter was the "o," which required a steady pressure. When she finished, it was not a perfect circle, but an upright oval, a cat's pupil. She bit her lip in vexation and gave the knife to her mother for the carving of the final "n".

Erik cut the dates of Jan Andersson's life, 1802-1839. The beginning and the end. It was written.

At last, Charlotta burst into tears. Erik held her while she wept, and she accepted his strength and authority just for the moment—the way a newly-broken horse accepts the bit— with the tremulous yielding of exhaustion.

***

In August, Erik's parents moved from their Torstuna home to a new house they had built in Osterunda parish. The handsome dwelling was called Klockaregarden, and it had double chimneys, a tile roof and a grand front door under a carved cornice.

Erik was to dedicate the new house, and the event would be the first outing for the family at Domta since the death of Jan Andersson. Charlotta and her sisters bathed in a big, wooden tub before the hearth and dressed in their best clothes, tying yellow mourning aprons over their skirts.

"It will do Mamma good," Carolina whispered, "she hasn't been out of the house for three months, and she's starting to act like an old woman!"

Charlotta shrugged. She felt like an old woman herself, and she couldn't sympathize with Carolina's yearning to resume the old round of dances and flirtations.

They walked toward Klockaregarden through the twilight in silent, almost military formation. When Sabina broke away to pull some moss from an old split rail fence, Mamma pulled her back roughly.

"There will be no laughing or acting foolish tonight!" she said sharply.

A candle glowed from every window in the new house, and Aunt Sara stood in the open door to welcome them. Inside, they dutifully admired the fine corner fireplace, saying it was the most beautiful *spis* they had ever seen. They praised the painted molding of scrolls and leaves and the niche built in the best room for Aunt Sara's pride, her blue tile stove.

When Charlotta was small, she had willed herself into the pictures on those stove tiles, walking on blue cobbled streets and gazing at strange and beautiful towers. She told Pappa about it once, and he nodded with a faraway look in his eyes. He told her that he had wanted to go to sea from the first time he saw the Baltic, but the land held him fast. She stared at the stove, trying to enter one of the blue scenes in the old way, but she could not. This room and the people in it held her fast.

Aunt Sara was saying, "Erik will ask the blessing on the house, and then we will eat."

"Where is he?" Sabina asked, casting an eager eye at the table.

"Praying in the bedchamber. He'll come when he's ready."

Charlotta fixed her eyes on the door and waited. When the door opened silently on its new hinges, Erik stood back-lighted by two lamps, taller than life. His eyes glittered. Ice chips in winter.

"Beloved friends," he said, "you all know what God has done for me, and He will do as much for you if you believe. The faithful are without sin and capable of healing—of casting out demons!"

"I thought he was going to pray," Carolina whispered, "and now he's preaching a sermon!"

It was all the same to Charlotta. She stared at the scrolled

molding and retreated into her own thoughts. Though she
conformed to the demands of religion, she didn't expect God
to do anything for her. At the very moment when she tried to
speak to Him, He was readying a great sorrow for her. Why
should she listen to talk of God?

Tiring of the molding, she shifted her gaze to the people in
the room. Sabina had tied knots in the corners of her mourning apron and bunched the cloth around her fist to make a
cat that wiggled its ears. Mamma, her mournful face framed
by the starched, white Västmanland cap, was turned to Erik.

Erik's brothers, Peter and Jan, sat with their wives and
children, leaning forward as they listened, but Karl, the
youngest brother, cleaned his nails with a pocket knife. Karl
was embarrassed by Erik.

Aunt Sara glowed with pride in her son, Uncle Johannes listened with calm satisfaction, and Maja-Stina gazed at her
husband with adoration, stroking the downy head of their
baby son also named Erik.

Two housemaids stood in the kitchen door, and the heads
and shoulders of the hired men could be seen at the open windows of the *formak.*

How was it possible that Erik, a sickly and ugly young
man who shunned company could now be heard with such attention and respect? He had a harsh and rasping voice that
annoyed the ear, and yet they listened to him as if to music.

"Beloved, you see in me a God-sent prophet, the vicar of
Christ on earth! God has determined to reveal through me
His mysteries, and I will shed the greatest light since the
time of the Apostles!"

What a thing to say! This man was her cousin, a farmer,
and he had teeth like a great, gnawing animal.

"Abide in me, and you are sinless—now and forever!"

No! she said silently, *No!*

***

Those who heard Erik preach at the dedication of Klockare-garden begged him to hold another service, and when he agreed to a meeting at Lötorp, his own home, the crowd was so large that he preached from a wagon in the yard.

One servant told another about that service, creating a clamor for still another conventicle in a forest clearing where there would be room for all. Erik chose the Troll Clearing.

Asked by a hired man if his sermons could substitute for Sunday services at Osterunda church, Erik leaped to one of Axel Pehrsson's boulders and shouted, "Listen to me, all of you! I do not preach to take the place of Sunday worship—I only give you more. As Swedish subjects, we are bound to the State Church. You who do not own property are subject to your patrons. Do not offend your masters by staying away from church!"

***

Pastor Nilsson mumbled through the opening liturgy from the steps of the altar, then climbed to the pulpit to deliver his sermon.

Charlotta listened while he announced the text for the day, the first verse of the 29th chapter of Proverbs. The priest's face was deep red, almost purple above the white ruff. Strange.

"He, that being often reproved hardeneth his neck, shall suddenly be destroyed, and that without remedy." He read with deep anger, then stared straight at the pew where the family from Lötorp sat. "How fitting are these words of Scripture! It comes to my ears that a farmer of this region is handling sacred matters without knowledge, without ordina-ton—" he paused for a deep, quivering breath and the awful color of his face deepened, "This is a scandal, a heresy—a—" with a throttled cry, he stiffened and toppled, sliding head-first to the bend in the pulpit stairs.

Shock paralyzed the congregation until the pastor's house-keeper gave a piercing shriek. Then two men sitting near the front of the church rushed to the fallen priest. One of them put an ear to his chest and got up slowly, shaking his head.

Erik silenced the rising confusion and took charge. He told the men at the pulpit stairs to carry the body to the parson-age and went to the big Bible.

"Beloved," he said, "in the 29th chapter of Proverbs we also read, 'The fear of man bringeth a snare; but whoso put-teth his trust in the Lord shall be safe.' Go to your homes in peace. The church authorities will send you a new pastor."

"Why can't it be you?" cried a housemaid, "This must be a sign!"

"I seek no signs. God speaks to me plainly, and I will share His truth where He directs. This is not the place."

The church emptied quickly and silently. Charlotta saw the pastor's housekeeper approach Erik and heard her say, "Did you strike him dead, Erik Jansson?"

"I have the power, but I did not use it today. God will let nothing stand in my way as I reveal His truth. *He* has van-quished this false preacher!"

Shaken by the events of the morning, Charlotta was more ready to respect her cousin's authority than before.

The University of Uppsala, September, 1839—

The professor crossed the arching bridge over the River Fy-ris to splash through puddles on the stone walk leading to the small restaurant where he took coffee after his first lecture of the day.

The proprietor greeted him respectfully and bore away the

stovepipe hat in hands wiped clean on a starched, white apron. The young woman who always served the professor scurried before him to wipe the already shining table she knew he would choose—in the back, away from the draft of the frequently opened door. She pulled out his chair with a bobbing bow, and he smiled at her absently, knowing his coffee would arrive without summons.

With the morning post in hand and as yet uninspected, even a cloudy day was bright with possibility. Putting aside a bill from his tailor, he unfolded newspapers from London and Paris to relax their creases while he read the letters, a treat deferred. He paid scant attention to the notice of a learned society meeting, winced at a dinner invitation from a colleague who employed a notoriously incompetent cook, and took up the remaining letter with resignation until he recognized the handwriting with a leap of pleasure.

Old J.J. Risberg, his classmate, his friend of shared lodgings when they were young enough to believe they could change the world, had written to him after long silence. He turned the letter in his hands, admiring the impression of J.J.'s signet ring in the red-brown wax of the seal. The initials were as sturdy and forthright as their owner.

Dear Jeremiah, whose name in no way fit, was not the man to "Go and cry in the ears of Jerusalem," but he was decent and helpful, demonstrating the love of God in a thoughtful, quiet way. J.J. was not an eloquent preacher—too diffident— but if just one of the professor's students became the pastor, the calm shepherd that J.J. was, he would die happy. He broke the seal and unfolded the letter.

"My Dear Jakob, I've been posted, unexpectedly, to Osterunda parish, Västmanland. Bengt Nilsson, who had the living there for so many years, died suddenly of burst blood vessels. He met his Maker in the pulpit, actually, terrifying his poor flock.

"My first official act was to refuse purchase of Nilsson's distillery. As you know, I have no head for business, and besides, I believe that a man with three glasses of brännvin in him is primed to do whatever work the Devil has in mind. Not that I object to spirits altogether—I have warm memories of the occasional glass you and I enjoyed together—but let the excess that human nature embraces be on someone else's conscience! Are you shaking your head at me, old friend?

"Now to my first unofficial act. Nilsson's good housekeeper, Manda by name, lingered at the door of my bedchamber the first night I slept in the parsonage. She stood with lowered eyes and great internal agitation, determined to do her duty, until I said "good night" to her firmly and knelt for my prayers. I cannot say that I was flattered by her infinite relief, Jakob, but she smiled at me with true human feeling in the morning and served me an excellent breakfast.

"My parishioners accept me provisionally, but they invest their emotions in another preacher. Tell me, Jakob, do you believe that God still speaks to man in the Old Testament manner? Five years ago, a farmer of this parish, who then lived at Torstuna, heard the voice of God in a field and was cured of seizures and rheumatism. He lived quietly with his miracle until recently, when he began to preach in private houses.

"This Erik Jansson appeals to the serving girls and the hired men, and they come to hear him in such numbers that he has moved his conventicles to the fields and forest clearings. The people believe that Providence has delayed the fall rains to let him be heard.

"I heard him myself. The people were frightened when I showed up in the clearing because they expect repression from the State Church and usually get it, but I was delighted with the man! His eyes blaze when he speaks of 'blowing the dust from the Scriptures.' He holds some of the views we

once cherished, Jakob, and I cannot fault him for wanting to
scrape away the moss of the centuries to reveal the ardent
faith of the early Church—as long as he gives God the glory.

"As God so often does, He has chosen an unlikely vessel.
The man is ugly, but I remind myself that the pre-figured
Christ of Isaiah was "one from whom men hid their face."

"Jakob, you could do wonders with him, and I went so far
as to suggest that he come to Uppsala and sit at your feet.
He didn't say yes or no, but I suspect a mere mortal's advice
means little to one who has heard the voice of God. But I
covet him for you, this man of fire who reads and studies until his eyes fall out. Like Luther, he is a rough fellow, but you
could refine him and make him a preacher of Pauline stature.
Your own fire deserves such a rich lump of ore just once,
Jakob! Yours in Christ, dear friend, J.J. Risberg"

The professor pushed his glasses high on his forehead and
rubbed the bridge of his nose. What a thing it would be to
teach such a man! Whether God truly had spoken to him or
not didn't matter—as long as this Erik Jansson believed it
was so. He would be above human ambition, open to learning,
a well-laid fire ready to blaze.

Contemplating the ideal balance of teaching and learning
was so pleasant that the professor drifted in it overlong.
When he finally looked at the clock, he knew why the proprietor, who knew his habits, was standing at the door holding
his hat with a look of anxiety. He quickly collected his mail,
dropped coins on the table and snatched his hat on the run.
Careless of his shoes, he splashed through puddles, crossed
the footbridge and trotted up the hill, fighting for breath. The
thought that he hurried to apply his "fire" to a heap of wet
moss made haste seem ridiculous, but he could do no other.

Västmanland, fall, 1839, to January, 1840—

The fall fair was another milestone in the first year without Pappa, a time for Charlotta to remember other fairs when he had carried her on his shoulders for a high view of the booths, the crowd, the horses with rosettes on their bridles, the rope dancers. When she was too big to carry, he took her hand and bought her decorated sugar candy. Last year, when she walked beside him in her new winter clothes, he bought her a lace-edged handkerchief, a more grown-up souvenir. If she stayed home from the fair, it wouldn't hurt so much, but she would merely postpone the pain until the next fall fair. His absence at special events must be lived through, time by time.

It was customary to wear new winter clothes for the first time at the fall fair, but Mamma considered new garments inappropriate for a family in mourning. Charlotta's best woven skirt from the winter before had inched higher on her shins, and the armholes of her blouse were so tight that they made red marks on her skin, but unlike the vain Carolina, Charlotta didn't care.

Carolina grumbled all the way to the small, temporary town that was the fair, but her crossness vanished in the noisy laughter that rang in the cold, bright air. Servants received a double ration of brännvin to celebrate the fall fair, and many of them dipped into their savings to buy still more. Sometimes they grew frighteningly drunk, but that should not happen this year. Spirits were more expensive since the pastor had refused to operate the distillery. The new owner had raised the price.

Tradespeople had decorated their booths with ribbons and sheaves of grain, and the displays of goods were beautiful: clogs, copper pots, woven goods, and sugar candy decorated with trolls, cottages, flowers and love poems.

"I'm going to the fortune teller's tent!" Carolina cried,

moving away from them so quickly that her white petticoats
flashed from the hem of her skirt.

"She wants to know if Ingvar will marry her, I suppose,"
Anna-Maja said.

"He's right over there," Sabina pointed out, "why doesn't
she just ask *him*?"

"That isn't the way it's done." Charlotta said, "Look,
Sabina, there's the organ grinder!"

"We'd better not let her out of our sight!" Anna-Maja said
with a worried look.

"She'll stay right there with the monkey—the way I always
did. I even got lice from it once! Come on, let's watch the
rope dancers."

"You go." Anna-Maja said, "I'll keep an eye on Sabina."

Charlotta joined the crowd around the rope dancers, standing on tip-toe to see the blurred patterns of the ropes in the
air and the fast, intricate footwork of the dancers. Their skill
saddened her obscurely, making her want to flee her own
plodding body. Her calves trembled with the effort of staying
on her toes, and when a staggering hired man jostled her, she
lost her balance and fell to her knees. Big hands on her ribs
lifted, then released her. She turned in embarrassed confusion
and recognized Anders Salin, the hired man Erik sent to
Domta to do the field work.

"Are you enjoying the fair?" he asked.

She nodded and tried to keep from staring at him. Usually
dressed in homespun and high boots, Anders was nearly un-
recognizable in a new blue coat, fawn-colored breeches and
low shoes with gleaming buckles.

"Would you like to see the horses?" he asked.

She nodded again, and they walked, wide apart, to the
stakes where the animals were tethered. They listened to the
spirited bargaining; watched prospective buyers pull back the
soft, quivering lips to inspect teeth and run their hands over

rumps and hocks.

"That's a nice chestnut mare," Anders said, speaking softly to the horse and stroking her gleaming shoulder.

I wish I were that horse! The thought flashed into Charlotta's mind without warning and unsettled her completely. She wanted to run, but she stood still. Why did he stay with her? He could have pulled her to her feet and gone on his way. It occurred to her that he might be waiting to be thanked. She hadn't managed to utter that simple word. The earthy horse scent swirled in her nostrils, and she forgot that she meant to say thank you. Other words came.

"We used to have a horse—old Mayrose—but she was twenty years old, and she died—"

"I guess *I'm* your horse now!" he said with a grin. His hand cupped her elbow, and they walked, "Someday I'll have enough money to buy my own farm, and then I'll buy a mare like that at the fair!"

As they moved through the crowd, Charlotta's friends greeted her with a look of surprise. Erik had brought Anders from Vappeby, but they all spoke to him as if they knew him.

"You are well-acquainted here," she said.

"I meet people at the Saturday night dances. Why don't you ever come?"

"We're in mourning, as you know."

"I'm sorry—of course."

Why did I have to say it like that? In the long silence that followed, Charlotta was unhappily aware of her outgrown clothes, her brown hair, her peaked eyelids. Why was Anders wasting time in her company? She turned to leave him, but he took her elbow once more and guided her to a candy booth. After long consideration, he chose candies decorated with flowers and gave them to her with a bow.

"Thank you," she said at last, "for helping me up and for these." She was both relieved and disappointed that he had not selected the love poem candies.

"You don't talk a lot, do you?"

"I don't have much to say."

"Maybe not, but it's all in here," he tapped his forehead.

For the first time since Pappa's death, Charlotta felt an understanding that sought her out—came to meet her. Overwhelmed, she was almost afraid to believe in it. "I—I must go home," she said, "Will you tell my sisters I've gone?"

"I'll tell them—Charlotta."

Go quickly—before you ruin it! She whirled away from him, taking his face with her, the wide-set blue eyes beneath wheat-colored brows; the strong, straight nose and the full mouth. Why had she never really seen him before?

Walking back to Domta, she reviewed each moment of their time together. She recaptured the sensation of his hands on her ribs, enjoyed the expressions of her friends when they saw her with him, felt the brush of his fingers when he gave her the sugar candy, lingering longest on the memory of him tapping his forehead and saying, "It's all in here!"

As she approached the house, she hoped Mamma would not want to talk. She wanted to go on remembering, but Mamma saw her on the path and called out, "Back already? Where are the others?"

"They'll be along soon." Then she heard Mamma speak to someone else, and when she entered the kitchen she saw Karl, Erik's youngest brother, seated at the table with a cup of coffee. Ordinarily, she resented Karl because Mamma doted on him and probably pretended he was the son she never had, but now she was glad to see him. He could keep Mamma company while she went to the room she shared with Anna-Maja and Carolina to think about Anders.

"Sit down, Lotta," Mamma said, "Karl went to the big fair at Uppsala with Erik, and he's just now telling me about it."

Charlotta stifled a sigh and obeyed. She had one fair on her mind and no interest in any other, but one did not argue with Mamma. Karl seemed upset, but that was nothing unusual. He often talked to Mamma about things he couldn't mention to his own mother, and she didn't blame him. Aunt Sara was fierce!

Karl tugged at his ear and said, "We went to the library at the University, and we surely didn't belong there! Everyone wore robes and spectacles, and they looked at us as if we were pigs in the best room! Erik asked to see a certain book, and they wouldn't allow it, so he said, 'It doesn't matter, greater truth will come through me!' They all laughed, and I wanted to climb into a hole!"

"You mustn't be ashamed of your brother!" Mamma said.

"But that wasn't the worst of it! When we got to the fair—you wouldn't believe how much bigger it is than ours!"

"Size isn't everything," Charlotta said drily.

"Oh, but they had tumblers, dancers, music—and there were bad women everywhere!"

"You needn't go into *that*, Karl!" Mamma said.

"But I have to! Those women set Erik off. He was looking at a horse when this woman with loose hair and red on her cheeks grabbed his arm. He just went wild! He jumped on a barrel and yelled, 'Sinners!' Once everyone got quiet, he told them he was the only true preacher since the time of the Apostles and that he would do even greater work than Jesus and the Apostles! They all laughed, and I thought I'd die! Why can't Erik act like other people, Aunt Anna?"

"Because he's *not* like other people." Mamma twirled her coffee cup in its saucer. She looked troubled. "Are you sure he said he would do greater work than *Jesus*?"

"That's what he said—and he's going to stop farming and do nothing but preach!"

"How will they live?" Charlotta asked, "Has he thought of Maja-Stina and the baby?"

"He says his followers soon will be as many as the fish in the sea, and they will take care of him. Well, I'd better go home. I just thought you ought to know—"

Mamma saw him to the door. "Thank you for coming, Karl. Now remember, however things may seem to you, Erik is led by God." She returned to the table and sat down heavily. "And since Erik cares for us, *we* are in the hands of God. Who would expect such a thing from a fall fair?"

Erik will take Anders away! How soon? Charlotta went to her room to prepare her defenses. She denied the meeting at the fair until it seemed unreal. She hid the sugar candies deep in a trunk of bedding.

Anders found her at the well when he was bringing pails of milk to the house. Once more he wore wadmal and high boots.

"Charlotta, I asked your cousin if I could walk out with you, and he said you were too young. Then he told me that he's sending me away because he will have no money to pay me. I'll stay here for nothing, Charlotta, for you!"

She was cold inside, almost too cold to speak, but she managed to say, "No! You must work to earn money for that farm—for that mare—I don't want you to stay here!"

She unhooked her water pail and ran into the house, stricken by his expression of hurt and furious at Erik. *Pappa would never do this to me!*

***

By the new year, Erik's converts had multiplied so rapidly that no house in the parish was large enough to hold them all, and it was too cold for outdoor conventicles. The people took turns attending the services, sharing their preacher in Christian amity.

Pastor Risberg, who had come to some of the fall conventicles, had not been seen for several months, and as the family gathered in the kitchen at Lötorp before an evening of preaching, Charlotta's mother suggested, "His nose is out of joint because Erik is a better preacher than he is."

"More likely it's the weight of the offering basket!" Aunt Sara said with a sniff, "When they give to Erik, the church gets less."

Maja-Stina danced the baby on her knees as she said, "They haven't got much, but they're generous to us. Erik says it's always the lowly who open their hearts first, and that's God's truth! He must have talked to twenty housemaids about their troubles in the last week."

Aunt Sara raised her head haughtily. "I'm sure he's an expert on the troubles of housemaids!"

Charlotta saw the barb strike, but Maja-Stina managed to smile and say, "You know how it is with unmarried servant girls—lonely, away from home for the first time—"

And treated wickedly by mistresses like you, Aunt Sara! Christ was first Son and then Servant, but Maja-Stina had it the other way around, Charlotta reflected. Erik's love seemed to make up for it.

Erik had convinced Charlotta that Anders Salin was not for her by describing Anders' carnal attachments to other girls in the parish. She was now glad that Erik had intervened as soon as he did.

Carried along by the total belief of her family and neighbors, Charlotta had yielded to Erik's burning persuasion little by little until she was grounded in the True Faith and more comfortable than she had been while she resisted it. She was glad to be here tonight, at one with those who thirsted for Erik's message. As the new arrivals brought gusts of cold air into the house, she moved close to the fireplace for warmth. She was rubbing her hands before the flames when a veiled woman plucked at her sleeve and asked in a low voice, "Will you please ask Erik Jansson to come to me? I'll wait here."

As always, Erik was isolated in a bedroom to meditate before the service, but the woman's urgency made it seem necessary to interrupt him. She rapped on the door.

"What is it?"

"You're needed, Erik."

He could not move through a room without this person
catching his arm and that person tugging at his coat. Impatient with the delay, Charlotta grasped his hand and pulled
him after her. She presented him to the veiled woman and
started to move away, then saw the veil raised, revealing a
battered, swollen face.

"What has happened to you, Brita-Stafva?" Erik asked
quietly.

The woman's hands flew to the hurt face. "You—you told
us to purify our souls, so I—I—Arvid drank a whole jug of
brännvin and beat me—he said I had no right—"

"No right to do what, Brita-Stafva?"

"To—to keep him from my bed—"

Erik sighed, shaking his head. "That wasn't quite what I
meant. I'm sorry that you had to suffer because I did not
speak clearly. No matter what the body does, the soul is sinless. Do you understand?"

"No—" Brita-Stafva said mournfully.

Charlotta didn't understand it either, but she had learned
to accept much without understanding.

"Do you mean that we can do even those things that we
have been taught not to—"

Erik interrupted Brita-Stafva impatiently, "No, no, we
must behave well to give a good testimony to those who do
not understand this doctrine!"

"I must go—" the woman said nervously, "I only came to
warn you—don't let Arvid find you, or he'll hurt you!"

"Lower your veil and find a seat," Erik ordered, "It's time
for the service to begin."

"But I'm afraid—"

"You needn't be. I will deal with Arvid."

The *formak* was packed now. Anyone else who came would have to sit in the kitchen, where they could hear Erik but not see him. Charlotta's job was to admit latecomers. Swedish doors swung inward to keep a household from being trapped inside by heavy snow, and she had to ask the people seated in front of the door to move when others came.

After the opening prayer, Erik preached of the splendor of Solomon's temple, all overlaid with gold and carved with cherubims and palm trees and open flowers. He created it before their eyes, and when he said, "The two doors were of fir tree," he looked straight at Charlotta. Then he said, "But we, beloved friends, will build even more magnificently for our God. At a time which He will specify, we will build a new Jerusalem!"

Charlotta answered a soft knock at the door and was amazed to see Pastor Risberg. She whispered that she would find him a chair, but he shook his head and stood against the wall, pulling off his fur hat.

Erik seemed not to notice the pastor, continuing, "In the New Jerusalem, the faithful will abide in me. He who does not, shall be cast forth as a branch and shall wither!"

"Is he preaching from the Gospel of John?" the pastor whispered.

"No," a big farmer answered, "he is talking about us and himself and what we will do when God says it is time."

The pastor frowned, but he went on listening intently. When the service ended, he waited for Erik beside the door. Charlotta heard him say, "Perhaps you go too far. Are you leading my flock astray?"

Erik's eyes flashed angrily. "Hear this, false preacher! All authority hath been given unto me in heaven and on earth. If I so willed, you should at once fall dead at my feet and go to hell!"

"Will it, then," the pastor said calmly.

Charlotta caught her breath sharply, remembering what Erik had said when Pastor Nilsson died in the pulpit. If he killed Pastor Risberg, would it be murder in the eyes of God?

The eyes of the two men locked and held until Erik said, "Why should I consign you to hell? You're a better man than the last priest."

Charlotta breathed again with a deep sense of relief.

The men shook hands, and Pastor Risberg said, "I beg you to be careful about what you say to these people! Do you understand the responsibility of the influence you have upon them?"

"I do!"

"Good! I would not like to see bailiffs and constables brought into this situation. Good night, Erik Jansson."

Bailiffs and constables? The very thought terrified Charlotta, but Erik seemed unconcerned. He smiled at her and said, "Good night, my little door keeper!"

The University of Uppsala, February, 1840—

The professor, wrapped to the eyes in a long, woolen muffler, picked his way across the icy foot bridge, stopped at the stationer's shop to buy a new journal, and cautiously made his way to his lodgings. The woman who cleaned his rooms always left him a cold supper and a small fire in the grate, which made homecoming worthwhile.

And he had a number of books and pamphlets to inspect: a book on prison reform by Oscar, the Crown Prince, who also was Chancellor of the University; an essay on Francois Guizot, the new Minister of France; a piece on the return of exiled writers to Berlin at the order of Frederick William IV, the new King of Prussia; and a treatise by Robert Baird, an

American Presbyterian who had visited Sweden twice.

With his stockinged feet on the hearth fender, the professor sipped a glass of brännvin to thaw his brain and chuckled at a sentence in the French essay, "Guizot does nothing, and that is the secret of his preservation." That *bon mot* could be applied widely.

It seemed somewhat indecent to drink spirits while reading Baird, the Temperance man, and he started to put the piece aside, but a paragraph near the bottom of the page caught his eye: "Mr. Laing seems to think that the Swedish church has an advantage in having no schism or sect to resist. We think differently on this point also. If there was an active and zealous secession party; in other words, if there was a goodly number of churches independent of the State—"

The gist of the paragraph reminded the professor of the letter from J.J. Risberg that he had found no time to read that morning. The hour when he usually took coffee and read his mail had been devoted to a sullen student who was determined to throw up the ministry and go to trade. He had not tried to dissuade the young man from peddling herring, thinking this was as close as he was likely to get to the sign of the fish, but just listening to the fellow's justifications and agreeing with him took time.

He slapped his pockets until he found the letter, then collected a sandwich of smoked salmon and cheese from the sideboard before sitting down to read it. Could it be that J.J. had managed to steer his bucolic preacher to Uppsala?

"My Dear Jakob, I am of half a mind to come to Uppsala and find out which supercilious dons refused to allow Erik Jansson to look at the Codex Argenteus. Upon learning their identity, I would kick their scholarly behinds!"

"At the time of the fall fair, Jansson entered the University Library to view this marvel, half-persuaded that formal learning was a good thing, and he was rebuffed and insulted. As a result, he has chosen to go his own way, and he has given up farming to devote all his time to preaching. Unfortunately, his pronouncements become more heretical by the day, and my poor simple parishioners believe every word he utters. His converts are legion.

"He calls me a Pharisee, a hypocrite and a whited sepulchre, which is unpleasant, I confess, but my concern is for the people.

"Your meek Jeremiah is not helpless in this situation. With God's help, I stood up to him. I wish you had seen it! For a time, I thought it best to ignore his conventicles, but when I heard that he was usurping the authority of Christ, I walked to Lötorp and listened with my own ears. What I had heard was true.

"After the sermon, I spoke to him—gently, of course. I suggested that he might be going too far. Jakob, the look he gave me would have withered any fig tree! He said that if he willed it, I would fall dead at his feet and go to Hell.

"And can you believe that I said, 'Will it, then!'? He chose not to consign me to Hell. This may seem humorous to you now, but it wasn't at the time, I assure you. It was a bad moment. Before I left him, I wielded the big club of the State Church, making a veiled threat of bailiffs and constables. I didn't scare Jansson, but some of the others took note, and attendance at the conventicles started to fall off.

"Yesterday Jansson asked me for a paper of permission to travel to Helsingland. When I asked the reason, he said, 'God has told me to leave the stony ground of Osterunda parish and carry the true faith elsewhere.' I told him he must have a temporal reason for his travels, and he said he would sell wheat flour. I wished him well and asked him to tell me about his experiences in the north when he comes back. He will return, as he leaves his wife and child here. I would warn the pastors in Helsingland about him if I could, but he was extremely closemouthed about his itinerary. At least there will be peace in this parish for a time.

"But he makes me wonder, Jakob, am I truly cleaning the outside of a cup and platter that are foul within? Am I jealous of this self-taught farmer who touches hearts while I buzz about the ears like a bottle fly? Pray for your troubled friend, J.J. Risberg."

The professor sighed, brushing crumbs from his lap. The pendulum was shuddering at its sticking point. He polished his glasses on his shirt front and picked up the Baird treatise.

"But we come to the last cause of the existing depravation of morals in Sweden: which is the want of a thoroughly efficient presentation of the Gospel throughout the length and breadth of the land, and yet not for the want of a sufficiently numerous public ministry, nor for the want of human learning on the part of that ministry."

Skewered by Baird, the outsider with the disinterested eye, the professor felt uncomfortably defensive and put aside the treatise in favor of the essay on Guizot. It was easier to maintain a sense of superiority in secular matters, particularly those of a foreign nature.

Osterunda parish, April to June, 1840—

While Erik was away, Maja-Stina and the child lived with his parents at Klockaregarden, and Charlotta was appalled at the way they were treated.

Aunt Sara would not let Maja-Stina sit at the family table, reducing her to her former housemaid status, and when the cow strayed and Maja-Stina asked Uncle Johannes to help her find the beast, he said, "Find her yourself! *You* lost her!" In spite of all this, Maja-Stina remained cheerful, sharing her letters from Erik with his parents.

I wouldn't! Charlotta thought as she sat in the kitchen at

Klockaregarden listening to Maja-Stina read aloud.

"Per Norin, a leader of the Norrala Readers, said I was an imposter and asked me never to return, so I shook the dust of that place from my feet as the Bible directs, but I was most welcome elsewhere." Maja-Stina paused, frowning.

"Well," Aunt Sara said impatiently, "go on!"

"He writes of a shrew from Utnäs who follows him from village to village saying that he lies—"

Aunt Sara snatched the letter. "How dare she? And what's this? He's traveling with a girl from Delsbo?"

Maja-Stina blushed deeply. "He explains it, as you see. He says she needs the strength of his companionship to wean her from an immoral life."

"That's indecent!" Aunt Sara snapped.

"If it were, he wouldn't have told *me*, would he?" Maja-Stina defended.

"Ah, but you weren't going to read us that part, so you must think—"

"No! I trust Erik completely! Give me my letter!"

Aunt Sara thrust it at her contemptuously and left the room.

Charlotta touched Maja-Stina's hand. "Why don't you go back to Lötorp? How can you stand it here?"

"Erik wants us here, so we'll stay." Maja-Stina smoothed the letter with loving fingers, "What she *doesn't* know is that he's coming home!"

***

Erik returned on a Saturday, and the next day he took his place in the family pew at Osterunda church. He was greeted with glad affection by the followers who had missed him. The church seemed filled with gladness.

And then the atmosphere changed. Just before the service

was to begin, the King's bailiff walked down the aisle and took the pulpit.

"Hear this proclamation! The instigators of the heretical religious movement spreading through Sweden will be arrested and fined for any activities contrary to Church law!"

Erik listened without expression, but many of the people obviously were terrified. When the service ended, they left the church with apologetic glances, afraid to speak to him.

Cowards! Charlotta thought furiously. She was afraid too, but she lifted her chin and went to Erik, asking him, "What will you do now?"

"Plow the fields and wait for God's instructions."

***

Before the plowing was done, Uncle Johannes died. Erik wanted to preach the funeral sermon and bury his father at Klockaregarden, but Aunt Sara would not hear of it. She wanted him laid to rest properly, she said, and Erik deferred to her.

The coffin was carried to Osterunda church, where Pastor Risberg met the mourners and carried out the customary funeral rites. He was their enemy now, but Charlotta had to admit that he conducted the service decently and spoke kindly to the widow.

As the family left the church yard, Erik said, "Come walk with me, Little Pine Tree. Now we both know what it is to lose an earthly father."

Charlotta nodded sadly and asked, "Will you stay here now and care for your mother?"

"No. God has given me the understanding of Solomon, and I must go north to preach in the summer pastures at Delsbo and Forssa."

"They have bailiffs in the north, too."

"Yes, but the people there are not the kind who will set them on me! In Söderala I found good souls who read the Bible diligently — men like Jonas Olsson, the Devotionalist reader at Ina, and his brother Olof. They have made a start, but there is much they do not know.

"I stayed in the house of Jonas Olsson all of a Saturday and Sunday, and not once did I see him hold devotions with his servants. He even asked me to sell his sister some wheat flour on the Lord's Day! Lotta, do you know what they call me in the north?"

She shook her head.

"Wheat Flour Jesus!"

Domta - June, 1840—

Birch boughs crowned the doors of the parish houses for Midsummer's Eve, but Domta was without adornment, wrapped in mourning again.

After supper Charlotta stood at the door to admire a sky of luminous blue and yellow that looked like a huge, Swedish flag stretched above the earth.

Carolina was pouting because Mamma had forbidden them to dance all night at the home of the most prosperous farmer in the parish. It would be unseemly so soon after the death of Uncle Johannes, she said.

"We won't even see them raise the Maypole!" Carolina complained.

She'll be even crosser when the music starts, Charlotta thought, *and they probably would crown her Midsummer Bride if she went.*

"You're just mad because Ingvar will dance with somebody else," Sabina said.

Carolina swatted Sabina's backside.

"That's enough, girls!" Mamma said sharply, "Why don't

you make the magic pancakes? Right here in our kitchen with
no one to see, you can't be accused of dancing on your uncle's
grave, at least."

Carolina brightened, hurrying to find a bowl, a big wooden
spoon and the iron spider. "Go find Anna-Maja," she ordered,
"we need three."

"*I* make three," Sabina said.

"You're not old enough, and besides, who would marry a
mouthy creature like you?"

Charlotta left them to their quarrel and went to find Anna-
Maja in the milking stall.

"I don't know why I should make myself thirsty all night,"
Ann-Maja said, "I never dream at all."

"Oh, do come! I don't really believe in it either, but it will
make Carolina easier to live with for a little while."

The mixing of the magic pancakes required absolute silence,
and nothing must be spilled. Carolina carefully measured a
spoonful of salt, handing it to Anna-Maja, who gave it to
Charlotta. Holding her breath, Charlotta dumped the salt into
the bowl. Not a grain was spilled. After two more spoons of
salt came the triple handling of three portions of flour and
three of water. The sisters took turns at the stirring, commu-
nicating with gestures.

The batter, poured by three hands, was tricky to manage
without spilling, but with artful juggling, they pooled three
portions in the pan and returned the ladle to the bowl without
an accident. When the cakes bubbled, they flipped each one
with three hands on the wooden paddle, silently counting together to coordinate the lift and twist.

Sabina did her worst to make them break silence. She made
faces, danced up and down and even tugged at their skirts
until Mamma ordered her to leave the room.

They ate the over-salted pancakes with wry faces, but the
object of the whole procedure was to go to bed thirsty. The

men who offered them water in their dreams would be their future husbands.

Charlotta went outside to look at the well with longing. All she could think of was water — cold water. Anna-Maja joined her, and they stared at the handle, the rope, the bucket.

"Maybe we could sneak out here when Carolina is asleep?" Anna-Maja whispered.

"Lowering the bucket makes too much noise."

The deliciously dripping bucket floated before her eyes, tantalizing her, and she pulled her sister away from temptation.

In the kitchen Mamma was drinking coffee — hot, wet coffee. She looked at her daughters with amused sympathy and said, "Is the prophecy worth the price?"

"Not when you're paying for somebody else's prophecy," Charlotta said with a groan, "I'm going to bed."

"Don't cheat, now," Carolina warned, "I'll be watching."

Charlotta undressed, loosened her hair from its braids and got into bed. How hard it was to fall asleep in a room as light as morning. At first she lay on her back, hands folded on her breastbone. Water. She turned on her side. Milk. She tried the other side. Coffee. She flopped onto her stomach, pressing her parched lips to the bolster, trying not to think about drinking, but it was her only thought.

Anna-Maja came to bed with the unhappy news that Carolina planned to stay up most of the night. She gave Charlotta a stone to suck, but it didn't help. Then the music began, faint and far away. It was *The Fire Polka Waltz.*

Charlotta allowed herself to think of Anders, a dangerous indulgence, but she must overwhelm her raging thirst. At Vappeby Anders was dancing away the longest day in the year, smiling at someone in this white night. As the distant fiddles played *Father and Mother and Petter,* she stepped into his arms, and they danced — not more than a few steps before she remembered she was not alone. How could she bring

Anders into her head with her sister lying beside her?

"Anna-Maja?" she said softly.

No answer. Asleep was nearly as good as absent, Charlotta supposed. The music still played, and she brought Anders back to dance until she also slept.

Charlotta woke at dawn to find Anna-Maja dressed and sitting beside the bed.

"Well?" her sister said.

Charlotta looked at her blankly, then licked her dry lips and remembered. She clutched her head, trying to capture the dream before it slipped away. There had been a man, dark-haired and covered with dust. He gave her a drink of bitter water from a bottle encased in rough cloth. Describing him to Anna-Maja, she said, "I didn't know him. Did you dream?"

"You know I never do! I've brought you water."

Charlotta drank it gratefully and said, "I suppose Carolina dreamed about Ingvar?"

"No, Pehr Ericsson, and she's furious!"

"I was so sure it would be Ingvar! Ah well, I suppose the magic pancakes are just foolishness. Erik says God will choose our husbands."

And yet she believed in the magic pancakes—just a little— as much as was natural in a country where dim memories of the old gods tangled with knowledge of the Hebrew Jehovah.

The University of Uppsala, June, 1840—

After a breakfast in the old gardens with nearly three hundred colleagues and distinguished citizens, the professor took his place in the procession to the Cathedral for the promotion ceremonies.

The usual bottleneck developed at the Cathedral entrance. The wait would be more pleasant if he could look up at the first spire above a Gothic window, but he could not do so

without dislodging his hat. Instead, he fixed his eyes on the
green, sphere-topped dome of the Gustavianum medical theater and moved them downward to enjoy the play of the morning sun on the tawny, salmon walls of the building.

The long crocodile had moved slowly under the warm sun.
His brow was moist. When he first joined the faculty, he had
not known how to extricate necessaries from beneath his robe
with dignity. The student expedient of hiking up the hem to
reach a pocket was out of the question for a professor, and he
could not bring himself to ask a colleague how to manage, so
he devised his own method, a folded handkerchief tucked inside his shirt cuff. He removed it now and patted his forehead, enjoying the fresh-laundered scent.

Passing from sunlight to the rich dimness of the Cathedral
interior, he felt the presence of the invisible company of
saints, hosts that defied the present passion for numbering
things. He basked in their benevolence.

The Promoter, Professor Geijer, took his place below the altar, and the professor watched him closely. This position of
honor was rotated in the faculty, and one day it would fall to
him. Of course he couldn't expect to equal the stature of Geijer,
who was mantled with honors. He was not only the author of
a history of Sweden and numerous poems, but a composer of
serious music. The ninety young men who awaited their degrees would tell their grandchildren that Geijer had crowned
them with laurel. Hoping his own turn would wait for a kind-
lier contrast, the professor sat back in a pew worn smooth by
six centuries of contact with devout bottoms. Or at least he
supposed they had been devout.

Only the graduates in Philosophy received their Master of
Arts degrees publicly. Other faculties conferred degrees in
private. No wonder the best minds gravitated to Philosophy.
Surely it was more glorious to be loosed on the world with
speeches and cannon fire than to be sent off as surreptitious-

ly as illegitimate issue?

No matter how many times he witnessed it, the presentation of the first degree thrilled him. The laurel crown was placed on the graduate's brow, the Promoter read the conferral in Latin, and the cannon outside boomed at just the right moment. How did the cannoneer manage it? By watching for the sexton's signal from a window.

After about forty cannon rounds, the ceremony became tiresome. The professor saw that the crowns were beech leaves, not laurel. The deep, green leaves of the beech were a passable substitute, but not the real thing, not the true crown of the victor. He was disturbed and cross with himself because he felt that way. Always caviling at details! Why could he not be at home in his own age?

When the exercises finally ended, the procession re-formed for the march to the New Botanical Gardens for dinner. The food would be excellent, but he begrudged the hours he would have to spend listening to tiresome speeches and toasts.

When a colleague handed him a glass of brännvin and a string quartet beneath the ash trees started to play Mozart, his spirits lifted. And when another colleague passed him an issue of the *Norrlands Posten*, he grew positively cheerful. With a drink, music, and something to read, he would not be wasting his time at the celebration.

Provincial newspapers interested him greatly. Their tone could be as personal as a private letter, and they dealt with issues of true importance to their readers with none of the kow-towing puffery of some city papers. Scanning the page, he saw a familiar name. But why familiar? Jansson—Erik Jansson? Ah, J.J.'s rustic preacher!

The brief account began, "A family at Forssa accuses a man from Västmanland of fraud because he undertook to heal their 29-year-old crippled son and failed. The young man was malformed at birth, but Jansson assured his parents that

God had given him the power to heal their son. On Wednesday, Jansson said the cripple would leap like a deer on Thursday. The parents bought a new suit of clothing for him, placing it beside his bed, but when Thursday came, he was as twisted as ever and could not rise to clothe himself. Jansson claims that the fault lies with the young man, who did not have the faith to be healed.

"This man Jansson claims to be a messenger from God, bringing new revelations. He frequently preaches in the fields and has made many converts to what he calls the True Faith. At this writing, Church authorities have declined to comment on the matter."

"Knut!" the professor called, "May I tear a bit from your *Posten?*

"Take it all! I've read it, Jakob."

He must send the cutting to J.J. Risberg. The two of them had discussed miraculous healing exhaustively. They finally agreed that Christ healed as a sign of His Messiahship to the Jews. The Apostles carried on the sign gifts to validate the Gospel, and when the Biblical revelation was complete, the gifts of healing, tongues, and raising the dead were revoked. After I Corinthians 12:13-14, the gifts were never mentioned again. Why, if they were meant to have a place in the Christian life, were the sign gifts not included in the great Church epistles, Ephesians and Colossians?

Jansson could not heal the cripple because the young man had insufficient faith? Paul, the great man of faith, asked thrice to be healed of the thorn in his flesh, and it remained. If the faith of the afflicted was necessary to healing, what about the people Christ healed who never asked for healing, who never participated in it with their own hope?

J.J. was quite right to be disturbed about this man's heresies! He himself was so agitated that he neglected to bow his head when the Promoter asked the blessing on the food until his friend Knut nudged him.

Osterunda parish, August, 1843—

Pehr Ericsson had not started to court Carolina for more than a year after the dream of the magic pancakes, but it now seemed certain that they would marry. Charlotta wondered if the ceremony could be held in Osterunda church? They still attended services there, but the atmosphere was strained. It seemed that each time Pastor Risberg heard of Erik's successes in the northern provinces, he grew colder toward them all.

Then Erik returned to Osterunda parish and announced that he would sell his farm and move to Helsingland immediately. Maja-Stina sent for Charlotta to help with the packing, and when she arrived, she found a buyer in the kitchen at Lötorp discussing terms.

"I stopped by to pick up the post," Charlotta said, "and there was this letter for you, Erik."

His face hardened as he read it. Then he told the buyer, "I'm sorry, but I can't sell Lötorp after all—not now."

The man went away, bewildered, leaving the coffee cup Maja-Stina had just filled for him untouched.

"Drink it, Charlotta," Maja-Stina said, "it's real coffee and shouldn't be wasted. Now, Erik, what's this all about?"

"Risberg thinks I have come back to stay, and he threatens me with fines and imprisonment! Well, stay we shall! Furthermore, I intend to call a conventicle for the hour of the Lutheran mass!"

"Oh Erik," Maja-Stina said, "can't we just go to Helsingland in peace?"

"Not in the face of this challenge!"

The Sunday morning conventicle was sparsely attended, but when the pastor heard of it, he nailed a paper to the

Church door that read, "Erik Jansson and his followers are forbidden the sacraments from this day forward."

Erik countered by serving the Lord's Supper at Klockare-garden. Charlotta participated with a sense of dread. Would she be damned for taking a bit of hardtack as the Lord's Body and drinking His blood from a cup of hammered silver that had been in Aunt Sara's family for generations and used for wedding toasts?

"This is what we must do, Beloved," Erik said, "return to the simplicity of the early Church."

When he said the age-old words, it seemed all right to Charlotta, more meaningful than before.

But her courage was tested severely on the night when Erik led his followers to the parsonage to pray for the conversion of Pastor Risberg. Though they were more than twenty and the pastor was just one man, he held the power of the Church. Charlotta hung back, terrified by Risberg's huge shadow thrown against the wall of the *formak* by a single lamp.

"Kneel!" Erik told them. Then he shouted, "False prophet, hear the words of your salvation!"

The pastor came to the open window. Charlotta always had thought him kindly, but now his face was twisted with anger as he said, "Be careful what you say to a minister of God!"

"I speak in mercy, Risberg! You have strayed from the truth, and I have come to seek and to save that which is lost. I am the vicar of Christ on earth, and you would do well to listen to me!"

"God pity those who listen to you! How dare you keep these people from the Church and from the Sacraments?"

"They are not lacking in either, as they will tell you if you question them."

Charlotta made herself as small as possible, hoping the pastor would not choose her for questioning.

Risberg leaned from the window and his pectoral cross clanked on the sill. "Why do you listen to this man? Go to your homes before the constable breaks your heads!"

Erik moved close, and with his face inches from the pastor's, he said, "I have changed my mind about you! You are not worthy of salvation! Make the most of the life that is left to you, for you will burn in Hell soon enough!"

"Bless those who curse you—" the pastor said in a voice that held no benediction. He turned from the window to blow out the lamp.

***

Not content with one service a week, Erik's followers pressed him to preach in the forest clearing at night when the farm work was done.

Charlotta found a seat on a fallen log next to Sophia Schön. Mamma never had allowed her to associate with Sophia before Erik converted the girl, but it was all right now. Sophia had changed. She no longer spent the hours of the Saturday dance behind a haystack.

"Beloved friends," Erik said, "the idols from which the heart is to be cleansed are, first and foremost, the idolatrous books—particularly Luther's and Arndt's."

The people murmured, and one farmer was so outraged that he stalked away through the forest gloom.

"There!" Erik cried, "You see with your own eyes that the Devil had to get out—for it is impossible for him to hear the word of God preached in its purity! The Bible alone is the guidepost to salvation!"

"Is Nohrborg bad too?" a woman asked.

"An empty barrel with both ends closed! He echoes the wails of Satan!"

"Then what are we to do?" an old man asked, "Throw our

postils on the manure heap?''

Erik's eyes kindled. "In the 19th verse of the 19th chapter of the Acts of the Apostles it is written, 'And not a few of them that practiced magical arts brought their books together and burned them in the sight of all!''

Magical arts? Charlotta thought, *Who in the world has such books? Surely Luther, Arndt and Nohrborg had nothing to do with—*

"Lanterns!" a small boy cried, "It's the constable and his men!''

Erik hastily raised his arms in benediction, "Beloved, God see you safely to your homes. We will meet again soon!''

Charlotta looked for her family in the scattering crowd. Mamma had been right over there with her sisters, and Carolina and Pehr had sat near one of the big boulders, but she could not see them now. Where had they all gone so quickly?

Maja-Stina caught her arm. "Come to Klockaregarden, Lotta, it's closer than Domta. Your mother and sisters are already on the way there.''

They hurried through the trees, scaring rabbits and roosting birds as they trampled dead branches. Behind them, lanterns bobbed ominously. Klockaregarden was dark, but Aunt Sara was waiting for them at the door. "You're the last, thank God!" she said, pulling them inside and barring the door after them.

By the light of a single lamp covered with dark cloth, the women were spreading pallets on the floor, preparing for siege.

Charlotta was sent to make coffee. Measuring the roasted rye into the pot, she wondered what Erik had meant to say about burning books? To her, any book was precious. Besides her Bible, she had just one—a thin volume about the death of Baldur in a worn cover of dark green cloth. And she was afraid for Erik. It was his custom to linger in the forest to pray after a service, but he shouldn't have done that tonight!

The women's voices were high with tension and the children cried peevishly, not understanding the strangeness of the night. Aunt Sara ordered everyone to bed, seating herself beside the door to lift the bar when Erik came.

"Are you scared, Lotta?" Sabina whispered, "I am!"

"The door is new and strong," she said, but she wondered, *What will happen now? Will we be beaten? Arrested and taken to jail?*

The knock at the door nearly stopped her heart.

"Who is it?" Aunt Sara called sharply.

"The bailiff! Open up!"

"Go away, you're waking the children!"

"Open, I say!"

Silence, men's voices muttering in consultation, then the grunting sounds of exertion and a shuddering blow to the door. Aunt Sara couldn't bear to see her new house ruined and lifted the bar. Three men came in with lanterns held high.

Women shrieked and children cried as the men searched among the sleepers on the floor who slept no longer. One of the intruders put his lantern on the table and pulled Sophia Schön to her feet. "A nice hussy you are!" he yelled, striking her with the flat of his hand.

When Sophia threw up her arms to protect her face, he clutched at her hair, pulling until she screamed. Maja-Stina rushed between them, and he abandoned Sophia, taking his lantern to the bedroom. Bolsters and covers flew as he raved. "Where is he? Where is the whore-monger?"

"Of whom do you speak?" Aunt Sara said coldly, "There is no such person here!"

The other men stepped back sheepishly, ready to apologize and leave, but the violent one grabbed Sophia and thrust her at them. "Take this woman to the sheriff's house!"

"Why?" Maja-Stina cried, "She has done nothing!"

"I know you now!" Sophia said to him, "At the fall fair two years ago—you laid hands on me, and I—"

"Take her away!" he yelled.

Sophia wore nothing but her shift, and she was without shoes. She begged, "Let me cover myself!"

"Never mind that, your body is a public monument!"

"Not any more! I am without sin!"

Charlotta pulled a woven coverlet around herself tightly, feeling Sophia's shame as if it were her own. *Oh Erik, come back!*

When Erik finally did come, the women were hysterical. Aunt Sara was shaking so fiercely that she could not speak, and Maja-Stina sputtered with rage.

"Can *anyone* tell me what happened?" he asked impatiently.

Charlotta spoke with forced calm. "Three men came, and one of them hit Sophia. They've taken her to the sheriff's house."

"Then I must find a rich believer to buy her back." He left immediately. Within an hour, he returned with a sobbing Sophia wrapped in a coverlet.

"God has told me to move my family to Forssa tonight." he said, "And He has brought many women to Klockaregarden to help us prepare for the journey. Will you come with us to Lötorp?"

Couldn't God bring us together without scaring us to death? Charlotta sighed and put on her clothes, longing for her bed at Domta.

Uppsala, August, 1843—

The professor returned from his holiday on Lake Mälaren earlier than he had planned, catapulted home by the energy of a new term's infinite possibilities. He forgot the inevitable let-down of other years as a woman forgets the pain of childbirth.

His string of days beside the water was an amber necklace to be put away in a drawer. Restless and uneasy at first, he gradually had enlarged his holiday capacity for doing nothing until a mid-point, when that capacity started to diminish with the thought of return. Now the quiet, sunny days were past, stored away for winter remembrance.

The fusty air of rooms closed tight for several weeks was repugnant to him. His lungs had learned to demand better at the shore. He threw open the windows, frowning at the dust on the sills and knowing that he would ignore such trivia when his mind was engaged once more.

He turned to the accumulated post, newspapers tied in bundles and a slender sheaf of letters. Swedes took summer seriously and let nothing interfere with the enjoyment of its brief span. Personal correspondence lagged in the summer, except in Axelina's case. His querulous sister had written to him twice while he was away. He opened one of her letters, then put it aside, feeling in no mood for her litany of complaints.

The other letters were just as unappealing: a request for a letter of recommendation from a student he could scarcely remember, the notice of a pre-term faculty meeting, and a bill from his stationer. Nothing from J.J. Risberg. Since his old friend had routed his untutored rival, he had been silent.

The professor sighed and picked up his pen. He must write to the char woman, advising her of his early return. He preferred the old-fashioned quill to a steel tip. Words written with a quill from the wing shaft of a goose were more likely to fly, in his opinion, and besides, the quill responded to infinite variations of pressure and angle, producing any line that suited the fancy.

Opening a bottle of ordinary ink, he thought of the sympathetic writing fluids of the ancients. Arab priests wrote the name of Mohammed on stones, and the hot hands of the faithful caused the name to appear. That would be a fine trick for J.J.'s miracle man! Unfortunately, no one knew what the Arab ink was—or at least *he* didn't. All he knew was that Ovid had instructed lovers to write in milk, dusting soot over a seemingly blank page to learn its message.

Such nonsense! He dipped the quill and wrote, "Dear Madame, I returned to Uppsala this morning, Monday, and I look forward to the resumption of your ministrations. Yours faithfully."

The clutter of his writing table offended eyes accustomed to the neat shoreline of Lake Mälaren as he searched unsuccessfully for the blotting sand. He put the note on the sideboard to dry on its own and started to make orderly piles of the papers. As he picked up the *Hudiksvalls Weckoblad*, a small heading leaped at him with more force than its size warranted. "Book Burning at Tranberg."

The sense of holiday well-being vanished. He beat the stubborn folds of the paper flat and read, "A large pyre of books was burned on the shores of Lake Viksjön Tuesday by a group of religionists known as *Erikjansare*. Books, pamphlets, and postils by Luther, Nohrborg, Lineroth and Pettersson fed the flames while the leader, Erik Jansson, read from the Book of Revelation. Those who had no books threw Temperance tracts on the flames.

Jansson said, 'Satan had a jubilee when Luther's writings were published, and when they are burned, the Devil will be in mourning!'

"He said further that God has ordered him to transcribe the Bible anew, and he is taking subscriptions for his translation of the Scriptures. A large sum of money has been collected.

"After the book-burning, the *Erikjansare* met in a field, where they were attacked by unknown assailants. Jansson was unhurt, but others, including many women, were severely injured."

Alternately hot and cold with outrage, the professor deplored the purity of his vocabulary. He could only express his fury by comparing book-burning to bedding one's mother—urinating on a grave—eating excrement. How satisfying it would be to say "God damn Erik Jansson!", but it was forbidden.

He threw the paper from him and clasped his hands to stop their trembling. "Satan had a jubilee" indeed! How dare this Erik Jansson burn his betters? And what gall to announce that he would transcribe the Bible! Without Hebrew? Without Greek? It was laughable! The fools who gave him their money might not live to see the "true translation." Luther had spent eleven years transcribing the Old Testament alone, the Berleburg Bible was sixteen years in translation, and the King James was the long effort of a commission of bishops!

He paced, fighting for control, reminding himself that Luther's God "potently does everything in everything." If Luther could hail the power of God in the likes of Attila the Hun, surely *he* could find some vestige of that power in this book-burning wretch? Could this black act at Tranberg lead to some good, or was it only a sign that the dark forces of ignorance were in the ascendant?

Someone was at his door. He pulled the knob fiercely, forgetting to turn it, and was balked. *I must get hold of myself!* He took a deep breath and turned the knob.

"Ah, Jakob! I'd heard you were back. I brought my fiddle—can we play a bit of something?"

"I'm *just* back, Olaf, you must have been watching the post house." He felt himself unfit for company and considered turning his friend away, but the mere sight of Lovgren's civilized face seemed to relieve him, and he said, "Come in, come in!"

While the professor took his violin from its case, Olaf arranged two chairs and a wooden stand near a sunny window. They played Bach, best defended against charges of frivolity by clerics who liked to play the fiddle.

The professor's part began with an eighth note rest. He listened to Olaf's note for the space of a quick breath, then launched into the phrase of liquid eighth notes that meshed with the sustained tone. That first small silence had calmed him, prepared him to soar. What could be more blessed than a well-placed rest?

Stenbo, June, 1845—

Charlotta stayed close to Maja-Stina in the jostling, high-hearted crowd gathered at Stenbo to celebrate Midsummer's Day. She couldn't believe that she actually was here in the North with Erik and his family, that she had survived the ordeal of asking Pastor Risberg for a travel permission paper, that he had consented.

Erik had gone on ahead to find the best spot for preaching the sermon he intended to deliver to this large gathering from many parishes. Though he had been imprisoned twice and beaten repeatedly for holding unauthorized religious meetings, he would not be silent. Charlotta admired his courage, but she wished they could just have a happy time, as in the old days.

Hired men pressed close to laughing girls massed on the high bridge that led to the village hall. She watched them, feeling a fishhook of envy in her vitals. The man of her magic pancake dream had never appeared, not in all these years.

Much had happened since that dream, but little or none of it had happened to her. Carolina had married Pehr Ericsson; Maja-Stina had given birth to two daughters, first Mathilde and then Charlotta, named for her; Erik's brother Peter had lost his beautiful wife to tuberculosis; the old King had died, and the Crown Prince took the throne; and Maja-Stina had petitioned King Oscar for Erik's release from jail, an act that even Aunt Sara had to admire. The only change in Charlotta's life was her strengthening belief in Erik's True Faith.

"There he is," Maja-Stina said, "on the steps."

Charlotta saw him the dark frame of the village hall's open door. Excited by the crowd, which was not yet aware of him, he seemed ready to explode with his message.

"Beloved friends!" he shouted.

People glanced at him idly, then continued to laugh and chatter.

"Hear me!" The noise lessened, and he continued, "You have noticed, I suppose, that it has not rained for many weeks?"

Why was he talking about the weather, Charlotta wondered? He had more important things to say.

"It will not rain for three years and six months!"

The people gaped, then stirred and murmured uneasily. A man shouted, "Why? Why won't it rain?"

"Because I have prayed to God to withhold the life-giving rain from an evil people until they turn from their wicked ways!"

Oh Erik, what have you said? What if God won't stop the rain for you? Charlotta was ashamed of her doubt, but she couldn't help feeling it.

Maja-Stina left her abruptly, pushing through the crowd to Erik and shouting, "Run, Erik! It's the King's bailiff!"

Charlotta could not see the bailiff until some of the people stepped down from the bridge and others shrank back to let him pass. He was a cruel-looking man with red veins snaking all over his large nose, and the men who followed him carried clubs.

Now Erik saw the bailiff too, but he did not run. He stood on the steps with his head high, waiting.

Charlotta watched, pressing a fist against her mouth. *Don't let him take you!*

"You are my prisoner!" the bailiff shouted, reaching out to grasp Erik. At that moment, a woman lunged at the bailiff's legs and pulled him down. Erik darted away, across the bridge.

When the bailiff got to his feet, he had no idea which way Erik had gone, and his men had been too busy helping him up and cursing at the woman who tackled him to notice. The crowd did not betray Erik, and the officials decided he had entered the village hall. In they went with their clubs, followed by six or seven of Erik's burly converts. The door banged open and shut as they fought.

A hand closed on Charlotta's arm, and she gasped in terror, then saw that it was Maja-Stina.

"Come, Lotta," she said in a low voice, "but walk slowly. Those who run are often chased."

Tense with the effort to show no haste, they lost themselves in a noisy crowd of country girls and their swains. When they were well away from the village, they started to run.

Exhaustion eventually slowed their pace, and Maja-Stina motioned wordlessly toward a cow barn. They entered the cool dimness and sank to the straw gratefully.

While their breath still came in sobbing gasps, they heard drunken voices.

"Into the straw pile, quick!" Maja-Stina hissed.

Charlotta burrowed frantically, and Maja-Stina covered her, neglecting her own safety until all she could do was make a dash for the dung trap in the barn floor. Charlotta clawed a peephole in the straw and saw a man's shadow appear as the trap door banged shut. She held her breath, hoping he had not seen or heard, or that he was kind and it wouldn't matter.

"Ha ha!" he said, "We've caught a rat!" He strode into the barn and pulled at the trapdoor. Maja-Stina tried to hold it down, but there was no handle on the underside.

Three other men joined him to pull Maja-Stina from her filthy hiding place, and one of them was ordered to cut some beech saplings outside.

"It's the madman's wife, all right!"

"Shall we teach her a lesson?"

"Why do you think I sent Swan for the saplings?"

The fellow named Swan came back with the sticks, slashing them about like a small boy playing soldier. They pulled off Maja-Stina's wooden shoes and struck the soles of her feet, again and again. Charlotta winced with each blow. *If I had a pitchfork—*

"I have done nothing to you!" Maja-Stina said.

"Oh? You feed and bed a man who breaks the law, and we are law-abiding citizens!"

Swan, a mere boy with peach fuzz cheeks, scooped up a handful of dung and threw it at Maja-Stina, spattering the man who held her arms.

"Idiot! Look what you've done to me!"

Too drunk to remember what they were about, they started to fight among themselves until the stumbling battle moved out of the barn and became a new quest for brännvin.

Charlotta sprang from the straw and went to Maja-Stina, who sat silently with her arms around her knees, her face buried in her skirt.

"I'm sorry, Maja-Stina—I should have tried to help—"

"What could you do? They might have done worse to you!"

"I should have tried!" Charlotta tried to place the wooden shoes on Maja-Stina's feet, but Maja-Stina cried out with pain. Her soles were swollen and hatched with angry red marks, some of them bleeding. Charlotta tore strips from her apron to bind the poor feet.

They started for home slowly, making their cautious way through fields and behind haystacks. If anyone pursued them now, they were lost.

But they reached home safely and found a small boy waiting with a memorized message. "Olof Stenberg took the Prophet across the lake in a boat. He will take him to Jonas
Olsson at Ina."

"Thank you, my dear," Maja-Stina said, "come in and have
a sugar cake."

"What happened to your feet? the boy asked.

She smiled crookedly. "I stepped on some sticks."

Tears rolled down Charlotta's cheeks as she bathed the injured feet. "Tell me what more I can do for you!"

"Just stay with me a few more days and help with the children until I can walk comfortably."

Charlotta went outside to relieve the girl who had cared for
the children while they were at Stenbo. Dust devils danced in
the road, and Erik and Mathilde felt gritty when she took
their hands. Maybe God *would* withhold the rain.

Before they went to bed that night, several farmers who
were more superstitious than religious came to call on Maja-
Stina, begging her to persuade Erik to pray a new prayer
before their crops died in the rock-hard soil.

"How can I?" she said, "He knows best, and besides, I
don't know where he is."

When they had gone, Charlotta said, "But you do know
where he is—at Ina."

"Perhaps, but we are allowed to lie to good purpose. I feel
Erik won't be taken this time. God gave him time in prison to
write the new hymns and the catechism, but that's done now,
and it's best for him to be free to preach."

***

Soon after Charlotta returned to Domta, a notice was
posted offering thirty crowns for the capture of Erik Jansson.
In worried consultation, the family agreed that thirty crowns

was a great deal of money in a time of drought.

Hearing a knock at the door, they changed the subject quickly. Charlotta opened the door to a tired, dusty woman and courteously asked her to come in. Off came the bonnet and shawl, and a strangely buxom Erik clasped her to him.

He had traveled by night in clothes borrowed from Jonas Olsson's wife, and he was glad to be himself again, but he realized he would have to hide, and they discussed possible places for nearly an hour. The best choice seemed to be a space under the floorboards of a nearby dairy barn.

"It isn't much bigger than a coffin!" Charlotta warned him.

"That's big enough. I once saw a toad hop away happily after being walled up in a churchyard for years."

Charlotta took him to the barn after midnight. When she had lined the space with a quilt, he climbed in, and she replaced the boards. As she was kicking straw over the floorboards, she was startled by his eery, muffled, "Good night, Lotta!"

"Good night, Erik. Can you live without food until tomorrow night?"

"Of course. And bring me some writing materials then."

"You can't see to write!"

"I'll find a way."

She stood still in the barn, testing the feeling of the hidden presence. It seemed very strong to her, but she *knew*. Someone else would sense nothing but the munching and shuffling of the cattle.

The next night when she brought food, a damp cloth to freshen Erik's face and hands, and the writing materials, he asked her what day it was.

"It's Thursday, July 20."

"Ah, then my trial is to be tomorrow." He laughed softly, "Let them try a ghost."

After he had walked about the barn to stretch his legs, he

went to the door and sniffed the night air. "Dry." he said, "Dry as gun powder!" Charlotta had brought a small cutting board for him to write on, and he squatted to scrawl brief letters to Ina, Forssa, Alfta and Soderala. The moon gave the light he needed, as if on command.

The following night, he wrote more letters, and Charlotta asked, "What do you tell all of these people? Not that it's any of my business!"

"Ah, but it *is* your business! The time has come to make the New Jerusalem real, Lotta, God has told me to take the faithful to North America—to a place called Illinios near a great river."

She was speechless, unable to grasp the strangeness, the distance.

His letters finished, Erik stepped outside the barn. When Charlotta followed to warn him to be careful, a drop of rain struck her cheek.

"It's raining! Erik, how can this be?"

He raised his face to the quickening shower and said, "It rains because I have taken pity on the faithful and prayed a new prayer—let it rain on Sweden!"

"Oh Erik, then we won't have to go—our crops will grow, and we can stay in Sweden!"

"No, Lotta, I tell you, God is leading us out of Sweden! I have prayed, preached, healed, burned vile writings—and yet these hard-necked people have not repented! We will shake the dust of Sweden from our feet!"

"If this rain goes on, it will be mud we shake from our feet! Now please go back in your hole—sometimes when people can't sleep, they leave their beds and wander. You might be seen!"

***

Near the end of July, a new hired man began his duties at the farmstead where Erik lay hidden. The man was carrying a load of hay to the mangers when his boot caught on a protruding board. He swore and kicked at the projection, dislodging the board.

Erik had been sleeping, but the sudden streak of light alerted him to his danger, and he gave a low, unearthly moan that scared the wits out of the hired man. He laughed as he told Charlotta how the hay flew, then sobered and suggested a new hiding place.

"How about Soldier Blom's house?" she said, "They have an upstairs room they never use, and they are trustworthy."

He agreed, and Charlotta hurried away to wake Aina, Blom's wife. When they had collected a featherbed, a big needle and some strong cord, they went to the barn to wake two hired men who were believers.

The four of them stole back to the dairy barn, and the men stood watch while Charlotta and Aina sewed Erik into the featherbed. After his fit of sneezing among the feathers subsided, the men carried what looked like a heavy bed roll to the upstairs room at the Blom house.

The secret seemed to be safe until Soldier Blom had a visitor from his old regiment who asked pointed questions about "that devil, that heretic!"

"Erik Jansson must have had his ear to the floor," Aina told Charlotta. "When I brought food in the morning, he was gone."

The Bloms took down the knotted bedsheets Erik had used to escape and preserved then with pride, the Prophet's ladder.

Uppsala, September, 1845—

The professor awoke with a neck so stiff that he had to use both hands to lift his head from the bolster. Groaning, he wished for the privilege of the late Professor Oedman, who lay propped up in his bed to lecture to the students who crowded his bedchamber.

Oedman had lived in obscurity until his *Natural History of the Bible* created a stir in England, prompting Gustavus III to appoint him to the faculty at Uppsala. Now Oedman's portrait in a half-recumbent pose hung in the Academy of Science at Stockholm. He was immortal.

The professor once hoped that his own writing would raise him to eminence. A decade earlier, he had started a manuscript on the liberal experiment of Fourier in France, but the whole business faltered when Fourier died, and though his newspaper, *Le Phalange,* still published, it was forced to report failures, large and small.

It seemed feasible, establishing large groups of people in common houses to perform work they liked and could do well for the benefit of all, but selfishness crept in. Members held unequal shares of capital in the enterprise. Those with property and inheritances lorded it over the others. Somehow, Fourier had not gone far enough. Why? Perhaps he was intimidated by the violent reaction to his plan for abolishing the institution of marriage.

The professor had planned to compare the phalanges with the early church at Ephesus, where the people were exhorted to live in the bond of peace, each to practice his own gift for the good of all. "Let him that stole steal no more: but rather let him labour, working with his hands the thing which is good, that he may have to give to him that needeth."

What hopes the professor had cherished of capturing the notice of the Crown Prince with this work! He *should* have been interested with a French mother and a wife who was the granddaughter of the Empress Josephine. Oscar was young then—open to new ideas. *If I had finished the book then—*

Now that Oscar was king, his earlier liberality had turned

slow and cautious, disappointing those who had awaited the old King's demise with unseemly eagerness. The professor could sympathize with a man forced to wait in the wings until the peak of his manhood was past. Long deferrment was detrimental to performance, whether in the matter of loving a woman or assuming power.

The professor himself had given up hope of either, content to occupy the obscure niche where God had placed him. He, like Oscar, was hardening in reaction. The rising tide of religious unrest actually shared many of his own views, but like a spoiled child, he did not want to share. When one of his own students, Carl Rosenius, broke from the mold and fled to George Scott, the English Methodist missionary in Stockholm, he resented it deeply.

Though the professor agreed with Robert Baird that the Swedish clergy was secularized to the point of impotence, he was made peevish by the man's obnoxious insistence upon America's manifest destiny as the religious and moral leader of the world.

Scratching his ribs through his nightshirt, he looked through the book shelves for Baird's book, *A Traveller's and Immigrant's Guide to the Mississippi Valley*. He had to stoop to reach it, and the movement gave his neck an unholy twinge.

"The Valley of the Mississippi is a portion of our country which is now arresting the attention of not only our own inhabitants, but also those of foreign lands. Such are its admirable facilities—the influence which it is undoubtedly about to wield in giving direction to the destiny of this nation...The soil of this state is generally very fine, and exceedingly productive...no country in the world has greater advantages for raising livestock...Illinois is of easy access by the most convenient and cheap modes of removal."

Let Baird have them, all the troublemakers! The headbreaking anger in the provinces was an offense to God! The

professor only hoped they would not be afraid to go—after
the shipwreck off Oregrund that claimed fifty lives the week
before. Cramming the dissenters into ships and casting them
off in his imagination pleased the professor greatly and relieved
the painful tension in his neck. He would be able to deliver
his lecture on the presence of Christ in the Lord's Supper,
Luther's "real presence," without severe discomfort.

Domta, Forssa and Gefle, October, 1845—

Erik's plan to move the faithful to North America, written
while he hid at Soldier Blom's house, told how the people
would hold everything in common like the early Christians.
They were to sell what they owned in Sweden and put the
money into a fund that would pay for their removal to the
new land. At Domta, the family discussed what must be sold
and what could be kept.

"Do we really have to give up the clothes that let people
know we are from this parish?" Sabina said, "Why do we all
have to dress alike in the New Jerusalem?"

"Because the Bible speaks against vanity." Mamma said,
"I wish we had more to sell. They tell me that some of the
faithful are giving thousands of crowns to the common fund."

"That may be so," Charlotta said, "but others can't leave
Sweden until their debts are paid, and they are taking money
out of the fund."

"I don't want to go!" Anna-Maja said, "I've heard that
North America is filled with dragons and wild beasts!"

"Who told you such foolishness?" Mamma asked crossly.

"They were talking about it at the post house—"

"You should know better than to listen to those worthless
hang-abouts!"

"I don't care if there *are* dragons and things!" Sabina said
stoutly, "Erik won't let them hurt us! Besides, he said we'll

eat figs and wheat bread and as much pork as we like! Won't
that be fine?"

Perhaps there would be neither dragons nor figs and wheat
bread, Charlotta thought, but at least they would be together,
a small army of believers. Erik's followers numbered in the
thousands now. When they said "yes" to the all-important
question, "Wouldst thou be saved?", Erik wrote their names
in a book, and that book was fat with names.

But there would be sad partings when they left. Erik's sister had married and moved to the south of Sweden, where she
lost interest in the True Faith. Karl, his youngest brother,
would stay in Sweden because he had a wife who refused to
leave. She had told Karl to go without her, but he would not.

Erik had sent Jonas Olsson's brother Olof as a scout to
North America to find a place for them. When a report from
the new land arrived, they would leave Sweden forever. Charlotta thought of Pappa's grave in Osterunda church yard and
swallowed hard.

Charlotta was distressed to hear that Erik had shown himself openly in Forssa and had been served with a summons to
appear in the county court of that parish on October 11. How
could he be so careless? Now she must arrange to go north to
care for the children while Maja-Stina attended his trial.

This time, Charlotta did not ask the pastor for a paper of
permission to travel to another parish. When the post house
official asked her for it, she smiled, blushed and convinced
him that she had lost it and couldn't wait for another. After
all, Erik said that lying was not only permissible but praise-
worthy when the lie was to the glory of God. Surely this lie
was.

The journey was without incident, though she expected to
be detained and questioned at every post house. She found
Erik and Maja-Stina calm, even cheerful.

The next morning they set out for the trial as if they were going to a wedding or a christening, leaving Charlotta to hide her edginess and dread from the children as best she could. Unhappily, they felt it, as children do.

I must stop this! She forced herself to sing with the children and play games with them until she nearly conquered her sense of foreboding.

Then Maja-Stina came home alone.

"They would not let the faithful testify, Lotta, only those who were against us were heard! But the judge has set a new trial at Delsbo in November—"

"Where *is* Erik?" Charlotta asked fearfully.

"Talking to people about North America. I wish we were there now!"

"I'd better write to Mamma and tell her I'll be staying for awhile—"

***

The Delsbo trial was a repetition of the proceedings at Forssa, a guilty verdict and the judge's reversal of the finding with an order for a third trial. This time, Erik was jailed for his own safety until he could be tried again.

Maja-Stina told how she wept outside the courtroom and how a big man with Lapp features said, "Put your mind to rest about your husband. Just be ready to do what we ask!"

Three days later, a housemaid Maja-Stina never had seen before brought a basket of eggs to the house. As Charlotta transferred them to another basket, she found a letter, folded small, which told how Erik had been bound and placed in a carriage for the trip to Gefle prison. At Lynäs, several masked men blocked the road. They cut the reins from the horses of Erik's captors, knocked the deputies unconscious, and took Erik into their own carriage. A woman rushed from a nearby cottage to pour a bucket of goat's blood in the road to make the reviving deputies believe that murder had been done. Maja-Stina's unnamed friends wanted her to reinforce that impression by driving to Gefle, supposedly in search of her husband's corpse.

"Lotta, find the mourning aprons while I harness the pony to the cart! We may have to pinch the children to make them cry, poor lambs!"

Charlotta got out the mourning aprons and a black armband for young Erik. She fashioned a black rosette for the pony's bridle and even tied a black ribbon to the strings of the baby's cap. She rubbed her eyes red and told the children to do the same.

"Why?" young Erik asked.

"We're playing a game—to see who can act the saddest. Like this—" she wailed loudly.

"Is somebody dead?" Mathilde asked.

"No, thank God!" Maja-Stina said, "But we must put on a fine show!"

Maja-Stina drove and Charlotta held the baby. The older children howled and moaned with gusto until they were told to save it for Gefle. When Maja-Stina stopped the cart near Gefle church, Charlotta poked young Erik. "Now!"

He shrieked so convincingly that a crowd gathered to hear Maja-Stina wail, "Has anyone seen the body of my poor husband? He was murdered last night near Lynäs—how can I see to his burial when there is nothing to bury?" She covered her face with her shawl and shook with imitation sobs.

The people listened and shook their heads, hurrying away to tell the sad story to others.

Maja-Stina drove on to the town hall and repeated the performance. The children actually were crying now, caught up in the power of their own make-believe. Charlotta made herself weep by imagining Erik truly dead.

Near the lumber piles of bright yellow pine at the wharf, Maja-Stina called to men who were unloading drays, "I have nothing but his memory! If you should hear of a corpse with one finger joint missing—"

The men took off their caps, nodding respectfully.

"Now," Maja-Stina said under her breath, "now maybe they'll leave him alone!"

***

After Charlotta returned to Domta, frequent letters from Maja-Stina kept her informed of Erik's whereabouts. Their elaborate play-acting at Gefle had bought some time for him, but rumors of his death were discounted as he continued to preach.

Erik narrowly escaped arrest at Voxna Mills and spent a cold week under a barn floor at Ofvanaker. Then he went to Alfta, where they knew so much about North America. His last letter came from Dalarna, the home of Swedish liberty, where he received a large sum of money for the common fund from a rich farmer. He said he was wearing women's clothing again, and he might have chosen a better province for that! The shoes worn by Dalecarlian women had a high heel in the middle of the arch, and he teetered on them awkwardly. The short petticoats revealed too much of his legs in the Dalecarlian red stockings, and the yellow cap on the back of the head would not do. He wore the white sun-bonnet instead.

Charlotta and her sisters laughed at the thought of Erik in such garb, but they sobered and shuddered as the letter continued, "Erik knocked out his front teeth with a maul. He has so often been recognized by his teeth that he thought it best, but he says the cold air on the broken stumps is most painful."

They heard nothing more from Maja-Stina until January, when she wrote to say that Erik had crossed the mountains to Norway on skis and had sent for her and the children. They were to meet him in Christiania and board a coastal schooner for Copenhagen. They were on their way to North America!

Uppsala, February, 1846—

The professor's afternoon lecture had gone well, but only because he delivered it as unto God, foregoing all hope of satisfactory human response.

He had spoken of the emergence of the *regnum gloriae* ringingly: "The Kingdom of Glory is based upon the militant church. The struggling church is transformed into the finished dominion of God, not with a pessimism that underestimates God's power nor with an optimism that ends in Utopian dreams, but with the perception that it is *God* who wages our warfare!"

Walking home past shop windows that hid their wares behind curtains of frost, he tested his own belief in what he had said. Any don worthy of the calling must revise his offerings when they no longer reflected his thinking. Otherwise, he was nothing but a lazy parrot, coasting on old effort. Once he had believed in Utopian dreams, thinking that the Divine Will could be realized in the circumstances of life on earth, but apotheosizing the earthly had brought him little satisfaction. Could it be that he now leaned to pessimism? God forbid!

The professors at Lund were, as he was, critical of the established church. However, their approach to change was pietistic, an attempt to reproduce original Christianity. They were doomed to fail. History did not repeat itself, and God had a new message for every age. He believed that God was at work in the present painful turmoil of the Swedish Church, plunging it into the refiner's fire of conflict, but he could not see the outcome. *Faith is the substance of things unseen.*

Alone in the hallway of his lodging house, he hiked up the hem of his robe and brought out the long key to unlock his door.

Hanging his coat on a hook, he pulled his chair close to the grate and warmed his feet while he looked through the newspapers he had found no time to read during the day. He was forever subscribing to new ones, trying to keep abreast of what was happening in the provinces.

Erik Jansson had left the country at last, and a paper from Söderala carried his farewell address to his native land. The professor polished his glasses, poured himself a glass of brännvin, and read.

"Merciful God, open the eyes of Sweden's king that he may see how the devilish teachings of the clergy bring their hearers to the damnation of Hell—"

Oh, come now, Jansson!

"O Lord of all, lend to the Government light to see the darkness that enshrouds the earth, as related in Isaiah 60 and to see that the devil's preachers have caused darkness to descend over a whole people—"

The devil take you!

"Farewell, Sweden's princes and powers that be, who soon enough, as recorded in God's Word, will bite your tongues because of the woe that will overtake you—"

The professor quickly pulled his tongue from between his teeth, furious at yielding to the power of suggestion.

"Farewell, ye ravenous wolves, who have brought Sweden's people to the unfortunate state that they must pay several thousand *riksdaler* to those who reject and banish those who have been faithful to God's commandments—"

Ravenous. He walked to the sideboard for a bit of bread and herring.

"But peace be unto those who have received and do receive

him in the name of a prophet."

The professor reached for his Bible and turned to the book of Deuteronomy. "If there arise among you a prophet or a dreamer of dreams, and giveth thee a sign or a wonder, and the sign or the wonder come to pass, whereof he spake unto thee, saying, Let us go after other gods, which thou has not known, and let us serve them; Thou shalt not hearken . . . And that prophet, or that dreamer of dreams, shall be put to death—"

The professor closed the Bible abruptly. Why did he bother to apply the test of a prophet to Erik Jansson? The man's signs and wonders had not come to pass. He could not heal consistently, though people *did* say he had effected a cure or two. Rain had fallen before the time he had appointed. He had not transcribed the Bible as he promised. Why did so many believe in him, suffer for him, accept his fantastic claims?

That knock at the door must be Lovgren, whom he'd invited to supper. He poured another glass of brännvin and extended it to his friend as he opened the door.

Olaf laughed as he took the glass. "Are we in such a hurry for sweet oblivion tonight? Let me take my coat off first, at least!"

They settled before the fire for the easy conversation their long friendship made possible, and Olaf said, "Do you remember our old classmate, Sture Ruth?"

"The one from Norrland who doubted his calling?"

"Ah, you do remember Sture. He went into the import business with his uncle in Stockholm, and I visited him last week. He asked me to greet you."

"Sture was wise to abandon the clerical life. Even with a strong calling it can be difficult, and without that, it must be impossible! How *is* Sture?"

"Distressed, as a matter of fact. His son Johan got into

some kind of trouble—forged the old uncle's name to some
notes in payment of gambling debts, it seems. Sture managed
to get him into the army, hoping for foreign service—at least
until this business blows over. We never have a war of our
own, Jakob, are there wars anywhere to occupy young Johan
Ruth?"

"If not, there soon will be! And don't complain about our
lack! Like the Orientals, I want nothing to do with an inter-
esting history!"

Olaf laughed, then sobered. "I am sorry for Sture, though.
I hope the army will solve this problem for him."

"I wouldn't count on it. Sending the young man away may
chase the unhappy circumstances from Sture's mind, but the
army may bring out the worst in the boy."

"He's not really a boy, Jakob, and I suspect that his worst
has surfaced already."

They fell silent, watching the flames. The professor remembered the woman who refused his proposal of marriage, the
only one he ever made. The delicate oval of her face appeared
in the fire, and he raised his glass to it in silent thanks.
Because of her, he had no son to bring him shame. *God works
in every sorrow.*

Domta, Spring, 1846—

The long-awaited letter from Erik's scout, Olof Olsson, had
been copied in many hands. Carolina, who had the best handwriting in the Domta family, had made theirs, as well as one
for herself and Pehr.

They had read and re-read the letter until the words were
etched in their minds and the paper was limp from much
handling.

"Read it again, Charlotta," Mamma said.

"When I in Jesus' name went ashore upon the New Land,

it was a great joy for me! We had not our feet upon land during three months and three days—"

Mamma always looked worried at this point, saying, "What a long time to be on the sea!"

Charlotta continued, "The Communion Table is spread for you upon the New Earth. Everything is ready, so that it can be said in truth to each other when you set foot upon the Blessed Land, 'Come, let us go up to Zion!' Help the poor servants over. Money is of no value in America except to buy land. A good woman or maidservant or one of our farmhands is worth far more than money. They quickly work off their debt. This is a land like the Heavenly Kingdom. It is a land for action, a land where worker as well as Regent may eat wheat bread!"

Sabina clapped her hands. "When can we go?"

"As soon as we can get ready and find a ship to take us."

Mamma said, "Read that list of what we need again, Lotta."

"You must bring only the strongest clothes, dry bread, pork, meat, peas, butter, wheat flour, rice, salted herring, treacle, figs and vinegar. You may be on the water for a long time, and you would do well to bring dried fruit to save you from scurvy—"

"What's scurvy?" Sabina asked.

"I hope you never know!" Mamma said, "I've seen sailors with swollen gums and black and blue spots all over their bodies. That's scurvy!"

Anna-Maja said, "Aina Blom says that Erik has promised we'll all speak English as soon as we set foot on North America. Is that true, Mamma?"

"*I* never heard of such a thing!"

Aina was a good soul, Charlotta thought, but she was likely to get things wrong. Erik probably had said God would help them learn the language quickly.

"Here comes your cousin Jan," Mamma said, "I wonder

what brings him to us when it's still light enough to work in
the fields?"

"Why should he plant what he may not harvest?" Charlotta said.

Erik's oldest brother brought news of a sailing from Stockholm in early July. He said, "Jonas Olsson from Söderala will
sail then, and it seems like a good time. I've already talked
with Carolina and her husband—they're for it. Do you want
to go then, Aunt Anna?"

"Oh let's Mamma!" Sabina cried, "I'm so sick of waiting!"

"Hush, Sabina," Mamma said, but she nodded to Jan.

"Good! That makes four of you, six with Carolina and Pehr,
nine with Peter and his children, fourteen with my family,
and fifteen with our mother. Let's finish our selling and begin
to pack!"

***

With so many people leaving the parish, a buyer's market
prevailed. Houses and land brought meager prices because
the owners could not wait for better offers, and Charlotta was
glad Pappa had not lived to see the cheap sale of his family
home.

The common fund dwindled when money was withdrawn to
buy believers out of military service and to pay the debts of
others, but when those found wanting in faith and expelled
from the emigration parties tried to get their money back,
they were refused. Erik had left orders that the fallen away
must forfeit their contributions to the common fund.

After this separation of the sheep from the goats, those
who were in good standing prepared for departure in earnest.
The men gathered adzes, hatchets, mauls, chisels, planes,
hammers, sticking and skinning knives and fishing gear.
Women collected wool cards, knitting needles, sheep shears,

woollen clothes, needles and thread, drinking cups, wooden plates, spoons, knives and forks. Baskets were filled with dried, smoked and salted meat; rye meal and barley loaves; tubs of salted butter; honey; cheeses; coffee; sugar; dried apples; salt and pepper; stick cinnamon and wormwood seed.

Mamma walked among the jumble of trunks and baskets at Domta, checking and re-checking what had been collected. "Now what have we forgotten?"

Anna-Maja consulted the worn letter. "Pots of soft soap, Phosphor salve for lice, and fine-toothed brass combs for taking vermin from the hair, it says here."

"I have the soap," Mamma said, "but we have never had need for lice salve or fine-toothed brass combs for such a disgusting use! The very idea!"

"What do lice look like?" Sabina asked.

"I'm sure I don't know!" Mamma said indignantly, but she sent Charlotta to the village to buy the weapons against vermin, just in case.

***

When the emigration party from Osterunda parish reached Stockholm, Jan led them straight to the harbor. Charlotta was disappointed. She had hoped to see the Royal Palace, the Hall of Knights, and the Swedish Pantheon where the old kings were buried, but she supposed she might as well start weaning her heart from Sweden immediately.

The air at the wharf smelled of tar, fish, new rope and the sea. It made her think of Pappa and how he had wanted to be a sailor. She couldn't imagine him behaving like the sailors who were everywhere on the dock, flirting with the housemaids sent to buy fish from a fresh catch. Such winking, smiling and bold talk never had been Pappa's way. One of them seemed to be looking at her with unmistakeable invita-

tion. She responded haughtily, only to realize with embarrassment that his eyes were on Sabina, who stood just behind her
and smiled saucily.

Mamma had seen the interchange too, and she said, "Keep
your eyes down, girl! What would Erik say if he saw you carrying on like a bad woman?" Roughly she dragged Sabina to
Cousin Jan, who was guarding a mountain of baskets, chests,
boxes and knapsacks until the loading began, "Keep an eye
on this one, Jan!"

Charlotta joined Cousin Peter, who was trying to amuse his
two young children during the wait. She asked him, "Which
ship is ours?"

"Over there," he pointed.

"How small she is! Do you really think that ship can cross
an ocean?"

Peter laughed. "She has, many times, and with a full load
of iron!"

The brig had seen years of service, judging by her dirty
sails. They were the color of long-used potato sacks left out in
the rain, and the white of the hovering gulls made them look
even filthier.

Another group of emigrants reached the dock, and Peter
said, "That's Jonas Olsson, the reader from Söderala."

Olsson couldn't have been much older than Erik, but to
Charlotta, he looked like a Bible patriarch. His eyes were far-
seeing. Heavy cheekbones, a strong nose and a firm mouth
gave him an air of authority. All he lacked was a flowing robe
like the Moses in the steel engraving in her Bible.

Olsson's party of twenty-eight from Söderala was small
compared to the fifty-six from Osterunda and Torstuna, but
he was clearly in command. Even strangers from the Bolnäs
group moved close to him. He went about the dock counting,
and when he was satisfied that all passengers were present,
he raised his hands high and offered a prayer.

"Oh kind and loving Father, we ask Thy protection from the perils of the sea and beseech Thy blessing on our lives in the new land. In the precious name of Jesus, Amen!"

The brevity of the prayer startled Charlotta. It certainly was not Erik's way!

The scout had asked that his crippled young son be brought to him in America, and the child was the first to board the ship, carried in his grandmother's arms. Charlotta waited patiently for her turn.

Once aboard, she went below with her mother and sisters to explore the compartments of bunks separated by canvas partitions. One section was for families, another for unmarried men, and the third for single women.

"We're staying together by parishes down here." Jonas Olsson's wife told them.

A lurch and a sway meant the anchor had been hoisted. Charlotta and her sisters hurried on deck, looking for a place at the crowded rail to watch Stockholm fade in the distance.

A servant girl made room for Charlotta and told her, "I'm waiting to see it sink!"

"To see what sink?"

"Sweden! It's heavy with wickedness, and when we are safely away, it will sink into the sea and disappear!"

"Who told you that?"

"The Prophet!"

Charlotta started to correct her and decided against it. Erik was so often misunderstood because people put words they wanted to hear into his mouth—the way they twisted the Bible to mean what they wanted it to mean. She could argue until she was blue in the face, and nothing would be changed.

Very soon a crew member went among them clanging the supper bell. They were so many that they could not expect to sit at tables, and they carried their food to any sheltered spot they could find.

Then Jonas Olsson preached a sermon on the deck. He had none of Erik's spell-binding qualities, and Charlotta found herself listening to the slap of the sea against the sides of the ship and the sound of the wind in the bellied sails. This was her first experience of the sea, and it was both exciting and terrifying. *The sea either carries you or kills you!*

As Olsson preached on, she looked at her fellow-passengers with interest. Anders Thorsell, the shoemaker from Torstuna, was alone on this journey with his six-year-old son. His wife had refused to leave Sweden. Charlotta did not know that handsome woman with the thin daughter, but she had heard they were not believers. They were going to America to promote the girl's singing career.

Two former soldiers sat tailor-fashion with their backs to a coil of rope, and the woman next to them was a spinster from Soderhamn. The most important person on the passenger list was Anders Larsson from Hällby. He had been a juror, and he had given up a fine house and valuable business property to join Erik's followers. Larsson sat beside an illegitimate maid servant and offered her his coat when the wind blew cool, showing that he was no respecter of persons. Charlotta reflected that God probably would not reward Larsson for his kindness because he took so much pleasure in the public act. *What a strange ark we make!*

***

The first few days of sailing were calm. Charlotta stood at the rail for hours gazing at mingled shades of blue, gray and green in the waves and staring at the line where sky and ocean met.

When she tired of looking at the sea, she played with Peter's children on the deck or watched a growing romance between a girl from Gävleborg and one of the sailors. She had looked the sailors over herself, but how could she expect to find a dark and dusty man at sea?

The worst part of the voyage so far was their introduction to the common louse, an experience that brought their mother low. They all smelled strongly of Phosphor salve.

Charlotta was on deck when the sky darkened and the strong winds blew up, tossing the brig about like a leaf in an autumn gale. Terrified by the solid walls of water that threatened to entomb the brig and all its occupants, she rushed below.

She soon wished she had been brave enough to stay on deck. The combination of stale air and the sound of retching on all sides was too much for her. She vomited until she was certain her stomach had turned inside-out, and when those around her prayed aloud to die, she added a feeble "Amen!"

Jonas Olsson walked through the compartments, laying his hands on the sick in prayer and encouraging those who were simply sick with fear.

The juror from Hällby thrust his head through the curtains and said, "Jonas Olsson, it does no good to pray for the sickness to end! Pray instead for better weather!"

Their eyes met and locked, and Olsson said, "I will follow my inner testimony!"

Charlotta had heard Erik use just those words so many times. Where was he now? Had he been sick like this in crossing, or had God spared him? And how had Maja-Stina managed with the children in such awful circumstances? What if they arrived in America only to learn that Erik was dead? *Oh God, help us!* She doubled up, clutching her abused stomach. She must think the storm away, concentrate on something else. She tried to envision Illinois and could not. She summoned Anders, but he would not come. In her weakness, she allowed an unforgiveable thought to form, *I wish I'd stayed in Sweden!*

***

The brig survived the storm. The sea was flat and green once more between the swells that were gentle hills. The passengers moved about shakily, amazed to be alive.

The women had sloshed countless buckets of sea water across the floor of the sleeping compartments and scrubbed until their fingers were wrinkled, but they could not entirely vanquish the odor of vomit.

"We'll just have to stay on deck as much as we can," Mamma said.

The brig was only forty paces long and eight paces wide, and the deck seemed more crowded than a busy city street. Longing to be alone, Charlotta ventured into the hold.

A sailor who was shifting the cargo for better balance told her passengers were not allowed in the hold.

She apologized and started to leave. When she bumped against what looked like a basket of dirt, she turned to ask what it was.

He seemed reluctant to answer, and she persisted, "Does the Captain plan to grow something in it?"

"It's for the burials—"

"But we're at sea!"

The sailor scratched his head and tried to explain. "It's something the captain got into his head to make it more like dying at home. He throws a handful of Swedish soil on the shroud before it goes into the water."

Now that the storm had passed, the thought of death was far from Charlotta's mind. Of course some of the passengers were old, and a woman in the Bolnäs group was quite sick—*No!* She tossed her head and said, "You won't need it on this voyage! We will all die at home—in North America!"

"It will save the Captain a lot of bother if you do!" the sailor said crossly, "Now, will you get out of this hold?"

She took a generous pinch of the soil of her homeland in her fingers and ran. For all her brave talk, she couldn't really think of North America as home.

New York, September, 1846—

While he waited for his baggage, the Rev. Robert Baird stamped his feet to re-acquaint them with the feel of solid ground and looked about for a news boy. From the beginning of his journey to Stockholm for the international Temperance conference, he had prayed daily for President Polk, asking God to give him wisdom in the conduct of the Mexican War, and he now felt an entirely human curiosity as to what God's answer had been.

An urchin with a bundle of papers approached, but the child was selling Bennett's filthy sheet, and Baird would have none of it. Horace Greeley was his man. The "cheap but moral" New York Tribune championed the under-privileged, opposed slavery, and carried book reviews, reflecting his own views rather well. He shook his head at the boy. What a look of resentful disappointment! Baird reached into his pocket for a coin, hoping to alleviate the harshness of this young life. The boy probably would be beaten at home if his sales were insufficient. The child took the coin, rewarded Baird with a brief smile, and rushed away, shouting his wares with the anxiety that must be his habitual state.

A lad like that should be in school! Ironic that one of the nation's older cities allowed its children to grow up like wild beasts while frontier towns established schools before they built permanent homes. He had founded many of the frontier schools himself, drawing on his vibrant conversations with Philip Lindsley, the Greek and Latin tutor at the College of New Jersey at Princeton. Lindsley's ideas for college students could be adapted to younger children.

Lindsley attributed the student disorders at the College of
New Jersey to the fact that the school made them "so delicate and bookish as to be ill-equipped for living." he believed
in education that would combine the strength of Hercules and
the wisdom of Minerva. A thin, ascetic-looking creature himself, Lindsley believed in hard work and athletics as well as
book learning, and Baird never would forget the night when
Lindsley jumped to his feet in the basement of Nassau Hall
and cried, "Pupils should breathe an intellectual atmosphere,
live in a learned society, witness new experiments, share with
professors their enthusiasms and their thirst for knowledge!
Then how liberal and enlarged would be their views!" *Dear
Philip!*

Ah, one trunk was coming down, but there were others.
Baird had traveled to Stockholm heavily laden with Temperance tracts and other printed material, and their space was
now taken by beautiful Swedish woven stuff and knick-
knacks for Fermine, his wife of twenty-two years. The very
thought of Fermine made him disbelieve his own age and
hers. He was forty-eight, old by some standards, but Fermine
was ageless and made him feel the same. The attributes of
French women that he deplored were present in Fermine in
such delicate and perfect distribution that they seemed vir-
tues, and they were perpetuated with delightful variation in
their children.

"Tribune! Tribune!"

Baird stepped forward to buy a paper from a spunkier lad
who did not tempt him to pity. Resting his elbow on a high
piling, he read a dispatch from Santa Fe. General Kearny had
occupied the city in August while he was away. *Lord, let it
end!*

At last his baggage was collected, but he stayed. A Swedish brig was coming through the Narrows to the Upper Bay,
and it looked like one of the iron vessels used to transport

emigrants. Baird knew that it was when he saw the Rev. Olaf
Hedstrom, a convert of his old friend George Scott. Hedstrom
had made an old schooner in the harbor into a floating mission, the Bethel Ship. He preached the Methodist Gospel and
sent as many emigrants as he could to Baird's beloved
Mississippi Valley.

"Good morning," Baird called to him, "have you come to
meet a shipload of fine, new citizens?"

Hedstrom nodded with a smile. He had come to the United
States in 1833, but he was still diffident about his English.

"And will they be Methodists before they start west?"
Baird teased gently.

Hedstrom shrugged and went on smiling. "That is in the
hands of God. I do what I can for them."

The brig flying the blue and yellow flag of Sweden nosed
close to the dock, and Hedstrom hurried to the spot where
the gangway would be lowered.

Baird looked up at the people lining the ship's rail and
thanked God for their safe arrival. They were physically
weary but glowing with hope, strong and beautiful people,
ideal colonizers. They had perseverance, a spirit of personal
freedom and independence. They waited patiently while the
captain re-checked the manifest, and when Hedstrom went
aboard, they surrounded him with glad cries.

Baird followed, wishing that he could speak Swedish fluently.
In his three visits to Sweden, he had not mastered the curious singing of the language, but he could say "Welcome!"
perfectly, and he did.

When a woman caught his arm and spoke to him urgently,
he was at a loss. He tried to tell her so, but she persisted,
shaking his sleeve.

"Olaf!" he called to the busy Hedstrom, "Come and help
me!"

The woman transferred her attention to the Bethel pastor,

and after Hedstrom gave a lengthy response in Swedish, she
staggered away from him, devastated. She sank to a bound
trunk and threw her apron over her face.

"What was that all about?" Baird asked.

"She says Erik Jansson told them they would speak English the moment their feet touched the American shores, and
I have had to disappoint her."

"I have heard of the man," Baird said, "and while he seems
to be unorthodox in many ways, I can't believe he would say
a thing like that!"

"I don't think so either." Hedstrom said, "He was here in
the spring, you know, and he has gone on to Illinois. He does
have a curious power which becomes even greater in the
minds of his followers—"

"Olaf, those two men over there—they seem to be locking
horns about something."

Hedstrom sighed. "Yes, two strong men who quarrelled
about doctrine on the voyage. They want to go west in separate parties, but we have only one interpreter to send, so I
must persuade them to forget their differences. And they
want to begin the journey this instant. I suppose they think
Illinois is just over the hill!"

"Do you have lodging for them in New York?"

"Yes, we have a certain number of beds aboard the Bethel,
and I know some Swedish women who run boarding houses
where they will feel at home."

Baird impulsively offered a banknote, then wondered if he
would have enough left to get to Philadelphia? As Hedstrom
took the contribution gladly, Baird found a large bill in
another pocket and scolded himself for the momentary worry.
Oh ye of little faith!

"Do you need more Swedish Bibles, Olaf?"

"Yes, always!"

"I'll have them sent, and *you* be sure to send these people to the Mississippi Valley!"

"That won't be hard! They speak of nothing else. They tell me that God has summoned them there through Erik Jansson."

As Baird left the ship and hailed a cab, he had a vision of a clean, Swedish village in the fertile flatlands of Illinois. His book, *Religion in America,* opened with a description of the Mississippi Valley as "a wonderful display of wisdom and beneficence in the arrangements of Divine creation and providence." Surely the religious schism in Sweden which sent these people to America was another design of Providence.

The boarding house and the Bethel Ship, September, 1846—

What Charlotta saw in New York on the way to the boarding house seemed normal enough—men and women going about their business. They had encountered no fearsome beasts, only a small, brown dog not too different from Swedish dogs.

The woman who met them at the door of a narrow house of several stories was a plump widow from Gefle who called herself "Mrs. Nystrom." She talked busily as she showed them to their rooms, telling how she married a seaman whose most frequent port of call was New York.

"If I wanted to see Nils, I had to come here, but God rest him, he was lost at sea five years ago."

"Why didn't you go back to Sweden?" Sabina asked.

Mrs. Nystrom shrugged. "This business is too good to leave, and besides, I like it here. Nobody tells me what to do! In this country, you can do anything you can pay for! You'll want to wash yourselves, I know, but after that, sleep or do whatever you like. I'll call you in time for supper."

The smooth, white sheets were tempting, but Charlotta thought it indecent to lie upon them with a dirty body, and

she would die of shame if she brought a small, gray louse into
this immaculate dwelling. She removed her clothes and inspected each piece carefully. Then she poured water from a
big china pitcher into a matching basin and washed herself
properly for the first time in weeks. She didn't know what to
do with the dirty water until Anna Maja discovered a china
slop jar decorated with roses, too lovely for such low use. She
used it.

The sun shone into the bedroom through lace curtains,
throwing shadowy rosettes on the gleaming floorboards and
beneath Charlotta's eyelids in after-image as she fell into a
deep sleep, cleanly naked on the fresh bed.

Mrs. Nystrom's voice seemed to echo from a deep canyon
when she called them to supper in Swedish. They woke, confused, and finally remembered where they were.

The entire family was seated around the big dining room
table: Carolina and Pehr, Aunt Sara, Jan and his family,
Peter and his children, Mamma and Sabina.

"This must be a very big house!" Charlotta said.

"I've given you all my rooms." Mrs. Nystrom said, "The
Swedish common fund pays as well as any sailor!"

The meal was a feast of meat balls and gravy, mashed potatoes, a sauce almost like lingonberry but not exactly,
canned green beans and burnt sugar cake.

The children filled their stomachs with milk and had little
room for anything else, but their eyes grew so big at the
sight of a decorative bowl of apples in the parlor that Mrs.
Nystrom passed it among them. They dealt with the apples
according to their natures. Peter's son bit into his immediately, but his daughter rubbed hers on her dress and looked at
her face in the shining skin. She fondled it, love it, and saved
it. Jan's children hid theirs in pockets and under aprons.
Someone had stolen their knapsack of toys while they waited
to board the ship in Stockholm, and the theft had left its

mark on them.

When Charlotta saw Carolina excuse herself and hurry upstairs, she quickly ran after her sister, calling, "What is it,
Carolina?"

Carolina looked about furtively. "Shhh! Someone might
hear! Come into my room—"

The bedroom was exactly like the one Charlotta shared
with Anna Maja, even to the china basin Carolina was bend-
ing over to vomit. She hurried to hold her sister's head.
"What's wrong, Lina?"

"Oh, I'm so sick! I think I might be—" Carolina bit her lip,
blushing.

For a moment, Charlotta didn't understand, but when she
did, she blushed too. "But you weren't—when we left
Sweden—" *How could they—with people so close—in such a
smelly, awful place?* Aloud, she said, "I suppose it's God's
will—"

"Pehr's will had something to do with it!" Carolina said drily.

"Are you all right now? Shall we go down?"

They found the others getting ready to leave for a service
on the Bethel Ship, which was quite near Mrs. Nystrom's
house.

The floating mission welcomed them with winking lights
and the sound of singing wafting through open portholes. The
schooner rode low in the water, and the partitions below the
deck had been removed to create a church on the bay. Hedstrom's congregation greeted them warmly, offering them
seats and strange-looking hymn books.

"Are they Lutherans?" Charlotta whispered to Peter.

"No, Methodists."

"I don't know what that is—"

"I don't either, but they have some in Stockholm, I hear."

Pastor Hedstrom preached with enthusiasm, comparing the
journey of the *Erikjansere* to the wanderings of the children

of Israel. He said, "Unlike Moses, your leader has crossed
over into the Promised Land, and you will be with him soon!"

After the closing prayer, the women served real coffee and
what the North Americans called cookies. Charlotta watched
Sabina drink two cups of coffee and eat three cookies while
she flirted vivaciously with a young Swede who had emi-
grated the year before. *Why shouldn't she have her fun? We'll
be gone from here before anything comes of it.* Charlotta
worked through the crowd to Mamma and blocked her view
of Sabina.

Maja-Stina's housemaid was talking to Mamma indignantly,
"He said nothing about Erik Jansson's mission to bring the
true light!"

"No," Mamma said, "but he has been kind to us, and I will
not criticize him. I don't see Sara—did she come with you?"

"I thought she was staying in the same house with you—"

"Well, she is, but—now I remember! She went upstairs to
get her bonnet, and she never came down. There were so
many of us walking together that I didn't notice! Come, Lotta, let's go back quickly and see how it is with her! The voyage was hard on Sara—"

The landlady at the boarding house met them with the
news that Erik's mother was dead. She helped them wash
and dress the body, and she closed Aunt Sara's eyes and
weighted them with American pennies.

Coffin-making was a trade in America, it seemed. Peter and
Jan went to a shop to buy one, placing it on trestles in the
parlor. Charlotta watched for a moment when she could be
alone with Aunt Sara in the parlor. She had something to say
to her, something to give her. When the opportunity came,
she hurried to the coffin and whispered, "You were a hard
woman, Aunt Sara, but I loved you anyhow! Here—" she had
wrapped the pinch of Swedish soil from the ship's hold in her
best handkerchief, "you never had a chance to make a new

home, so I brought you a bit of the old—" Aunt Sara's clasped hands were cupped just enough to conceal her offering, and they were cold, so very cold!

The Hudson, September, 1846—

The interpreter, Knut Lundeen, led the emigrants aboard the steamer Elmira bound for Albany on a clear, quiet evening. The river was still as glass, but even so, many members of the party groaned at the prospect of more travel by water. The most reluctant travelers went below immediately, hoping to sleep through some of the ordeal.

Charlotta remained on deck to watch the stern wheel's churning motion. When that palled, she watched the Americans in their endless variety. Beautifully dressed women who belonged on a more expensive deck strolled among the Swedes making much of the children. Some American men wore top hats and high winged collars, but other men were dressed in well-worn leather garments. Could they be of the same nationality? Of course they must—the leather might betoken a certain province, and the men in top hats must be professors.

Lundeen paused beside Charlotta and said, "Don't let anybody sell you anything! Swindlers make this trip just to take advantage of the greenhorns."

"What is a greenhorn, please?"

"A person who doesn't know the customs of a place. One without experience."

"How can they sell me something when I don't know what they are saying?"

Lundeen laughed. "You'd be surprised at what can happen with sign language!"

Charlotta saw a bright flash of green beyond Lundeen's shoulder and gaped at a woman in green, shining stuff followed by a small person in green and gold livery. The little creature had a black face! Not black, really, but a deep brown, the color of wet bark. Speechless, she looked to Lundeen for an explanation.

He turned to see the object of her amazement and grinned. "I'm surprised you didn't see Negroes in New York. We sometimes have southern visitors who travel with their slaves."

"Slaves?" she said, not certain that she had understood him.

"Yes, the blacks are bought and sold like property. That woman—" he nodded toward the retreating undulation of green, "—is probably on her way to Albany to meet the man who gave her the human pet."

Charlotta was horrified. *What kind of country is this? They told us of the freedom here, but never of the slavery!* With a clutch of fear, she asked, "Will someone take *me* and sell me?"

"No," he said with a laugh, "you're the wrong color!"

Relieved, Charlotta watched the woman and her slave round the corner of the deck. From what Lundeen said, she gathered this was a bad woman like Solveig in Osterunda parish. No one ever gave Solveig anything but the price she asked—probably because she didn't have this woman's dangerous beauty.

"I must leave you," Lundeen said. "It's time for Jonas Olsson's English lesson. Would you like to learn too?"

"No—not yet." She was not ready to struggle with the language that came from the back of the throat and held the lips so still—not until she had absorbed many other new things, such as the fact that a Swedish mile made six American miles.

***

They took a canal boat to Buffalo, and on that stretch of the journey, many were sick with dysentery. It was the strange food, they all said, and they ate hardtack and dosed themselves with pepper brännvin.

They were fewer now. The desertions had begun in New York, the separation of the sheep from the goats. It was now apparent that some had professed a false faith in return for passage to North America. More left the party at Albany, and at Buffalo the number of the faithful dwindled further. Those who remained believed the deserters had lost their souls.

Anders Larsson blamed Jonas Olsson, saying he should have taken more care in screening the emigrants, but Olsson merely said, "Many are called but few are chosen."

Carolina was desperately sick, and Jan's wife expressed her doubt that they would find Erik alive in Illinois. It was a bad time.

The days aboard the Agrippa on Lake Erie were long and unmarked. Such a lake Charlotta had never seen. In Sweden, a lake was a bright, blue basin one could see across.

The nights were growing chilly this late September, and most of the trunks were too well secured to yield the wraps the travelers would have welcomed. The days, at least, were crisp and sunny.

At last they came close to land, and Charlotta asked Lundeen what it was called.

"Michigan. Soon you will see the orchards."

She thought of the firm, transluscent astracan apples of Sweden and sighed. They had been without fresh fruit for so long that they craved it sinfully. She smiled at the thought of Jan's little girl hoarding her wrinkled apple from Mrs. Nystrom's parlor bowl.

As the ship moved closer to shore, she could see the green crowns of the trees bent low with fruit. The children danced beside the rail, begging for apples, and the captain called to Lundeen from the bridge.

"He says we are ahead of schedule, and we will put in for a few minutes. He's the father of many children and knows how it is."

The steamer nudged the shore, the gangway went down, and the children dashed into the trees. Their elders followed at a scarcely more dignified pace. Carolina, whose pregnancy was too new to make her clumsy, out-distanced Charlotta to seize apples with both hands. The apples were thick-skinned with opaque, white flesh; tart enough to pucker the mouth. Charlotta ate hers greedily, watching Jan's son bite and chew like a wild thing, juice running down his chin and onto his shirt. Even the infants balanced on their mothers' hips managed to puncture the glossy, red skin with baby teeth and gnaw avidly.

Then Jonas Olsson strode toward the happy, laughing company with an angry look. "Come here to me!"

They obeyed, holding the fruit behind their backs in sudden guilt. Given the chance, they would have hidden as Adam and Eve did when the Lord God called, "Where art thou?"

"My dear brothers and sisters," Olsson said sternly, "these trees belong to someone. We must not take what is not ours."

Charlotta and Carolina looked at each other guiltily. What they had picked could not be put back on the trees. In this big land, everything seemed free, the gift of God. What wrong had they done?

Olsson pulled a purse of treasury money from his coat and went off to search for the owner of the orchard. Lundeen ran after him, trying to dissuade him, but Olsson was determined, and the interpreter shrugged and went with him.

As the passengers returned to the steamer, some of them continued to eat the apples they had picked. Others threw the fruit away in a fit of conscience.

"What's the use of that if he's going to pay for them?"
Sabina said, taking a juicy bite.

"You're right," Carolina said, "I'm going to eat mine for
the baby's sake."

Torn between the alternatives, Charlotta hid her apple in an
apron pocket.

Jonas Olsson was gone for a long time, and the captain
blew the Agrippa's whistle impatiently until they appeared.
No one dared to ask if their mission had succeeded.

The passengers remained subdued until they caught sight
of Detroit. Here, for the first time, was a clean city that
reminded them of Sweden. The houses on high banks above
the lake were neat and well kept.

"The whole city burned about thirty years ago," Lundeen
explained. "Then L'Enfant laid out a new one. He's the
Frenchman who designed Washington, our capital."

"Is that where the king is?" a child asked.

Lundeen laughed. "We have no king. Our most important
man is a president—James Polk. Well, it won't be long before
we're in Chicago."

"Does it look like Detroit?"

"I'm afraid not. It's a nasty, little village in a swamp."

Lundeen was right about Chicago, Charlotta thought when
she saw it. The settlement had only three decent streets with
yard-high stumps standing in the others. Cattle grazed between the houses, which were new but gray for lack of paint.
The wind blew mournfully over this desolation, speaking of
the winter to come. With a pang, she thought of the snug
house at Domta painted with the red ochre of Falun. It looked
as warm as it was.

Then men were gathering to discuss the arrangements for
the last leg of the journey, and Anders Larsson announced
that he would remain in Chicago.

"We will make *our* New Jerusalem here! Who will stay with

us?"

A few hands were raised, some defiantly, others with shame. Charlotta was shocked to see Erik's brother Jan step over to Larsson's side, but she realized that she shouldn't be surprised. His wife had been full of doubts and complaints from the moment they set sail. What disturbed her more was the sight of Carolina plucking at Pehr's sleeve and whispering to him urgently. *Don't do it, Carolina!*

At last the lines were drawn, the majority staying with Jonas Olsson. He said calmly, "Leave us, then."

"First you must give us our contribution to the treasury!" Larsson demanded.

"That you will not have! You may not take back what has been given to build a stronghold of the faith on the land Erik Jansson has chosen!"

"Then keep it! You'll need it in the howling wilderness! God will help us make it up, the money you've stolen from us!" Larsson signaled to his followers with a rough wave of his arm and stalked away.

Jan looked back at his brother Peter. Finding no understanding or forgiveness in Peter's stony face, he turned in anger, yielding to the pull of his wife's arm. Charlotta wanted to run after them, plead with them, but she knew that Jan's decision could not be changed. He had his pride. *Erik's own brother!*

Jonas Olsson dismissed the traitors to Erik's cause as if they never had existed, and Charlotta thanked God that Carolina and Pehr were not among them.

"Now we must make plans for reaching the Prophet's land near Victoria." Olsson said, "We will hire wagons to carry our possessions, but every able-bodied person must walk."

"How far is it?" someone asked.

"About twenty-five miles."

Swedish or American miles? Charlotta couldn't bring herself to ask, but somebody else did, and the answer brought a collective groan. *Swedish miles!*

Olsson said he had picked up enough English to get them to Victoria without an interpreter, and they would begin their journey the next morning, on the Lord's Day.

Lundeen found them boarding houses for the night, and Mamma was shocked at the expense. Even though the money came from the common fund, she resented the price paid for dirty linens and bedbugs. With the four of them crowded into one bed, they could not even toss and turn when they felt the fiery bites of the filthy insects.

At daybreak, Carolina came to their room weeping. "Oh Mamma, I can't go! I'm so sick—every day, Mamma! Pehr has gone to take our things off the wagon—we'll have to come later—after the baby—"

Tight-lipped, Mamma said, "I never expected such weakness in you, Carolina!"

"Oh, Mamma," she wailed, "I can't help it!"

"Very well. Erik's own brother has deserted him with less reason. I will explain it to Erik."

Carolina sobbed as if her heart would break and embraced them all until even Mamma wept and said, "There, there, Lina, it's only for a little while."

She went to find Pehr, promising to come to the livery stable for a final good-bye.

***

The wagons were loaded and waiting, hitched to huge, patient horses that snorted gently, rippling their velvety muzzles. *Each of them would make two Swedish horses,* Charlotta thought.

Pehr arrived with Carolina, and he scarcely knew what to do with her. When she shrugged off his comforting arm, he came to stand beside Charlotta, silent and miserable.

"She can't blame you, Pehr," Charlotta said, "after all, *she's* the one who—"

"First it's stay and then it's go! I've had our belongings off and on that wagon three times already!"

"Where are they now?"

"Off, and that's where they'll stay! I'm not a weather-vane!"

Jonas Olsson pulled his big, onion-shaped watch from his pocket and asked, "Where is Hans Dahlgren? Everyone else is here."

"He means to go with us." Peter said, "His goods are loaded."

"If he does not come in ten minutes, we will go without him."

Charlotta shivered with the vicarious horror of being left behind, and then a shout from the road announced the arrival of the missing man.

"What kept you?" Olsson asked.

"I found a church where the people were singing hymns, so I went in. When the preaching began, they locked the doors, and they wouldn't let me out! I tried to tell them I was start-ing a journey, but they couldn't understand me—"

"What did you do, climb through a window?"

Dahlgren laughed. "I sang a Psalm in Swedish at the top of my voice—they opened the door to get rid of me!"

Everyone laughed, and even Carolina smiled through her tears.

"Let's be on our way!" Olsson shouted, "May God lead us safely to the New Jerusalem!"

The driver at the head of the line-up yelled, "Ohaw!", flick-ing his long whip, and the wheels turned ponderously in the direction of the open road.

"Jan might have come to say good-bye—" Charlotta said.

"No," Peter said, "he's too ashamed."

Carolina heard what he said and sobbed aloud. Charlotta hugged her sister one last time, blinking away tears. Carolina always smelled like new-cut hay—clean, golden and so very dear. "Come to us soon, Lina!"

"Good-bye—" Carolina said, her voice breaking, "God be with you!"

Philadelphia, October, 1846—

Robert Baird folded the New York Tribune in neat quarters for breakfast table reading. This arrangement permitted him an unobscured view of Fermine and the whereabouts of his cup of breakfast chocolate, which she had refilled three times.

"You are not at all temperate about chocolate, Robert!" she said fondly.

He loved the way she said his name, "Ro-bair," and the gentle teasing that kept his self-importance within bounds. They were well-met; she the descendant of persecuted Huguenots and he the posterity of hounded Covenanters. They never forgot that earlier generations had suffered for their happiness nor that they must savor it fully in gratitude.

"Temperance is an odd word, Mina." he said, relishing another mouthful of the hot, velvety drink, "A man in Sweden once asked me why we use it when we don't mean what it says. Why say 'moderation' when you mean 'not at all'?"

"Well, why *do* you?"

He reflected, stroking his mutton chop whiskers. "Probably because the right word sounds nasty—challenging. The human reaction to the word 'Prohibition' is instant resistance and—" he saw her eyes dancing above a carefully grave mouth and broke off, "Oh Mina, you and your *clarte!*"

She smiled. "A useful quality—as I trust you learned in Paris!"

"I did indeed!"

Fermine had guided him through the labyrinth of French manners and appearances so expertly that he felt equally at ease with a shop keeper and Louis Philippe. Sent to Paris to encourage the Protestant church in France, he bowed and smiled when the citizen King complimented him on his "truly catholic spirit." Without Fermine's *clarte*, he might have bridled at the term.

"I will leave you to your paper, Robert." Fermine said, "We are meeting this morning to arrange food baskets for the poor at Thanksgiving."

He lifted his face for her kiss. "Ah, charity is so pleasant to dispense and so difficult to receive!"

"I know that, Robert! We send the baskets with a messenger who does not stand about waiting for abject gratitude— old Bertie, who's deaf as a stone!"

"Of course you would find the perfect means, *mon coeur,* I meant no criticism!"

"Until lunch, then," she said, adjusting the rose-patterned Dalarna shawl he had brought her from Sweden. Baird appreciated how well it suited her until she vanished from his sight.

Correspondence for the Foreign Evangelical Society awaited him, and his speech on the Stockholm Temperance convention needed polishing, but Baird had accomplished his daily Bible-reading, prayer and meditation. He believed that God might allow him the brief indulgence of reading a book review—or two.

He did miss the writing of Margaret Fuller, who had gone off to Europe while he was away. Fermine had kept Miss Fuller's farewell to America for him, and he remembered it well because he agreed with it heartily.

"I go to behold the wonders of art and the temples of old religion. But I shall see no forms of beauty and majesty beyond what my country is capable of producing in myriad variety, if we have the soul to will it!"

Miss Fuller was an excellent teacher, and he sympathized with her passion for social reform, but he deplored her association with Emerson. That man, once pastor of Cotton Mather's church in Boston, was ruining a whole generation of Americans with his ringing but hollow affirmations! He deified man, challenging the omnipotence of God.

Baird folded his paper to the book review section, and a piece on George Sand's *Le Meunier d'Angibault* reminded him of another bone he had to pick with Miss Fuller. In her book, *Women in the Nineteenth Century,* published the year before, she had said women could be anything they wished, even sea captains! Fermine had made him admit the possibility of it, but he didn't like it. In his view, women should be spared all hardship.

What upset him more was Margaret Fuller's insistence that George Sand was the triumphant example of female emancipation. He had seen the Baroness Dudevant swaggering along Rue St. Augustin in trousers and tall hat, and he had forgotten all the manners he ever knew to stare at her arrogant dark eyes, fleshy nose and sensuously full mouth. Curiosity propelled him to a bookstall to buy her novel, *Indiana,* but he found it a silly, romantic book about misunderstood women and untrammeled love. Of course one couldn't blame Mme. Sand for what she had become. While at the Convent of English Augustinians in Paris, she had yearned to take the veil, but her fierce, old grandmother stopped that by whisking her off to the country and force-feeding her with Deism.

He glanced through the review by an unfamiliar writer and smiled at the closing verdict: "A mystico-socialistic book that offers a self-indulgent prescription for reform." *Ah, Aurore, Miss Fuller would have dealt with you more kindly!* One might not approve of George Sand, but she reflected the restless discontent of France, and someone should take heed.

Re-folding the paper to the front page, he noticed a small story he had missed; how, he couldn't imagine; with a heading of "Slave Sues for Freedom." As he read the piece, he realized that he knew the man! On one of his visits to the Mississippi valley, he had dined at the home of Dr. John Emerson in Davenport, and the slave, Dred Scott, had pulled out his chair with the elegance of a European footman. At the time, Baird had seen the tall, well-favored black man as the personification of Rousseau's Noble Savage and had laughed at himself for the notion. He didn't hold with the view that primitive simplicity equaled virtue.

Emerson, an Army surgeon at Fort Armstrong until that military outpost was closed, had treated his slave well, but Baird could see that he was disturbed about owning another human being. Not sufficiently disturbed to set the man free, however. Now Emerson was dead, and Dred Scott was suing for his freedom in the state of Missouri, claiming that living on free soil in Illinois, Iowa, and Minnesota had made him a free man. *And so he should be*! But he could imagine the effect of such an outcome on the slave-holding South, and it made his skull prickle with apprehension.

Ten years before, he had talked with the late Swedish King Charles about the maintenance of the Union. The old King had warned that civil war would follow division, and in the end, despotism would take the place of freedom. At the time, Baird thought it strange that the reactionary Swedish monarch should show such an interest in the United States and its progress while he allowed his own country to stagnate, but, he supposed, other peoples' problems were easier to solve than one's own.

Could the Union be maintained while slavery existed? Baird despised slavery, but he preached patience in dealing with it for the sake of that strained Union, "Help as much as you can, but don't bring the matter to open warfare!" And people did help. Most of the new towns on the prairie had their hiding places for slaves on the way to Canada. Baird had hoped the procedure could go on until the South literally was bled white, but now the noble and not-so-savage Dred Scott had thrown the gauntlet in a wonderful but terrible gesture sure to bring suffering to many of his brothers in the faith.

Baird thought of men like George Washington Gale, who founded a town to nurture a college in the Old Military Tract of Illinois. Gale hid slaves in his church and passed them along to the North. Picturing the thin, dyspeptic Gale, Baird smiled ruefully. He had been a guest in the big, square home of his Presbyterian brother in Galesburg, and he didn't wonder that the man had a bad stomach. Mrs. Gale, a plain Quaker who had removed the ruffles from her husband's wedding shirt, was an abominable cook! Accustomed to Fermine's culinary skill, Baird had felt a bit seedy by the end of the visit.

But the inner man was well-nourished in Galesburg. Most prairie homes and business houses were made of logs and raw boards, but Gale's new town was painted white, symbolizing pride in an ideal.

The name of the college was Knox. Baird had asked if it was named for the great Calvinist, and Gale said, "If you choose. There are those who think it was named for General Henry Knox, our first Secretary of War. We have enough problems without quarreling over a name, so we leave it open to interpretation."

At Knox, students paid for their education with manual labor, but they still had time for the literary societies, the Adelphi Lyceum and Gnothautii. The college came as close to Philip Lindsley's ideals as any Baird had seen.

And Gale had chosen his land well. The Old Military Tract was a rich cornucopia of land between the Mississippi and Illinois rivers set aside as bonuses for the soldiers of the War

of 1812. Most of them thought it too remote and were eager
to sell their patents.

The party of Swedes Baird had seen at New York harbor
was headed for that country. He knew how they had forced
their marginal farms in the north of Sweden to high yields by
ditching swamplands and overcropping, and he was sure they
would perform miracles with the rich land of Illinois. They
would work harder than any black slave under the whip and
do it gladly because they were free. *Oh Lord, bless their journey and their labors!*

Illinois, October, 1846—

Charlotta and her sisters walked beside the wagons as gaily
as if they were headed for an outing in the Swedish woods.
They were done with ships and boats, and the distance that
remained seemed insignificant in comparison with the miles
that had been put behind them.

The gentle flats of the countryside were still green, but
clumps of trees here and there flared in an unbelievable brilliance of reds and yellows. A mellow gold was Sweden's bright-
est autumn hue.

Little Jonas, the scout's crippled son, rode on a high wagon
seat with one of the drivers. His grandmother was wedged in
with the baggage until she complained that the trunks were
crushing the life out of her and asked to be lifted down.

Noticing that her mother was panting as she walked, Charlotta said, "Why don't you take that place in the wagon?"

"I can walk!" Mamma said proudly, but Charlotta noticed
her look of relief when the caravan stopped beside a stream
for the noon meal. They ate hardtack and cupped their hands
to drink the strangely salty water from the stream.

"I thought we were to have white bread and figs in America!"
Sabina complained.

Jonas Olsson's wife looked at her reproachfully. "By faith, famine becomes a feast! We will have better fare when we reach Erik Jansson's settlement.

Sabina sighed. "I wish I had another Michigan apple!"

"Shhh!" Charlotta said, wanting no reminder of that incident.

Jonas Olsson was studying the map, not to find the way, but to measure their progress. They could scarcely get lost on a road without turning. And it wasn't really a road, just deeply-rutted wagon tracks with shoulder-high grasses on either side moving in the wind like seawater. Charlotta sometimes looked back, expecting the grass to close behind them like the Red Sea, but there was no need. They were not pursued, thank God!

Olsson was on his feet, impatient to move on. Charlotta hurried to help her mother rise and was alarmed at how pale and exhausted Mamma looked. How many days would the journey take? Could Mamma stand it? Charlotta walked with an arm around her, supporting much of her weight.

The afternoon stretched long, and at nightfall they spread covers on the ground beneath the wagons. The bedding was odorous from the ocean voyage, but Charlotta was too weary to notice the smell or to hear the strange night sounds of Illinois. She slept and dreamed that she was dancing. In the dream, her feet didn't hurt at all.

***

Day followed day, and when they slogged along the muddy trail with no protection from a pelting rain, the children started to sneeze. Charlotta tucked Peter's children between boxes and trunks on one of the wagons and paused to tear her petticoat to bind her blistered feet. The caravan moved so slowly in the rain that she caught up with her family easily.

"How much farther?" Sabina whined.

"Let's not ask." Charlotta said, "If it's far, we'll just feel worse for knowing!"

That night they were too cold and miserable to sleep, and they heard the strange howls and hoots of wild things. Wolves? Charlotta's heart felt squeezed. Lynx?

Anna-Maja huddled close and whispered, "Maybe some monster we've never heard of lives in this ocean of grass—"

"God wouldn't bring us this far and then let something keep us from Erik!" Charlotta said stoutly.

She was more worried about the howl of a real wolf and the cough Mamma had developed. Would they ever be warm and dry again? Somewhere a woman cried softly and a child screamed in a nightmare. *There will be better days and nights!*

***

The ground was white with frost the morning the party reached Victoria, and Peter said, "Thank God we haven't far to go! The winter is almost here!"

"Olof writes that it is nothing like Swedish winter," Jonas Olsson said. "It comes late and goes away early."

Charlotta was pleased to hear it, and she would be even more pleased to find a warm hearth and a place to wash. Her hair and skin were filthy, and she had worn the same clothes for nine days.

"Look," Sabina said, "someone is coming to meet us!"

The man was clean-shaven with bright eyes and an upturned mouth. He spoke in strangely garbled Swedish, searching for words, but they finally understood that he was Jonas Hedstrom, the brother of the Bethel Ship's pastor, the missionary who made his living as a blacksmith.

"I have almost forgotten my native tongue," he said in smiling embarrassment, "I find no use for it here. How is my brother?"

"He is well." Jonas Olsson said, taking Hedstrom aside for consultation.

While the caravan waited, Charlotta looked at the small, unpainted buildings that lined the road at wide intervals. Curious faces at the windows and in the doorways looked back, and a woman who was hanging her washing from a line stretched between two young trees waved.

"This isn't much of a place!" Sabina said.

Charlotta answered, "I like it better than Chicago!"

At Jonas Olsson's signal, the wagons moved again. Hedstrom walked with them for a mile or so, then he raised his hands in benediction and went back to Victoria.

The caravan moved faster, energized by the knowledge that the Prophet was very near. They sang some of his hymns, startling a farmer in his field.

Expecting to reach Erik's settlement by midday, the people were disappointed when Jonas Olsson signalled for a late morning stop.

"We will eat before we arrive." he said, "We have not come here to be a burden to Erik Jansson."

They ate their hardtack, telling each other that this would be their last wretched meal. The New Jerusalem was at hand.

"All of this land with no trees!" Mamma marveled, "If only Jan had lived to see it!"

Charlotta nodded sadly. She had wanted to bring Pappa's bones to North America, but the others convinced her that Pastor Risberg would never allow it, and besides, Pappa's soul was free to come to North America. She did feel that he was with them now.

They had not gone far beyond the place where they stopped to eat when Erik galloped from the north to meet them, shouting, "God be praised! You're here!"

As Erik dismounted, Jonas Olsson stepped forward to clasp

his shoulders and say, "These people are in your hands now, Erik Jansson!" Erik embraced him.

How strange Erik looked with his tusk-like teeth broken to stumps, Charlotta thought, but how beautiful, even as he was, in their reunion. She saw him turn to his brother Peter, and her gladness dimmed. *He'll ask about Aunt Sara. We've had time to get used to her being gone, but he—*

"Well, Peter, where is our mother—and Jan?"

"Mother died in New York—"

Erik closed his eyes as if he had been struck, but he quickly recovered and said in a firm voice, "Peace be to her dust!"

"And Jan decided to stay in Chicago. It was Sara Beata who—"

Erik cut off the explanation with a short, harsh laugh. "First he chops off my finger joint, then my teachings! So be it! Come, let us go to the church and give thanks!" He remounted and urged his horse forward, leaving the dusty caravan to follow.

Then others rode out from the settlement to meet them. The men were dressed alike in undyed wadmal. One of them asked for the scout's mother-in-law, and as she spoke with him, she gave a piercing shriek and ran to Jonas Olsson weeping.

Charlotta was going toward the woman when she was caught and lifted off her feet in the exuberant greeting of Nils Helbom, Erik's hired man.

"Welcome to BiskopSkulla!" he boomed, "We have named the New Jerusalem for Erik Jansson's birthplace in Sweden, and we are learning to call it Bishop Hill—the way the Americans do!"

"Nils, you scared me!" she said, standing down, "I was just going to see what the trouble was over there—"

Helbom's high spirits vanished. "Ah, it's bad! Olof Olsson, his wife, his mother, and his children—all dead from some strange ailment. The wife is not yet in the ground!"

The terrible news paralyzed Charlotta for a moment, and then she thought of Jonas, the little cripple. What would become of him with his whole family dead? She found him sitting on the ground playing with a stick, forgotten in the confusion. *Oh, my little lamb, you don't know your mother is dead!* "Come!" she said, holding out her arms to him, and he gave her a brief, bright smile that nearly broke her heart. He was heavier than he looked, but she refused Helbom's offer to take him and carried him the rest of the way in aching arms.

As they entered the settlement from the south, she saw a cross-shaped structure of logs and canvas among tall oak trees with two log houses and four large tents farther on.

"Erik Jansson is waiting in the church." Helbom said.

Charlotta stumbled into the cross-shaped building and put the boy down on one of the log seats. The huge enclosure was lighted only by the candle on the log pulpit, where Erik waited to speak to them.

"Why is it so big?" she asked Helbom.

"We built it for all who mean to come to us. It was the first building we put up."

Maja-Stina rushed in carrying the infant born in New York. Mathilde and little Charlotta clung to her skirts, and young Erik was close behind. Greeting her relatives with glad cries, Maja-Stina asked, "Where is Erik's mother?"

"Gone." Mamma said, "She died in New York."

A large, round tear coursed down Maja-Stina's cheek, and Charlotta marveled that she could mourn a woman who had treated her so unkindly until she realized that Maja-Stina was grieved for Erik's sake.

"My poor man!" Maja-Stina said, as more tears followed the first.

"Beloved friends!" Erik said.

At the sound of his voice, the company fell silent, and when he launched into his sermon, Charlotta was convinced that his power had grown in the new land.

"Our fathers had the tabernacle of the testimony in the wilderness. Even so will we preach and testify as we build the New Jerusalem! Here we will hold all things in common, rejoicing in the—"

The words blurred and faded, and she could no longer see the single candle flame. At a choking, tickling sensation, she opened her eyes to stare in confusion at a bunch of feathers tied to a long stick. Ashamed that she had fallen asleep, she sat bolt upright, blushing furiously. The feathered stick withdrew, and its opposite end, fitted with a wooden ball, rapped the head of a sleeping man in the next row. Such an object had not been necessary when Erik preached in Sweden, Charlotta thought. Did they sleep now because they were no longer afraid of violent interruption? She was determined to keep her eyes open, but her mind wandered, distracted by tempting thoughts of food. After days of hardtack, she could scarcely wait for a proper meal.

***

The first meal served to the newcomers to Bishop Hill was pea soup, the traditional Thursday night fare in Sweden, and it was not Thursday. Charlotta disliked pea soup, but she was hungry enough to eat it and wish the helping had been larger.

Maja-Stina explained, "We came too late to plant a crop. These are the dried peas we brought from Sweden."

After the meal, Erik took his relatives to his own quarters in the north end of one of the cabins. The night was chilly, and they crowded around a fireplace of stones mortared with dried mud.

"This is a better cabin than Olof Olsson's in Victoria!" Young Erik said, "When we stayed there, rain came in through the roof and snakes crawled in through the cracks in the logs!"

His father said, "Something worse than snakes and rain had crept into Olof Olsson's cabin—Methodism! I spent weeks re-converting him to the True Faith!"

"What a time that was!" Maja-Stina said, "They were at it morning, noon and night, and once Olof threatened to throw us all out of the house! He could have done it, too! What a big, strong man he was!"

"If he was so big and strong, why did he die?" Sabina asked.

"God alone knows. The children were taken with chills and fever, and then Olof, and Anna Maria died just yesterday. They have diseases here that we know nothing about!"

"What will become of little Jonas?" Charlotta asked.

"He'll be cared for by his grandmother—and by all of us. Tonight they have taken him to see his dead mother. He would have seen her alive if you had come just a few hours sooner—"

When Erik's relatives left his cabin to go to their beds in a cold tent, the Söderala people were just returning from the burial. Little Jonas was white with exhaustion and bewildered grief.

Later that night when Charlotta was remembering the kind Methodists of the Bethel Ship and wondering why Erik condemned their beliefs, she heard little Jonas screaming in his sleep in the next tent. *Oh God, how can You be so cruel to a child?*

***

The routine of life in the New Jerusalem was established immediately. Everyone rose at five o'clock in the morning, broke a skim of ice from their wash basins, and prepared to attend 5:30 matins in the tent church.

Candles were too precious for common use, and the people found their way to the church in the dark. The log seats nearest the fire were reserved for the old and the sick, but no one was in the bloom of health. The food supply, scanty when the new party came, had dwindled further, and the race to finish new shelters before the worst of the winter arrived slowed as the workers grew hungrier and used up their reserve of strength. Charlotta coughed and lusted for both food and sleep as she took her place on one of the log seats.

"Beloved friends," Erik said, "all suffering, sickness and hunger is merely a prelude to an existence more glorious than you can imagine!"

Charlotta tried to listen, but a two-hour sermon was too much for her when she was cold, hungry and exhausted. She kept her eyes open to avoid the feather bundle, but her mind drifted, fixing on nothing but how miserable she was.

At last it was over! Thanking God for the final "Amen!", she hurried to the dining tent, where she stood with the others before the long planks that served as tables and prayed Erik's prayer before meals. They fell upon the hardtack and rye coffee with true gratitude, and the scant rations were consumed all too soon. Then they prayed, "I thank Thee, my God, who has taken away my sins and satisfied me both to soul and body, with Thy rich blessings which I always own and enjoy, for the name and death of Jesus Christ. Amen!" *God, I am not satisfied!*

Erik stood at the tent door, giving out work assignments. The colony had more women than men, and they were expected to do every kind of hard labor. None complained. Charlotta was sent to dig into the banks of a ravine that wound southward from the Edwards River. They were building *Jordkulor*, dugouts to be lined with logs and fitted with fireplaces. The strongest of the women dug, and the rest passed buckets of earth to the outside. Charlotta was proud to be a digger, and she quite enjoyed the rich, moldy smell of the excavation.

As soon as a cave was finished, the men brought logs from Red Oak grove to split and saw for the inside walls. Most of the dugouts were eighteen feet wide and thirty feet long with two tiers of bunks along the sides. They sheltered thirty colonists. A few were built to accommodate fifty people.

Knowing that she was working on the dugout that would be home to her, her mother and her sisters, Charlotta fought her exhaustion and worked an extra hour that day.

***

When they moved in, the dugout seemed roomy. Many of the bunks were empty and could be used for storing trunks and cases. Light filtered in from the two windows in front, dispelling Mamma's fear of living like a mole, and she began to take pride in the dwelling. She swept it thoroughly with a birch twig broom brought from Sweden and even swept the spaces between their dugout and the ones on either side.

But then the earth's dampness began to seep through the log walls. One morning Charlotta found Mamma so stiff that she couldn't rise from her bunk. Alarmed and not knowing what else to do, she ran to find Erik.

He prayed with Mamma, and she improved enough to sit up and say, "That was just what I needed! I can get back to work now."

"That's right, Anna," he said, "if you have faith, you will not be sick."

Charlotta could see that Mamma believed what Erik said, but she wasn't sure that she did. Olof Olsson had returned to the true faith and died.

***

Philadelphia, December, 1846—

At the postman's ring, Robert Baird went to the door in his shirtsleeves. "How are you this morning, Mr. Bundy?" he asked and shivered in the cold draft as the postman made earnest, literal answer.

"Rheumatism bothers me a mite. It's the damp cold that does it, Reverend. The Missus is a little peaked too—don't think she's got thick enough blood for these parts. If it wouldn't be too much trouble, Reverend—"

"Not at all, Mr. Bundy, I will be happy to remember you both in my prayers. Thank you and good day!" He closed the door firmly. *Oh Lord, before I forget, if it be Thy will, heal the infirmities of the Bundys.*

He sorted the mail on the hall table: Temperance to the left, American Bible Society to the right, and school correspondence in the middle. It occurred to him that the arrangement might be inappropriate, and he shifted the Bible Society letters to the center.

One envelope remained, a letter from Illinois. That careful handwriting belonged to Ithamar Pillsbury, the Presbyterian minister responsible for at least three new towns in Illinois. For the past five years, Ithamar had served the church at Andover, a town patterned after New Haven, Connecticut, and he was working to establish a public school system there.

Baird carried the letter into Fermine's solarium, thinking the warmth of the winter sun through many windows might toast away the chill he had taken at the open door. It was shameful that he should even take note of such a small physical discomfort! Ithamar certainly would not. Just before Baird's second visit to Sweden, Ithamar had written that the people of Davenport, Iowa, asked him to come to them and organize a Presbyterian congregation. A neighbor had borrowed his horse, and it was not returned in time for the jour-

ney, so Ithamar walked twenty-six miles to perform his duty
and walked home again. *Would I have done as much?* Baird
sighed and opened the envelope.

"My dear Robert, Andover flourishes. We now have a plain
but adequate house of worship, and Mrs. Pillsbury is thankful
that the services have been removed from our house, as she
has quite enough on her hands with the school classes in our
dining room and parlor.

"The school is by subscription because I have not yet been
able to convince the populace that every child should be educated at public expense. May I use your successful arguments to the Legislature of New Jersey on the benefits of
free schools? Perhaps you will be good enough to send me a
transcript of your remarks in Trenton eight years ago—if you
still have such a thing.

"The new town of Cambridge for which I gave thirty-six
acres of land three years ago seems loathe to grow, even
though it is the seat of Henry County. Poor mail service is
part of the problem, I believe. Few of us would choose to live
in a place cut off from the rest of the world, and the mail
route from Wethersfield to Geneseo has altered, leaving Cambridge out. The carrier throws the mail bag from his wagon
ten miles east of town, and a boy must be hired to fetch it.

"The real reason for this letter, Robert, is the plight of the
new Swedish settlement at Bishop Hill southeast of Cambridge. Knowing your deep interest in the Swedes, I feel that
you will want to pray for their relief. A third party of immigrants arrived there in late November to be greeted with the
proclamation of a five-day fast! This after a stormy crossing
and a cold overland trip! Some of the younger ones were so
angered by the fast that they left Bishop Hill.

"The few who passed through Andover could not speak
English, and I sent for Jonas Hedstrom, the Swedish missionary at Victoria, to serve as an interpreter. Hedstrom had

some personal knowledge of the situation, and it all adds up to a deplorable state of affairs. The people are crowded into caves, which promotes the spread of disease, and the settlement has no doctor because their leader insists that faith will keep them well. Furthermore, this Erik Jansson told the deserters that they were damned when they left his New Jerusalem, and Hedstrom and I were hard put to correct that awful impression. The fact that they would leave, so believing, means that conditions at Bishop Hill are truly unbearable. Our congregation has sent a supply of epsom salts, quinine and bitters, but I fear this will not be enough. Please help as you can in substance and spirit. Yours in Christ, Ithamar Pillsbury"

Baird's eyes misted with tears at the memory of the hopeful emigrants debarking at New York, and a verse from the book of Numbers came to him, "Is it a small thing that thou has brought us up out of a land that floweth with milk and honey to kill us in the wilderness—"

He remembered Njutanger in the north of Sweden where the people so gladly received his praise of the Mississippi valley. He had told them, "The climate of Illinois is delightful, and unquestionably healthy."

He remembered the people of Norrala, who sang such sweet hymns and thanked him for telling them of religious liberty in North America. Were they now held prisoner in Bishop Hill? This man Jansson sounded as oppressive as the State Church of Sweden, if not more so, calling down damnation when the fate of any soul other than his own was not in his hands! Baird recalled a comment made by the pastor of the Bethel Ship, "That fellow has more power than a good man would want and more power than a bad man ought to have!" Baird got to his feet and paced, deeply agitated.

Fermine came into the solarium and took his tightly clasped hands in her own. "What troubles you, Robert?"

"I have had a letter from Ithamar Pillsbury—"

"The son of Aaron from Illinois?"

"Yes, Fermine, and it carries bad news about my Swedes."

"*God's* Swedes, Robert, put them in His hands!"

"Oh, I do, my heart, I do! But *we* are His hands—I must send a bank draft to Ithamar immediately!"

"I have been very thrifty in the house this month, Robert, and when you write the draft, please add the cost of your Christmas gift to me."

He lifted her hands and kissed them. "We are not yet *that* poor!"

Bishop Hill, December, 1846, to summer, 1847—

The fourth party of emigrants brought new illnesses to Bishop Hill, and when the newcomers were crammed into the already crowded dugouts and cabins, their diseases spread with alarming speed. Those who were weakened by hunger went down with chills, fever and diarrhoea. Others had hard cases of measles.

At least we have seen measles before, Charlotta thought, but when she found Peter's daughter hot and raving, she was frightened and sent Peter to find Erik.

"It's only the measles!" Erik said, "Remember how we had them when we were young in Sweden? Just keep her in the dark so her eyes won't be harmed."

Peter laughed bitterly. "That won't be hard! This cave never sees the light of day!"

"Are you complaining, Peter?" Erik asked with ominous calm.

Peter held out for a long, stubborn moment, then he bowed to his brother's authority. "No, I'm not complaining. I believe we are doing God's work, and He will not forsake us."

Erik showed his broken teeth in a smile and clasped his

brother's hand.

***

Peter's daughter recovered, but a small boy from Bolnäs died of measles or what followed them, and many others died of ailments that had no name. The dugouts were pits of contagion.

Each morning Erik assigned men to carry out the corpses. No planks were available for coffins, and the bodies were wrapped in winding sheets. Erik stood beside the wagon that served as a rude hearse, giving directions to the men of the burial detail.

"Will you speak over the dead?" Charlotta asked.

"There is no time. They die too fast! I cannot spare the men to dig a grave for each—they must be buried together, but God knows where they lie!" He left her abruptly to follow the burial wagon to the hillside east of the village.

***

In spite of the deep sadness of Bishop Hill, the colonists took heart at the coming of Christmas. Fathers lost precious hours of sleep carving wooden animals and mothers made dolls from wooden spoons and bits of cloth. All were moved to remember the Prophet at Christmas, digging into carefully hoarded provisions to find a bit of soap or a single beeswax candle to carry to his cabin.

Charlotta cut up one of her petticoats to make a nightcap for Erik. Biting the thread after the final stitch, she sighed and said, "Remember when we gathered hazel nuts to put on the tree?"

"Hazel brush grows above the ravine," Mamma said, "Next year we can—"

"What I remember is the sweet and sour limpa!" Anna-Maja said, licking her lips, "How I wish we could celebrate *Jul-Afton* with coffee and *doppa* in bed!"

Charlotta nodded. "If we only had the time!" In Sweden, there had been *some* time to do as one pleased, but here there was nothing but work. Erik had to convince them it was God's work, or they would think they had died and gone to Hell!

They celebrated *Julotta* by rising in the black, early morning and lighting candles for a procession to the tent church. The candles were an extravagance they might regret, but it was Christmas!

After Erik lengthily praised God for the gift of the Saviour, they walked out of the church and formed a circle under the bare oaks for the unveiling of the big bell ordered from Chicago. Nils Helbom slid a heavy rope through the metal loop at the top, and with the help of another strong man, suspended the bell between two big oaks.

"Here is the voice that will call us to worship!" Erik said, setting the bell swaying.

Listening to the sweet peal on the wintry air, Charlotta wondered how much the bell had cost? How much food would its price buy?

Two days later, the colony buzzed with news of the first birth in Bishop Hill.

"It's a girl!" Sabina said, hurrying into the dugout and shaking the snow from her shawl.

"Will she live?" Charlotta asked, thinking of the many babies Maja-Stina had lost.

"Oh yes! She's as plump as a little duckling—and pretty!"

"What will she be called?"

"Mary, like the mother of Jesus."

***

Little Mary Malmgren was baptized in the tent church on New Year's Day, 1847, and as Erik held her in his arms for the blessing, a great storm of rain, sleet and snow broke over the canvas roof. The congregation, sensing a bad omen, exchanged glances of dread, but the baby sucked her fist in complete unconcern.

Erik shouted above the wind, "I have something more to say to you, beloved friends—God has given me a new testimony. From this day until I tell you otherwise, the single are not to marry, and the married are to refrain from embracing."

The atmosphere of the tent church was heavy with shock, but not one spoken protest was heard. The wind still moaned, but the heavy pelting on the canvas roof stopped. The people departed silently into a dense, wet snow.

When they were well away from the church, Charlotta heard one woman laugh bitterly and say, "He needn't worry! My old man is too worn out to make mischief these nights!"

"Not mine!" said a younger wife, "I don't see how we can obey Erik Jansson—but if we don't, we're sure to get caught. Every spring, one baby climbs out of the cradle to make room for the next, and how can I hide it?"

Sabina tugged at Charlotta's shawl and hissed, "Isn't life hard enough without this?"

Charlotta knew that her sister had eyes for a young man in the fourth party, and she tried to comfort Sabina by saying, "Maybe it won't last long." As far as she was concerned, it didn't matter. She was twenty-two years old and nearly resigned to spinsterhood—nearly, but not so completely as Anna-Maja.

The dugout was noisy with passionate discussion of the new edict, but Charlotta held herself apart from it. She was unbraiding her hair before going to bed when Sabina grabbed her arm and pulled her along.

"Come and help me, Lotta! It's Hilda—I can't make her

stop bellowing to find out what's wrong!"

The girl was sprawled on her bunk, sobbing loudly. When Charlotta touched her shoulder, her distress increased.

"Stop that, Hilda! You must tell us what's wrong!" Charlotta said in a stern voice.

Hilda stifled her sobs and dug her fists into her eyes. Gulping and sniffling, she said, "Tore and I were just going to ask Erik Jansson if we—if—oh, what are we going to do?"

"Wait, I suppose," Charlotta said, repeating what she had told Sabina, "maybe it won't be long—"

"We *can't* wait!" Hilda's eyes were full of terror, "I'll have to kill myself!"

"Oh no! You'll go to Hell if you do that—promise me you won't!"

Hilda promised readily, relieved to be saved from self-destruction, and they all went to bed.

In the morning, Hilda was gone, and there was an empty place in the men's crew wagon leaving for Red Oak grove. Erik demanded to know why, and though Charlotta and Sabina knew, they said nothing.

***

Charlotta was greatly impressed by Sophia Pollock, who taught the English kindergarten in one of the dugouts. Erik admired her too, which was somewhat surprising. He believed in elementary education but thought that anything beyond that was likely to make a person conceited. Apparently it hadn't in Mrs. Pollock's case.

She had been a teacher in a private academy in New York, and she and her husband came west with Erik and his party, but Mr. Pollock sickened on the journey and died just outside of Victoria. He was her second husband, and she was twice widowed when she came to Bishop Hill.

Sophia Pollock was an orphan raised by a wealthy family from Goteborg, and they had brought her to America when she was fifteen. Shortly thereafter, she married a Swedish sailor who was lost at sea on his first voyage after their wedding. She then attended Pollack's Academy, taught there, and finally married the headmaster. Charlotta had the story from Erik, who knew the history of each colonist in detail.

Mrs. Pollock wore American clothes, promising she would dress like the others when her wardrobe wore out, and the sight of her was a welcome change from the monotony of un-dyed wadmal. She walked to her dug-out classroom with a firm step, and Charlotta waved to her from the bank above. Mrs. Pollock returned the greeting with a gray-gloved hand, smiling.

Charlotta's job for the day was digging chalk stone clay from the bank. Phillip Mauk, one of their American neighbors, had told Erik that the clay could be made into adobe bricks. Working beside Maja-Stina, Charlotta filled her pail rapidly and emptied it into the wagon. As Erik approached, she worked faster, hoping for his nod of approval as he walk-ed the bank.

Then Phillip Mauk called up to them and climbed to the place where they were working. "Hello, Mrs. Jansson!" he said.

Erik answered.

"No, no, Mr. Jansson, I'm talking to your wife! In America, the wife takes the name of her husband."

Charlotta remembered the New York boarding house and the woman named Nystrom who seemed to have a peculiar first name. She still didn't understand.

Neither did Erik, it seemed. He took Maja-Stina's arm and asked, "What is her name, then?"

"Mrs. Jansson—Mrs. Erik Jansson, just as my wife is Mrs. Phillip Mauk—or Elvira Mauk."

"Ah," Erik said, "then she is Maja-Stina Jansson!" He went among the women, touching their shoulders as he christened them with their husbands' last names. When he came to Charlotta, he turned to Mauk and asked, "What about unmarried women?"

"They take the name of their father."

"Then I am Charlotta Andersson?" she said.

"No," Erik said, "you will take *my* name! I now stand in your father's place."

I'm sorry, Pappa! Charlotta Lovisa Jansson? How strange it sounded.

"Come, Mr. Mauk," Erik said, "I'll show you what we're doing here. The people are building a red frame house for my family, and the *Flickstugan* will be over there—"

"*Flickstugan?*" Mauk was puzzled.

"Ah, I forgot that you don't know Swedish! It means Girl House. They will have a single large room and a garret, and another building like it will be put up for single men and boys. Now tell me—if we mix coarse grass with the chalk stone clay, will that make a good brick?"

"I reckon so."

Sabina started to sing, "Yankee Doodle came to town—riding on a po-nee—"

Mauk's eyes widened. "Where in tarnation did she learn that?"

"From Mrs. Pollock." Erik said proudly, "Her English is a good as any American's."

Better not praise her to Maja-Stina, Charlotta thought.

***

By the calendar, American winter was shorter than the Swedish season, and perhaps it would have seemed so, Charlotta thought, if they had brought their snug, Falun red cottage from Domta to shield them from it. As it was, spring found the survivors dazed and scarcely able to believe that the warm sun had come back. They were like the savage people of ancient times who could not be certain that the sun would rise each morning.

Working with the brickmakers, Charlotta shared the growing determination to put the bad times out of memory. She sang as she packed the forms with clay and even cut flowers into the wet bricks to celebrate the season.

Sighting a column of dust far off on the road to Cambridge, she straightened and shook the damp clots from her hands. As the horses and riders came nearer, she recognized the colony dress of undyed wadmal. Erik's missionaries were back! He had sent them out weeks before to convert the heathen.

Entering the village, they rode past the brickmakers toward Erik's house. From the way their shoulders were bent, Charlotta knew something had gone wrong. Leaving her job was risky, but she ran into the hazel scrub and emerged behind Erik's house. He was on the porch with the missionaries, and she edged as close as she dared to listen.

"Good boys!" he said, "You're back in time to put in the crops!"

"At least *that* is something we have done before!" one said glumly.

Another said, "The Yankees are too busy chasing the dollar to attend to their souls!"

"Are you telling me that you have brought your nets up empty?"

"We did everything you said, but it was no use!"

"Then we will take care of our own and let them go to the Devil! Come to the log house for small beer!"

Charlotta wished she could join them. Brick-making was thirsty work. An American neighbor had given the colony some malt and molasses, and the women cooked it in a big caldron, added yeast, and let the mixture ripen in a cellar for two days. She swallowed hard, told herself she was not thirsty, and got back to her work.

At suppertime, she sought out one of the missionaries and listened to his story of persecution by the North Americans—jeering, clod-throwing and general abuse from heathen who wanted no part of Erik Jansson or his doctrines. Now, at least, they could let those pagans be damned without the slightest feeling of guilt. They had tried.

Charlotta vaguely remembered something in the Bible about turning the other cheek, or was it forgiving seventy times seven? But she supposed she had no right to make applications of Scripture. That was Erik's place.

***

The helpful Phillip Mauk convinced Erik of the importance of maize, but Erik was not impressed by the yield from Mauk's planting procedure. He prayed for the revelation of a better method, and it came to him.

Calling the people together, he said, "This first crop is precious to us, and every kernel must count. Two men will carry poles with a knotted rope marker. Ten women will move between the knots on the cord, carrying a planting stick and a seed sack tied to the waist. Each woman will press her planting stick into the ground, drop two kernels into the hole, and drag the dirt over it with her foot. Do you understand?"

They did, all but Lena Sandell, who never understood anything.

"Walk beside Lena and help her, Lotta," Erik said, and Charlotta sighed. Being the Prophet's cousin and ward had its drawbacks.

The men had ploughed the fields laboriously with a thirty-six-inch blade pulled by eight pairs of oxen, turning up the

black-brown earth to receive the seed. The ground smelled
fresh and rich, like the air after a cleansing rain. The teams of
twelve lined up for the entire width of the field. Lena was on
Charlotta's right and Anna-Maja on her left. The two men on
the ends held the rope taut and stepped forward. When they
stopped, the women stopped and pressed the planting sticks
into the earth as they thrust their free hands into the sacks
tied around their waists. The kernels dropped, their feet
replaced the earth with a quick sweep, and they moved on. At
first, they lurched and staggered on the uneven footing of the
plowed field, and Lena was so slow that the rope left her at
the point of a sharp angle, but when the rhythm of it caught
them all, it became a slow dance.

At midday, Erik called the workers together in the grove
and told them that morning and evening services in the tent
church would be suspended until after the harvest. Instead,
they would meet briefly for worship at noon.

"God sees our labor and finds it good!" he said.

Labor? We're dancing! Did God see that too?

***

How the corn grew! This crop which was strange to many
of the Swedes from the North could be eaten by both man and
beast, Erik said. The tiny, green spears burst through the
earth in perfect rows, unfolding long, pointed leaves in the
warming sun. Every kernel planted seemed to sprout, which
didn't surprise Erik, but Phillip Mauk was amazed.

When the ears still were young and tender, Mrs. Mauk told
the women how to cook them in boiling, salted water and
chew the buttered kernel from the cob.

"It tastes good!" Mamma said, "If only my teeth were better!" She dropped the cob on her plate with three others,
creasing her buttery cheeks with a smile, "God is good! I

haven't eaten so well since I left Domta!"

Mrs. Mauk gave the women recipes for cakes, pudding and mush made from corn, and these were a success, but the Swedes did not like cornbread. The first batch of corn run through the grist mill owned by an American pastor lasted for a long time because the bread baked from the meal was gritty and unpleasant to the taste of the colonists.

The oats grew well too, and beyond those fields were the acres of flax. When the flax was ripe, the girls would pull it up by the roots and stack it in piles. Then the older women would bind it, sitting on little stools to make the bundles. A mile to the east was a large pond more than ten feet deep fed by a branch of the Edwards, and here the flax bundles would be submerged to rot until the woody portions came away easily. A scraper was being made to remove the seeds, and a work crew was building a flax mill for drying and scraping the bundles.

The whole process moved too slowly for Sabina, who coveted a new dress.

"Well, my fine lady," Mamma said, "we have little time to worry about our looks around here!"

"But it would make me so happy!"

"Would it?" Charlotta asked teasingly, "With no color?"

Sabina looked crestfallen, but she recovered quickly. "Can't we find some berries in the woods and dye the linen?"

"There's no time, Sabina," Mamma said, "and besides, those berries are strange to me—they might ruin perfectly good cloth! Can't you be satisfied with the blessings you have?"

"It's all very well for you, because you're old! But we can't marry, we can't dance— I wish I'd stayed in Sweden!"

Charlotta was dismayed by Mamma's hurt expression. She seized Sabina's arm and said, "It's milking time, come on!"

When they were out of Mamma's hearing, Charlotta gave

Sabina's arm a shake and said, "You hurt Mamma's feelings!
For shame!"

"I didn't mean to—I just get so sick of—oh Lotta, will you
come dancing with us tonight? Gunnar Olsson made a fiddle
from a box and some wire, and we're going far into the grove
where no one can hear us!"

"If Erik finds out, it will go hard with you!"

Sabina made a face. "It goes hard with me no matter what!
Gunnar is bringing some of the butcher boys, and I'm going
with Catherina Skogland—"

"Then be careful! Remember what happened to Hilda!"

Sabina tossed her head. "As if I'd ever!"

***

At breakfast the next morning, Erik said, "I thought I
heard music last night."

Sabina nearly choked on her porridge, but she quickly recovered and said, "I did too. The Americans must have had
visitors."

He nodded and turned his attention to something else.

I wish I had gone, Charlotta thought, *will I ever dance
again?*

Philadelphia, November, 1847—

Robert Baird denied himself a third cup of breakfast chocolate and leaned back in his chair to read Margaret Fuller's
latest letter from Europe. She was visiting many places that
he knew well, and while her impressions did not match his
consistently, they interested him.

"Listen to this, Fermine," he said, "she writes, 'The American in Europe, if a thinking mind, can only become more
American.' "

"I suppose that's true."

"And then she talks about the three species of Americans in Europe—the servile type who goes abroad to spend his money and indulge his tastes and who has all the thoughtlessness and partiality of the exclusive classes in Europe without any of their refinement—"

"We have such people." she said dryly, "Does she name our type?"

"I haven't found us yet! I'm just reading about the 'conceited American, instinctively bristling and proud of—he knows not what'—and listen to this—" he chuckled, "with great clumsy hands, only fitted to work on a steam engine, he seizes the old Cremona violin, makes it shriek with anguish in his grasp—then says there is not really any music in these old things; that the frogs in one of our swamps make much finer, for they are young and alive.' "

Fermine laughed. "But surely there is an American type Miss Fuller approves?"

"Ah, here we are! 'The thinking American is a man who, recognizing the immense advantage of being born to a new world and on virgin soil, yet does not wish one seed from the past to be lost.' "

"Yes, I like that! I will admit to being that type."

Baird read on, sobered by Margaret Fuller's assessment of a "hollow" England, of a France "shallow and glossy still," of a "lost" Poland, of Italy "bound by treacherous hands," of Russia with "brutal Czar and innumerable slaves," of Austria with a royalty "that represents nothing" and a people "who, as people are and have nothing." Did she exaggerate? Deep down, he feared that she did not.

He read aloud to Fermine, "If we consider the amount of truth that has really been spoken out in the world, and the love that has beat in private hearts—the public failure seems amazing, seems monstrous."

"She's quite right." Fermine said, "Why can't all this separate truth and love be joined?"

Having no brief answer, Baird dropped his eyes from Fermine's passionate gaze to the newspaper. Miss Fuller excoriated "the horrible cancer of slavery, and the wicked war that has grown out of it." *A war of the mind and spirit thus far,* Baird thought, but God alone knew what lay ahead. He read on, "I listen to the same arguments against the emancipation of Italy that are used against the emancipation of our blacks; the same arguments in favor of the spoliation of Poland as for the conquest of Mexico."

Baird looked at Fermine, troubled. Margaret Fuller's description of the mood of Europe made him think of their son, Henry Martyn, at school in Switzerland. Perhaps they should bring the boy home before conditions worsened.

Feeling his eyes on her, Fermine looked up from the section of the newspaper she was reading. "Robert, did you read this notice of the appointment of a Mexican peace commissioner to negotiate with our Mr. Trist? Peace is in sight, thank God!"

"Peace?" The word was at odds with his thoughts. "Fermine, what do you think of bringing Henry home to finish his studies, perhaps at the new Free Academy in New York?"

"Oh Robert, I would love to have him near!"

"Of course instruction has not begun there officially, but I know some of the organizers, and perhaps some sort of tutoring can be arranged for Henry until regular classes begin."

"Wonderful, Robert!" She clasped her hands at the base of her throat, a gesture of delight that he loved. Then she narrowed her eyes and asked, "But why? Are we too poor to keep him abroad?"

"No, my Love," he said, not wanting to worry her with his own concern for a fifteen-year-old boy encircled by gathering revolution, "it's just that I miss him." That, at least, was true.

"My cup runneth over!" she said, "My son is coming home, and we are nearly at peace in this country!"

Baird smiled at her, but his mind leaped ahead to the problems of peace: men trained to kill roaming the country—trying to take up their interrupted lives—drinking to blunt their sense of dislocation. God's challenge to the Temperance cause was clear.

Bishop Hill, November, 1847, to July, 1848—

The first harvest at Bishop Hill was bountiful, but the arrival of a fifth party of emigrants, four hundred adults and many children, put the colony on short rations again.

The newcomers had floundered on the Atlantic for five months, and many of them had scurvy, which rotted the flesh from their bones and caused them to scream with pain at the slightest touch. Charlotta worked in the sick house, doing her best to care for the sufferers, but she could do little for the black and blue spots that welled under the skin, the bleeding gums, and the teeth that loosened and dropped out. Elvira Mauk thought tomatoes might help, but the victims of the disease could not bear the sting of the tart juice in their mouths.

Within two weeks, thirty died. Those who were conscious to the end departed with Erik's assurance of a place in Paradise. *Could I die so bravely?* Charlotta doubted it. Harsh as her life was, she preferred to keep it, and Mrs. Mauk had told her that scrubbing with strong soap after caring for the sick was the best way to stay healthy.

She was carrying a square of strong lye soap to the basin to scrub when Erik entered the sick house.

"Don't waste the water," he said, "the level of the Edwards is down, and I can't spare horses or boys to tread the water wheel."

"But—I don't want to get what they have! I don't want to die like that!"

"You won't. You have not been on the sea for five months."

Charlotta put the soap away, brooding over questions she would not ask aloud. Could it be that God knew Bishop Hill could not feed five hundred new mouths? Could it be that He caused Erik's followers to destroy themselves like lemmings rushing into the sea? Was the progress of the New Jerusalem more precious to Him than thirty lives? How could one hope to understand God?

At the sound of hoofbeats, Erik went to the window. "A fine time for our friend from Victoria to call!" he said crossly, "He'll think we're in desperate straits!"

We are! Charlotta clamped her lips tight on the words she dared not say. She went to the door to watch Hedstrom dismount and shake the dust from his black cloak. He started up the walk, then stood aside for a burial crew carrying a woman's body to the hearse wagon. Charlotta had grown accustomed to flesh mottled with blackish bruises and the staring eyes of the dead, but she sympathized with Hedstrom's revulsion. She stood aside to let him enter.

Hedstrom crossed the room in broad strides to confront Erik. "Have you no doctor here *yet*?"

"God heals whom He will."

"You expect Jesus to step down from heaven and touch these poor creatures?" Hedstrom wheeled angrily, his cape swirling, and crossed the road to the dugouts.

"This is not his affair!" Erik said.

The Victoria missionary emerged from the first dugout with blazing eyes and pinched nostrils. He returned to the sick house and spoke to Erik in a voice of choked anger, "How can you confine human beings in such holes? No wonder they die!"

"I did not expect so many," Erik said, "I am doing the best I can."

"Your best is not good enough!" Hedstrom said, "You must get a doctor for these people!"

"I will pray about it."

"You will do more than that, or I will bring legal proceedings against you!" Hedstrom departed abruptly to re-mount and kick his horse to a gallop.

"I thought this was a free country!" Erik shouted after him.

In the quaking silence that followed, Charlotta steeled herself to say, "Maybe we *should* get a doctor—"

"Where is your faith, girl?"

But he did go to the tent church to pray about the matter, and at the evening meal he announced that brännvin would be distilled for medicinal use. It was to be called Number Six and kept under lock and key.

Charlotta accepted Erik's compromise with Hedstrom's demand as better than nothing. At least the sick would have a dose of brännvin to dull the ills that faith would not cure.

***

In the early spring, soon after the ice went out in the Edwards, the man in charge of the distillery forgot to lock the room where the Number Six vats were stored, and a party of young men took advantage of his negligence. They roared drunkenly through the settlement late at night, waking the inhabitants of every house.

Wrapping herself in a shawl, Charlotta stepped outside to see what was happening. Erik, bare-footed and in his night shirt, held a lamp high and shouted for the culprits to come to him. Too drunk to be cautious, they came to the light like moths. He identified them, told them they were no better than swine, and sent them to their quarters.

When the incident was discussed at breakfast the next morning, many of the colonists remembered sowing wild oats of
their own and were inclined to be amused, but Jonas Olsson
threatened to leave Bishop Hill if such a thing ever happened
again, and he demanded that the six young men be punished.

"I have read the King's Book about the evils of drink!" he
said in a shaking voice, "The one written by the man named
Baird! He says what I, too, believe—and have since I saw
brännvin passed in a mockery of the Lord's Supper at a country dance in my youth!"

"I will deal with it immediately, Jonas!" Erik said, and he
called out the names of the drunkards, sentencing them to
tread the water wheel on the Edwards from sunrise to sunset.
He ordered every colonist to go to the river and witness their
disgrace at some time during the span of punishment.

Charlotta was sure that Erik would not have been so harsh
if Jonas Olsson had not insisted upon it. She decided to go to
the river immediately and get that unpleasant duty behind
her.

The six strained against the wheel on shaking legs in the
early light, and she pitied them, especially the two who were
too young to have known spirits before. Their shirts were
stiff with vomit, and they looked ready to faint. She turned
and walked away quickly, considering the blessings of moderation. Brännvin was not bad in itself. If the dwindling deaths
were any indication, it seemed to be of some use as medicine.

***

At haying time, the men went to the fields with scythes,
and the women walked behind them, tying the grain into bundles. *Stoop, gather, tie, forward,* Charlotta chanted to herself,
enduring the itch of the chaff inside her clothes. There was no

time to shake it away, not with Erik shouting for them to hurry in the face of gathering rain clouds. *We can never finish before the storm!* Already the sky was gray-black, and the wind was blowing in sharp gusts.

Astride his horse, Erik raised his face to the dark sky and shouted. "If you, O God, do not give good weather so we can finish the work we have at hand, then I shall depose You from Your seat of omnipotence and You shall not reign, either in heaven or on earth—for You cannot reign without me!"

Charlotta gasped and dropped the bundle she had just tied. The girl beside her threw herself to the ground in terror, but Charlotta seemed rooted where she stood. She squeezed her eyes shut, fearful of seeing the field scorched by the wrath of God. She heard the wind and far-off thunder, but nothing else, and she dared to open her eyes. The fat, black clouds had blown rapidly to the south. A slant of water fell on fields beyond the earthen boundaries of the colony's holdings.

"Get on with your work!" Erik shouted, "God has heard me!" He spurred his horse and rode toward the rain. He galloped his horse back to them, laughing out loud with the proof of his power. His hair was plastered to his head, and his coat was soaked through.

Stooping to fill her arms with hay, Charlotta realized that she was trembling. Why was Erik so careless of the danger of challenging God? The reckoning might be delayed, but it would surely come.

***

Charlotta was pleased that her mother had been allowed to move to one of the new adobe houses and that Mamma's skill at spinning a mile of perfect thread spared her the heavier work of the colony. Never one to spare herself, Mamma would have worked at the pile-driver if Erik had asked it of her, even though she panted like a bellows after climbing a few steps.

Charlotta had told Mamma that she would stop by and walk to supper with her and that she would come early to give them plenty of time. Why didn't Mamma answer her knock? She opened the door and found the room empty. Strange. She went on to the dining hall, but Mamma was not there, either. Neither Anna-Maja or Sabina had seen her. The supper bell was ringing.

"I saw her going to the tent church about half an hour ago." Maja-Stina said.

Mamma is never late! Suddenly frightened, Charlotta ran to the church. It was dark and seemingly empty. "Mamma? Are you here, Mamma?" The door had closed behind her, and she could see nothing. The only thing she could find to prop the door open and let a bit of twilight in was Erik's pulpit Bible, and she did not hesitate to use it. The shaft of dim light fell on Mamma, lying beside the first row of log seats.

"Mamma!" Charlotta shrieked, dropping to her knees. She pressed her ear to her mother's chest and heard the erratic beat of a living heart. *Thank God!* Then she ran for help.

***

At the adobe house, Erik prayed beside Mamma's bed while Sabina sobbed and Anna-Maja huddled miserably in a corner. Charlotta stood beside Erik, feeling cold inside.

"Oh Erik," she said, "can't we send for a doctor? Look how gray her face is—and she scarcely breathes!"

"I have had a new revelation—" he said slowly, "all of us may be better for having a doctor."

"Oh Erik, thank you!" Charlotta cried, stepping aside to let Maja-Stina place hot bricks wrapped in towels at Mamma's feet.

"Maja-Stina," Erik said, "send Nils Helbom to Victoria for a doctor, and if none can be had there, tell him to try at LaGrange."

"Listen!" Charlotta said, "She's trying to speak!"

"Oh Jan," Mamma murmured, "if we could just be young again and together here—it's hard sometimes, but it helps to know that we're pleasing God—in Sweden I didn't always know—did you?"

Charlotta seized the cold hands. "Mamma, do you have pain?"

"Arms—chest—Jan, why don't you answer me?"

"Hush, Mamma, a doctor is coming."

But he didn't come for hours, and when he did, Mamma wanted nothing to do with him. The cold instrument he placed on her chest made her whimper and struggle to cover herself.

The doctor's speech was different from that of their American neighbors, and there was a sweetish smell about him.

"I can't understand him!" Charlotta cried, "Can we send for Mrs. Pollock?"

"I'll get her myself," Erik offered.

Sophia Pollock had no difficulty understanding the doctor, but she hesitated in her translation for Charlotta and her sisters.

"It's—it's her heart, he says. I'm afraid he thinks her heart is too badly damaged to—to go on—"

"You mean he says she will die?" Charlotta said dully.

"Oh, I'm sorry, my dears!"

"Is he a good doctor? Does he know?"

"He was trained in England," Sophia said, looking down at her shoes.

"Erik!" Charlotta cried, "Don't let her die!"

"Lotta, I believe that God wants to take her now. Be reconciled to His will."

"No! Go away, all of you! I'll care for her, and she'll live!"

"Mrs. Pollock and I will go, but your sisters will stay here with you. They have that right."

And so the vigil began. Mamma's labored breathing mingled with the weeping of Sabina and Anna-Maja in Charlotta's ears as she sat beside the bed, cold as a stone, holding her mother's hand.

Eventually, her sisters slept, and she whispered to Mamma, "I remember how you held me while Pappa read to us and kissed the top of my head. You thought I was too little to know, didn't you? And I remember how you wove a tiny shawl for my doll on a funny little loom you made yourself— oh Mamma!"

Mamma opened her eyes and smiled. She strained forward as if she was trying to see better and fell back, still smiling, but with the light gone from her eyes. Fearfully, Charlotta took Mamma's face in her hands. The faint warmth of life was still in those cheeks, but the eyes—the eyes! That light gone out—was it the soul? *Come back, Mamma, come back!* Nothing changed. Charlotta knelt beside the bed, and sometimes it seemed that Mamma breathed, but she knew this was a cruel illusion. After a long time, she stood and woke her sisters.

Watching them express the grief for which she had no outward sign, Charlotta numbly considered what must be done to prepare Mamma for burial.

Now I have only Erik.

***

After the funeral, Erik told Charlotta to move to the second floor dormitory of the milkmaids and join them in their duties at the log dairy house northeast of the village.

She didn't care what she did and thought she might as well be miserable while milking cows as doing anything else. Each morning she went to the milking pen with her pail and small stool, leaning into the fresh-smelling warmth of a cow as she wrung streams of rich milk from a swollen udder. When her pail was full, she climbed a stepladder to empty it into a huge tub suspended in the wagon and returned to the stanchions to fill it again. With fifty girls milking, nearly two hundred cows could be attended to in half an hour.

Charlotta had no appetite herself, but she realized how much the dairy herd meant to the colony. Once more there was milk soup with dumplings and cheese to go with the hardtack. The children drank milk with every meal, and the grown-ups ate butter three times a day. In the two terrible winters, they had seen butter only on Sundays, if then.

And now they had fish. When Erik learned that no fish worth eating could be caught in the Edwards, he sent a party of men to establish a fishing camp on the big river to the west, the Mississippi. They came back laden with catfish, all gutted and cleaned except for one—a hideous thing with ugly whiskers. Charlotta saw it before Erik made them cut the head off. He said it would ruin everyone's appetite, and it certainly had spoiled hers!

She was coming back from the dairy house when she saw the wagon from the fishing camp unloading a new catch. The women had brought pots and caldrons from the kitchen and they were making a game of catching the slippery fish in them. At the frantic clang of the church bell, they froze like a scene in a tableau.

"Fire!"

The shout came from the south, where black clouds of smoke rose above the trees. Charlotta caught her breath sharply. *The tent church! God wouldn't do such a thing to Erik!*

Some of the women at the fish wagon ran toward the fire, but those with better sense emptied the fish from their kettles and hurried to the river for water. Charlotta, still carrying her milk pail, joined them.

Erik formed a line of colonists from the church to the river to pass along buckets of water. Charlotta changed places until she was close enough to see the church. The canvas roof, rotted by weather, was blazing hotly, and some of the logs in the walls had caught fire.

"How did it happen?"

"An old man smoking a pipe. Sparks flew into some sawdust—he was making a new pulpit."

"He should have chewed snoose instead!"

"Maybe God wants a new church?"

The fire died down, only to start again, and by sundown, the tent church was a charred ruin.

"Don't grieve, beloved friends," Erik said, "we can worship under the trees—in a church such as God provided for us in Sweden!"

***

In less than a week, Erik had drawn plans for a new church that would include added living space. The outlines of the structure were roped east of the dugouts along the street that became the road to Cambridge.

The digging of the basement, which was to consist of ten rooms opening off a wide corridor, was a hard, hot job. The workers consumed gallons of small beer. Ox boys were sent to Red Oak grove for the larger timbers of walnut and oak, but other materials were to be bought in Peru, Rock Island and Chicago.

Hearing that a supply wagon was leaving for Chicago, Charlotta wrote a short letter to Carolina for the driver to deliver. She had received no reply to her letter telling Carolina of Mamma's death, which led her to distrust the mails. However, Carolina had waited months to write of the birth of her son, and now it was clear that she did not intend to keep her promise that they would come to Bishop Hill after the baby was born. Carolina was silent because she felt guilty. *Poor Lina!* Charlotta signed her name quickly and hurried to the stables with the letter.

The driver raised his whip in a salute, twirling its sixteen-foot lash in a vicious spiral. "I'm going to get me some rattle-snakes this trip!"

The ox boys had a running contest to see who could kill the most snakes with a whip. One expert crack could kill a rat-tler, and the boys prided themselves on their eye, their aim, and their wrist action. A snake carcass could be twined around a wagon axle for lubrication if nothing better was available, and Phillip Mauk said that some people ate rat-tlers. Charlotta shuddered at the thought. She wished the driver luck and begged him to keep his trophies out of her sight.

With the morning milking behind her, she went to the new church site to make bricks of chalk stone clay. She wasn't as quick at it as some. The fastest brick-makers had time to add the decoration of a flower, their initials or the date, but she merely filled and smoothed the forms while her mind probed the loss of Mamma as the tongue seeks the break in an acci-dentally bitten inner cheek. She pushed the hurt to its limits.

She supposed that others also grieved as they worked. It could not be otherwise, because every colonist was involved in the building of the church, the only excuses being death or child bed. They dug, made bricks, or soaked hand-hewn strips of wood for accordian lathes. Even the smallest children col-lected straw to mix with the clay.

They knew exactly what they were making because Erik had explained the plans to them in detail. The first floor would be the twin of the basement with ten rooms opening off a corridor the length of the building. The second floor would be a sanctuary for a thousand worshippers with double stairs at the north end, and it could be used for classrooms when religious services were not being held. Bigger than an American barn, the new church would be as simple in design with bonneted eaves. It would look nothing like the churches of Sweden.

The work stopped as Erik came on the site with a rolled-up paper and beckoned to everyone. He knelt to unroll the design for another big building, explaining that it would be three stories high with ninety-six rooms.

"What for?" somebody asked.

"To live in! Nothing like this has been seen in western Illinois, but we must get our people out of—what did Hedstrom call them?"

No one but Charlotta knew, and she thought it best not to remind Erik. He had been furious when Hedstrom called the dugouts "holes."

He went on with happy enthusiasm, "These kiln-dried bricks are turning out well! We'll use them for the new building—in fact, why not call it Big Brick?"

"Where will it be?"

"Where the dugouts are now. We'll show Hedstrom that we can rise above the ground!"

Charlotta stared at the row of cave dwellings, trying to visualize Big Brick, but the image that came to her was their old home at Domta. A long-delayed pang of homesickness took her by surprise. Somehow it seemed that Pappa and Mamma were together at Domta again. Her eyes filled with tears, the first since Mamma died.

Virginia, July, 1848—

Robert Baird marveled at the endurance of the sturdy

mountain mare that pulled his rented hack steadily upward to Front Royal. His own Dorcas would blow and heave with such an effort, and that was why he had left her in her own comfortable stall in Philadelphia.

Baird was on his way to address a gathering of mountain people on the subject of Temperance, and his friends in Washington had warned him that they would be difficult, if not dangerous. His invitation had come from a small minority in this timeless pocket of semi-civilization, and he would be speaking to mountaineers who distilled their own lethal spirits and consumed them for comfort, for celebration, and from sheer emptiness. He would plead with them to substitute Spirit for spirits, and he had prayed for the power to convince them, a power that must come from God.

As he drove along, he thanked God for the good, little mare and praised Him for the beauty of His creation—the varying greens of the pines and the glossy-leaved young oaks at the roadside; the soft, blue spine of the mountains before him. He also prayed for the future of his young nation. During his brief stay in Washington, he had heard General Zachary Taylor touted for the presidency on all sides, and he felt some qualms about a military man leading the country during a time of peace.

The hack passed a break in the trees, and when Baird saw the flash of sun on the Shenandoah River far below, he stopped the mare and backed her to the best viewing point. The river was a snake of polished pewter in the deep, green valley—so beautiful that he wished Fermine were beside him to share the sight. The scene suffered from the absence of her gaze, and it occurred to him that Adam could not have known the full beauty of Eden until God created Eve.

How would the Mississippi River look from such a height? Only God could know. Mere mortals could not achieve a high view of the broad river that flowed through flat lands—right past the door of some.

He was reminded of Archibald Allen, a young Scotsman who lived with his wife Lamette in a cabin called Caanan above Port Byron on the Mississippi. Secure on his claim, Archie Allen supported his family by hunting and fishing. He took orders from no man, only from God.

Baird had felt a kinship with Archie Allen. They came from the same stock, they both revered their Maker, and they had married magnificent women of French descent. Unhappily, Lamette had died young, but Archie went on, strong in her memory and beholden to no one.

Archie Allen was an affront to the principles of the Communist Manifesto brought out by Marx and Engels in February. Henry had brought his father a copy of it when he returned from Europe, and Baird had read it thoughtfully, trying not to dismiss its philosophy with American impatience. After all, nations where social class was a factor were likely to receive the Manifesto gladly. Those without property naturally would favor abolition of private ownership.

One measure of the Manifesto appealed to him greatly: free education for all children in public schools. However, it was all or nothing with Marx and Engels, he supposed, and some of their prescriptions were unconscionable. How could they say the family was based on private gain and should be abolished? He, certainly, did not see in his wife "a mere instrument of production," and he viewed an openly legalized community of women as an abomination! As for the economics of the Manifesto, Christianity could be just as revolutionary—if applied. The early church was not forced to share but was constrained by love to do so.

Actually, economic Communism was being practiced at Bishop Hill, according to a recent letter from Ithamar Pillsbury. Ironic that the Swedes should come to America and live contrary to one of its basic principles, but of course they were free to do as they pleased in such matters. It might be well if someone told them of the Brook Farm experiment near Boston. For a time, the residents worked, thought, wrote and discussed happily, but individual responsibility was somehow lost. When a fire destroyed one of the main buildings, the brave experiment ended. Heaven on earth was an illusion.

Baird clucked at the mare, and she started off willingly without a slap of the reins. When he had driven a mile or so, a man in a shapeless hat and clothes bleached colorless by many washings stepped into the road. He carried a rifle as naturally as if it were a third arm and all men were born with three.

"Be ye the preacher man?'

"I am, Sir, how may I serve you?"

"They's feudin' 'round the church, and I must carry you to another house across the ridge for the speakin'. I'll cover your buggy with branches alongside the road over there, and you can lead the mare."

"I'm sorry if my coming has caused trouble."

" 'Tain't you. One of the Clegg boys run off with a Hyatt girl, and they's bad blood between the families."

"Why, if I may ask?"

"The Hyatts got a duke way back, and they don't want no trash in their clan."

Baird smiled wryly as he climbed from the hack to unhitch the mare. *My classless America!*

Bishop Hill, summer and fall, 1848—

The stumps and log seats were taken when Charlotta reached the grove for Sunday services, and she sank to the ground tailor-fashion, tucking her skirts around her folded legs.

Erik took his place at the stump pulpit and raised his hands for silence. The people bowed their heads, expecting prayer, but he said, "Beloved friends, God's mercy toward us has been great. The crops flourish, the cows give a goodly yield, and the slaughter animals are fattening. God tells me that our people may now enter wedlock, multiply themselves and replenish the earth!"

The startling announcement did not affect Charlotta personally. She watched the reactions of others with a certain wistfulness. A young man stifled a whoop of joy. Eyes searched, found and held other eyes. Secret loves became shyly visible; some she had guessed at, but others surprised her.

Erik spoke again, "On Sunday, July 23, I will unite in matrimony as many as feel the true promptings of the heart and those marked for each other by my inner testimony."

Charlotta saw Sophia Pollock nod solemnly at Lars Gabrielson. Erik's brother Peter beamed at Anna Christine Lindbeck, who was not as beautiful as his first wife but alive and in love with him.

Sabina had come late to the service, and she cautiously lowered herself beside Charlotta to ask the reason for all the excitement. The answer brought a dazzling smile.

"Oh Lotta, now I can marry Gunnar!"

"Has he asked you?"

"No, but he will!"

***

A Saturday night rain broke the shimmering heat that had baked Bishop Hill for a week, and on Sunday the grove had a new-washed sparkle. Orioles answered the distant calls of meadowlarks. Butterflies looped lazily among the wild flowers at the edge of the trees. The fragrance of red clover perfumed the outdoor altar.

The brides, twenty-four of them, were dressed alike in undyed homespun, but they showed their individuality in the bridal crowns planted like tiny, up-turned baskets on their heads. In Sweden, a bridal crown was laced with the traditional wedding myrtle, and some of the women had brought myrtle roots to plant in Bishop Hill, but they had died. These new world brides chose leaves of the wild grape and the oak entwined with buttercups and cornflowers.

Sabina was among the willing and happy brides, but Charlotta saw others who looked as if they had wept the whole night before. They were the victims of Erik's inner testimony, marrying at his command. *I would refuse!* But the thought of defying Erik was frightening. Not one of the brides had dared.

When Erik called the couples to take their places before him, Sabina seized Gunnar's hand and skipped forward eagerly. Charlotta watched her younger sister fondly, forgetting how exasperating she could be. *I'm glad she's happy!*

"Beloved friends," Erik said, "I have written a new service of marriage, since the one by which most of us were wed has been consigned to the flames. You who are to be husbands— take the hand of the woman God has given you."

The hands were joined, some gladly and others with resignation. Charlotta put her own hands behind her back with a heady sense of belonging to herself.

"The man is the head of the woman, as Christ is the head of the faithful. Do you women promise to subject yourselves to these, your husbands?"

"We do—do—do—" came the ragged answer.

"Do you promise to be faithful to your husbands and serve them with heart and hand?"

They watched each other and answered in better unison, "We do—"

"Do you promise to obey your husbands in all things?"

The call of a catbird blended with their answer, giving it a mocking sound.

"Men," Erik said, "do you promise to be followers of Christ that your wives may respect you?"

"We do—"

"Do you promise to be diligent in the up-building of the New Jerusalem for the good of your wives and your seed?"

"We do—"

Charlotta was surprised to see Erik raise his hands in benediction. Why did the women have to make more promises than the men?

"Oh Christ Who turned water to wine at Cana, bless these unions made in Thy sight! Amen!"

Confused by the brief prayer, the couples stood motionless, waiting for the ceremony to continue, but when Erik told them to come forward and sign a paper to be taken to the Henry County courthouse, they knew it was over. A few embraced shyly, but not Sabina. She seized Gunnar's face in both hands and kissed him vigorously on the mouth.

Sabina and Gunnar were the first to turn toward the log house where the wedding feast was waiting. As they ran, hand in hand, Sabina's bridal crown tumbled sideways and Gunnar righted it, kissing her eyelids.

Charlotta watched them with a queer kind of pain that she recognized as envy. There would be more and more weddings now, and she must find a way to keep from wanting one for herself. *Imagine Erik ordering you to marry a horrible, old man,* she told herself, and she was so thankful he had not that she laughed out loud.

***

At harvest time, the colonists amazed their American neighbors with the speed of their labor. In one day between sunrise and sundown, two Bishop Hill men cradled fourteen acres of grain. Charlotta was one of the women who walked behind them to gather and bundle the grain.

The next day she was stiff and thankful for a chance to straighten her back when Jonas Hedstrom came to the field. She watched him for awhile, saw that he talked only to the men, and went back to her work.

During the noon meal, she asked one of the men what Hedstrom had wanted, and he would not answer until she pressed him, "I know he was angry with us when everyone was so sick, but what is it now?"

"He says that the country is big—land can be had for almost nothing. He says we can do better on our own!"

"Do you believe that?"

The man shrugged.

Word of Hedstrom's visit was not long in reaching Erik. He strode to the shade trees where they were eating and said, "So the devil has been among you! I tell you this—there is no salvation outside the New Jerusalem! Depart at your own peril!"

A man of more than sixty stood up and gave Erik a long, hard look. Then he walked away.

Erik called after him, "God has determined to reveal through me His mysteries! He who does not abide in me shall be cast forth as a branch and shall wither! Don't you remember the day I ordered God to stop the rain?"

Charlotta did, and she thought, *I would not like to be alone in this strange country, saved or damned!*

***

Hedstrom's seeds of discontent produced a heavy crop of deserters. The old man who left first made it easier for others, and within a few weeks, two hundred colonists had left Bishop Hill. They were allowed to take nothing with them.

"We are fewer now," Erik said grimly, "and we must work

harder!"

Charlotta stifled the resentful question, *how can we work any harder than we have?*

***

Toward the end of October it grew too cold for outdoor church services, and the dining room became the temporary church. Charlotta had arranged to go to worship with Sabina and Gunnar, and at the first sound of the bell, she hurried toward their room in the basement of the new church building. Some of the living quarters had been finished before the sanctuary.

She took deep breaths of the crisp, fall air, appreciating it keenly as she remembered the choking closeness below the deck on the sailing brig and the fuggy dampness of the dugouts. She looked at the trees blazing with color in the bright morning sun and knew that as long as she lived, she would never tire of this American autumn, a season that had been nothing but a dreary introduction to winter in Sweden. Just a few days before, they had experienced what the Americans called "Indian Summer." This unseasonable heat did not come every year, they said, and Charlotta supposed that some North American summers were so strong that they refused to die when the calendar said they should. But hard frost was as certain as daybreak, and it left the weather cool and beautiful—so beautiful that she would be sorry when this day ended.

Two years had passed since she first walked into a settlement of primitive log buildings. Now Bishop Hill was a substantial village of buildings that would stand longer than any of them would live, even the new babies. More houses and more graves, though mercifully, death no longer was commonplace in Bishop Hill. To forget the intrusive thought of death, she looked up at the intense blue of the October sky, a brightness pleasurably painful, then stumbled, half-blinded, down the steps to her sister's room.

She found Sabina taking off one dress and trying another while Gunnar waited, arms crossed. "Aren't you ready yet? We'll be late!"

"Don't boss me, Lotta, I'm a married woman now!"

Charlotta stifled a retort and leaned against the door frame, her arms crossed like Gunnar's. Sabina seemed to inspire that gesture.

How cozy the room looked, she thought. The bedstead with turned knobs, a big chest, and a graceful rocking chair were Gunnar's handiwork, and Sabina had done the needlework and the weaving that warmed and softened the dark-toned wood. Together they had made a true home, something Charlotta believed she had lost when she left Domta and which she believed she would not have again.

Sabina was ready at last. They reached the top of the steps from the basement as the last peal of the bell died away. They heard the sound of horses' hooves in the still morning and wondered who it might be, but there was no time to wait and see.

When they reached the dining room, Erik was praying. They stood just inside the door until the "Amen!" and then tried to find seats without attracting notice. Maja-Stina moved over to make room for them.

In the middle of a hymn, the door opened again, and Charlotta stopped singing at the sight of the man who entered. She stared at the gun-belted stranger in a dusty, broad-brimmed hat with a sense of recognition that puzzled her. She felt that she knew him. Why? The two men who followed him were rough-looking with suspicious, sliding eyes, and Charlotta dismissed them from notice after a brief glance. Only the first man interested her. He swept his hat off, revealing a head of heavy, dark hair. His eyes were blue; a curious, faded blue. Part of his clothing seemed to be a uniform of some sort.

As soon as the hymn ended, Erik said in English, "Welcome to Bishop Hill!"

Charlotta was so amazed to hear the stranger answer in Swedish that she nearly missed what he was saying.

"—name is John Root. I heard that my countrymen had settled in Illinois, and I have traveled far to find you."

"Take off your guns and worship with us."

Root unstrapped the belt that held a long-barreled pistol and dropped it to the floor. His companions watched, making no move to follow his example until he spoke to them sharply in English. Then they removed their guns.

"This is Wester," Root said, touching the arm of the short, squinting man. He identified the taller balding man who shifted a wad of snoose from cheek to cheek as Zimmerman. Then, seeing no place to sit, Root slid to the floor and clasped his arms around his tall, dusty boots. His companions did the same.

Erik preached on the goodness of God and how He supplied the fruits of all labor, but Charlotta scarcely listened. Her eyes and her mind were on John Root. His speech had the cultured accents of a city, and yet his rough dress and unkempt beard were not characteristic of a Swedish gentleman of quality. Who was he? Why did she think she knew him?

When Erik was in the second hour of his sermon, Root pulled a canteen from inside his coat and drank. As Charlotta watched him, she felt the mystery lifting, recognized the dark stranger of her Midsummer's Eve dream in Sweden so long ago. She reddened at the realization and was sure that everyone near her noticed. She wanted to run away and hide, but that would be even more noticeable. It was impossible for her to look at Root now, but she was painfully aware of him.

At the end of the service, Maja-Stina said, "Lotta, we must move the tables back in place for dinner."

"Oh—yes—"

Erik was talking with Root and his friends, and Charlotta could see that they meant to stay for the meal. The scarcities of the first two years had made hospitality in Bishop Hill impossible, but now there was plenty for all. She saw the hand of Providence in the timing of John Root's arrival. She watched him as she worked, seeing no need to make herself known to him. He would come to her. It was ordained.

The meal consisted of catfish from the Rock Island fishing camp, potatoes, and beer soup. The butter was sweet and fresh, and when Charlotta placed a pat with her own imprint before John Root, he moved in such a way that he touched her arm. She pulled back, trembling.

"When I take a wife, she will be a Swedish woman!" Root said, "They know how to provide the comforts of life."

"Are you looking for a wife?" Erik said, "We have many unmarried women here and not enough men to go around!"

Root laughed but said nothing.

Charlotta moved along with her butter plate, suffused with happiness. *So he isn't married!* Then she scolded herself for being ridiculous. How could he be married when he had been marked for her so many years ago?

Wester sat near the end of one of the long tables, and when he chucked a young girl under the chin as she filled his coffee cup, she jumped back in alarm, spilling coffee on the floor. Charlotta didn't blame the girl. The man was disgusting! *God help the women of Bishop Hill if those two want wives from among us!* Charlotta returned the butter plate to the sideboard and carried wheat bread to Erik and his guests.

"When did you come from Sweden?" Erik asked Root.

"A year ago in the spring. I was with Winfield Scott at Veracruz." Erik and the others responded with blank looks, and Root continued, "Surely you read about the Mexican War in the newspapers?"

Erik hastily explained, "The Bible and the Catechism are the only reading matter in Bishop Hill—except for the simple exercise books we use in the school."

Charlotta remembered that Elvira Mauk had offered her an American newspaper one day, but it was incomprehensible to her. She inspected it as one would look at a weaving pattern and gave it back with a polite smile.

Root was shaking his head in wonderment. "Then this is your world—the rest doesn't exist?"

"It's world enough for us!" Erik said proudly, then changed the subject. "You were a soldier?"

"Yes, a sergeant in the Swedish Army. You know the custom—we never seem to have a war of our own, so we find a foreign conflict and fight for the experience. The American war is over now—"

"Then the King will expect you to return to Sweden?"

Root gave Erik a quizzical look. "Would *you* go back to Sweden?"

"Never!"

"Nor will I. I'm tired of being a soldier—I have killed enough dark, little men to satisfy the blood thirst of a Genghis Khan! To tell you the truth, Pastor, I'm tired of everything!"

Jonas Olsson coughed to gain Root's notice and asked, "What was the war about?"

"Land."

"But there is so much land here! When you can buy all you need, why kill for it?"

"When a man gets the idea that something is his, he will kill anyone who tries to take it from him. Nations are the same."

The meal ended, and Root sought out the cooks to compliment them. Unused to praise for doing their duty, they blushed and hung their heads.

Erik watched Root strap on his gun and asked, "What do you call that weapon? I have not seen one like it."

"This is the Colt revolver. The Texans call it 'the difference.' Would you like to try it?"

They went outside, and Charlotta quickly started to clear a table near the windows to keep them in view. Root found a broken piece of brick and set it up as a target. Erik hefted the strange hand gun and aimed. The shot went wide. Then Root fired, shattering the brick fragment. They walked toward the hitching post, out of her sight. She rushed to the dishwashers and volunteered to bring fresh water from the pump.

She worked the pump handle slowly, making the task last as long as possible. She had an excellent view of Root as he gentled his handsome bay horse and dug into a saddle bag for a fold of felt. It was a hat with its wide brim fastened to the crown front and back, foolish-looking actually, Charlotta thought, but it made John Root look like a ruler of some grand and ancient time. He removed the fastenings, and the brim fell in a wide circle that shadowed his face completely.

"The Andrews hat," he said, "Great for campaigning in the desert!" He plopped the hat on a small boy's head, and the other children who had clustered around the hitching post to stare at him laughed with delight when the crown covered the boy's nose and mouth. Charlotta smiled, pleased by Root's easy way with the children, but she sensed, as they did, that he would stand for no over-familiarity.

"Tell me, Erik Jansson," he said, "have you a place where I can stay the night? I can pay for my keep." He reached into his pocket and poured a stream of gold coins from a leather bag into his palm.

"Some of the rooms in Big Brick are finished, and we use

them to accommodate travelers. Will your friends stay too?"

Root glanced at Wester and Zimmerman, who lounged against the outer wall of the dining hall smoking small cheroots. They returned his look inquiringly, alert as wild animals.

Charlotta tensed as she waited for his answer. *Oh, send them away!*

Root said in Swedish, "They were good companions in war, but now that I have found my own people, I think it best to part from them. Their habits would not please you, I'm sure. By the way, I have noticed that American religious people often shun spirits. Do you lean to that, or have you maintained the Swedish way?"

Charlotta's heart sank, only to lift again at Erik's surprising answer, "We believe in moderation in all things."

"Fair enough! I like a bit of brännvin now and then. It makes me laugh to see how shocked some Americans are when I tell them that Swedish pastors own distilleries! Well, I think I'll stay. Please excuse me while I send my friends on their way."

He approached the men and spoke in abrupt English. They scowled and argued, but when Root narrowed his eyes to slits and touched his gun, they shambled to their horses and mounted. Just before they turned north, Zimmerman twisted in his saddle, drew his gun with incredible speed, and put a bullet through the high crown of Root's hat. The lower edge of the bullet hole was dark with his hair, and Charlotta's knees went weak at his close brush with death.

Root drew his own gun instantly, but Erik held his wrist and said, "We live in peace here! You will not stain the New Jerusalem with murder!"

The angry contortion of Root's features smoothed instantly and so completely that Charlotta almost thought she had imagined it. He laughed abruptly and said, "Sorry—they objected to being driven from your little Eden here!"

"How did you persuade them to go?" Erik asked.

Root hesitated, then chuckled and said, "I told them that on All Soul's Day, the Swedes practice human sacrifice—three victims—that you already had one, and that they, being non-Swedes, were likely prospects for the other two."

Erik was taken aback, but then he smiled slightly. "Ah well, the Lord allows us to lie to good purpose. The Old Testament abounds in lies that carried out the Divine Will. Come, I'll show you to your room in Big Brick."

"Lotta!" Maja-Stina called, "Where is that dishwater?"

She stooped to lift the pan, trembling so hard that she spilled half of it and had to pump again. So long in coming to her, John Root nearly had died before her eyes. *Oh God, don't scare me so!*

***

The leaves fell, the first snow lay on the village like a quilt, and John Root stayed in Bishop Hill. He had not paid particular attention to Charlotta, but she knew that he would in time and was content to watch his comings and goings, memorizing the pattern of lines at the corners of his eyes and the hollows behind his ear lobes where her thumbs would just fit. Sometimes her certainty was shaken, and she worried that he would grow weary of idleness and move on. She was almost glad that he gambled at cards with the English doctor in the unfinished parlor of Big Brick. It passed the time for him.

Her own time was well filled, but she gave up hours of sleep to wash her hair and rinse it with vinegar until it squeaked, to launder all her collars and stiffen them with potato water for a crisp finish. She remembered Carolina's trick of pinching color into the cheeks and practiced it before any possible encounter with John Root.

"What's gotten into you?" Anna-Maja asked.

"I don't know what you mean. I think I'll go to the red house and visit with Maja-Stina. Do you want to come along?"

"No, I must go to the cobbler for my shoes."

Charlotta's shoes had been finished the week before, and they were so stiff and new that the freshly-tanned leather bit like a vise. She endured the discomfort because the new shoes were better-looking than her backless wooden clogs, and she had a new concern for her appearance.

"Aren't you supposed to be working at the church?" Anna Maja asked.

"Not until the carpenters make more spindles. I've sanded all that were finished."

The air was clean and cold, drawing chimney smoke upward in straight pillars as Charlotta walked past the church, the meat storage house, and the north end of Big Brick. It made her blood race pleasantly.

She found Maja-Stina mending undergarments and took a shift of Mathilde's from the work basket to help. As she settled herself beside the kitchen fire, she heard voices in the next room, Erik's and John Root's. Would he think she was pursuing him? Truly, she hadn't known he was here and could only suppose that Divine leading was responsible for her inspiration to visit Maja-Stina. If she strained her ears, she could hear what they were saying, except when Maja-Stina covered their voices with talk of young Erik's cough and the baby's colic.

She heard Erik say, "Perhaps you would like to invest in our enterprise here?"

Charlotta suspended her needle, waiting for the answer, and Maja-Stina said, "Mrs. Mauk says a mustard plaster might help the chest, but if you leave it on too long, it burns the skin—"

Root's speech out-lasted Maja-Stina's, "—too restless to settle down."

Charlotta bit her lip in disappointment, and as chairs scraped in the next room, she became intensely interested in her mending. The men were coming into the kitchen.

"Maja-Stina," Erik said, "have you any more of that pie Mrs. Mauk brought us? Mr. Root might like to try it."

"I don't believe I have met this lady," Root said, nodding toward Charlotta.

"Then let me present Charlotta Lovisa Jansson, my cousin and my ward."

Finally—he knows my name!

"I am honored, Miss Jansson!" Root bowed with an exaggerated courtesy that filled Charlotta with confusion. She had scant experience with fine manners. Unable to speak, she nodded an acknowledgement and rose to take the pie plates from Maja-Stina with hands that shook embarrassingly.

Root looked at the pie doubtfully, but he took a bite and rolled it on his tongue with evident pleasure. "What is it?"

"Pumpkin." Erik said, "A strange American fruit that grows on a vine—sometimes they get as big as wash tubs."

Seeing that only the men were served, Root offered Charlotta a bite from his fork. The gesture was so intimate that she could not accept it in the presence of witnesses. She shook her head dizzily, faintly aware that Erik was watching her with a strange look. She had known his fondness and his disapproval, but never this expression of calculation.

"Charlotta," he said, "perhaps Mr. Root will see you to your quarters. It's almost milking time."

"With the greatest of pleasure!" Root said.

Bewildered by such a suggestion in a place where women walked everywhere alone, Charlotta fumbled for her shawl on the back of a chair. Root took it from her and draped it carefully around her shoulders, increasing her confusion. He put on the Andrews hat, and she caught her breath at a flicker of firelight through its bullet hole. She stood back from the door while he said his good-byes, waiting for him to go out first, but he swept her ahead of him with a firm arm.

Outside, she said, "There's really no need—I only live in the dairymaids' house to the east—" *What am I saying? I have wanted to be with him for so long!*

"I wish it were farther!"

Charlotta smiled at him uncertainly, noticing that he really was not much taller than she was. His partial uniform with the stripe gave the illusion of height. "Where did you live in Sweden?" she asked, just to have something to say. She knew the answer and felt slightly guilty about deceiving him. The seemingly casual questions put to anyone who had talked with him were anything but casual. She knew he had lived in Stockholm, but his family originally came from Norrland. Now he was putting the same question to her.

"We lived at Domta, Osterunda parish, Västmanland."

He smiled. "Ah, Västmanland! I was there one Midsummer's Eve, and I danced until sunrise with a girl who had hair like ripe flax."

"A true daughter of Svea!" Charlotta immediately regretted the sharp tone of jealousy in her voice and hoped he would not notice.

He laughed. "I have learned to appreciate Svea's darker daughters. Everyone knows there is more depth and passion in the dark Swede."

She wanted to ask if he had been taunted about his dark coloring, but she didn't dare. It might lead to a discussion of her own sufferings on that score and make him value her less. She stared intently at the toes of her shoes, noticing a pale scratch in the new leather.

Disturbed by her long silence, he said, "Have I said something to offend you?"

"No—"

"I might, you know. I have been away from women of your
gentle nature for too long!"

As they walked on in silence, Charlotta took small steps to
stretch out their time together—not that she was putting it
to good use! She was happy just to have this man by her
side—handsome, well-spoken, mysterious, and hers by a
decree of fate—or by the will of God.

When they were close to the dairymaids' house, he said, "I
saw you that first day. You stood out, somehow, and I
wanted to know you, but you can't rush at a Swedish woman
as if she were a Mexican whore—"

Charlotta stiffened and blushed painfully.

"Now I *have* offended you, but please make allowances for
me—I have been among rough soldiers!

"I—I must go. I have work to do."

He bowed and left her.

Why couldn't I have said something to make him love me?
I thought it would be so easy once we met!

She changed her clothes and went to the milking stalls,
where the cattle lowed plaintively, pleading for release of the
pressure in their full udders. She pressed her cheek to a
warm, hairy side and stripped jets of milk into the pail.
"There's help for you twice a day," she told the cow, "but I
might burst with love before he takes it!"

***

Charlotta worked at the church, sitting on a small stool to
rub hand-turned maple spindles for the pews. She dreamed as
she worked, scarcely hearing the hum of children's voices
from the classes in the north anterooms. She saw a bed with
posts that were hour glass shapes spread with Mamma's indigo coverlet. That priceless piece of weaving had gone to

Anna-Maja, the oldest daughter in the family, but Anna-Maja
had given it to her. If Anna-Maja ever married, which she
swore she would not, Charlotta would give it back, but for
now it pleased her to imagine it on her own marriage bed, a
sign of her parents' blessing.

"Good morning, Miss Charlotta!"

She turned with a rush of gladness and saw John Root in
the light blue, yellow-striped trousers of the army uniform
and a new coat from the colony tailor. His beard was trimmed,
and he smelled of the English doctor's bay rum. She hated
the scent on the man who had failed to save her mother, but
the unpleasant association faded in her appreciation of John
Root.

"I'm going to take a look at the Red Oak land this morning," he said. "Will you be my guide?"

"I—I can't leave my work."

"I've already asked permission from Erik Jansson to take
you with me."

She looked at him doubtfully, and he laughed. "I knew you
wouldn't believe me, so I asked him for a note. It says, 'Charlotta Lovisa Jansson may be excused from her duties at Colony Church to accompany John Root to Red Oak grove.' "

"Let me see it—"

"Don't you trust me?"

She nodded, reaching for the paper at the same time.

"What a hold that man has on you!"

Recognizing Erik's signature, Charlotta stood and brushed
the fine sawdust from her hands. Root wrapped her wool tip-
pet around her as if she were a child, and she gloried in the
attention.

Hugo, his bay horse, stood untethered outside the church.
He stood like a statue while Root lifted Charlotta into the
saddle. She clutched the big, western horn and held her body
forward to make room for Root behind her, holding that tense

position until they were well out of the village and he pulled her back against him, explaining, "This will balance us better for Hugo."

The horse's hooves rang on the frozen ground, the only sound in this bright morning. Two snows had fallen and melted partially, leaving tawny patches in the fields and white collars at the base of the bare trees. The land was stark but beautiful.

Encircled by a warm arm, Charlotta did not mind the chill wind in her face. This was her first holiday since she left Sweden, and she was happy as a child, but some of her feelings were by no means childish. She was intensely aware of the body of the man who held her and slightly frightened of her pleasure in the contact.

At the end of their three-mile ride, Root helped her down, and they searched for a place where they could eat the cheese and hardtack from his saddle bag. Root spread his outer coat for her in a hollowed shelter in the bank of the Edwards. He broke a skim of ice on the water and tried to bring her a drink in his cupped hands, but it trickled away, and she laughingly dipped her own hands into the icy stream.

He pointed out a soaring hawk, told her that the pale sun made her hair the color of Hugo, and warned her that she should not associate with a bad man like himself.

She admired the hawk, smiled at the thought of being compared to a horse, and laughed at his warning, responding more by expression than word. Enchanted by John Root, she was still afraid to offer any part of her private being to him, afraid of the power of the word in naming what she felt.

When they had finished lunch, she said, "This is the first land we bought. Olof Olsson chose it, and he wanted the village to be here, but Erik preferred the place where we are. Come, I'll show you what is here."

Root helped her up the bank and walked beside her, looking

at dugouts that had been converted to food storage space and pausing to listen to the urgent sawing and chopping in the timber, where men were working to cut as many logs as possible before the heavy snows.

"Why did you want to come here?" she asked.

"I don't like living elbow-to-elbow with other people, do you?"

"I don't mind. We have our own rooms."

"But they aren't yours! They belong to everybody!"

"Erik says it won't be that way always. As soon as the New Jerusalem is established, we can go back to the old ways—owning property the way we did in Sweden."

Root laughed shortly. "What makes you think he'll ever let go? Once a man has power—"

"The power comes from God. He gave it, and He will take it away when He wishes."

"How fine it would be to have a simple faith—or any faith at all!"

Charlotta looked at him with alarm. "Surely you—"

"I've seen all I care to here. Shall we ride out?"

Hugo carried them eastward rapidly, and Charlotta dreaded the ending of their day together. After his remark about faith, John Root had closed himself to her, and she did not know what to do about it. She needed time, the time that was fast running out. And then he pulled the horse to a stop and turned her face to his. He took her hand and brushed it with his lips. *A hand so red and rough!*

"Charlotta, do you feel anything for me?"

She lowered her eyes, trembling and unable to speak in this miraculous reprieve from his rejection.

"Look at me with those eyes so marvelously made!" He traced the peak in one eyelid with his finger, "I have never seen such eyes!"

"Erik says they are like—like little pine tree tops—" she

said shyly.

"Always Erik!" He dropped his hand and turned from her in anger.

"John Root," she said softly, amazed at the words that crowded to her lips, demanding to be said, "I dreamed of you one Midsummer's Eve—after eating the magic pancakes—"

"It's not possible!" he said in a choked voice.

I've made a mistake. Oh God, let me take it back!

Hugo started forward again at a touch of the neck rein. Root did not speak, and Charlotta could not. The silence of their constraint had become nearly unbearable when it was broken by the rumble of cart wheels. The ox boys with their laughter and their singing whips made enough noise to bear them along to Bishop Hill with no possibility for utterance.

At the dairymaids' house, John Root lifted Charlotta from the saddle with impersonal courtesy. He bowed and said, "Thank you for being my cicerone today."

She did not know what he meant, but she nodded stiffly. *Why was it wrong to tell him what is true?*

Root did not appear in the dining hall that night, and Erik gave Charlotta a severe look as she took her place at the table. Heavy-hearted, she wondered how she had failed Erik? She must take care to avoid him until his annoyance, whatever its reason, was forgotten.

***

In spite of the disastrous ending of the day at Red Oak grove, Charlotta was unprepared for the sight of John Root escorting the blonde and beautiful Marta Blomberg to Sunday worship. She felt as if a huge hand had squeezed her heart dry.

Root and Marta parted at the north door and moved to the center of a back pew from opposite side aisles, making it very clear that they were together, though separated by the partition between the men's and women's sides of the church.

Charlotta, do you feel anything for me?" The remembered words mocked her, and when Erik took his place at the pulpit, she could scarcely concentrate on what he was saying. The sanctuary was unheated, like that of all Swedish churches, but somehow it seemed colder here. Damper, at least. She shivered, pulling her shawl close, and came so close to weeping that she held her eyes wide open to discourage the formation of tears.

She looked at the hollowed wooden sticks piled beside the pews, thinking of the next day's work. Her job would be to lay string through the sticks and fill the hollows with melted lard, making lights for evening worship. She could not worship in her present condition, and it might be that she could not work. If she could persuade Anna-Maja to tell Erik that she was sick, she could crawl off like a wounded animal and try to recover—but then Erik would send the doctor, and that was the last thing she wanted! What symptoms could she give him? People did die of broken hearts. Mr. Pollock, Sophia Gabrielson's second husband, had, people whispered. It broke his heart when Sophia dragged him away from everything he cared about to follow Erik.

If I could only go the forest! She longed for the comforting sound of wind in the pine branches, the patient solitude of the big trees. But the only pines in Bishop Hill were the small seedlings in the graveyard, too young to sing with the wind. *The graveyard—Mamma is there!*

"Anna-Maja," she whispered, "will you take my place in the kitchen before the noon meal? If you will, I'll scrub the bath house for you."

"But your name is on the roster."

"If the job is filled, nobody will look at the roster!"

"All right, but if we're caught, you'll have to take the

blame!"

Leaving the church without facing John Root and Marta was a problem for Charlotta. They were part of a crowd listening to Jonas Olsson's wife complain that the ceiling of the entrance hall was too low.

"The balcony comes down too far!" she insisted, "It knocks off my father's hat!"

Big John Johnson nodded, waving the tall "cake" hat that was his pride. He loved it because it reminded him of the professors' hats in Sweden.

Gilliam, the carpenter and coffin-maker, said, "But if we raise the balcony, it will be too cramped for any good use!"

John Root listened to the argument with amusement, watching Gilliam and Mrs. Olsson in turn as the smiling Marta clung to his arm. Charlotta passed behind them quickly, rushing down the outside stairs without looking back.

A light snow was on the ground, and Charlotta's feet slipped as she ran, hoping to be out of sight before the witnesses to the balcony dispute came out of the church. Her mother's grave was not far from the western boundary of the cemetery. She approached it panting and knelt to clasp the wooden marker. *Oh Mamma, I shouldn't have dared to want him!* She clung to the cold slab and cried until the snow melted beneath her knees and soaked through her skirt.

"Lotta, what on earth are you doing?" Sabina stood above her, hopping from one foot to the other as she hugged the ends of her shawl to her body.

"Leave me alone!"

"I will not! You're behaving very strangely, and I'm not the only one who has noticed!"

"Who else?" Charlotta asked, stung by the thought that her feelings were public property.

Sabina ignored her question and said, "It's John Root, isn't it?"

"Don't mention that name to me!"

"Why not? Erik wants you to marry him, you know. He wants Root for the colony because he's educated and he has money—and he won't join us for any other reason, so—"

"So?"

"So Erik is clever enough to remember how we got the German mason!"

Charlotta remembered too. The mason had stopped overnight in Bishop Hill on his way to a job in Galesburg, and he was so smitten by the girl sent to light him to his room that he never left. Urgent messages from the Galesburg employer were ignored. She was angry that Erik meant to use her in the same way, and she said, "I will not be bait for a trap! Besides, if John Root stays, it will be for Marta Blomberg!"

Sabina laughed. "You don't know anything at all about men, do you?"

"I know what I see."

"And that's precious little! I don't know what happened that day you spent with him at Red Oak grove, but whatever it was, he decided he needed to make you jealous. Why did you let him do such a thorough job of it?"

"I haven't!" Charlotta lied, "I don't care what he does!"

Sabina laughed and pulled at Charlotta's arm. "Come away from this cold place before you get sick and hurry back here in a box! You want to be a bride, not a corpse!"

As she allowed Sabina to guide her down the hill, Charlotta tried to determine whether she was relieved, angry or hopeful. She decided that she was all three.

Philadelphia, December, 1848—

Hearing the swish of Fermine's skirts in the hall outside their room, Robert Baird quickly covered the small jeweler's box on the dressing table with a handkerchief. Not given to taking pleasure in concealment, he enjoyed that rare experience as his wife's face appeared in the mirror, then vanished behind his own when she caressed the back of his neck above his collar with cool fingers.

"Are you tired after your meeting, *Mon Cher?*" she said, "Perhaps you should lie down before tea."

"Only if you will lie beside me, Mina."

She lifted one eyebrow, smiled, and planted a high-laced shoe on the bed step. "Is my company worth the effort?"

"Your company is worth infinitely more!" He bent to untie and loosen the lace. *What a glorious ankle! What a sublime limb! But I would love her if she walked on piano legs!*

When they were stretched out on the counterpane like twin tomb effigies, Mina sighed luxuriously. "When we were younger, Robert, you would not have stopped at my boots, but there is something to be said for just being together so beautifully!"

"Which do you prefer, my dear? I am capable of either."

"Just talk to me, Robert, about anything."

He looked at her hands folded on her breastbone and imagined how the ring in the jeweler's box would look on her right hand. Fermine's hands were not delicate, but they were white, firm and capable. Beautiful hands. The ring, a wide band of gold with lilies, was inscribed, "Ever Thine, Robert, 1848." He had borrowed another ring from her jewel box to get the size, and the gold was as pure as could be managed. Though Mina deserved absolutely pure gold, it would never do—too soft. How hard it would be to withhold the ring until Christmas!

"You haven't said anything, Robert, shall I let you sleep?"

"Oh no, I was just thinking—"

"Of what?"

Of what, indeed! "Of gold."

"Ah, you mean President Polk's announcement in his annual message?"

What a fortunate escape! "Where was it? California, I know, but—"

"At Coloma on the south fork of the American River, the newspaper said, and it's a rather important find."

"Ah, do you remember when they found gold in northern Georgia, Mina? It was the year I was ordained."

"Of course I remember! I remember everything about that year! As I recall, there wasn't much of it in Georgia, and most of the people who rushed down there to make their fortunes were disappointed."

"Yes, a small amount of gold, but it resulted in a great amount of evil—stealing, killing. Why are people so mad for gold?"

She turned her wedding ring on her finger. "Because it's beautiful, it warms to the skin—and because we've been told that the streets of heaven are paved with it—"

"So they are! The Book of Revelation says, 'and the street of the city was pure gold.' "

"Oh Robert," she turned to him earnestly, "I may be a heretic, but my heaven has nothing to do with gold and precious stones—it's just being with everyone I love forever and ever without sickness or crying or ever saying good-bye! Is that wicked?"

"You know it isn't, Mina! In that same chapter of the Book of Revelation, the first mention is of the new Jerusalem, a place where God will dwell with men, 'and He shall wipe away every tear from their eyes; and death shall be no more; neither shall there be mourning, nor crying, nor pain, any more.' My love, you could *never* be wicked!"

"It's just that some parts of the Bible are dearer to me than others, and I suppose I should love it all—equally."

"Mina, dearest, all of the Bible is equally inspired, but not all of it is equally inspiring. I myself have trouble whipping up enthusiasm for the 'begats,' necessary as I know them to be!"

Fermine edged close and kissed his forehead, her eyes sparking with mischief as she said, "Thank you for the absolution!"

"And now will you absolve me?"

"Of what?" The mischief remained, "You are perfect!"

But Baird was serious. He said, "I often wonder if I should have taken a church instead of going into education and Temperance. Have I betrayed my ordination, Mina?"

She sat bolt upright. "I have never heard of anything so silly! Philip Lindsley is an ordained minister, and education is his very life! How many times have you heard him quote Blake, 'To labour in knowledge is to build up Jerusalem'?"

"Ah yes, but Philip is accomplishing so much at the University of Nashville—doing a mighty work in spite of his loss of Margaret. Without you, I couldn't go on!"

"Don't even talk of being without me! I pray that we will die in the same moment—be taken together, so that neither of us will have to mourn! How did we ever get onto such a terrible subject?" She lay down beside him once more and reached for his hand.

"In the beginning, we were talking about gold. 'If I have made gold my hope...I should have denied the God that is above.' "

"You're quoting, Robert, I recognized the tone."

"Yes, from Job, and now from Proverbs, 'How much better is it to get wisdom than gold!' And from the Psalms, 'The ordinances of Jehovah are true, and righteous altogether, more to be desired are they than gold, yea, than much fine gold.' "

"Robert, let me tell you the kinds of gold I love—Henry's hair when he was a baby; a shaft of sun through the solarium windows; that nice tea you brought me from England served in a thin, china cup; the forsythia that blooms below our window in the spring; and most of all—the reflection of firelight in your eyes when the children are in bed and we sit together thinking of the day we have lived—I thank God for such gold!"

He gathered her into his arms and held her for a long moment, then released her so abruptly that she gave a small cry of protest and bounded from the bed to bring the small box from the dresser.

"I can't wait!" he said, "Tell me if you like it!"

Fermine opened the box and gazed at the softly gleaming circlet in its green velvet slit. Before she put it on, she turned it in her fingers to read the inscription, knowing there would be one.

"Oh Robert, I'll wear these words as long as I live!"

Seeing the rich, gold band on her hand, he briefly felt the lure of the yellow metal, knew the strength of the compulsion to have it and give it. And yet, it was the "word fitly spoken" that won her praise, "like apples of gold in network of silver."

"Is it late?" he asked, pleading with his eyes.

"Not very." she said. The carved lilies gleamed as she unfastened her high collar.

Bishop Hill, winter, 1849—

One cold morning in early January, Charlotta stood near the high ladder of Gilliam the carpenter, handing him the tools necessary for raising the floor of the church balcony (Mrs. Olsson had won), and she nearly dropped the hammer she was holding when John Root came in with a gust of cold air.

Root nodded to her stiffly and addressed the carpenter, "Mr. Gilliam, I've been assigned to help you."

"Now maybe we'll get somewhere!" Gilliam said, "All they

ever give me is women, and they expect me to do a decent
job of building with that kind of help! Get a ladder and start
tearing planks from the other end of this flooring."

Charlotta resented Gilliam's remark, and she left him to
hand tools to John Root. It was obvious to her that Root
never had handled tools. He worked clumsily, asking for the
same things he heard Gilliam request from the other girl on
the job, and they were not always appropriate for his task, as
Gilliam was farther along. Charlotta took wicked satisfaction
in handing him the wrong thing with a face carefully devoid
of expression. She slapped the tools hard into his hand, careful not to touch his skin.

When Root hit his thumb and suppressed a stream of
curses with difficulty, she said, "Perhaps you should have
asked for an assignment to the weaving house." Marta Blomberg worked there, and she knew he would take her meaning,
but he said nothing, doggedly pulling at the planks and piercing his hands with splinters.

A young girl brought boiled grain coffee to them, and Root
climbed down, holding out a hand reddened by seeping blood.
"Miss Charlotta, could you pull this small log from my palm?
Of course, if it sickens you—"

"I've seen a lot worse!" she said scornfully, but she was ex-
asperated by the trembling of her own hands as she extracted
the splinter and washed the wound with coffee.

Gilliam ordered them back to work, and through the rest of
the day, they stole glances at each other, looking away in
confusion if their eyes chanced to meet. When the dinner bell
rang, Charlotta snatched up her shawl and hurried out of the
church, confused beyond measure.

Root came after her and fell into step beside her. He sighed
deeply and said, "I'm not very good at that kind of work."

"Then why don't you find a job that is not so hard on
you?"

"I want to be where you are."

"I thought you wanted to be where Marta was!"

He pulled off his hat and ran a hand through his hair. "How can I explain this? I thought that loving you was *my* idea, and then you told me I'd been roped by fate. I couldn't bear that, and I tried to break loose, but—"he shrugged, "well, you see how it is with me."

Charlotta steepled her hands at her lips, trying to catch and hold the explosion of joy that rocked her being, and he took the hands away to kiss her hard on the mouth, *Right in the street, with everyone watching! Oh, now he is mine!*

"We will go to Erik Jansson tomorrow," he said. "There must be a wedding of some kind—whatever he requires."

***

John Root wore the full uniform of the American Army for the all-important visit to the red house. He squeezed Charlotta's hand before he left her in the kitchen and went to talk with Erik in the next room. Before the door closed, she saw him click his heels smartly and heard him say, "I've come to ask for the hand of your ward, Charlotta Lovisa Jansson."

Maja-Stina was not at home. Who would know if Charlotta crept close and listened? The temptation made her stomach flutter, and the Mora clock, ticking in heartbeats, seemed to urge her forward. She yielded recklessly and tip-toed to the door.

"Are you a believer?" Erik asked.

Charlotta held her breath through John's hesitation, and when he finally said, "I am.", she went limp against the wall.

"Do you love her?"

"I do."

"Will you stay with us?"

"As long as we're content here."

"Your answer prompts me to include a proviso in your marriage contract—something to the effect that should you choose to leave Bishop Hill, your wife may make the choice of going with you or staying here."

"I have no objection to that. With all due respect, I have confidence in my own qualities."

"Do you agree to add all monies in your possession to the community funds?"

John chuckled. "Such as they are, yes."

"But you have gold—I've seen it! You have paid me some of it for your keep!"

"And that nearly wiped out the small stake I had to show, I'm afraid."

Charlotta tensed with dismay. If Erik wanted John for his money and there was none—

"—may have deceived me in that respect, but not in another! The colony has uses for a man of your type, but I warn you—do not forge my signature again!"

"I apologize! The charms of the lady overwhelmed me."

What is he talking about? Charlotta frowned with puzzlement until she remembered the note of permission John had showed her the day they went to Red Oak grove. It would be impossible to duplicate Erik's signature so perfectly—and yet John seemed to admit it—

"What *can* you contribute to the colony?" Erik was asking, "It's clear that you have never known hard work."

"I'm an excellent shot. I can hunt game—and perhaps I can help you interpret the American laws of property and of commerce."

"Very well, you may have her."

Charlotta sagged against the wall in happy relief, then was startled to hear John say, "Your new teeth are quite handsome." *Why is he talking about teeth at a time like this?* A Chicago dentist had replaced Erik's broken stumps, and they all agreed that the false teeth were remarkable, but John's compliment was an odd response to Erik's consent to their marriage. She heard the chairs scrape and moved away from the door quickly to take a seat near the fireplace.

Erik came into the kitchen and kissed her cheek. His lips parted, and the false teeth were cool against her skin. "I wish you every happiness, Lotta."

"And she will *have* every happiness!" John said, offering her his arm.

When they were outside, she asked him why he had mentioned Erik's teeth at such an important moment.

"Because he was waiting for my abject gratitude, and that is something he will never have! No one will ever have it!"

She accepted his explanation and asked another question, "Did you really sign Erik's name that day?"

"Yes. I became quite skilled at forgery in Sweden."

"Why?" she asked, shocked.

"To increase my uncle's philanthropy," he said with a laugh. "As long as you're taking *me* to task, may I ask where you learned to listen at keyholes?"

She blushed and said nothing. John had told Erik that he was a believer, and if that were so, what he had done in the past no longer mattered. *I love what you are and what you will be!*

In the little time that remained before the wedding, there was much to do. Sabina brushed Charlotta's hair until it crackled and threw her worn undergarments into the rag bin. Anna-Maja had been sewing replacements for days, but she did it sadly, viewing Charlotta's marriage as a desertion.

"Better rub some lard into those hands," Sabina advised, "they're rough enough to tear even a soldier's hide!"

"If we had married in the right order, you wouldn't be so high and mighty about what you know!" Charlotta said.

Sabina laughed. "Tomorrow you'll know everything I do,

and if I'm any judge of men, you might know a bit more!"

Charlotta reddened and said, "I wish Mamma were here!"

Maja-Stina knocked and entered without invitation, the little boy born in New York balanced on her hip. She shook the snow from her shawl and said, "What will you do for a bridal crown, Lotta? Surely there's nothing green in this whole white world!"

Sabina suggested the sheaf of wheat she had arranged in a copper pot at harvest time, but Charlotta shook her head. With all her heart she wanted a crown of green, the color of eternity.

"The pines!" she cried, "The little pines in the cemetery!"

"No, Lotta!" Sabina said, horrified, "Don't you remember how they spread pine boughs near the houses of the dying in Sweden?"

She nodded, recalling the branches that muffled the noise of rolling wheels, horses' hooves and wooden shoes, allowing the dying to depart in peace. She, too, wanted peace. "It doesn't matter," she said, "we are no longer in Sweden. Besides, I love the pine! Erik gave me its name when I was a little girl."

Maja-Stina sighed heavily. "Yes, I guess it's different here. If you have your heart set on pine, I'll send young Erik to the cemetery for some branches. He's just outside playing with that dog Mr. Mauk gave him." She went out to speak to the boy.

Sabina brought a pot of sand from the banks of the Edwards to the table and commanded Charlotta to rub her hands in it to wear away the callouses. They spoke of other weddings they remembered, and Sabina told her she was lucky to have one all to herself.

Then young Erik hurried in with the boughs of tender, young needles, saying "John Root gave me his hunting knife to cut them."

"Did you tell him what they were for?" Charlotta asked.

"Yes, and he looked kind of funny, but then he laughed and said he was glad his bride wasn't stitious. What does that mean?"

Maja-Stina's lips trembled as she said, "Why don't you ask Sophia Gabrielson?"

Charlotta knew that Maja-Stina was deeply jealous of Sophia's influence over young Erik, and she saw by the boy's expression that he was pained by tangled loyalties. She touched them both in a silent plea for reconciliation, but it was too late.

"I *will* ask Mrs. Gabrielson! She knows everything!" Young Erik spoke so vehemently that cords stood out on his neck.

"You might as well go and live with her!" Maja-Stina cried.

"Oh don't! Not on my wedding day!"

But the atmosphere was hopelessly jangled. Young Erik ran from the room to hide the tears that shamed him, and his mother departed heavily, too grieved to say good-bye.

In the silence that followed, Charlotta picked up the pine boughs to weave her wedding crown. A dead needle pierced her finger. She stared at the liquid ruby with vexation and dread, struggling against seeing it as a bad omen, then sucked it away and went on with her task.

***

It was dark when Charlotta's sisters escorted her into the church. Candle boys stood at the windows tending the wooden lights, some of them made by her own hands. As she walked with Sabina and Anna-Maja down the women's aisle to the front of the church, she saw her friends of the voyage so dimly that she nearly paused to ask for more oil in the wooden forms. *No, it's my own eyes.* A deep, internal trembling affected her legs, forcing her to walk slowly, and this accorded with her sudden doubts about the step she was taking. At the first pew, she felt John's presence across the partition, but she could not look at him.

"Charlotta!" he whispered urgently.

She raised her eyes and saw him through a mist of tears. He wore a new suit made by a tailor in Cambridge, and it was outlandishly styled in comparison with the simple clothing of the colony men. His beard was freshly trimmed, and the scent of bay rum crossed the partition and mingled with the fragrance of her pine crown.

The wedding service began with a hymn, and Charlotta stilled her own shaking voice to listen to John's. *How beautiful, how strong!* When Erik began to preach, she could not get the sense of his words. He was having trouble with his false teeth, but Charlotta knew that was not the reason for her incomprehension. *I am not here!*

Breathing the scent of pine, she was in the forest near Domta, then at Osterunda church, where the dead sat in the family pews looking very much alive: her father, her mother, Uncle Johannes, Aunt Sara. *Will they hear me if I speak to them? If I say—we are free now, but I wonder if our faith is as strong as it was when we were fined and beaten—this man who sits on the other side of the partition—this man who claims me—how can he know what it was? How can he know me?*

At the clatter of a wooden candle toppling on the sill, the dear faces vanished, and Charlotta made a strong effort to listen to Erik. When he called them forward to take their vows, her voice was steady in promising to subject herself to her husband, to be faithful to him and serve him with heart and hand. She promised to obey him in all things. John promised to follow Christ and to be diligent in the up-building of the New Jerusalem.

Charlotta was not sure how she got from the church to the log house dining room for the wedding feast, but suddenly she was there, smiling and shaking hands beside her bridegroom. At long last, the line of well-wishers dwindled to nothing and the guests moved to the serving tables to help themselves to the venison roasted in the big ovens at the bakery. John had brought down the buck with a single shot.

"We should have music and dancing!" he said.

Charlotta smiled regretfully. "We don't dance in Bishop Hill, and our only music is our own voices."

"Then will somebody please sing a polka? I'd like to dance with my wife!"

"Oh, John!"

He scowled at her tone of wifely reproof and looked around the room restlessly until he saw the English doctor beckoning to him from the door. Then he bowed to Charlotta and said, "Excuse me, Mrs. Root, I must see what my good friend wants."

Mrs. Root! To a woman of twenty-five who thought she never would marry, the new name was music. John had disappeared with the doctor, and she went to a window, scraping frost away to see if they were outside. Two dark shapes moved in the direction of the hospital. *Don't leave me now!* But he had. Holding her head high, Charlotta moved among the colonists, laughing and talking feverishly to hide her embarrassment at being abandoned at her own wedding feast.

After what seemed like hours, John returned, stamping the snow from his boots. He drew her hand through his arm and said, "Well, Mrs. Root, shall we repair to our quarters?"

Our quarters? Our home!

Dairymaids crowded the door, giggling behind their hands, and the oxboys made suggestive remarks until Erik scattered them with a roar.

Outside, the snow was brilliant in the moonlight, so bright

that it made Charlotta's head ache. She pressed her temples and asked, "Why did you leave me?"

He answered by blowing his breath in her face. "The celebrations of Bishop Hill are a bit tame for me. I would have taken you with me, but surely you don't drink?"

"I once had a piece of hardtack soaked in brännvin—"Her eyes misted at the memory, and she heard Pappa's voice, "Sometimes we find we do not like what we thought we wanted, Lotta."

They were close to the dual stairway that led to John's room in Big Brick. Charlotta had a wild impulse to run away, but instead, she hung back until John realized she was not beside him and turned.

"Are you afraid of me?"

"N-no—"

"Come, then!" He lifted her and climbed the stairs, opening the door with the hand that passed under her knees. He dropped her on the bed with a bounce. He lit a candle, then another and another in a wasteful blaze that illuminated the sturdy colony bed, two straight chairs, a massive chest of drawers, and a Mexican saddle heavily worked with silver. This was a man's room with no hint of a woman's touch.

He came to her and lifted the crown of pine from her hair. She stifled a small cry when the needles caught and pulled, taking the crown in her own hands to work it loose. He took her shawl and threw it on a chair. He removed the brooch at her throat, Mamma's brooch, and though he had gone gloveless in the winter night, his hands were warm. The moment Charlotta realized that he meant to take all of her clothes from her, she squeezed her eyes shut tight in an agony of embarrassment, and when she was naked, she bent forward, trying to cover herself with woefully insufficient hands and arms.

"Open your eyes!" he commanded, "What have you to be

ashamed of?"

She obeyed, but the sight of him fully dressed while she
stood naked increased her shame, and she turned her back on
him.

"Oh my God!" he said, and she cringed at the exasperation
in his voice. A drawer banged open. She felt a cool silkiness
on her body and gratefully gathered it around her, a huge
shawl of crimson, yellow and poison green.

"I bought that in Saltillo. I hope it makes you act the way
it makes you look!" Holding her gaze, he undressed.

Startled by the first male nakedness she had ever seen—except for infants—Charlotta closed her eyes again. *I should
have asked Sabina what to do!*

***

Though Erik had excused Charlotta from her duties at the
dairy the first morning of her married life, she awoke at the
usual early hour. John still slept heavily. She touched him
with a diffident tenderness, and he stirred, reaching for her
without opening his eyes.

"Rosa—" he murmured.

She went stiff in his arms. "I am Charlotta!"

"Uh?" One eye opened, "Oh, yes—Mrs. Root—"

"Who is Rosa?"

"I can't imagine, and in any case, it's none of your concern."

She pouted, he kissed her, and it began all over again, the
rough loving that had so amazed her the night before. She
was lost in it until the morning worship bell sounded, and
then she struggled to break from him.

"Stay with me."

"I can't, and you must come to the service too."

"Not on your life! I'm too tired—"

"But you promised to uphold the—"

He stopped her lips with his hand. "Are you quarreling with me so soon?"

"No, I love you!"

"Then go to church if you must—but let me sleep!" He rolled over and closed his eyes.

Sighing, she rose to dress and was horrified to discover red marks on her body. Did every bride rise from her marriage bed like this? Fortunately her clothes would cover the branding.

Walking to the church alone when everyone expected her husband to be at her side was embarrassing, but she straightened her back, held her head high, and pretended that there was nothing unusual about it. Sabina saw her enter the church and moved over to make room for her.

"Where's John?" she whispered.

"He—he's not feeling well." Charlotta was amazed at the ease of her lie.

"Was it you, or too much Number Six?"

"Sabina!"

"Well, I saw where he went with the doctor, who just happens to have a key to the medicine closet, but it *could* have been—"

"Hush! The service is about to begin!"

***

John did not appear at breakfast either, and though it was against the rules, Charlotta planned to carry food to him before she began her work at the church. She took two of everything, much to the amusement of the serving women, and she bit back an angry reply to their ribald whispers.

Concealing the food in her apron, she hurried back to Big Brick, entering John's room like a polite visitor. *I will have to learn that I live here!*

Roused by what she thought was a quiet entrance, John

groaned, "Can't I have a moment's peace?"

"I'm sorry—I thought you would be hungry."

He got up, making no effort to cover his nakedness, and took the food. After one bite, he complained, "Hardtack! This is a fine breakfast!"

"It's better than nothing! If you won't get up for breakfast—"

"I thought you would take care of me—see to my comfort—"

How sorry he is for himself! A spark of anger heated her tone, "I'm doing my best! Bringing your breakfast has made me late for my work at the church, and Erik will—"

"You should be working for *me*, not Erik Jansson!"

"Both of us must work for the New Jerusalem!"

"I'm used to a better life! I must have been mad to marry and bind myself to a place where a man can call nothing his own—not even his wife!"

"I'm yours, John," she said in the voice she would use to cajole a cross child. *When night comes, I'll give you everything you want!*

***

The days were difficult for Charlotta. Troubled by her husband's savage boredom with colony life, she praised his marksmanship and encouraged him to hunt game in the woods. This was one of the skills that had recommended him to Erik, perhaps the only one that John was willing to exercise, and though she was now close to thinking that her marriage had been a mistake, she had to go on believing that Erik's reasons for it were sufficient. No proof to the contrary could be considered.

According to colony rules, all food except that in Erik's house and the hospital was to be consumed in the dining hall. Charlotta took the risk of smuggling cheese, hardtack and apples wrinkled from winter-long storage to their room to pack John's lunches, but her sense of relief when he rode off on Hugo for a day of hunting was well worth the guilt she felt at disobeying Erik. When John stayed in the village, his discontent made her physically sick.

In the early spring John bagged several deer, but more often he brought back a few rabbits—or squirrels, which were hard to clean and dress, scarcely worth the ammunition. Charlotta knew that he spent more time in a Cambridge saloon than in the woods. He came home late, hours after game could be sighted, bringing the harsh smell of spirits into their room.

One night he returned in a black mood, having shot nothing and having lost at cards in Cambridge besides. He pushed past Charlotta and fell into a chair. Tossing his empty game bag into a corner, he commanded, "Take off my boots!"

Unmindful of the mud, she grasped one boot willingly and pulled. She felt John staring at the back of her neck, that space between the coil of her braids and her collar. Could it be dirty? She always tried to wash thoroughly, even the places she couldn't see, holding to cleanliness as her only appealing quality when John told her about the city women he had known—women in silk dresses. Why wouldn't the boot come off? She gave a sharper tug.

"You're breaking my damned ankle!"

"I'm sorry." She altered the angle and tugged again. As the boot came off in her hands, John planted his other foot on her backside and sent her sprawling. Enraged, she glared at him. "Why did you do that?"

"Because I'm sick of Erik Jansson and his female followers! This is no life for a man! If it weren't for you, I'd be off and away—free!"

"Work is the life for a man, but you play like a child!"

"Play, do I? I put plenty of meat on the table here!"

Oh, why doesn't he just go away and let me have some peace? He treats me like a towel thrown damp in a heap to moulder! But Erik wants him, needs him. She forced herself to speak calmly, "Yes, John, you provide a great deal of meat."

Her switch to meekness made him angrier. "I'm going to join a lodge in Cambridge. If I don't see some real men somewhere, I'll go out of my mind!"

What do you know of real men? From what he had told her of his father, she had decided that Sture Ruth was not much of a man. Silently she pulled off the other boot.

"Clean them for me. I'm going out."

"But you just came home!"

"So I did, but how can I enjoy the company of a woman who lets herself go to fat?"

"With good reason!" she snapped. She was almost sure but had been too shy to mention her suspicions to the other women for confirmation.

He looked at her closely, and then a slow smile spread over his face. "I was beginning to wonder why nothing had happened! When I think of the times I've dreaded to know—and now—my God, what a feeling!"

Charlotta covered her face with her hands and tried not to cry, but tears squeezed her closed lids. *Other women—how many?*

"Lotta, please!" He took her in his arms more gently than he ever had, drinking her tears with his tongue, "I won't go out tonight after all."

Then he cleaned his own boots.

***

When Erik arranged a cattle buying and missionary expedition to the Shaker settlement in Pleasant Hill, Kentucky, some of the men returned to tell their wives of the brilliantly dyed cloth they had seen in the south. The women were so excited that they spoke of little else for days, and Erik was moved to preach a sermon on the evils of vanity. He did, however, allow Jonas Olsson's daughter Carin to journey to Pleasant Hill for the secret of the Shaker colors.

Carin Olsson returned with moist bundles of earth-bound plants and enough mysterious packets of powder to dye a few bolts of linen. The wool would have to wait until the Kentucky plants took root and multiplied in the soil of Bishop Hill.

Charlotta joined the women who were questioning Carin about the Shakers at the weaving house.

"Their furniture is very much like ours," she said, "but they are strange people. They see spirits! The men and women do not live together, and at the worship services, they make their bodies shake and shiver. The first time I saw it, I was frightened by the way they danced and hopped about, singing and howling. Some of them went on with it until they fell down in a faint!"

"Do they believe in God?"

Carin wrinkled her brow. "I guess so, but they think that God came to us as a man in Christ and as a woman in their prophetess, Mother Ann."

"God *can't* be a woman!" Maja-Stina said, "That's blasphemy!"

Bored with the scandalized chatter about Shaker theology, Sabina said, "If the men and women never come together, soon there will be no more Shakers! What happens when they all get old and die?"

"They make converts from the outside."

Sabina laughed, "Well, they'll never get *me!* They really *are* strange!"

Carin smiled. "Many people think *we're* strange. Aside

from the Mauks and the Mascalls, our American neighbors look at us the same way."

"Yes," Charlotta said, "I suppose we have brought a little piece of Sweden to Illinois." *Will we ever belong here? Is that what I want? I should want it, because I can never go back, and my child will be an American.* She realized that she was thinking "my child" rather than "our child" and sighed deeply. With Mamma and Pappa, it was always "our daughters."

***

Carin Olsson dyed three sample bolts of linen, one green, one brown and one red. On the May morning of Charlotta's birthday, John gave her a length of the deep red cloth.

Delighted, she draped it around her body and longed for a sizeable mirror. "How in the world did you get this? It wasn't to be given out until there was enough for everyone!"

"Communism only works for those who believe in it. Let's say that Miss Olsson and I came to an understanding."

She looked at him doubtfully, unable to believe that Jonas Olsson's daughter would do anything questionable. Could John have forged Erik's signature again to get the linen?

"Get busy and make it into something!" he ordered, "I'm sick of looking at the drab things you wear. Make yourself a red dress, and I'll take you to Cambridge and show you off!"

"Not now, John! I'd look like a walking Big Brick in red, and why hide this beautiful linen behind a forty week apron?"

"It's impossible to please you, I see."

"That's not true, John, this is a wonderful gift, and I thank you for it!" *You please me when you leave me and set me free from displeasing you.*

"To hell with it!" He strode to the door.

"Where are you going?" She needed to know how long she would be free.

"I'm not a child to be questioned!" He returned to the table for a small leather pouch and went out, slamming the door.

She knew where he was going. The pouch meant a game of cards with the doctor. They gambled frequently, and John had won a good deal of money. After he learned that she was expecting the child, he bought her presents in Cambridge or Victoria with his winnings. She was pleased, of course, but she told him she preferred that he put the money into the colony fund. He refused, and the gifts stopped coming as well— until today. Charlotta held the fabric to her cheek and sighed. John did try, she supposed, but it just wasn't in him to be the husband she had hoped for and confidently expected—a man as strong as Erik.

A man's mother was largely responsible for what he became, Charlotta believed, and she had asked John to describe Ingrid Ruth (John now spelled his name the way Americans pronounced it). She could scarcely imagine such a woman. John's mother did nothing more strenuous than lifting food to her mouth. The work of the house and the cooking was done by servants, and Ingrid Ruth even had a maid to help her dress and to arrange her hair. How did she fill her days? By drinking tea with her friends in a blue drawing room, lifting a cup of the Vasa pattern delicately to her lips and bemoaning the behavior of a son she never scolded. Charlotta clamped her own lips tight at the thought, vowing to do better by her own child.

She unbraided her hair and brushed it, thinking she might as well go to bed. The doctor had the key to the medicine cabinet, and he and John would drink Number Six and play cards for hours. She would be better off asleep when he came home. She undressed and looked at the swell of her body with interest. The thought of another life hidden within her was amazing. Did the baby know when she was happy or sad? If so, the poor little one must have a poor view of the world out-side. She must make a better effort to be cheerful.

When she first felt the kick of life, she had the impulse to talk to the child, but she didn't, she merely directed her thoughts to it. *It?* That didn't seem kind, but how was she to know if it would be "he" or "she"? John wanted a son, she supposed. Most men did. She herself would be more comfort-able with a girl after growing up in a family of sisters. If the baby turned out to be a girl, they would stand together against John's disappointment. She pulled on her night shift and patted it to her body as if she were tucking the child be-neath a coverlet. Then she blew out the candle and climbed into bed.

She could not sleep immediately, and she stared into the darkness, wondering how she would have fared as the wife of Anders Salin? She hadn't thought of Anders in years, but now she wondered how it would seem to be bearing his child instead of John's? It probably was wrong to think of it, but she couldn't help remembering Anders as he had looked that day at the Fall Fair. And that was not wrong—not when it re-leased the tight anxiety that signalled distress to the baby, her little *flicka.* As close to content as she had been in months, she slept.

Jarred awake by John's cursing as he stumbled into the dark room, Charlotta got up quickly to light a candle. As the light flared, he continued to curse, throwing his clothes in all directions. She saw that he was not only drunk but angry.

"What is it, John?" she asked, flinching in anticipation of his answer.

"That damned sawbones has accused me of cheating at cards! I ought to put some lead into his liver!"

"The doctor must be mistaken. We'll see Erik about it in the morning."

"What good will that do? Jansson will take the side of his

medicine man! Maybe I'll have to tell what I know about the good doctor—about those mysterious absences of his!"

"Erik knows that the doctor still treats a few people outside the village—" Charlotta said, puzzled.

"Have you ever noticed how little interest he has in women? Those outside patients are not sick, and they happen to be young males!"

"I don't know what you mean."

"Do I have to spell it out for you? My God, woman, what you know about the human condition could be written on the head of a pin!"

"John, please come to bed. Mamma always used to say that everything looks better in the morning."

"Thank heaven or hell that I was spared knowing her! If there's anything I can't stand, it's an old woman full of tedious, country wisdom! I never should have come here—happier in the barracks with Wester and Zimmerman and tequila—wonder where they are now?"

Smarting from John's insult to Mamma, Charlotta went back to bed and tried to shut her ears to his stream of tales about his old comrades. His speech had the careful precision of a man who knows he is drunk and tries to prove otherwise, and it came in torrents. If the doctor had consumed as much Number Six as John had, neither of them would remember the cheating accusation by morning.

***

Erik met them at the door of the red house, and Charlotta knew by his expression that the doctor had been there first. Before either of them could speak, Erik said, "So you cheated my doctor, John Root?"

"See, Lotta? John said, "What did I tell you?"

"Erik," she said, "you can't make up your mind before you

hear John's side of it!" She had to defend the husband she had promised to serve with heart and hand, her child's father.

"Be still, Charlotta!" Erik said, "I have given you to a bad husband—"

"No, Erik!" she lied.

"I say it is so! Look at you! Just a few months ago, you were a beautiful woman, and now your face is thin, your eyes are sad—and you are not my Little Pine Tree!"

Crushed, Charlotta fixed her eyes on her shoes, which seemed to waver through unshed tears. "We didn't come to talk about me, Erik, but about an accusation against my husband. Couldn't it be that the doctor cheated and tried to cover it by accusing John?"

"Lotta, you know very well that I can see into the hearts of men, and I find the doctor innocent. He has served us well, healing the sick and advising us in matters of their care. What has this man done but loaf and roister?"

"He shoots game for you, and he—"

"Enough, Charlotta! Is he not man enough to speak for himself?"

With a short, bitter laugh, John said, "Why should I bother? You are clearly on the side of your pederast doctor, and you do not wish to know the facts!"

Charlotta did not understand the strange word John used, but she could see that Erik did. He went red and pushed the stump of his mutilated finger against his false teeth.

"John Root, I should drive you from Bishop Hill, but I would not willingly break the marriage of my ward and vows made in the sight of God. Therefore, you will pay your debt to the doctor and begin to work on a regular schedule like the others. You may go."

"Erik," Charlotta pled, "I can't have you think that John is dishonest! Please believe him—believe us!"

Erik turned his back and left them. Maja-Stina studied him

as he passed her and signalled her sympathy to Charlotta with a meaningful look and an almost imperceptible shrug.

Charlotta took John's arm and turned him from the door they had not entered.

"God damn!" he said, "I should shoot him down like a dog!"

"Don't say that! You are a Christian man, and Erik is the Vicar of Christ!"

"The hell I am! The hell he is!" John ran from her toward the barn, leaving her alone on the path. Moments later, he rode out to the north on Hugo without a glance in her direction.

Charlotta stood motionless, feeling hollow and heavy at the same time. Had Lot's wife experienced this feeling when she turned to a pillar of salt? *Oh child, child—you may never see your pappa—and I loved mine so!*

***

No explanation was given for the disappearance of John Root, and Charlotta presented such a hard face to the village that no one dared to ask her about it. She was fierce in keeping the secret of her desertion.

She was weeding in the vegetable garden when Erik's brother Peter called her name. She sat back on her heels, striking the clots of mud from her hands, and waited for him to speak.

"I have word of your husband."

Her heart jolted fiercely, and she struggled with mixed feelings. A sudden dizziness made Peter's face swim in her gaze as she asked, "Where is he?"

"Heading north. A Jewish peddler passing through Cambridge hired John Root to be his guide and bodyguard."

"He's well, then—"

"I don't doubt it! *You* know the toughness of the dark Swede."

Peter's big hands lifted and steadied Charlotta as she tried to rise on cramped legs, and he said, "I wish things were better for you, Lotta—"

His sympathy was almost more than she could bear. She wanted to throw herself at her cousin's chest and weep, but pride would not allow it. She took a deep breath and asked, "How is your wife?"

"Sick every morning. I worry about her!"

"You needn't worry—that's the way it is with some women. I'm just lucky—or maybe it's because I'm a dark Swede. She is luckier, though, you'll be with her when—"

"If I can ever help *you*, Lotta, you have only to tell me how."

She nodded and tried to smile, kneeling among the feathery carrot tops to go on weeding. She had longed for some news of John, and now that she had it, she was desolate. *No one can help me!*

Philadelphia, summer, 1849—

Robert Baird carried the mail into the garden and sat down on the rustic wooden chair their son Henry had made for the spot beside Fermine's prized Austrian Copper rose bush. Fermine joined him, and since there was only one chair, he rose immediately and offered it to her.

"Ah no, Robert, I just came to see if there was anything of interest in the post. I'm on my way to a meeting for the relief of the cholera orphans."

The word "cholera" alarmed Baird. "Mina, promise me that you won't go into a house where they have had a cholera case! I couldn't bear it if you—"

She laughed lightly. "My esteemed theologian, you are the very one who always tells me that a person cannot die until God decides his or her mission on earth is finished. Whatever my job is, I can't imagine that it is done, but if it is—" she gave the Gallic shrug that normally delighted him, "Well, what about the post?"

He shivered in the warm June morning. "Promise me!"

She snapped off a rose and smelled it with delight. "Very well, Robert, we'll see if God can arrange to take me off some other way—since cholera upsets you so!"

"This is no joking matter! A cholera victim dies in agony!"

She turned serious instantly, letting the rose fall from her fingers. "I know, Robert. I've seen them."

"Then you've already exposed yourself to the contagion! When?"

"A month ago in a house on Chestnut Street. If God meant me to have cholera, I would be dead by now, but I promise you I won't go again. I'll help from a distance. Actually, I couldn't bear to see another—" her voice faltered, and he took her in his arms, "Robert, why does God permit such a plague?"

"I don't know, my love, He doesn't speak to me as he is said to have done to a farmer in Sweden not long ago."

"That man who brought your Swedes to Illinois, yes?"

"Yes. And they don't even know they're in America—they live to themselves almost entirely."

Fermine opened the gold watch pinned to her bodice. "I didn't realize it was so late! And you still haven't told me about the letters!"

"Only one would interest you. Philip Lindsley has married again—"

Fermine clapped her hands. "Oh, wonderful! I remember that sad letter he wrote about the silence in his house, about having no one to care and feeling like a grown-up orphan. I'm

so glad, Robert! Let's think of a glorious wedding present for
Philip and—what *is* her name?"

"Mary Ann, I believe. Yes, that's it. As for the present,
you must say what it is to be. I'm no good at that sort of
thing."

"Nonsense, Robert!" She twisted the gold ring carved with
lilies to catch the sun, "This is the loveliest gift ever!"

"I can only think of gifts for you! 'Where your heart is—' "

"Robert, you're quoting again!" She kissed him quickly,
"Au revoir!"

He watched her go, thinking that the ring was even more
beautiful after six months of wear. Warmed by Fermine's vibrant life, it glowed more richly now than when it was new.

He started to fold Philip Lindsley's letter and realized that
he had not read it all, stopped by the marriage news. The second page began, "I feel quite certain that Mary Ann is part
of God's plan for my life, but I had no idea of that when I
left Nashville to teach in Indiana. I merely thought my
Maker graciously had decided to relieve me of the painful
sight of slavery in practice. Of course I never saw the worst
of it. A University professor is exposed only to what they call
"house niggers" in the normal round of events, and cruelty to
fieldhands is out of sight and out of mind.

"I tried to instill a concern for the education of the Negroes
in some of my students, but they are children of the South
and insist that Negroes 'smell.' With that pronouncement,
they close their minds to any reasonable discussion of the
matter. Oh Robert, it seems so long since you and I talked
about the theories of Pestalozzi and expected sweet reason
from every moldable mind! As much as I despise extremism,
I find myself wafting toward the Abolitionists like a moth
bent on incinerating itself in a candle flame. What are we all
coming to? But for the gentle charms of Mary Ann, I would
be a pessimistic old party. Yours, Philip."

Baird folded the letter thoughtfully and breathed the sweetness of the Austrian Copper roses. When he had tried to promote the education of the Lapps in Sweden, a young teacher
had told him, "One cannot bear to be in a closed room with a
group of Lapps. They smell of rancid fat, dirty bodies and oily
wool so strongly that it quite turns the stomach!" When
Baird scorned such delicacy, the teacher rounded up enough
Lapps to prove his point, and they *were* rank. With no hope
of changing the nomadic, unwashed ways of the Lapps, Baird
was roundly thwarted. Why hadn't he thought to suggest instruction of the Lapps in the summer pastures? Erik Jansson
had taught and persuaded in fields and clearings. Or perhaps
Sweden could trade its Lapps to the South for the Negroes.
The Swedes were fascinated by black faces. Once when he
spoke at Hudiksvall, a woman traveled for miles to hear him.
She had heard that black men lived in America, expected him
to be one of them and was bitterly disappointed.

Philip's comment about the Abolitionists reminded him of
Margaret Fuller's latest letter from abroad, in which she
wrote, "How it pleases me to think of the Abolitionists! I
could never endure to be with them at home, they were so tedious—so narrow, always so rabid and exaggerated in their
tone. But after all, they had a high motive."

Baird shared her feeling. When he had not met an Aboli-
tionist for a time, he was more kindly disposed toward them.
To him, the ideal solution to the problem was to wrest the
slaves from their owners—buy them with tax money if necessary—and ship them to some far place where they could be
free and live in peace. However, the thought of administering
such a program was enough to make an angel weary.

Just the day before, Baird had written to George Gale advising him to break with his Southern Presbyterian brethren
rather than countenance slavery, and it was a hard piece of
advice. Baird reasoned that churches were man-made, while

justice was an attribute of God and infinitely more worthy of
being served. He would not have foisted his opinion on
George Gale if the man had not asked.

A cloud scudded across the sun, throwing Baird into brief
shadow. Cholera. The disease seemed like an Old Testament
punishment visited upon a nation where slaves were kept
with no hope of a Year of Jubilee.

*Oh God, I pray Thee, forgive us and withhold the visible
marks of Thy displeasure!*

The sun returned and warmed his up-raised face.

Bishop Hill, summer and fall, 1849—

In the last weeks of June, Big Brick's guest rooms were filled
with travelers. Erik ordered the parlor cleared of furniture for
dancing in the evenings, and when Jonas Olsson criticized
such frivolity, he was told, "We must be more friendly with
outsiders. We have goods to sell now, and they have things
we need. We must please our paying guests." The guests in
turn were a welcome diversion for the colonists.

The music drifted from the parlor to Charlotta's room, and
though she was tired from the work of the day, she changed
her clothes and joined the children who sat on the steps leading to the parlor to watch the dancing. The children were not
permitted to move from the stairs, and she did not choose to,
considering her condition.

"They did this in the old country, didn't they?" Peter's
daughter said.

"Every Saturday night." Charlotta told her, tapping her
foot to the music of homemade fiddles played by two of the
ox boys. If John were here now, she thought, he might find
Bishop Hill more to his liking. She imagined them dancing together, she in a dress made from the red linen and John in

the best of his army uniforms. *If we could only start over again, it might be better, but we can't, so why think of it?*

When the music stopped, two men approached the vat of small beer on a table beside the stairs. Charlotta supposed they were drummers who traveled about selling goods, and she had been told that some sold harness for horses and others sold harness for ladies.

The short man with gold-rimmed spectacles said, "Did you hear what happened to that Jew we ran into at the Cambridge House?"

Charlotta could speak very little English, but she understood a great deal. The words "Jew" and Cambridge" riveted her attention to the conversation.

The other man hadn't heard, and the spectacled drummer informed him with relish, "They found him dead under the floor of an empty cabin a ways north!"

Charlotta scarcely breathed. She gripped the stair rail so tightly that her knuckles showed white, pulling herself up to meet whatever she must.

"Somebody shoot him?"

"No, knife through the heart. Whoever did it stole him blind too, all his gold trinkets."

"He should have carried a little persuader like mine." The man pulled out a gun small enough to fit in the palm of his hand.

"Jews don't go in for killin', or so they say. I heard he hired himself a bodyguard, though. Do you suppose *he* done it?"

Charlotta leaned over the stair rail and started to speak in Swedish, but then she realized the men could not understand her and struggled to find English words. If only Sophia Gabrielson were here! "The Jew only—dead?"

After she had repeated it for the third time, the spectacled man said, "Just the Jew, Ma'am. Nobody else around."

She nodded her thanks and sat back among the children, light-headed with relief. Even if John didn't love her and didn't care about their child, she didn't want him dead. She still wanted a last word with him somewhere, sometime—to salvage her pride. But if John had killed the peddler as that man seemed to suggest—*no! I won't even think of that!* She tried to distract herself by trying out names for a baby girl. *Anna for Mamma? No, too many Anna's here.* She disapproved of John's mother, so it would not be Ingrid, and when one called "Carolina," dozens of women and girls answered. Sabina was uncommon, but she certainly didn't want her child to take after her younger sister!

"What is that song they're playing?" a child asked.

"The Siri Waltz." Charlotta answered absently. *Siri? Siri Root? No, think again.*

***

Just when the summer field work was the most demanding, Erik announced that the sixth party of immigrants had left Chicago with a guide he had sent to meet them. This group included a number of Norwegian converts.

Stirring a bubbling pot of fruit soup in the miserable heat of the communal kitchen, Charlotta discussed the expected newcomers with Maja-Stina. "At least the ones who come in the summer aren't sick, and we have enough food for them this time."

"Yes," Maja-Stina said, "but it still won't be easy. They're usually not worth much for awhile after they get here."

Charlotta stepped back from the fire and wiped her face with her apron. She wondered if the baby was as hot as she was? Perhaps not. It would be dark there. She walked to the door with what she knew to be a false hope of catching a breeze. The day was so humid that the outside air felt almost

like the steam from the soup caldron. Shading her eyes from
the early afternoon sun, she saw a barefoot child running
toward the cook house. From a distance, she couldn't tell who
it was. All the little boys dressed alike and had hair the color
of pale butter. It pleased her to think that her child was sure
to be dark; recognizable from any distance.

"They're coming! They're coming!" the boy cried, and she
recognized the voice of Peter's son. She picked up her skirts
and moved her thickening body as fast as she could to the
church, where she would have a good view of the road from
Chicago. Since that first long journey to Bishop Hill through
Victoria, Erik had learned of a better route, an old Indian
trail to the north.

The other women joined her to watch the shapes of wagons
and weary horses emerge from clouds of dust. The people who
walked beside the wagons staggered as if their strength were
at an end. Then a lone horseman broke from the procession
and galloped toward the village shouting, "Get the doctor!"

No one knew where the doctor might be, and it occurred to
Charlotta that he was never around when he was needed. Six
boys were sent in as many directions to look for him as the
caravan came on, heading for the hospital building. The
women of the village ran ahead of the wagons to be ready to
help.

Charlotta gasped at the sight of a young girl who was trying to climb down but was too weak to hold to the seat until
her feet touched the ground. Charlotta caught her as she fell
and all but carried her to a bed inside the hospital. Hot as the
day was, the girl's skin was clammy and cold to the touch.

Charlotta tried to help a man who doubled over and clutched
at his stomach, but he motioned for her to keep away and
promptly vomited. An old woman thrust a swollen tongue
through cracked lips and begged for water. What, in God's
name, was wrong with them all?

When the hospital beds were filled, Maja-Stina sent children to bring linens from Big Brick, and the women made pallets on the floor, folding coverlets to use for pillows.

The doctor, who had been awakened from a nap, entered the hospital yawning. He bent over a young boy on the bed nearest the door, then backed away, shaken. "Where's Jansson?"

"Outside talking to the leader of the party." Maja-Stina said.

The doctor rushed out, tying a handerchief over his nose and mouth as he ran. Charlotta watched from the door as he grasped Erik's arm and said, "My God, man, it's cholera! They shouldn't have been brought here!"

"They are here by the will of God. Heal them, Doctor, I believe in you!"

I don't! Charlotta looked at the masked doctor scornfully, remembering how he refused to fight death when Mamma was stricken. If only Herta Olsdotter were here! Herta sometimes lost to death, but she fought.

As much of the doctor's face as could be seen above the handkerchief was gray as he stood outside the door stammering his orders, "No-no water. They—they must have absolutely no water or other liquid—th—that's how the thing spreads!"

"Cholera?" The word was passed around among the women and no one knew what it meant.

"Maybe it's like the plague in the old days." Maja-Stina said, "Just look at those poor souls!"

The women stayed in the hospital for the rest of the afternoon, wiping fevered faces with wet cloths and covering those who shivered. They heated stones and wrapped them in towels to ease cramping. They spoke words of sympathy, but these people were beyond comfort. The doctor had forbidden their one desire, water.

"You'd better step outside for some air," Maja-Stina told

Charlotta, "you look like death itself! And someone in your condition has to be careful!"

Charlotta walked quickly to the well for a drink. The constant pleas for water had made her thirsty. She took deep breaths of fresh air to replace the stench of the crowded hospital. The newcomers carried the smell of long journeying, an odor she remembered all too well, and when it mixed with the smell of sickness—she swallowed hard, fighting nausea.

"How do, Charlotta!" Elvira Mauk called from the seat of her one-horse trap, "I brought you folks a mess of tomatoes. We've eaten so many we're sick of 'em, and it's too close today to bottle 'em for winter."

"Thank you, Mrs. Mauk," Charlotta said, holding to the edge of the well to steady herself.

Elvira Mauk climbed down with the basket of tomatoes and started to tie up her horse. "What's going on at the hospital?"

"Most of the new party is sick. The doctor says it's chol—I can't remember the word."

Elvira dropped the basket, and tomatoes rained from it, some splitting and others rolling into the road. "Dear God, the milk sickness!" She jumped back into the trap and put the whip to her horse, turning the vehicle on two wheels. "Get away from here as fast as you can!" she shouted over her shoulder.

Elvira Mauk was afraid of nothing, or so Charlotta had thought, and now she was running away, pale and wild-eyed, and telling Charlotta to do the same. *I can't go!* The thought of abandoning Erik was much more frightening than whatever the newcomers had brought to Bishop Hill. She hurried to the cook house to find a bit of clove to tuck under her tongue and returned to the hospital with a sense of having armed herself. Besides holding nausea in check, the clove resembled a tiny stick in a letter of a medicinal Rune.

A parched young boy caught at her skirt and begged for water so piteously that she defied the doctor and held a cup to his lips.

"Charlotta, what are you doing?" Maja-Stina said sharply, "Didn't you hear the doctor?"

Guiltily Charlotta pulled the cup away, but the boy clawed the air, reaching for it, and she gave it back to him. "Look at him, Maja-Stina, can it matter? If it does, *you* take it from him!"

Maja-Stina's face crumpled with pity, and she looked the other way.

The boy finished the water and fell back, seemingly relieved. Charlotta smoothed his hair and his hot face, and he called for his mother. *Mother. What a word that is!* She stayed with him, furtively giving him water when he cried for it. A great sweat broke out all over his body, and when she had sponged him dry and changed the sheets, he slept.

"See what water has done for him?" she told the others, but they refused to listen. Erik Jansson's doctor had forbidden water.

No one died that first day, but the next morning a six-month-old baby was discovered lifeless at the breast of his barely conscious mother.

Maja-Stina said, "A little one like that is a candle in the wind! He was born on the ship and came all this way in a wagon—cream in a butter churn. Poor lamb!" She gathered up the tiny body to wash it for burial, "Fetch the christening gown from the red house, Lotta, I may not need it again, and he must be properly laid away."

After a long search, Charlotta found the beautiful, little garment at the bottom of a bound chest. The intricate white embroidery on sheerest linen had been worked by Maja-Stina before the birth of her first child, long dead now. Breathing the smell of camphor from the chest, Charlotta suddenly was terrified for her own child. She clutched her body protectively and was comforted by a pulsing kick.

***

The colonists quickly learned the English word "cholera" and knew that it meant death. The sickness was a palpable presence in the village, an enemy to be fought, and yet life went on. The women came and went between the hospital and the communal kitchen, bearing the burden of extra work without complaint, and the men met the unceasing demands of fields and crops.

Charlotta always scrubbed thoroughly when she left the hospital, and the clothes she wore to tend the sick were soaked in vinegar, the only disinfectant she had. If everyone followed her example, the vinegar wouldn't last through the epidemic, but they thought her scrubbing and soaking was foolishness. She was trying to gauge the amount of vinegar left in the jug when Sabina burst into her room, crying like a child.

"Lotta! Gunnar is gone!"

"Gone where?"

"He's—I can't say it!" Sabina collapsed on the bed, muffling her sobs in the bolster. When Charlotta sat beside her and touched her shoulder, the words tumbled out wildly, "He was fine this morning at breakfast—Gilliam says he worked hard for two hours—then he—he just—Lotta, I must be dreaming! Please tell me I'm dreaming and I'll wake up and it won't be so! He wasn't sick, didn't we just—"

"Oh Sabina—" Charlotta said sorrowfully, opening her arms. They held each so tightly that bone met bone as they wept together. Charlotta's thoughts were bitter. *Gunnar, the good husband, is dead—John Root lives.*

Six others joined Gunnar in death that day, and they were buried before the sun went down in an attempt to imprison the contagion in the earth. Gilliam the carpenter put aside all other work to make coffins. The doleful hammering rang from his workshop in Colony Church until Charlotta covered her ears with her hands. Fear was growing. Erik went among the people praying aloud and commanding them to have courage.

The next day, a woman who helped prepare the noon meal was dead by late afternoon, and a member of the morning gravedigging crew was buried at nightfall in his own excavation.

The doctor's treatment seemed worthless. Why bleed these suffering creatures? Since the doctor gave his orders from a distance, Charlotta felt free to ignore them. A few of her patients had died, but not all, and the boy who drank water that first day was well on his way to recovery. Now a few of the other women were breaking down and giving water to those who pled for it.

"If they're going to die anyhow, why shouldn't they have what they want?" Anna-Maja said.

Erik conducted burial services day and night, and the horse cart used for a hearse never was unhitched. The horse ate from a nose bag, standing patiently between the shafts while the coffins were loaded, and the driver was given a special ration of Number Six to drown the smell of death.

Charlotta went to her bed exhausted but too tired to fall asleep. The child kicked vigorously, and she sent the thought, *Don't come into this world yet—let me keep you safe. Are you hot? I am! The air is so heavy!*

When the door creaked, she sat up in alarm, bracing herself for the news of another death. *Not Anna-Maja or Sabina, please, God!*

"Lotta?"

She recognized the coarse whisper with grim satisfaction. *You couldn't leave me after all!*

He closed the door and came to her in the darkness, smelling of tobacco, leather and sweat. His thick beard smothered her, and the handle of his Bowie knife pressed painfully into her side.

"I heard there was cholera here—you've got to come away with me, Lotta!"

"No, I'm needed here. Besides, I can't leave. Have you forgotten the paper you signed when we married?"

"What's a paper when your life is in danger? Don't be a fool!"

"You left me!" Humiliation put an edge in her voice.

"Not you, him! I should have taken you then—listen, are you all right? You're not vomiting or cramping, are you? I've seen cholera, and it's not pretty!"

She smiled grimly in the darkness. *No, it's not pretty, but what death is?*

"Lotta, answer me!"

"I'm fine, John, just tired. My time is getting nearer—"

He passed his hands over the swell of her body. "Then come away—for the child's sake!"

"The child's life and mine are in the hands of God."

"What kind of a God would want you to stay here and die?"

"If God wanted me to go, He would have told Erik."

"Erik! Always Erik!"

"I would feel it inside too, but I feel I should stay."

"Oh Lotta, I've missed you! I want you to be with me—make a life with me—and forget all this nonsense about the New Jerusalem!" He stood, and she knew that he was trying to remove his gun belt and knife sheath noiselessly.

"You needn't be so quiet," she said wryly, "you have a right to be here."

He laughed. "So I do!" Then he threw his coat down and the buttons clattered on the floorboards.

Charlotta rose to light a candle. "Where have you been?"

"Up north." He stooped to feel in the pocket of his coat and placed something in her hand.

Charlotta stared at the small, gold cross on a fine chain that gleamed in her palm. *"All his gold trinkets."* The drummer's voice echoed in her memory chillingly, but she quickly told herself that the peddler could have given the cross to John before—

"There's no one like you, Lotta!" He bore her down, weighing too heavily on the child, "We'll go in the morning before it's light."

Charlotta said nothing. She knew her duty at this moment; welcomed it, in fact. When John kissed her and rolled away from her to sleep, she lay awake, weighing a decision she had not expected to make. After she had resigned herself to a life without John, here he was, asking her to go away with him. Her first feelings for him re-surfaced and set up a clamor, not because their bodies had joined again, but because he had shown a tender concern for her and the child.

But what would happen to them if they left Bishop Hill? Would they be damned as Erik said? If so, Heaven would be a sparsely populated place. Bishop Hill was such a small part of the world. She might take the risk if it weren't for the little *flicka.* Just then the child moved strenuously in her body. *Is it go or stay, little one? Ah, how can you know? I must decide. Dear God, give me a sign!*

She fell into troubled sleep and dreamed that Pappa stood in the door of the room, barring her from leaving it when John called to her from somewhere outside. She woke with a start and eased from the bed without waking John and wept silently as she dressed.

She longed to find his lips for one last kiss, but then he would wake and prevent her from doing what she must. *Now.* As she carefully opened the door, she resented the new, freshly-oiled hinges that refused to cry warning, providing a way for her to stay with him that was not her doing. If John awoke and carried her away without her consent or connivance, surely God would not blame her—nor would Erik—but John slept on.

The night was still, hot and heavy. She crept down the stairs and stood still, uncertain of what she must do next. It came to her that she had the sign she had asked for, and she must act on it. She took a deep, quivering breath and walked resolutely toward the hospital, knowing that John would not dare to storm the house of plague to take her away.

The night nurse she relieved was touchingly grateful for the unexpected chance to rest. Wiping brows, cleaning up vomit, and giving water to the sufferers, Charlotta felt numb, and this surprised her. Somehow she had expected to feel some lift of the spirit as a reward for her hard choice. The night passed slowly.

Though Charlotta expected that John would leave the village before it was light, she stayed away from the room until after the noon meal. Even then, she opened the door slowly, looking for him with mingled hope and dread. He was gone, and she wondered if she could have dreamed his presence until she saw the tiny gold cross and a small tobacco pouch. Believing she had seen her husband for the last time, she threw herself on the bed, buried her face in the impress his head had made on the pillow, and sobbed herself into resignation. Then she got up and fastened the chain around her neck, dropping the cross inside her dress. She tucked the tobacco pouch among the woollens to keep the moths away.

She wanted praise from Erik for what she had done, but telling him of it would reveal that she had been tempted to doubt his edicts. He must not know.

***

In the second week of the plague, Erik ordered all who were
well to accompany him to the farm he had bought from the
doctor. It was some distance from Bishop Hill near
LaGrange.

"How can we leave the sick?" Charlotta asked.

"Whatever we do for them doesn't seem to help, so they
must manage on their own." Erik said, "God has told me
that we must go."

The tents used in the first months in Bishop Hill were aired
and re-folded, and the wagons were packed with supplies.
Once more the colonists were on the road, and it was a grim
journey in the heat and the dust for all but the irrepressible
ox boys. Charlotta found herself clinging to Anna-Maja like a
child, and her silent sister glowed with pleasure at being
needed.

They arrived at the farm just after sundown. The men raised
the tents while the women started supper over open fires.
After the meal, Erik preached in the firelight, and then they
spread their pallets on the hard ground of the pasture land to
sleep.

Charlotta tossed restlessly, sat up to pull hard clods of dirt
from beneath her pallet, and decided that she was thirsty.
She tip-toed through the tents to the barrels of water brought
from the Bishop Hill well, but it was warm and brackish. She
spat it out.

Some of the men still sat around the dying fire, and she
heard one of them say, "This land is poor. I think the doctor
cheated Erik Jansson!"

If the soil never grew a decent crop, it was worth whatever
Erik paid for it, Charlotta thought. What could be more valuable than a haven from cholera? She returned to her tent,
prayed for the sick at Bishop Hill, and thanked God she did
not have to look at them for a time. She slept and woke in
the middle of a dream that her arms had grown lamb's wool.

Terrified, she touched herself and found that it was not so, but there was a bleating somewhere. She crawled to the tent flap and looked out. The noise came from a woman who lay prostrate at Erik's feet clutching his ankles.

"Bring him back! You can make him live!"

Anna-Maja came into the tent and knelt to put her hands on Charlotta's shoulders. "We've brought the cholera with us."

"Oh God, no!"

***

In the days that followed, seventy died at LaGrange. Without the services of the carpenter, there could be no coffins, and the bodies were wrapped in sheets or quilts and buried in a long trench. This dreadful planting became so commonplace that tears ran dry.

Erik consulted with the doctor and announced that all were to be examined. Those free from any signs of the disease would accompany Erik and his family to the Rock Island fishing camp. While the examinations were going on, a woman who had been certified as healthy died, and Erik realized the futility of trying to anticipate the swift enemy that gave no warning.

"God tells me that we must go alone." Erik said.

The doctor caught his arm. "Will you take me too?"

"God did not mention you, but you may be of some use."

Maja-Stina lifted the children into the wagon and climbed to her place beside the driver's seat. "Until we meet again!" she said.

After the doctor was settled on a trunk in the back of the wagon, Erik took the reins and turned the horses to the west. "God keep you!"

He has taken us out of Bishop Hill, and we do not seem to

be damned yet. It is not the place, then. And if it is his pres-
ence, why does he leave us? Troubled, Charlotta watched
Erik's wagon grow smaller and smaller in the distance.

When the wagon was out of sight, Jonas Olsson said,
"There's no sense in staying here. Let's go back to Bishop
Hill."

They entered their ghost village at dusk. Charlotta went
straight to the hospital, expecting the worst, but only one
child had died and some of the patients actually had improved.

"I drank half the water barrel!" an old woman crowed,
"And it gave me enough strength to lay out the little Ander-
son girl for burying."

"Who dug the grave?"

"The Nelson boy. Right out by the steps because he wasn't
strong enough to go far. I said a few words over the little
flicka myself—'The Lord is my shepherd, I shall not want—' I
think I can go home in a day or so, praise God!"

Why did we run? It was better here!

***

On the first day of September, Charlotta stood beside the
open grave of the woman who had prepared the baby girl for
burial. She had survived cholera and died of something else.

Andrew Berglund, the preacher who served the colony in
Erik's absence, stood ready to speak the words of committal.
He was a gentle man with the far-seeing eye of a visionary,
and the spirit that filled him was a glowing candle compared
to Erik's raging fire. Berglund suited the people who were
tired and grieved, past rallying to Erik's demanding challenges.

"This day the spirit of our dear one is with the loving
Father in heaven, and we who mourn are comforted by His
mercies—"

Lulled by Berglund's voice, Charlotta let her eyes wander

over the fields, still green but layered with the dust of this hideous summer. The very leaves of the trees had witnessed such horror that she would be glad when they fell, removing their mute testimony to what had happened here.

Sabina had turned to stare at Gunnar's grave. The mound of earth had sunk and cracked, and the flowering weeds Sabina had laid on it early in the morning were wilted. Sabina had wilted too. She no longer cared how she looked, and Charlotta and Anna-Maja nagged her about bathing and brushing her hair. *Oh, my little sister!* But was Charlotta herself any less widowed? No kiss, no touch, no presence. At least she had the promised child. Sabina had nothing.

After the final prayer, Charlotta left the grave. She could not bear to hear the dirt strike the coffin lid. As she walked back to the village, she heard wagon wheels rattling along the road from the north. She went to the Colony Church to watch the road, and when the burial was completed, the others joined her, straggling from the cemetery to stand and wait. At one time, the approach of a wagon would have inspired excited chatter, but now the people were silent, too tired and too sad to speak. All wagons looked alike, but when the horses climbed the last rise, Charlotta recognized Erik at the reins with Mathilde and young Erik huddled forlornly beside him. He stopped the wagon at the church and jumped down to hand the reins to Nils Helbom, then raised his arms for their attention, which he had without asking for it.

"Beloved friends," he said slowly, "God has seen fit to take my wife and my two younger children. Blessed be His name!"

Raw grief seized Charlotta as she remembered Maja-Stina's cheerful farewell, "Until we meet again!" *Not on this earth.* The loss of her namesake, the little Charlotta, pained her deeply, but somehow she could accept the fact that God had taken the baby. From the first time she saw him, he had seemed temporary, as if he were destined for an early departure from life, and she never thought of him by name. He was just "the baby." Surfacing from her own shock, she recognized fear in the others. If the Prophet could not save his own, what could he do for them? But they loved him, and they grieved with him, clasping his hands and shoulders and murmuring their sympathy.

"The colony must not be without a spiritual mother." Erik said, "Let the women of Bishop Hill who have no husbands search their hearts, and if their inner testimony prompts them to come to me, I will examine that testimony and learn the will of God."

Charlotta glowered at her cousin. *Couldn't you mourn for a little? She loved you so much!* Then she realized that the children still were hunched on the wagon seat, forgotten. She stood on a wheel spoke to raise her cumbersome body and put her arms around them. She could find no words to offer them.

"The doctor said he would save them—" young Erik said, "but he let them die of thirst!"

"No, no—it was a disease. Why didn't the doctor come back with you? Did he die too?"

"He didn't die, he ran away."

Mathilde spoke in a tired, thin voice, "Pappa put them in the ground at the fishing camp. We won't ever see them again."

"That's not so, Mathilde!" young Erik said, "Father told us we'd see them in heaven."

"I'm not going there." Mathilde said, "I don't like God."

Charlotta started to say, "Whom the Lord loveth, He chasteneth," but she thought better of it. Erik could deal with his daughter on that score. "Come," she said, "I'll take you home."

The dead air in the red house was musty, and Charlotta opened the doors and windows, shaking her apron to move the staleness outside. When she turned to look for the children, she saw that they had collapsed on a bed and fallen asleep. That bed was made up by Maja-Stina when she was healthy and strong, and the copper pots still held the shine she had rubbed into them.

Charlotta passed her hand over the lid of the bound chest where she had found the christening gown, remembering Maja-Stina's words, "I may not need it again." Strange words for a woman capable of child-bearing whose husband was in full vigor. Had Maja-Stina somehow known that her death was near? Charlotta sat in a chair near the kitchen hearth, the chair she had chosen on the day she had met John Root. Throwing her apron over her face, she cried. The little *flicka* kicked and thumped as if in protest, but she could not stop her weeping, and she was so absorbed by it that Erik's hand on her shoulder startled her and made her jump with alarm.

"You mustn't grieve." he said, "We must trust God and accept what He ordains."

"If He loves us, how can He treat us so?" She knew the answer before he gave it.

"Whom the Lord loveth, He chasteneth."

Charlotta sighed deeply. "You'll have to do something about Mathilde. She says she doesn't like God."

"Poor *flicka!* When I find her a new mother—"

"That you'll never do! God gives us only one!"

***

The women of Bishop Hill searched their hearts, but none dared to approach Erik with unseemly haste, and in due course he invited them to come to him. Charlotta was amazed at the number of single women outside the red house waiting to tell Erik of their inner testimony.

Among them was Sophia Gabrielson dressed in a gown of brown watered silk from the old days when she taught at Mr. Pollock's academy in New York. Lars Gabrielson had been dead less than six weeks. Would Erik really listen to God in this matter? If so, the outcome might be a surprise, but if the choice were entirely up to him, the other women might as well go home. Erik had a special feeling for Sophia. Some of the others were younger and prettier, but Sophia was intelligent, and he admired that. Besides, she had worked and grieved herself to a becoming slenderness, and she had the sort of elegance that even John Root would approve.

Charlotta went on to the cook house, where baskets of wild pears waited to be preserved. As she peeled fruit and carried kettles to the fire, she listened to the other women talk about Sophia.

"She's a husband killer!"

"It's not *her* fault!"

"But she does put on airs with all her books and such—"

"Maja-Stina was jealous of her—"

With a touch of mischief, Charlotta said, "What if he chooses someone else?"

"He'll do that when it snows on Midsummer's Eve!"

"I like her." Charlotta said.

"And so we all must! This is our last chance to say what we feel about the woman. When she is our spiritual mother, we will have to hold our tongues!"

The marriage was announced at the evening meal in the log house. Under the circumstances, there was to be no celebration, but Sophia wore a radiance fit for a coronation. Young Erik sat beside his "new mother" at the table and gazed at her adoringly, but Mathilde would not look at her. When the meal ended, Charlotta congratulated Erik and wished Sophia joy. She smiled at young Erik and stooped to kiss Mathilde's small, closed face, whispering, "It will be all right, Mattie!"

That night Charlotta turned restlessly in her bed, finding no comfortable position. She thought wistfully of the days when her stomach was flat and of the nights when she first knew love. She imagined what was going on this night in the red house until she blushed in the darkness. Some of the colonists might think that Erik was too holy to enjoy a woman, but he was a man—a man of her blood.

***

In deference to Charlotta's heavy pregnancy, Erik assigned her to the seated task of sorting broom corn. Broom corn promised to be a profitable crop. One group of men went through the field breaking the stalks to simplify the cutting for those who followed, and wagon loads of the tops were brought to sorting sheds at the eastern edge of the village. The piles then were brushed through four large horse-drawn scrapers to remove the seeds and spread in the drying sheds. The marketable lengths were pressed into bales to be sold in Chicago, Peoria and New York, and the short lengths were kept to make hand brooms and brushes for the colony.

The days had grown shorter, and the sorting began by lamplight. Charlotta started for the sheds earlier than the other women because her ponderous body could not be made to hurry. Everything she did was slower, somehow, and she needed that early start if her pile of sorted corn tops was to equal the size of the others. Alone in the shed, she counted the days until the birth date the other women had helped her reckon. She was both eager and afraid now that the days were pared to seven. What would it be like? "Just like the pain of the monthlies, only a lot worse." Elvira Mauk had told her, "It's a natural thing—usually." *Usually.*

The arrival of the other women was a welcome distraction, and Charlotta listened to their voices without attending to the words until somebody said, "Nobody but Jonas Olsson would dare!"

"Dare what?" Charlotta asked.

"Didn't you hear? He went to the red house and told Erik Jansson that we don't have enough say about the way the colony is run."

"What did Erik say to that?"

"He said he runs the colony the way God tells him."

That's what he would say, Charlotta thought, but Jonas Olsson's challenge alarmed her. As long as everyone believed in Erik, she could too, but if doubt crept in, she might be the first to waver. She wanted to believe in Erik. Those she had leaned on had been taken from her, one by one, and he was her last support. She took a deep, frightened breath and coughed in the flying chaff from the broom corn.

Toward the end of the morning, Charlotta felt a wet heat on her legs. Alarmed and humiliated, she arranged her skirts to hide the puddle around her feet, but it was too late. The woman beside her jumped up from her stool and hauled Charlotta to her feet.

"Get to your bed, girl! Your time has come!"

"But—I thought there would be pain—"

"That will come! You're in for a dry birth now."

"Please—will you send for Mrs. Mauk?"

"If we can find a boy and a horse."

The walk back to Big Brick seemed endless, and Charlotta was terrified that her baby would be born in the road, but there was no pain. She changed her wet clothes for a night shift and folded a worn sheet over a heavy scattering of dry leaves on the bed. Peter's wife had told her to gather the leaves and have them ready to take up the blood. *Oh God, I'm afraid! The moss from Pappa's wound!* She settled herself on the rustling leaves and folded her hands on her breastbone. At the first dull pain in her lower back, she thought, *Now, my little one! Mrs. Mauk, please hurry!* Nothing happened. She dozed to be awakened by a sensation like the blow of a cloth-wrapped maul. Why hadn't she sent for her sisters? The pains grew sharper and more frequent. She clenched her teeth and whimpered.

Elvira Mauk arrived, smelling of bacon grease, and advised her to go ahead and yell. *No.* The clock ticked senselessly through the pain until the sun went down. Elvira knotted a towel around the bedpost for her to pull. Charlotta thrashed about, longing to roll away from the pain, but it clasped her like a lover. Then, mercifully, it stopped, and she knew nothing until someone shook her arm. She whimpered crossly and tried to burrow back into sleep, but the far-away voice would not be still.

"You have a son! A boy!"

The leaves no longer rustled beneath her, and the familiar hill of her body had flattened. Charlotta could not grasp the change until she felt warmth in the curve of her arm and heard a gurgling cry. With a fumbling hand, she uncovered the child and stared at the perfection of the miniature male body. *I called you flicka—no wonder you kicked so much!*

"Well," Elvira Mauk said, "how do you like him?"

"He's beautiful—a dark Swede—"

"And what will you call him?"

Charlotta had not thought about names for a boy at all, and the one that came to her lips surprised her and gave her pain, "John."

"Fine," Elvira said, "I'll write it on the birth paper. He was sixteen hours getting here—not bad for the first time!"

And the last. Charlotta pressed the small, seeking mouth to her breast.

"Your milk won't be in yet." Elvira told her.

"I know, but he doesn't, and I have to give him *something!*" Young John turned his damp, little head from

side to side, burrowing, curling his tiny fists. He was as
fiercely impatient as his father. *Oh God, if I must fail him
now, let it be the only time!*

Philadelphia, January, 1850—

At the sound of moist weeping in the hall outside his study,
Robert Baird blotted the line he had just penned and went to
the door to see what was the matter. The hall was empty. He
followed the diminished sound to the dining room, where he
found Fermine's Negro maid Pearl huddled against the sideboard. She wore what he considered to be a silly, white cap,
and it trembled with her suppressed sobs.
    "What is it, Pearl? How may I help?"
    "It—it's nothin', Sir—"
    "Nonsense! You wouldn't cry pitifully about nothing!"
    Pearl shook her head stubbornly, and Baird went in search
of Fermine, surprised that his wife had not heard the sounds
of distress and come to Pearl's aid. Fermine answered his call
faintly from her upstairs dressing room, and he took the
steps two at a time.
    "Fermine, Pearl is in a state, and she won't tell me—" he
stopped, shocked by his wife's wan look, "My love, aren't you
well?"
    She smiled slightly. "As an ancestress of yours might say,
Robert, I have a wee headache. It's nothing. I'll see to Pearl
immediately." She pulled the stopper from a scent bottle and
touched it to her temples, "We'll see her together."
    They found Pearl sniffling and taking shuddering breaths
as she wielded a feather duster and in the parlor. Fermine
touched her shoulder and said, "My dear, you must tell us
what is troubling you."
    Pearl held the duster behind her back and stared at the
floor, mute until Fermine lifted her chin with one finger and

smiled encouragingly.

"Oh Ma'am, he beat me again!"

"For what reason?"

"Well, I went to meetin' last night, and I—I—well, I got saved again. I didn't want to be worldly right away again, so my man said he'd just have to thump the holiness outa me—"

"Robert," Fermine said, "I think Pearl and I should talk alone, after all."

"Of course. Call me if you need me." He left them and tried to return to his speech-writing, but he was too indignant to get on with it. What kind of a man must Pearl's husband be? Striking a woman for any reason whatsoever was beneath contempt.

When Fermine entered his study, the frown lines between her brows were deep. "Robert, has it ever occurred to you that some women invite abuse?"

"Surely you don't think that Pearl—"

"I do! She thinks so little of herself that she thinks she deserves beating! I tried to tell her that anyone Christ died for cannot possibly be worthless, and that she is no longer a slave in any sense, but she doesn't really believe me."

"I hope you told her that salvation is once and for all? I was appalled to hear her say she was 'saved again!' "

"I didn't mention it, Robert, that's your department."

He tugged at his whiskers with annoyance. "These revivals! What pernicious things they are! Anyone who dares oppose them is regarded as an enemy of spiritual religion, but revivals do more harm than good. The emotionalism strikes like lightning and is gone. The hell fire preacher plants a tree that is never watered, and it quickly dies."

"I quite agree, Robert."

"Do you remember my telling you of the revivalist preacher in Indiana?"

She shook her head.

"I attended his service and watched the poor souls sobbing and yelling and throwing themselves down at the altar to be saved. Afterwards I asked him if the experience would have a lasting effect, and he said, 'Don't know, Reverend, I just hang 'em up green and allow for shrink.' Then, as friends were trying to help the converts to their feet at the altar, he turned and shouted, 'Leave 'em lay where Jesus flang 'em!' I find this disgusting! How much better it is to treat the lost as if they possessed all the powers of moral agency—as if they could choose to turn to God—and convince them that it is inexcusable for them not to do so!"

"I know how you feel about the revivalists, Robert, but they do mean well."

"The road to hell is paved—"

"With good intentions!" she chimed in. She smiled suddenly and said, "A miracle, Robert, my headache is gone! Now I can start my day properly!" She kissed him and left the room, but something of her remained in a cloud of valley lily fragrance.

What a bright spirit Fermine was! When Baird was away from her, his perceptions were less acute. He had realized this dramatically when he visited the cabin of Dr. Jeremiah Lyford near the Mississippi River. The doctor presented his bride, Mary Ann, and she reminded Baird so much of Fermine that the sun suddenly shone brighter, the river flashed blue-violet, and the bird-song swelled. Mary Ann Lyford, who pushed a cradle with her foot while she read Virgil, was an educated woman who lighted up the wilderness. Neither she nor Fermine would ever love punishment as his wife said Pearl did. Until Pearl and her people were as self-respecting as Fermine and Mary Ann Lyford, the nation that made them otherwise would be under God's judgment.

Baird heard the postman ring and forced himself to sit still until the man had gone. If he entangled himself in conversa-

tion, there would be no time to look at the newspaper before
the Bible Society meeting. When Mr. Bundy was safely out of
sight, Baird brushed a sprinkling of snow from the letter box
and carried the post to the hall table. The newspaper was
folded to display a story about Dred Scott's second bid for
freedom, a plea to the Circuit Court of Missouri. Four years
had passed since the first suit. *How long, Lord? How long?*

Bishop Hill, winter, 1850—

Sabina was one of the twelve brides married on February
11, and Charlotta was deeply thankful that her younger sister
had accepted a man whose love was quiet and deep. Charlotta
had made the red linen into a dress to celebrate the occasion,
and though it was the wrong weight for such a wintry day,
the color was warm.

The wedding feast also served as the dedication of the dining room in a new section of Big Brick. The food was bountiful, and most of the talk was of the gold discovered in California.

"I'd sure like to get my share of it!" one bridegroom said.

"You can't leave Bishop Hill," his new wife reminded him,
"you promised to build up the New Jerusalem."

"Maybe Erik Jansson will send somebody out there to bring
gold back—"

Sabina touched her forehead to Olof's and said, "We have
everything we need right here."

If only John had said that! Charlotta rocked her baby in
her arms, enjoying the sturdy bulk of his body. Peter's baby
girl, born just a few days after little John, had a sickly,
bluish cast to her skin.

The talk of gold went on, reminding Charlotta of the tiny
gold cross she no longer wore. Perhaps John had gone to California. Such an adventure would suit him very well. *But I*

have the real treasure! She smiled down at her baby.

***

On a Sunday in early March when the snow still lay in patches on the fields and the wind blew cold, Charlotta stopped at her room in Big Brick to nurse her baby before going on to the dining hall. Little John still was sucking and kneading her breast greedily when the dinner bell rang, and she had no intention of interrupting him. She would try to slip into the dining room unnoticed after the meal began. At last he was sleepy, milky-mouthed and content. She laid him gently on the bed and straightened to fasten her bodice.

The door flew open, banging against the wall. Charlotta turned, a scolding at her lips for the person who dared to wake her baby, and the words froze at the sight of John Root and three strange men.

"I heard you had the child." John moved toward the bed, "A boy?"

She nodded, abashed by the presence of the three strangers. It was right that John should see his child, but not like this.

"This is Mr. Stanley from Cambridge and two county officers." he said, "Get your things and wrap up the boy."

She looked at the men, saw their guns. "What if I don't want to go?"

"There's no time for argument. Get ready!"

She obeyed, afraid that the baby would be harmed if she resisted. Everyone in the village was at dinner in the basement dining room of Big Brick. Even if she shouted for help, no one would be able to hear her above the din of a communal meal. The last time John came for her, she had longed to be taken by force but now—"Sometimes we find that we do not like what we think we wanted." *Oh, Pappa!* Wrapping the baby warmly, she took her own shawl and walked to the wagon outside. John helped her up, then pushed her to the wagon floor and warned her not to raise her head.

John took the driver's seat beside Stanley and whipped the horses southward. As far as Charlotta could tell, the county officers were riding in the opposite direction. The wagon bumped unmercifully at high speed, making little John cry, and Charlotta shouted to her husband, "You're shaking him to bits! Slow down!"

The whip slashed at the horses, and they went even faster. Charlotta got to her knees and worked her way forward to pull at his coattail, when he turned and cursed, but he was not looking at her. She turned too and saw the horsemen: Jonas Olsson, Peter, and a sizeable number of colony men.

"Damn it, Root, they have guns!" Stanley said, "You told me there would be nothing to this!"

John lashed the horses to a dead run, but Jonas Olsson's chestnut was faster, cutting in front of the team and stopping the wagon with a grinding jolt.

"Stay down, Lotta!" John commanded. He drew his gun and said, "Get the hell out of the way or I'll shoot you down!"

"Don't!" Stanley begged, "There's too many of 'em!"

"Charlotta?" Peter called.

"I'm here!" She stood with the baby in her arms, and John put down his gun to push her out of sight.

Stanley and Jonas Olsson reached for the gun at the same time, and Olsson got it. He said, "We'll take the woman and the child."

"By what right? How can you take my legal wife and my child from me?"

"Ask *her*." Peter said.

"So I will! Charlotta, do you want to go back to Bishop Hill with these stupid louts, or do you want to live with me as you are obliged to do by the laws of God and man?"

She tried to speak and could not. Why must she choose again and again? The baby was wet, fretting in her arms, and the thought of trying to change him in a cold, jolting wagon steeled her. "I want to go back—for the child's sake." She could not bring herself to look at John's face.

Peter dismounted and helped her from the wagon, holding the baby while she climbed to the saddle of his horse. When little John was in her arms again, Peter mounted behind them with a flying leap. The horse shyed at John's angry shout.

"You haven't heard the last of this! Tell that Goddamned Erik Jansson I'll see him in court!"

The colony horsemen moved aside to let the wagon turn back toward Cambridge, and Charlotta stared at her husband's receding back, thinking that this parting was easier than the last. The baby made all the difference.

***

Charlotta was carding wool when a strange wagon entered the village. She heard the other women remark about it, but she did not go to the window to look.

"He's stopping at the carriage and wagon shop."

"Now all the men are coming into the street."

"Here comes Erik Jansson!"

Charlotta went on carding wool until Sabina rushed in to tell her, "It's the sheriff! At first he was going to take Erik to jail, but now he says he'll take you instead!"

"To jail? Why?"

"To be sure that Erik comes to Cambridge for a trial—and you're to be a witness. The sheriff read from a paper that said Erik restrained the liberty of the wife of John Root!"

Charlotta dropped the wool carders in her agitation. "Erik won't let him take me!"

"I'm not so sure! You know how he is about the law—"

Charlotta knew, and her hope died. She half rose, then sat down again. "What shall I do, Sabina?"

"You could hide, but then he'll take Erik."

"I'd better get my things." She ran to Big Brick with little John jogging on her hip, and she had just tied clothing for them both into a bundle when Erik came in to explain what she must do.

"He has a subpoena, Lotta, and that means that you must go. Don't be afraid, you won't go to jail—just to a safe place until I get there in the morning. God keep you!"

Charlotta nodded and followed him to the sheriff's wagon. Sabina held little John while Erik helped Charlotta to the seat, then she and Anna-Maja reached up for a last embrace.

The sheriff's eyes darted nervously from one silent Swede to another, and he gave a deep sigh of relief when Erik motioned for him to go.

Charlotta never had been to Cambridge, and she had some interest in seeing the town where John had spent so much time.

They rode for a time in silence, and then the Sheriff said, "I hope you don't take this personal, Ma'am, but I'm just doin' my job."

Charlotta smiled and said nothing.

"You don't know what I'm sayin', do you? Don't know what good it's goin' to do to have you stand up in court. Nobody'll understand *you*, either!"

I understand you, but why should you know it?

The baby cried with hunger, but Charlotta couldn't bring herself to uncover in the presence of a strange man.

"Don't worry none about me—I'll look the other way. I'm a family man myself." He struck his own breast and pointed to the baby, placing one hand at the side of his face like a horse's blinder.

Charlotta smiled to herself as she unfastened her bodice under the cover of her shawl, and she appreciated his kindness when he reached behind him for a hairy lap robe to spread over her knees.

"Do you love that husband of yours? Not that it's any of my business!"

She scarcely knew the answer to that question and was glad that she had given him no reason to expect one.

When they finally arrived in Cambridge, wagon traffic was heavy. They locked wheels with another vehicle that careened around a corner. The angry words frightened Charlotta, and she could not see how they would ever pull free, but after much grunting and straining by both drivers, they were disengaged.

"Sorry about that, Ma'am, I'd better get you to the Cambridge House before the drunks hit the streets!"

The hotel was a big, barn-like structure of unpainted wood, and Charlotta couldn't imagine why John preferred it to Big Brick. The sheriff ushered her through a bleak room filled with long benches occupied by men in muddy boots, and she blushed at the way they stared at her. At the desk, the Sheriff gave the man some money and asked Charlotta if she could write, pantomiming the flourishes of a pen. She nodded and put her name in the book, "Charlotta Root."

"If anybody asks for her, she ain't here, understand?"

"Right." the man said.

"Come on, I'll take you to your room." He picked up the long key and steered her by the elbow through a pall of liquor fumes and cigar smoke to a dark stairway.

The room was dark and dirty, furnished with a sagging bed, a rickety chair, and a cracked basin and water pitcher on a sloping table. A bug scuttled across the stained boards of the floor, and the Sheriff swore under his breath as he squashed it with his boot.

"I'll have food sent up to you," he said, backing from the room.

Charlotta heard the key turn in the lock. *Well, John, this is scarcely Stockholm!* She spread her shawl on the bed to keep the covers from contaminating the baby and tried to forget that she was locked in. She wished she had brought some knitting.

When the food came, her appetite went. A tired woman with stringy hair slammed a plate down on the table beside the wash basin and went out without a word, locking the door behind her. Supper was a leathery piece of meat crowned with two fried eggs, cold and stiff eggs. Charlotta couldn't eat, not even when she tried to produce an appetite by remembering the hunger of the first winter at Bishop Hill.

The window would not open, and the panes were too dirty to see through. "This is a jail, little John!" she said, sitting on the bed and patting his fat, little hands together as she chanted, *"Lilla Van, Lilla Van—"* The bed smelled of stale sweat, which offended her. Even if she were starving or sick, she would try to stay clean. The hotel people had no excuse for the way things were. Hearing a key in the lock, she curled her body around little John's protectively and stared at the door. The hall was as dark as the room, and she could see nothing until a match scratched on a boot heel flared. She glimpsed John's face before the match burned his fingers and he dropped it with an oath.

"It's me, Lotta," he said, touching a fresh match to the bedside candle.

"What are you doing to Erik?" she asked angrily, "And why are you making *me* go to court?"

He laughed. "Don't worry, my love, you'll be far away when the court convenes. I'd like to see Erik Jansson's face when you don't show up tomorrow, but I'll have to forego that pleasure!" He reached for her, and when she saw that the baby was securely positioned on the bed, Charlotta submitted to the embrace. He spoke against her ear, "God, how I've missed you! I never expected to feel this way about a woman—"

"Then come back with me—I'll make things right with Erik!"

John shook his head, releasing her to pick up the baby. He seemed almost afraid to hold his son, awed by the strong arching of the tiny back. He brushed the baby's head with his lips and said, "This is all very pleasant, but I think we'd better go."

"No, John, the law says I must go to court tomorrow, and I will!"

"You will do as I say!" He put the baby down and drew his revolver, pressing it against her ribs. "Get your things."

She stood, rigid. "You'd kill me?"

"I will not give in to Erik Jansson!"

Charlotta gathered the baby into her arms and lifted her bundle from the floor beside the bed. "I'm ready."

John holstered his gun and held the door for her politely, helping her down the stairs with a firm hand on her elbow. At the sight of the roistering men in the lobby, he cursed under his breath and ordered her to follow him while he shouldered a path to the door. They had nearly reached the exit when a drunken man lurched against Charlotta. John knocked him down and stood above him with an unsheathed Bowie knife that discouraged further contention.

The horse harnessed to John's light wagon was a strange black, and Charlotta asked, "Where is Hugo?"

"Lost him in a crap game. I miss the old boy!" He drove out of Cambridge to the east, and after a long time, he turned north.

Charlotta gauged direction by the position of the moon, and when she was fairly sure they were driving west, she said,

"We're going in a circle, John."

"We must go where the roads are, poor things though they be! I'm heading for the Rock River settlement, where I have friends.

They drove on until the first pale light of morning was at their backs. Charlotta remained silent, her head bowed.

"Why don't you say something? I'm almost asleep at the reins!"

"I'll drive if you wish—if you'll hold the baby."

"I'd rather drive!" he said hastily, "Listen, are you still worried about displeasing Erik Jansson? Let me tell you something —Jansson didn't invent God, and he has no right to—"

"What I'm worried about is that I have nothing to say about my own life—whether I go, whether I stay. Why did God give me a mind and feelings if I'm never allowed to use them?"

"Ah, Lotta, I'm too tired to be philosophical!" He took the reins in his left hand and put an arm around her.

"How can the same man hold a gun to my side and embrace me in a single night?"

The arm dropped. "Maybe it was better when you *didn't* talk!"

The silence stretched on until she asked, "How did you meet these people in the Rock River settlement?"

He hesitated, then spoke in an over-hearty tone, "Claus and Brita? I stayed with them several times when I was on government missions."

"You never told me about government missions—"

His arm came around her again. "We have yet to get acquainted, Lotta, and I look forward to it."

The flight into Egypt. Mary couldn't have known Joseph very well until the commotion of Christ's birth was past. How was it with them when the angels and the kings of Orient went away?

The sun was rising as John turned into a farm lane. Roosters crowed, and a sleepy man came from the house to begin the morning chores. At the sight of them, he called John's name with glad surprise and took them in to his wife, who was pushing a churn handle. Charlotta saw a gold cross identical to her own at the woman's creamy throat and pondered the matter in her heart.

Brita greeted them in Swedish, reaching for the baby. "Let me take the little lamb to the trundle."

Charlotta surrendered little John and looked around the room with a pleasure that surmounted her weariness. A cheery fire blazed in the corner *spies,* and a Mora clock ticked contentedly beside a shining array of copper pots.

"Will you eat or sleep first?" Brita asked.

"Oh—" Charlotta said faintly, "I'm so dirty—"

"Of course, a bath! Come with me."

Charlotta was amazed to find a metal bathtub shaped like a chair beside the bed in the next room. She undressed while Brita bustled back and forth pouring kettles of hot water into the thing. When John came in, Charlotta blushed and covered her breasts. "I have never seen such a bath! How good it is to be wet all over!"

He smiled. "The things I can show you! Maybe we'll even go back to Sweden someday, and you'll drink tea in my mother's parlor." He dropped gunbelt and clothes to the floor, climbing naked between smooth linen sheets that smelled of sun and wind. "Come to me, Lotta!"

She stood to dry herself, veiling her body with the towel as she reached for the night shift Brita had placed on a chair. Then she picked up John's clothes and hung them neatly on the chair back.

"My good Swedish wife—" he murmured, and she saw that he was asleep. She was shocked at the keenness of her disappointment.

***

Charlotta was close to happiness those first days on the Rock River farm, but John soon was bored with the peaceful routine, and he harnessed the horse to drive his family to Davenport, a bustling city on the Iowa side of the Mississippi River.

Dogs and pigs roamed the streets of Davenport, and many of the people spoke a strange language that John identified as German. However, English was spoken at the Mercantile Company, where John bought Charlotta a dress of shiny, mauve goods and selected a silver spoon for little John, and at the livery where he traded the black horse for a better animal.

As they drove east on the street along the river, John pointed across the water. "You can almost see Jansson's fishing camp from here."

Charlotta leaned forward eagerly, shading her eyes to peer into the mist of the far shore. "Could we go there? I would like to see the graves of Maja-Stina and the children."

"Why bother with the dead? You can think of them or stand at their graves until Doomsday, and they'll never know it!"

That's not true! Charlotta was silent, resigning herself to the denial of her wish, but she sent a thought across the water, *Sleep well, dear ones!*

John booked a room at the Davenport House, a long, wooden hotel, and they had supper in the hotel dining room. The food was too poorly prepared to be worth the money in Charlotta's estimation. Then they strolled along Front Street until she sagged with weariness from carrying the baby. It did not occur to her that John might have relieved her. A soldier could not stoop to carrying an infant.

"I'd better take you back to the hotel," John said, "I have business to attend to."

Charlotta doubted him instantly. She had seen his longing look through the window of a saloon where a game of cards was going on.

Back at the hotel, John shaved, changed his shirt and spattered himself with bay rum. He warned her to keep the door locked until he returned and left her eagerly. From the window, she watched his confident swagger as he walked toward the saloon. *Chance is your true love!* She turned her eyes from him before he was out of sight and stared at sunset bands of salmon, purple and gold doubled in the waters of the river, the only color in this cold and backward spring.

Charlotta slept, waking to the urgent rattling of the doorknob. "Who is it?" she called.

"Shhh! It's me! Hurry up!" John whispered hoarsely.

When she let him in, he continued to whisper, "Get dressed! We have to get out of here!"

"Why? What's wrong?"

"Just heard of a new case of cholera, and they said they were going to keep everyone here so it won't spread. We've got to get away!"

"You can't run from cholera—I know!"

"For the love of God, woman, put your clothes on!"

She obeyed, wondering why John was rolling up the limp hotel towels and thrusting them under his arm. When the baby started to cry, she gave him her knuckle to suck, knowing he wouldn't be satisfied with that for long. They crept down the back stairs in the dark, emerging in an alley.

"We have to pay for our room, don't we?" Charlotta whispered.

"It's all taken care of. Wait here until I bring the horse and wagon."

She drew her shawl close, shivering and straining her ears for the sound of the horse's hooves. The quiet looming of the wagon startled her, and when John lifted her to the seat, she whispered, "How could you be so quiet?"

"I filled the towels with straw and tied them on the horse's hooves—a little trick I learned in Mexico—but they'll soon pull off."

She sensed that they were driving west and asked where they were going.

"You have a sister in Chicago, don't you?"

"Yes, but that's in the other direction—"

"I'm headed for the Buffalo ferry. It's out of the way, but it's safer."

"You've had a lot to drink, John. Shall I take the reins?" As soon as she said it, she was sorry. He was in no condition to hold the baby.

"No thank you, Madame, I can manage liquor and horses at the same time without difficulty." He spoke with exaggerated precision.

"I'm glad you thought to pay the bill," she said, "I remember that first winter at Bishop Hill when they brought a load of flour Erik had ordered. He didn't have the money to pay for it, so he told them to put it back on the wagon—even though we were starving!"

"I don't want to hear about him!"

When they were away from the town, John lashed the horse to a run. The straw-filled towels worked loose and flew to the side of the road, no longer needed. John woke the ferry operator at Buffalo, refusing his demand for double fare when they reached the Illinois shore. The argument ended with a threatening flash of John's Bowie knife. By first light, they were well into Illinois.

The baby sneezed and fretted. Charlotta was exhausted and knew that John must be more so. He hadn't slept at all. If she could persuade him to stop at Bishop Hill for food and rest, perhaps he would see the wisdom of staying there. Each time she started to bring it up, the angry look in his bloodshot eyes told her the time was not right. She was sure that John had not thought what a burden they would be to him when he snatched them from the Cambridge House.

She waited a long time before she said, "I'm hungry, John."

He stopped the wagon and went into the trees, returning after some time with a rabbit skinned and cleaned.

"I didn't hear a shot—" she said, puzzled.

"Why rouse the countryside? I threw the knife."

Charlotta gathered wood and built a fire. When she pierced the carcass with a sharp stick to hold it over the flames, she saw the heart nearly halved by the fatal wound. What deadly aim!

Late in the afternoon, it started to rain, and Charlotta demanded that they find shelter for the baby's sake.

"We can't pay for a room. I haven't any money."

He lost at cards. Charlotta had not yet worn the new mauve dress, and she wished she could exchange it for its price, but that was not possible. But John could work for their lodging. She suggested it.

"Doing what?" he asked scornfully.

"Whatever needs doing."

"I'm not a hired laborer! We can sit under the wagon until the rain stops."

"This is the kind of rain that goes on all day. I can work, John, I can clean, wash dishes—anything—if you'll take care of the baby—"

"I don't know anything about babies!" he grumbled, but she could see that he was considering her offer. When they came to a settlement, he stopped the wagon near an eating house and told her to go in and ask about work.

"My English is not good. Will you ask for me?"

"Certainly not! It would shame me to sell my wife's labor!"

"Then take me to a place with rooms to let, a boarding house like the one where we stayed in New York. I could make beds or do something that would not require me to speak."

"I suppose even a God-forsaken hole like this has a hotel." he said, but they were a long time identifying the unpainted building with such a function. They were ready to give up when John spotted a small, hand-lettered sign that read, "ROOMS."

John surprised Charlotta by relenting and offering to do the talking for her. He jumped from the wagon with his usual agility, but when he reached the walk of wooden planks, he started to limp. Charlotta was puzzled and alarmed by his sudden disability. When an elderly woman answered his knock, John swept his hat off, standing bare-headed in the rain.

"Ma'am, I am a veteran of the Mexican War traveling to Chicago with my wife and infant son. We had the grave misfortune of being robbed at gunpoint soon after crossing the Mississippi River, and we are penniless and in great need of shelter. This downpour threatens the infant's health!"

Charlotta was stunned by the elaborate lie, but she had to admire John's ingenuity. He stood there humbly, the picture of gentility brought low, while the woman considered, scratching her scalp with a tortoise shell hairpin.

"I'd sure like to help you," she said, "but I can't afford charity. I'm a widow myself."

"I would offer to labor in any way you could employ me," John said, "but my wounds have made me less than whole. My wife, however, is accomplished in every womanly craft, and she is at your service."

The woman peered through the rain at Charlotta and said,

"Guess I *could* use some kitchen help. Fetch them on in here!"

"Thank you, Ma'am, we are everlastingly grateful!" John limped back to the wagon and helped Charlotta down. He even insisted on carrying the baby to the house.

"Name's Keller," the woman said, "Minnie Keller. Can you take stairs with your bad leg?"

"I'll manage." John followed her up the steps with an irregular thump.

Mrs. Keller showed them to a long, windowless corridor furnished with a narrow bed and nothing else. "Tain't much, but it's about what nuthin' will buy!" she said with a wheezy laugh, "Come on down to the kitchen after you get settled, Missus."

John explained that Charlotta spoke little English, but that she would understand directions.

Mrs. Keller threw up her hands. "Why didn't you tell me she was from the Old Country? *You* don't sound foreign. Well, guess she'd better wait on the boarders. You don't have to talk to slap food down. Say, Mister, do you want me to heat a brick to put on that leg of yours? Mr. Keller used to get the miseries in a gunshot wound on a wet day, and a hot brick helped him some."

"You're very kind," John said, "but it isn't necessary. I carry my own medicine for the pain."

When Mrs. Keller had left them, clucking with sympathy as she went, John laughed and pulled out a small bottle of spirits, "Want a bit to warm you?"

"No thank you," Charlotta said drily, "*I* have no war wounds."

When Charlotta came downstairs, she found the boarders assembled at the table. Most of them were old men. Mrs. Keller told them, "This Swede woman will be helpin' me for a while. She don't speak English, so if you aren't served to your liking, holler for me."

Charlotta carried serving dishes from the kitchen, keeping her face carefully blank as she listened to the boarders' remarks about her.

"I thought Swedes was yellow-haired—"

"Funny-shaped eyes, ain't they?"

"Well, she ain't a bad-lookin' woman, I say, and I seen a few in my time!"

When the meal ended, Mrs. Keller spooned leftovers onto plates for Charlotta to carry upstairs. "You'll have to come back for the coffee," she said, "ain't got a tray."

When Charlotta reached the top of the stairs, she found the baby crying and John asleep. Blazing with anger, she banged the plates down on the floor. "Is this how you take care of our boy? Here's food, which is more than you deserve!"

John roused himself and matched her anger. "Watch how you talk to me!"

"If I'm working for our bed and food, the least you can do is—" the hard blow to her cheek caught Charlotta by surprise, and yet she was not surprised. John turned his back on her and started to eat, but she knew she could not force food past the lump in her throat. She picked up the baby, rocking and soothing him until he was quiet, then returned to the kitchen to help Mrs. Keller with the dishes.

The woman's eyes went straight to her cheek. "Your man do that to you? Ah, you don't know what I'm sayin', poor thing! It's hard to believe—a nice-talkin' gentleman like that hittin' his wife. Many's the time Mr. Keller served me the same way, but what else could a body expect from an old prairie dog like him?"

Charlotta shut her eyes tightly against threatening tears. "How—how far is Bishop Hill from here?"

Mrs. Keller's eyes widened as if Balaam's ass had spoken, but she answered, "Never heard of it, Honey."

When the work was done, Charlotta went back upstairs, dreading the sight of John, but there was nowhere else to go.

He had no word of apology, just a complaint. "We have to get out of this hole! We'll leave in the morning!"

"Are you ever content anywhere?" she asked bitterly, "If I stayed with you, would it always be like this?"

"Of course not! We'll have a house—a proper home—just as soon as we get far enough away from Jansson!"

Charlotta stooped to pick up John's empty plate, thinking she would eat her own cold supper now and wash the dishes, but she discovered one plate stacked on the other. John had eaten both meals. *How could you*?

As if she had spoken aloud, he answered, "You left it! Ask the old woman for more."

"I'd rather starve than beg!"

***

When they finally arrived in Chicago, John's leg really was stiff from the false limp, but he had collected a few gold pieces from fellow veterans of the Mexican War on the strength of the false wound, and he rather fancied himself as the object of pity. Charlotta thought it was disgraceful, but she rubbed the real stiffness in his leg because she had promised to serve her husband with heart and hand.

In the four years since Charlotta had been in Chicago, some of the raw board houses had been painted, and the stumps were cleared from most of the yards, but it still was not much of a town.

"Now where does this sister of yours live?" John asked.

"On Illinois Street with some of the others from the ship. At least she did when we last heard. Carolina doesn't like to write letters."

After repeated inquiries, they found the house on Illinois

between Dearborn Avenue and State Street. The woman who answered the door told them that Carolina and Pehr had built their own house near Chicago Avenue.

When John stopped the wagon in front of the neat, frame house, Charlotta said, "You wait here. I'll explain our situation to Carolina."

John looked suspicious, which Charlotta supposed was natural. Things had not been good between them since he struck her, and she was not surprised when he said, "I'll keep the baby with me—just in case you had some thought of running out on me."

The thought had occurred to her—running inside Carolina's house and barring the door. She hurried up the plank wall and knocked at the door. Carolina opened to her with a look of polite inquiry that changed instantly to incredulous joy. The sisters embraced tearfully, then stood back to look at each other. Carolina was plump now, but her pale hair shone and her blue eyes sparkled. She still smelled like freshly-cut hay.

"How is Pehr—and the baby?"

Carolina laughed. "What baby?" She pulled a small boy from behind her skirts, "This is Jan, who made me so sick on the journey—who made us stop here instead of going on. I've never been sorry, bless him! Come in, Lotta, come in!"

"My husband and baby—"

Carolina's eyes widened. "You have a husband and child? You might have written!"

"Why should I? You never answered! Carolina, we have no money, and we need a place to stay—"

"Our house is small, but you are welcome in it! Bring your family in!"

Charlotta motioned to John, and he carried the baby to the house, preparing to charm Carolina with his best manners. Charlotta noticed that he no longer limped.

Carolina was all blushes and smiles when John complimented her on her personal beauty and the tastefulness of her
house. Flustered, she measured out coffee and told them to
sit down.

"It *is* a nice house." Charlotta said.

"We got the land for nothing," Carolina said proudly, "All
we had to do was promise to build a two-story house on it,
and Pehr earned the lumber by sawing wood. He makes good
money in the building trade, but things are dear! A barrel of
flour costs six or seven dollars, and I've paid eight cents a
pound for pork this winter!"

Charlotta smiled and shrugged. "In Bishop Hill, we know
nothing about prices. Erik takes care of everything, and no
one is in want."

"Nor in plenty!" John said, "Mrs. Ericsson, would you say
that business opportunities are good in Chicago?"

"Oh yes! Anyone can make money if he is willing to work!"

And he's not! Charlotta longed to tell her sister everything,
but she would have to wait until they were alone, and that
might not be for some time. John was settling comfortably in
a rocking chair and taking out a small cheroot.

"Do you mind if I smoke, Ma'am?"

"Oh—no—" Carolina said, disconcerted.

She minds very much, can't you see? Carolina's house was
as clean as fresh washing, and the pervading odor of cigar
fumes would lodge in the snowy curtains, in the braided rugs
on the polished floor. Charlotta tried to catch John's eye and
signal that he must put the cheroot away, but he refused to
look at her.

When Pehr came home, he welcomed Charlotta with genu-
ine pleasure, but he met John with reserve, less ready to accept him than Carolina had been. They all sat in the kitchen
while the women prepared supper. Pehr held little John, and
the baby tugged at the golden hair on Pehr's arms, gurgling

with pleasure.

Supper consisted of Swedish meatballs, lingonberry sauce and potatoes baked in the coals of the gleaming, black cookstove that was Carolina's pride.

When the meal was finished, the sisters talked about Sweden and the voyage as they washed the dishes. Then Charlotta described Bishop Hill and suffered through the details of their mother's death because Carolina had a right to know. When they were close to dissolving in grief, Charlotta quickly told of Sabina's second marriage and Erik's new wife.

"So many joys and sorrows at once—I don't know how to mix them!" Carolina said, wiping her eyes with her wrist because her hands were soapy.

John offered a cheroot to Pehr, who suggested that they go outside to smoke, and Charlotta seized the opportunity to speak to Carolina privately. She whispered, "Erik has told us there is no salvation outside Bishop Hill. How is it with your soul?"

"Well enough! We worship with Pastor Unonius, and he was a saint during the cholera epidemic!"

"You had cholera too?"

"It was everywhere, they said. Pastor Unonius opened the second floor of the parsonage as a hospital. He got money from the rich to help the sick, and when parents died, he saw to it that the children were taken in—"

"Have you forgotten Erik's teachings, Carolina?"

"No, but I now believe that others have some part of the truth too."

Charlotta wanted to question her further, but there was no time. John would be back at any moment. Quickly she explained her circumstances, and Carolina bridled with indignation, but for a reason Charlotta did not expect.

"I think it's wrong of Erik to keep husband and wife apart! If you love him, go with him!"

"If he loved *me,* he would stay in Bishop Hill!"

"The husband is the head of the wife, Lotta, and you're bound to him in the sight of God."

"But he signed a paper before we were married—it said I would not have to go away with him if he chose to leave—"

Carolina frowned. "Erik took Anders Salin from you, and that should be enough! Why must he play God?"

Charlotta wanted to tell her sister that John had slapped her, that he was impatient and abusive, that he was a peevish child in a man's body, but she was too proud.

***

For a time, Charlotta was content in her sister's house, but then she began to reflect on an old saying, "Company under one's roof is like a dead fish. After three days, both begin to stink." She and John slept on a fat pallet of quilts in the parlor, and John often lay abed until noon, which drove Carolina to distraction. Pehr had less and less to say to John, and it was just as well that they met only at supper. Immediately after the meal, John went out to "look into business opportunities."

One night after John had left, Pehr said, "The day is for work. What can he expect to find in the dark?"

Charlotta knew, but she would not say. "I'll sit up to unlock the door for him.

When the others had gone to bed, she rocked little John until he slept, them blew out the lamp and waited in the dark. She knew that John drank and gambled, but did he go to women? *Don't think of it. What you do know is bad enough!* She dozed, waking in confusion when he rattled the latch.

"For God's sake, open up!" he shouted.

Charlotta stumbled to the door and let him into the dark house. He fell over a chair, cursing.

"Shhh!" she said, "You'll wake everyone!" As she lit the lamp, her nose twitched at the strong smell of liquor he brought into the house. "Well, did opportunity come knocking tonight?"

His reply was a strong blow to her cheek that sent her staggering against the coal scuttle. The baby started to cry, and the clatter brought Carolina from her bed.

"What is it, Lotta?" Carolina asked with a yawn.

"I stumbled." John said, "Sorry to disturb you."

Charlotta looked at her sister through a haze of tears. Standing there with a candle, her hair in rippling kinks from her daytime braids, Carolina was Santa Lucia. *If we could only go back!*

When Carolina had returned to her bed upstairs, John seized Charlotta and tore at her clothes. She struggled fiercely but silently. *I could scream and Pehr would come, but I am no country girl attacked at a parish dance, he is my husband!* She stopped struggling.

"Don't lie there like a stone!" John said.

"You have turned me to stone."

"Bitch!"

Anger hot as wind from a prairie fire dried her body. He hurt her, and she bit her lips until they bled, but she would not cry out. *This is the end. So many times I have thought so and cried, but now I have no tears. I feel nothing but the wish to see him gone.* She lay beside him, careful not to touch any portion of his body.

Charlotta did not sleep that night, and as soon as she heard morning sounds in the kitchen, she went to Carolina.

"Lotta, for the love of God, what happened to your face?"

Charlotta looked into the small mirror above the wash basin. The blue bruise that stained her cheekbone gave her grim satisfaction. It would say what she could not. With a bitter smile, she said, "John stumbled."

Carolina gathered her into her arms, calling, "Pehr, come and look at this!"

Pehr took Charlotta's chin in his big hand and turned her face to the strengthening morning light. "He should be horse-whipped! I'll throw him out of my house!"

"No, Pehr," Carolina said, "he'll find a way of getting back at her if you do that. Erik will know what to do—I'll write to him!"

"Then do it quickly." Pehr said, "I'll post the letter on my way to the job."

It occurred to Charlotta that she could have written herself, but she didn't know how to send a letter in America.

***

One morning a boy knocked at the door with a hand-delivered envelope for Carolina, and Charlotta turned it over and over in her hands, her heart pounding, until her sister returned from shopping to open it.

"Mrs. Kallman on Illinois Street has invited us to come for coffee." Carolina said, "It will do you good to get out of the house, Lotta. Shall I accept?"

"Yes, for God's sake!" John said, "I'm tired of seeing you mope around here!"

Carolina glared at him and went to change her dress. Charlotta knew that John felt a difference in Carolina and Pehr. He had accused her of telling them things that should be private, shaking her until her hairpins fell out. He took a step toward her now, and she hastily left the room.

When they were ready to go, Carolina told John, "If you go out while we're gone, lock the door. I have another key."

"By all means, Ma'am," he said with a mocking bow, "if I can think of anyplace to go in this God-forsaken community!"

The walk to Mrs. Kallman's house seemed long because little Jan's legs were too short for a normal stride. The sisters took turns carrying the baby.

"A little company will make the waiting go faster." Carolina said.

"But the letter could be lost! And even if Erik got it, it's plowing time—they may be too busy—"

"Now Lotta, remember what Mamma always used to say? A slow wind will also bring a ship to harbor."

Mrs. Kallman invited them in with an air of excited conspiracy, saying, "I have a great surprise for you!" She led them to a dim parlor, heavily curtained to keep the rug from fading.

Her eyes still blinded by the bright sunshine outside, Charlotta did not recognize the two figures in the room until she heard a dearly familiar voice.

"Lotta, we came as soon as we could."

"Oh Peter!" She rushed into the arms of Erik's brother, weeping with relief. Then she saw Nils Helbom. "Nils! Have you come to take me home?"

Helbom nodded, grinning, "I'd like to see anyone stop us!"

Peter gave her a scrap of paper. "Here's the address of a livery stable where we will meet in an hour's time. We've stationed horses and wagons all along the road to Bishop Hill, and you will stop just long enough to jump from one wagon to another. The Devil himself couldn't have as many horses as we do!"

"Oh," she said faintly, "how can Erik spare so many men from the fields?"

"The women are taking their place. We all care about you, Lotta!"

Carolina plucked at Peter's sleeve. "How shall I explain this to John Root?"

"I hadn't thought of that—" Peter said slowly.

"I know," Charlotta said, "you must run into the house all
out of breath and say that I ran away from you. He can't
blame *you* for it—but even so, you'd better stay away until
Pehr comes home to protect you!"

The sisters arrived at the livery stable early, and the hang-
abouts who resented the presence of women in that male do-
main taunted them.

"Pretend you don't hear, Lotta," Carolina said, giving the
louts a cold and regal stare. She settled herself on the waiting
bench, finding a sweet in her reticule for little Jan. "With
that relay of horses and wagons, Erik must expect trouble."

Charlotta's heart thudded dully beneath the mauve silk.
"I'm only hoping for a good headstart. If John comes after
us, I want to be out of the range of his knife and his gun!"

"What kind of lingo is that?" a rough fellow asked, looking
them up and down insolently. He came so close that Charlotta
nearly gagged on his rank-smelling breath. She averted her
face and saw Nils Helbom coming into the livery. Nils was beside them in two gigantic strides. Wordlessly, he gathered a
handful of the man's jacket and raised him off the ground in
choking suspension.

"S-sorry, Mister! Didn't know they was friends of yours!"

Helbom dropped him like a pile of dirty rags and led the
sisters outside, where Peter was waiting with a wagon. Helbom started to lift Charlotta up, baby and all, but she struggled from his arms to embrace Carolina first.

"Hurry, Lotta!" Peter urged.

The sisters waved tearfully until they could no longer see
each other. As soon as the wagon left the city streets, Peter
whipped the team to a dead run, something he never would
do without fresh horses waiting. Charlotta looked back fearfully, but the road behind them was empty.

Jonas Olsson was waiting at the first relay station, and the
transfer was made quickly and easily. Little John slept

through it peacefully. Charlotta worried that John might overtake Peter and Nils where they rested their exhausted horses. Even Nils Helbom was no match for bullet or an expertly thrown Bowie knife. *Oh God, take care of them!*

It was raining when they came to the next relay station, and Sabina's new husband dropped the reins to cover Charlotta and the baby with a piece of canvas.

"Thank you, Olof, I'm so glad to see you!"

"Hungry?" he asked, handing her a round of hardtack.

Surprisingly, she was, and she gnawed at the round gratefully.

When they had driven some distance, the wagon wheels bogged down in heavy mud. The horses strained to no avail, and in desperation, Olof lay the canvas in the road and pushed from the rear with Charlotta at the reins until the wheels gripped the cloth and spun forward. Olof retrieved the canvas and sprang to the driver's seat, muddy from head to toe. At least the mud would hinder John too.

The next wagon carried cheese and small beer. Charlotta forgot how wet and cold she was as she ate and drank, and then she slept, dreaming of a birthday morning—Pappa coming to her room at Domta to ask, "How many years high is my *flicka* today?"

Toward the last, Charlotta was too weak and tired to climb to the waiting wagon. One of the men lifted her to the seat, and after one look at her, the driver told her to climb into the back and lie down.

When the final relay team galloped up the rise to Bishop Hill, Charlotta was numb with fatigue, but she marveled at the speed of the journey compared to the caravan that first brought her to Bishop Hill. It was late. The only light in the village came from the red house, and when the driver stopped there, Erik rushed out with a lantern.

"You're safe now, Little Pine Tree!"

She gazed at him through tears. His face was grotesquely shadowed by the lantern, but it was beautiful to her.

"We'll get you something to eat," Erik said, helping her down, "and then you must go to the hiding place we have prepared."

"Why must I hide? I'm home!"

"John Root will surely come after you. He has the Devil's own pride!"

While Sophia prepared coffee, fried meat and hardtack, Charlotta attended to little John. He was sodden and fretful, and his repeated sneezes alarmed her. When she put him to her breast, he fretted and turned his head from side to side peevishly. How hard his short life had been!

Charlotta could scarcely believe that she had been gone from the village less than two weeks. So much had happened that it seemed a year. And yet, this house and its people had a blessed sameness, as if no more a night had passed since she had seen them. *I never want to go away again!*

Sophia called her to the table, and as she ate, she asked Erik about the trial.

"We took the oath and said that Root violated the right of domicile—"

Whatever that means—so tired—

"We were able to get a warrant for his arrest, but his lodge brothers intervened. We've had men out looking for you ever since you failed to appear that morning, and if it hadn't been for Carolina's letter—"

"I'm so sorry, Erik! If I could have foreseen—"

"Never mind, God often turns loss to gain. John Root has the sheriff looking for Jonas Olsson, Peter and some of the others, and I have decided to send them to the gold fields of California to keep them out of harm's way. We could use some gold. Come now, it's time we got you to the hiding place we've prepared in the meat storage house."

They walked without a light. Erik explained that no one but the wagon driver knew she had returned, and he was sworn to secrecy. "Ignorance is the best keeper of secrets."

Inside the meat storage house, Erik lit a candle and guided her between hanging sides of beef to an area floored with sawdust, which he kicked aside to reveal the ring that lifted a trapdoor.

"Remember when you hid me under the barn floor? This will be more comfortable, I hope." He descended the ladder first, put the candle in a holder, and returned to take the baby while Charlotta climbed down on shaking legs.

She was relieved that she could stand in the enclosure. A small room had been carved from the dirt and lined with canvas, and its furnishings were a narrow bed, a chair and a small table. The air was damp and heavy, pressing the candle flame to a horizontal tongue, and it was dark, but she could bear it.

"I hope you won't have to stay here long." Erik said, "We can trust Anna-Maja, and I'll send her to you tomorrow." He climbed upward and turned to say, "Good night, Little Pine Tree, sleep in the Everlasting Arms."

The only arms I'll ever sleep in again! As the trapdoor fell shut with a muffled thud, Charlotta felt abandoned and afraid. She settled the baby and dropped on the bed like a dead woman, only to rise and remove the mauve dress. She would keep nothing that came from John Root—nothing but the child. Then she slept.

Waking in total darkness, Charlotta did not know where she was until she heard the heavy tread of the butchers beginning their day above her head. How could she have let the candle burn down and gutter out? Would Anna-Maja bring another? She nursed little John, then lay back on the smoothed coverlet to fight a suffocating sense of claustrophobia. The invisible walls seemed to press in on her. She tried to distract herself with pleasant memories, and somehow all of them were of Sweden. There was little happines in Bishop Hill to remember.

When the baby woke again and cried, she did her best to quiet him, but she heard a voice from above say, "What's that? I heard a cry—"

"The carcasses are speaking to Magnusson!" somebody said, and the men laughed.

"Shhh, John, please!"

The baby arched his back, crying all the louder. In desperation, she stood and paced the small floor space, glad to bump into bed and walls to dispel the sensation of walking off the edge of the world in the darkness.

"Some wild thing has crawled under the foundation!" Magnusson insisted.

"You're crazy! You know how solid that mason builds!"

The breakfast bell called the men away, and almost immediately a crack of light showed at the trapdoor.

"Lotta!" Anna-Maja called softly, "I've brought food and candles."

Charlotta stood on the ladder to take the basket, and when Anna-Maja had climbed down, they embraced.

"What is happening? Has John been seen yet?"

"Things are quiet so far, but Erik is sure that John Root will come."

Charlotta sighed. "I suppose so."

When Anna-Maja lit a candle, Charlotta saw tears in her eyes. "Peter's little girl died in the night—"

"Oh no!" Charlotta picked up her own child and hugged him fiercely.

"Erik says it's providential. He asked me to take little John to Anna Christina. John Root won't think to look for him there, and Anna Christina will grieve less with a baby in her arms—"

"More, maybe! And what about me? No! I won't be parted from my baby!"

"You must, Lotta, Erik has ordered it. Besides, this black hole isn't good for a baby! Think of *him!*"

This was a long speech for Anna-Maja, and she stood there so plain and earnest, wanting the best for them, that Charlotta was forced to consider. Little John *did* need light and fresh air. How could she be so selfish? Hugging the baby so fiercely that he yelped in protest, she thrust him at her sister.

"Wait until I'm up the ladder." When the child was in her arms, she whispered, "He'll be all right. Anna Christina has plenty of milk."

"But what if it's curdled by grief?" Stricken by the thought, Charlotta reached up to reclaim her child.

"If that's so, I'll bring him back." Anna-Maja promised, "Now get down! One of the butcher boys is coming!"

Charlotta climbed down and tried to eat the food Anna-Maja had brought, but she had no appetite. Accustomed to forcing herself to eat and drink for the baby's sake, she realized it no longer mattered. God alone knew when she would have her son back, and if too many days passed, her milk would dry up. *Maybe he'll never take my breast again! What have I done?* She threw herself down on the bed, muffling dry sobs until she fell into a sorrowful sleep.

When she woke, her breasts ached and itched, leaking milk that would form stiff stains on the front of her shift. She stripped to the waist and tried to milk the nipples with her fingers, but the pain remained intense. Hearing a scuffling noise above, she snatched up the hateful mauve dress and pulled it over her head. Why hadn't she asked Anna-Maja to bring another? The trapdoor opened, and she recognized Erik's boots on the ladder.

"How is it with you?" he asked.

"I need my baby!"

"I followed my inner testimony in giving him to Peter's wife, but Sophia has told me of the difficulty this will make for you. She sent me to Mrs. Mauk for an herb that will ease you." He gave her a twist of paper filled with a powdery substance.

"What will this do?"

"Dry up the milk faster, she says."

"Oh Erik, little John is the only baby I'll ever have! Please let me keep him with me!"

"It's not safe, Lotta, you must do as I say."

She touched her tongue to the powder and found it bitter, as bitter as her heart.

"I have had word that John Root is gathering a mob in the Rock River settlement." Erik said, "They should be here tomorrow, and if they do not find me—or Peter or Jonas Olsson—they will look for us elsewhere. They will *never* find you!"

Charlotta bowed her head. "It would have been better for all of us if I had been swept from the deck of the ship by a great wave—or if I had died of cholera!"

"You are alive because God wills it, and while I do not understand it entirely, I believe that you are important to *my* destiny. Take Mrs. Mauk's powder now, and here is a Bible to help you pass the hours."

When Erik had gone, Charlotta opened the Bible. Erik had used it so much that it seemed to open of its own accord at the Acts of the Apostles, his constant study. Her eyes moved dully down a page and paused to read, "They cast four anchors out of the stern, and wished for the day."

***

Charlotta learned to read the sounds above her like a clock. The clank of the coffee pail meant 10 o'clock in the morning, and how she longed for a steaming cup of coffee! Everything brought to her hiding place was cold when it should be hot and warm when it should be cold. Of course she should drink as little as possible to stop the flow of milk in her breasts. The powder had had some effect, but the drawing it caused was nearly as miserable as the pressure of the milk. She ripped a button from her dress and sucked it to relieve the dryness of her mouth.

The rapid firing of three shots nearly caused her to swallow the button. She could hear the butchers running to the door and windows, and there was shouting outside. For a time, all was quiet, and then she heard boots tramping on the floor above and the impact of something heavy striking the boards.

"It's live meat we're lookin' for," a rough male voice said, "but if Mister Root wants us to do some mischief while we're at it, that's fine with me!"

"Don't do that!" Magnusson pleaded, "You'll get sawdust all over those sides of beef!"

The heavy thud sounded again.

"Any luck here?"

John!

"Naw, but I'm goin' to cut me a pork haunch while I'm here—"

"Leave the looting until later!" John commanded, "Let's try the hospital. I seem to remember the doctor saying something about a secret cubicle—"

Then they were gone. Charlotta huddled on the bed, terrified, until Anna-Maja finally came to tell her what had happened.

"He had about seventy riders, and have they ever made a mess of things! Tore up floorboards, threw furniture around, made a hole in the hospital wall—I never saw such—"

"But they're gone now—"

Anna-Maja shrugged. "For a little while. John Root said he'd give us a week to deliver you and the baby to him in Cambridge. If we don't, he'll burn Bishop Hill to the ground!"

"Then I'd better go to him." Charlotta said heavily. *Will it never end?*

"Erik will decide what you should do. He has been hiding in the timber, and Sophia sent young Erik out there to bring him back."

The trapdoor lifted suddenly, and the sisters held their breath in alarm until they recognized Sophia's voice.

"Lotta, come quickly! We're going away, and I've packed some of your things—"

Charlotta climbed up the ladder, blinking in the light, and allowed Sophia to guide her to a wagon outside. Erik held the reins, and John Helsen, the colony tailor, sat on a stool in the wagon box. Young Erik was mounted on a saddle horse.

"Where are we going?" Charlotta asked.

"To St. Louis, Dear," Sophia said, "Erik has business there, and we're taking Mr. Helsen along to earn part of our expenses. He did, after all, have the custom of the Swedish aristocracy."

"Erik," Charlotta said, "if we're going away, please let me take my baby!"

"No, Lotta. We'll be traveling hard and fast, and besides, Root will have the whole countryside alerted to a fugitive young woman with a child."

"Is Mrs. Mauk's herb working?" Sophia asked in a whisper.

"I—I think so. I feel a terrible drawing in my breasts—as if they were shrinking."

"Then little John is better off with Anna Christina, isn't he?"

Charlotta nodded unhappily.

When they had driven for several miles, Erik stopped the

wagon at a copse of trees and beckoned to his son to take the reins. "I'll tie your horse to the back of the wagon. Now take good care of your sister while we are gone."

The boy nodded and gentled the team while Erik and John Helsen unloaded the trunks from the wagon. Then he drove off, and Erik followed, smoothing the wheel tracks with his boot.

Charlotta could not understand why they were standing in open country with their cases and trunks. *I don't understand anything anymore.*

Erik walked to a natural rise, and Charlotta could not imagine why he was up-rooting the young saplings there until she saw that they were cut branches thrust into the earth to hide the mouth of a cave. The air pipe, a low round of earth-colored tile, would never be noticed by the casual observer. They went inside, exchanging the sweet, spring air for the damp earth smell so well remembered from the early Bishop Hill winters. Four crude bunks lined the walls, and a stock of food was piled at the back.

"What are we doing here?" Charlotta asked, "I thought we were going to St. Louis."

"So we will," Erik said, "but John Root expects us to take to the river immediately. We'll wait."

For three days they ate, slept, and listened to Erik's sermons. At least it was less lonely than the room under the meat storage house floor, Charlotta thought, but she pined for air and sunlight.

At last young Erik returned with his horse tied behind the wagon, and he brought news. The Bishop Hill party had departed for California, all was quiet in the village, and John Root, after a fast ride to the Mississippi River, had returned to Cambridge.

"How is my baby?" Charlotta asked.

"Fine! I saw him laugh, Lotta."

For the first time. What else will I miss?

"It's safe for us to leave now," Erik said, "let's load the wagon."

When all was ready, young Erik embraced his father, kissed Sophia's hand with shy affection, and rode away on the saddle horse. Erik turned the team to the south. Charlotta knew that the Mississippi lay to the west, but she supposed that Erik had his reasons for driving south. She watched the first stars appear, then fell asleep.

The morning sounds of the birds woke her as they drove into a small river town. At the levee, Erik negotiated their packet boat fares to St. Louis, giving false names for the entire party, and Helsen went off to find a place for the team and wagon until they could be reclaimed.

Erik told Sophia, "You will share a sleeping space with Charlotta, and I will be with Helsen. That will save us the price of two compartments."

Sophia sighed, but she nodded in dutiful agreement.

The levee bustled with roustabouts, passengers and barking dogs, and Charlotta expected to see John's face under every hat brim. She was deeply relieved when Erik told them it was time to board the packet. She stood at the rail as the anchor was hoisted and the Becky Lee slowly moved away from the shore. The river seemed still, but a strong, invisible surge carried the packet along like a leaf. It occurred to Charlotta that life in Bishop Hill was like that—quiet but invisibly powered by Erik's will.

Sophia was saying, "I haven't been outside the village in four years, and I had no idea that fashion had changed so much! Look how much smaller the bonnet brims are, and those puffy sleeves tight from elbow to wrist—if we wore things like that at Bishop Hill, we couldn't all sit down in the dining room at once!"

Sophia had owned some beautiful clothes in the early days,

Charlotta recalled, but she was somehow surprised that
Erik's wife still had such a keen interest in fashion.

"We do look strange, Lotta!" Sophia said, "Come, let's
speak to Erik about it."

They found him at the paddlewheel, staring at the foaming
wake of the Becky Lee. Sophia thrust her arm through his
and said, "Charlotta and I will be conspicious in the clothes
we have, Erik, may we buy a few things when we reach the
city?"

Lost in thought, Erik said nothing, and Sophia was ready
to repeat her appeal when he said, "Helsen can sew for you,
can't he?"

"He's a man's tailor. What does he know of women's clothing?"

Erik sighed. "Do whatever you think best, Sophia."

Charlotta was amazed. This man who always answered for
everyone was leaving a decision to someone else, and to a woman, at that. Of course it wasn't a matter of any importance.

A few miles downstream, the Becky Lee approached shore
with a whistle blast, and the gangway was lowered. A farmer
herded half a dozen pigs aboard, and while crew members
were taking them below, one escaped and ran squealing
around the passenger deck. It fell to John Helsen, a man who
loved cleanliness above all, to capture the dirty animal and
hold it until he was relieved of the unpleasant task. Charlotta
had to smile at the expression on Helsen's face.

"Look over there!" Erik pointed to a big, barn-like building
on the shore, "The sign says 'Play-acting Tonight'. I'd like to
see that!"

Sophia looked at him in amazement and said, "I'm afraid
the packet won't wait."

"That's so," he said with an expression of disappointment,
"but maybe we'll find something like it in St. Louis."

I wish we had been there and were on our way home! I

want my baby!

Washington, D.C., April, 1850—

Robert Baird pulled the huge linen napkin from his collar, touched his lips with it and smiled at his luncheon partner. "That went down singing hymns, as my grandmother used to say! I don't know whether to thank God or Congress for such a chef—both, perhaps!"

The Rev. Elton Marberry looked at him quizzically. "And to think, Robert, you will never know what an excellent Rhine wine would do for such a meal!"

Baird's smile vanished. "If ardent spirits were not served in this city, our nation might fare better!"

"Come, come, Robert, can't you take a bit of twitting from an old Episcopalian? That man just rising from the next table certainly would not hold with what you've said—that's Henry Clay from the bourbon state!"

Forgetting his pique, Baird followed the old man from Kentucky with his eyes. "The Great Pacificator! What an experience it is to see him! I've been interested in his political career since he supported the Missouri Compromise thirty years ago."

"Ah yes, he's sponsoring a new measure now. They call it the Compromise of 1850. He came back to Washington last year to save the nation from Zachary Taylor, but I suppose this effort will end as all the others have—Clay is a perpetual also-ran."

"God does not demand that we be found successful, only that we be found faithful. What does this compromise involve, Elton?"

"Admission of California as a free state, abolition of slavery in the District of Columbia, the organization of New Mexico and Utah as territories without mention of slavery, payment of Texas for western land claims, and a most stringent fugitive slave law. Neither the North nor the South likes it, but what's the alternative?"

"Disunion."

"Quite right, and who wants that? I will say one thing for Clay—he isn't as philosophical as Calhoun or as profound as Webster, but he *does* understand human nature, and he is absolutely fearless in expressing his convictions!"

Baird smiled. "Surely one takes the latter quality for granted?"

"Robert, you lead a sheltered life! There is nothing like a term in Congress to teach a man to dissemble. He learns to like luncheons like the one we have just dispatched, he thrives on being called 'The Honorable So-and-So,' and in short, he does not want to go home. He says whatever he must to persuade his constituents to send him back to Washington, and once here, he is at the beck and call of those with money and influence."

"But not Clay?"

"No, not Clay."

Baird smiled ruefully. "Can we find nine more righteous men and plead for the Capital as Abraham pled for Sodom?"

"Let us hope so."

"Elton, do you know Gustaf Unonius of Chicago?"

"No, should I?"

"I should think you might—he's pastor of the first Swedish Episcopal Church in America."

Marberry laughed. "Somehow I can't imagine our service in Swedish!"

"Unonius seems to believe that the Episcopal Church represents the best elements of the Lutheran Church in Sweden without suffering from its faults and defects."

"I wouldn't have thought they could be compared!"

"Elton, I am disturbed that Unonius is going about criticizing the Swedish communities for worshipping in their own way, questioning the legality of their congregations and charging them with separatism."

"Perhaps he has cause."

"*You* might think so, but I spoke to so many of these people in Sweden—told them they could worship as they chose in America—and Unonius is making a liar of me!"

"Come now, Robert, why accuse our communion of legalism when your own Presbyterian Church has such a rigid structure—and it hasn't the virtue of being colorful, if I may be so bold!"

Baird smiled ruefully. "We do love order. Everything must be done decently and in order, but sometimes I feel—"

"Don't tell me that you lust for the zeal of the Baptists!"

"I'm weary of denominationalism!" Baird cried, "Why can't we all be Christian brothers, searching the Scriptures for our truth and heeding the call of conscience?"

Marberry sighed. "I don't think it's possible. The human instinct is to organize, and everyone does it differently. At least you and I have crossed the lines today—"

Baird placed his napkin beside the plate and took his bill from the waiter's small tray. "Delicious, but dear!"

"Allow me, dear friend, my parish is rich."

"Then put its money to better use than feeding me! I'll buy my lunch, and your church can buy Bibles. Come, we can discuss it as we walk on Pennsylvania Avenue."

Marberry laughed. "The American Bible Society is just the place for you, Robert, a mission where denomination doesn't matter, but I can't help thinking what a salesman the world has lost in you!"

"I don't sell, I just pass along a gift—the greatest gift!"

They walked out of the dim, panelled restaurant into the April afternoon discussing whether enough Negroes could read to make a distribution of Bibles among them a reasonable project for the near future.

St. Louis, April, 1850—

Charlotta gazed about her with awe as a hired carriage took them to the hotel Erik had engaged in St. Louis. She had formed enough bricks with her own hands to appreciate the miles of deep, red brick buildings with marvelous towers and projections.

"Aren't the carriages beautiful!" Sophia said, "I hadn't realized it, but I'm really hungry for elegance—" She immediately regretted her comment and asked Erik's pardon.

"No harm done, Sophia," he said, "in time, Bishop Hill will prosper bountifully, and you shall *have* elegance! Solomon was not above enjoying it, and neither am I!"

Sophia smiled radiantly. "I didn't realize—we'd never talked about that, and I just assumed we were—well, Puritan."

"I don't know what Puritan means," Erik said, "but we do not despise beauty."

Their hotel was small and quiet, and Erik told them that the shipboard sleeping arrangements would continue. Charlotta and Sophia had just started to unpack in a tiny room that overlooked a gloomy courtyard when a knock at the door frightened them.

"Who is it?" Sophia called fearfully.

"It's me!" Erik said, rattling the knob until she let him in, "Bring your things, Sophia, I've taken another room for us."

"Oh—I'm glad! But what about the money?"

"That Helsen is a wonder! He has already measured a salesman he met in the lobby for a frock coat, and the man paid him in advance!"

Charlotta helped Sophia collect her things with a foretaste of loneliness. She had learned to love Sophia and to lean on her, but a husband's claims came first.

"Dress in the best gowns you have tonight," Erik said, "we're dining at a French restaurant."

"Oh marvelous!" Sophia said, "I haven't had French food since I travelled with the Linders when I was a little girl!"

"I don't know what it's like," Erik said, "but those people have blended their blood with our royal line, so they can't be all bad. Besides, this is the only restaurant I know how to find!"

When they had gone, Charlotta fully unpacked the bound trunk for the first time. Aboard the Becky Lee, she had used only the garments folded in the top layers. At the very bottom she found the red linen dress she had made for Sabina's wedding. *Bless Sophia for bringing it!* The gown was creased and not at all in fashion, but the rich color would carry it off.

The restaurant Erik chose was called *La Sortie,* and Sophia explained that it meant a kind of outing. She and Helsen accepted the snowy table linens, the flowers at each table, and a strolling violinist as if they were used to such things, but Charlotta could see that Erik was as uneasy as she was. Even so, she wished that John Root could see her in this place.

"You do look lovely, Lotta," Sophia said, "but we must go shopping, you and I! Erik, would you like me to order? I may be able to decipher the menu and see to it that you get something you like."

"Yes, Sophia, please." he said humbly.

She studied a menu as big as a pillow case and then spoke quietly to the waiter.

"Sophia," Erik said, "have him bring some wine."

Trying hard to conceal her surprise, she nodded and asked for the wine list, another huge pasteboard.

Charlotta always had admired Sophia, but she was a new creature tonight. A woman of the world in her blue silk gown from the old days.

When the food was brought, Charlotta was suspicious of it.

Everything was covered with sauce, and she couldn't be sure of its identity. Still, it tasted good, and she recognized the beans, at least. "They *are* beans, aren't they, Sophia?"

"Yes," Sophia said with a laugh, "but they call them *haricots.*"

After the first glass of wine, Charlotta stopped feeling strange and countrified. She held out her glass for more and admired the glorious, red color. *Deeper than wild strawberries—about like my dress.*

Erik was warmed by the wine too, and she never had seen him so charming. Could this be the same man who consigned people to Hell? His false teeth glittered in a wide smile as he handed a bank note to the strolling musician.

"He wants to know what you wish him to play," Sophia whispered.

Erik sighed. "I suppose he doesn't know *Father and Mother and Petter—*"

"I think it unlikely, my dear."

"Then you choose, Sophia."

She beckoned to the violinist. "A bit of Mendelssohn, perhaps?"

He brightened visibly and played a song of such heartbreaking sweetness that Charlotta was near tears. She never had heard such music.

When it ended, Erik cleared his throat to mask deep emotion and said, "God was generous to that Mendel person."

"Indeed He was!" Sophia said softly.

When Erik saw the men at surrounding tables light cigars, he asked the waiter to bring one for him. Charlotta watched, amazed, as he lit the thing. To her knowledge, Erik never had smoked or even chewed snoose.

"I always wondered what one of these things tasted like!" he said, blowing a dense puff of smoke toward the ceiling.

"Well?" Sophia wrinkled her nose.

"Not bad!"

They returned to the hotel in good spirits, and when they collected their keys at the desk, the night clerk gave Erik a letter, which he carried to a deserted corner of the lobby. He motioned for them to join him.

"It's from Andrew Berglund." he said, "John Root came back with an even bigger mob—enlisted Mexican War veterans by telling them we were communists and should be burned out like the Mormons at Nauvoo. Root and his men camped in Buck's Grove for a few days waiting for the colonists to bring Charlotta and the baby to him, and then they rode on the village with torches—"

"Oh God!" Sophia cried, "Have they burned Bishop Hill?"

"No, Sophia, Philip Mauk and some of the other Americans met them outside the village and turned them aside. Mauk told them the colonists were peace-loving and harmless and had no part in Root's quarrel with me. Berglund writes that Root swore he would finish that quarrel and threatened to shoot me on sight."

Charlotta buried her face in her hands and wept. "I should have gone to him—"

Erik put his arms around her. "Take heart, Lotta, Root is a cheap braggart, and I'm not afraid of him. Listen to this— Berglund says your baby thrives and that Root has given up the search for him because he believes the child is dead—"

"W-why does he think that?" Charlotta said, stricken with dread at the thought.

"One of the women led Root to the grave of Peter's little girl and made him believe it was his son's grave. But he'll still be looking for you, Lotta!"

"How long must we stay here?" she asked tremulously.

"Until I have found more markets for the products of Bishop Hill. We have lived to ourselves too much, and now it is time to become a part of this country!"

Then God help you to do it quickly!

***

Charlotta and Sophia outfitted themselves at a small dress shop near the hotel. The woman who waited on them would have been patronizing if Sophia had not charmed her right out of her high-buttoned shoes.

Charlotta's gown was an Egyptian cotton of spring green with the modish puffed sleeves, and Sophia chose a shade called ashes of roses. Carrying their old gowns neatly wrapped in pink paper, they went on to a millinery shop and selected bonnets with pert, narrow brims decorated with fluting and flowers. Erik was so pleased with their appearance that he wanted to show them off and suggested a tour of the city.

"Wonderful!" Sophia said, "Charlotta, go and tell Mr. Helsen to come quickly."

Erik shook his head. "No, let him get on with his tailoring after all that spending!" He motioned for them to follow him into the street, where he hailed a carriage.

First they rode past the charred ruins of thirteen city blocks destroyed by a fire that had spread from a burning river boat the year before. Charlotta thought of John's intention of burning Bishop Hill and shuddered.

"They might have cleared away the rubble!" Erik said with disgust.

The driver took them to the courthouse and ventured the information that Dred Scott had sued for freedom there.

"He got it, I guess," the man said, "but then the other side said they would take it to the Supreme Court, so he's dangling between the Devil and the deep, blue sea! Serves him right, the uppity nigger!"

Erik helped the women down and told the driver to wait while they looked inside.

Charlotta, who never had seen the courthouse in Cambridge, asked if it was like this one, all stone and marble.

Erik laughed. "No, it's just a big, wooden building."

"Who is this Dred Scott?"

"A black man who was a slave. He lived in free states with his master, and he says that makes him free. I don't know why some states are free and others are not."

Sophia looked thoughtful. "Perhaps we *would* understand such things if you allowed newspapers in Bishop Hill, Erik."

"I'll ponder the matter." He pulled out his big, round watch and frowned at it. "We'd better hurry! I've made an appointment at a law office."

The name of Britton A. Hill, Attorney at Law, was lettered in gold leaf on a frosted glass door on the ground floor of one of the tall, brick business buildings.

As they entered a waiting room that smelled of musty books and heavily-used spitoons, Erik explained, "Hill will help me draft a letter to the Governor of Illinois asking him to secure the peace of Bishop Hill."

A young man emerged from the inner office and beckoned to Erik.

"Is that Mr. Hill?" Charlotta whispered, not thinking much of his looks.

"I doubt it," Sophia said, "probably his clerk."

Charlotta squirmed in a leather chair that sent a chill through her skirt and petticoats. She stared at a big, round clock that ticked loudly and jerked its longer hand from one minute to the next, spelling out the words on its face, S-E-T-H T-H-O-M-A-S. Then she looked at the distorted reflection of her sturdy Bishop Hill shoes in the shiny brass bulge of a spittoon. The shoes didn't suit her new gown and bonnet, but they bound her to Bishop Hill and all she longed for there.

When the big hand of the clock had lurched past thirty-three minutes, the inner door opened and a gray-haired man with mutton chop whiskers said, "Ladies, come in, if you please!"

Erik introduced them to Britton A. Hill, and the lawyer said, "Mrs. Root, will you please sign this affidavit?"

Charlotta looked at words written in a beautiful hand that meant nothing to her. She could understand English and speak a little of it, but she could not read it.

"Read it for her, Sophia." Erik said.

Sophia, who was near-sighted, held the paper close and read, "That about the 18th day of March, 1850, Charlotta Lovisa Root voluntarily left her husband while they were at Chicago and went to the Swedish Colony with her friends—" She paused, her eyes skimming rapidly, "I'll give you the gist of it, Lotta, much of it is in legal language that would mean little to you."

Britton A. Hill cleared his throat reproachfully.

Sophia read on, "left her husband on account of ill treatment and abuse... affiant (that's you, Lotta,) verily believes that said John Root will take her life if she returns to him, and she is afraid to do so. The people of the Swedish Colony have not had any influence upon affiant to induce her to leave her said husband. And affiant being afraid of her own life, declares that she will not live with her said husband any longer. He is a man of violent temper and terrible passions and affiant trembles in his presence."

"Will you swear to this?" Hill asked.

"How can I?" Charlotta cried in Swedish, "I am *not* afraid of my life, and I do not tremble in John Root's presence! It's only that I will not be treated—"

"Lotta!" Erik said sternly, "Do you think that Governor French is interested in your personal preferences? Sign the paper!"

She took the quill and fought the trembling of her hand as she wrote, "Charlotta Lovisa Root" on a line marked with an

"X".

From the lawyer's office they went to a newspaper, where the women waited on a hard bench while Erik was interviewed about life in Bishop Hill.

"What if John reads it?" Charlotta whispered urgently.

Sophia's lips curved in a smile of sympathy. "Perhaps you didn't perjure yourself after all! But don't worry, we're too far away. John will never see a St. Louis newspaper."

When the story appeared, they were treated with new respect at their hotel. The management readily accepted Erik's explanation of the false names. People of importance always protected their privacy.

Sophia read the story aloud to Charlotta, glancing up to catch her look of incredulity at the account of Utopian prosperity. "Ah, you think it's all a lie?"

"What am I supposed to think?" Charlotta said, "We all know that the colony is pressed for money!"

"It's simple, Lotta. Erik has given a monetary value to each man, woman and child in Bishop Hill, and we are worth a great deal! He knows what he's doing—you'll see!"

How much am I worth? Lundeen said I was the wrong color to be sold.

An hour later, Erik returned to the hotel bursting with excitement. He pulled a sheaf of official-looking papers from an inside pocket and waved them about jubilantly.

"I suppose you want me to ask what you have there?" Sophia said with an indulgent laugh.

"The newspaper has done well by us! I've been able to secure several large loans—"

"For what?"

"Railroad stock! $50,000 worth!"

Charlotta was stunned by the huge sum of money, and she didn't know what railroad stock might be. How would they ever pay such a loan back? And what would happen if they could not?

"The railroad will change everything!" Erik said, "They call it the Iron Horse, but it moves much faster than a horse, and it runs on wood and water. It can carry tons of goods—people, too!"

"Have you seen one?" Charlotta asked.

"No, but it is fully explained to me. My inner testimony tells me that it is a good thing! When our men return from the gold fields, we can pay back the debt, and in the meantime, the stock will do wonders to establish our credit."

***

After the stock transaction, Erik was much sought after, and the women saw little of him from the hour of morning devotions to supper time.

"Business agrees with him," Sophia said, "I wonder if he will be content to return to farming?"

"What shall *we* do today?" Charlotta asked.

"Go walking, I suppose. What else is there to do?"

They put on their bonnets and strolled along the shopping streets, pausing now and then to look at the goods displayed in the windows. Charlotta glimpsed her own discontented reflection and did not recognize herself for a moment.

"Sophia, I feel so usless—I wish we could go back—"

"Yes, I know. I feel guilty and restless too. If only I had some children to teach!"

"And if I had little John!"

"I'll speak to Erik about going home."

They discussed the matter at supper in a small, cheap restaurant near the hotel. In spite of his improved prospects, Erik's natural frugality had surfaced again.

"We can't go yet," he said, "Helsen has too many commissions to finish!"

"We'll help him, won't we, Lotta?"

"But they are paying for *my* work!" Helsen said, offended.

"Both of us are skilled needlewomen," Sophia said, "and who will know? Aren't you eager to go home?"

"Yes," Helsen said with a sigh, "but I do not like to be party to such a deception!"

"Just tell them it's good, Swedish workmanship," Sophia said with a disarming smile, "that won't be a lie!"

"All right, Helsen," Erik said, "you will take no new orders, and when the work in hand is finished, we will go."

The women hurried back to the hotel with Helsen, and he parceled out a coat to Sophia and a pair of trousers to Charlotta for the small details of finishing. They sewed in Charlotta's room, pricking their fingers in their haste because Helsen had man-sized thimbles that were of no help to them. When they had finished, they took the suit to Helsen and begged for more, which he would not give them until he had inspected their work critically. His compliment was reluctant but sincere, "Not bad—for women! I'll deliver it first thing in the morning."

"Oh, do it now!" Charlotta begged. The suit was intended for the man in room 14 just across the hall, and she wanted to see him accept it.

"Oh, all right!" he grumbled, putting the suit on a hanger.

Charlotta and Sophia watched through Helsen's slightly open door as the tailor knocked and made the delivery.

"Here you are, Sir, fine Swedish workmanship!"

Money changed hands, and within minutes the man emerged wearing the suit and strutting like a rooster. The women exchanged a gleeful look of conspiracy and accepted their next sewing assignment from the tailor to the aristocracy.

***

On their last day in St. Louis, Erik announced that he had bought seats at the playhouse for Edwin Forrest's appearance in "Jack Cade," a play by Robert T. Conrad.

"I went to great trouble to get the tickets," he said, "everyone is curious about Forrest, they tell me."

"Why?" Sophia asked.

"A man I did business with this morning told me that Forrest has a great rivalry with William Macready, the English actor. Last year he interrupted Macready's performance in New York and started a riot—two dozen people were killed and a lot more were hurt."

Sophia looked pained. "I'm not sure *I* want to see such a man."

"Never mind the man—it's the play. When will we have another chance to see one?"

"Never, I suppose."

"Not for a long time, maybe, but don't say never! If I find this play worthwhile, I may allow such things in Bishop Hill."

"Will wonders never cease!" Sophia said.

Charlotta never had seen a play, and she was excited at the prospect. Traveling players never came near Osterunda parish, and in American life there seemed to be no time for make-believe. A friend of hers once had seen a theatrical troupe perform in Uppsala and had tried hard to communicate the wonder of it, but words failed her. She could only repeat a line spoken by the heroine, striking her heart with a fist as she cried, "I wait for him—the hurricane!" *Oh yes, play-acting must be fine!*

In the carriage on the way to the theater, Charlotta was sure that she and Sophia were as well-dressed as any women in the city, but when they arrived, she was not so sure. St. Louis women dressed differently at night. Gaslight flickered on bare shoulders and gleaming jewels; the scent of mixed perfumes was heavy in the air. Ivory fans held by hands gloved in white kid moved languidly before rice-powdered faces. Taffeta skirts rustled in the aisles and satin skirts were gathered close to allow passage in the rows. Again, Charlotta felt out of place. She removed her bonnet to be less conspicuous among the bare-headed women with their elaborate coiffures. Sophia followed suit, as a courtesy to the people behind her, she said.

The heavy, velvet curtain opened to a thunder of applause, and the actors entered in the costumes of an ancient time. Edwin Forrest (identified by the increased applause when he stepped forward) was a jowly man of middle years with a heavy mustache and a mere spot of a beard in the middle of his chin. His eyes flashed, and his voice rolled like ocean breakers to the far corners of the long, narrow theater.

At first, Charlotta could understand nothing, but when she grew accustomed to the cadenced speech, she gathered that Jack Cade was leading a rebellion against a government that treated the common people cruelly. She remembered the king's bailiffs with their clubs and gave her sympathy to Cade, rejoicing as his rebellion succeeded. His men were noble, thinking only of the cause—like the people of the New Jerusalem.

Then something strange started to happen. Cade's men were doing terrible things to other people, the very things the government had done to them. Uneasy, Charlotta stole a glance at Erik. He was frowning, pressing his mutilated finger agaist his false teeth. The lines of the play became meaningless to Charlotta. Something within her was closed to it, and she couldn't say how it ended. The final curtain surprised her.

After loud and long applause, the players took their bows, and Edwin Forrest finally appeared alone to a thunder of clapping. Charlotta was impressed by the loud, hollow sound made by striking cupped hands together and tried it herself.

"Think you're as good as Macready?" someone shouted.

Forrest's jowls tightened, and he started forward as if he meant to step over the footlights and attack the owner of that voice. A man in evening dress ran from the wings and tried to pull Forrest off-stage, but the actor thrust him away, shaking his fist.

Erik herded Sophia and Charlotta into the aisle, then stepped in front of them, elbowing roughly to break a path for them. Women shrieked as their gowns were trampled, and Charlotta was struck by the difference between this hysteria and the tight-lipped terror of the faithful when they fled their persecutors in Sweden. Even so, she was frightened by the mindless shoving and pummeling and held fast to Sophia's hand in the struggle toward the exit. By the time they reached the street, the waiting carriages all were taken. They would have to walk the long distance to their hotel.

"Thank God we *can* walk!" Sophia said, "I'm glad to escape with my life!"

She has never been threatened and clubbed!

Erik was silent. A palpable heaviness was upon him. When they were some distance from the noisy confusion of the theater, he spoke, as if to himself, "Perhaps there *is* a time when good becomes evil—when the oppressed becomes the oppressor—"

"It was just a play, Erik, you needn't take it so much to heart!" Sophia said.

"Just a play? God sent me to that theater, Sophia, and I have found the truth He put there for me."

Realizing that Erik had made the comparison she was afraid to face, Charlotta was ashamed. It was clear that Jonas Olsson and the other men were rebelling against Erik as he had rebelled against the Swedish Church, and the situation frightened her.

***

Charlotta walked the deck of the packet Arabella impatiently. The river still was shrouded in mist this soft May morning, and she could not see the wake that measured their
speed, but she knew the up-river journey would be slower.
I'm coming, little John, I'm coming!

When the sun burned the smoky pall away to reveal the
new leaves and snowy blossoms of trees along the river
banks, the Arabella left the center channel, moving towards
the east bank, where chimney smoke rose in slender columns.
That settlement must be Oquawka, where Erik had asked
Anders Andersson to meet them with a wagon. They could
have stayed on the Arabella as far as Keithsburg, but Erik
thought John Root would be watching the most likely landing. Charlotta hurried to her cabin to collect her belongings.

The four of them stood at the rail with their possessions piled
around their feet, holding their ears against the whistle blast,
and Andersson waved at them vigorously from the landing.
As soon as the gangway connected, he rushed aboard.

"I came last night and slept in the wagon!" he said, "I
didn't want to make you wait, not even for a minute!"

Charlotta stared hungrily at Andersson's simple colony
dress, and she could see that he was abashed by their city
clothes. Erik's insistence upon uniform dress in the colony
made more sense to her than it had before.

"Is everything all right in Bishop Hill?" Erik asked.

"All's peaceful."

"Thank God!" Erik said, but his heavy mood did not seem
to lift, and Sophia was keenly aware of his state. Maja-Stina
would have said, "Well, Erik, what is it with you?", Charlotta
thought, but Sophia always waited for him to say the first
word.

The day stretched long, and it was dark when they drove

into Bishop Hill. No lights showed anywhere. Charlotta lit a candle in her room and hurried down the long corridor to Peter and Anna Christina's rooms at the opposite end of Big Brick. She could not wait until morning to see her baby. Pounding at the door until the sleepy Anna Christina opened to her, she cried, "Where is he? How is he?"

Peter's wife turned groggily, setting down her candle to bring little John to his mother, but Charlotta pushed past her and snatched him from the cradle. "Oh John, my little John!" He gave an angry squeak at the sudden awakening, and she laughed, hugging him to her fiercely. Then she saw Anna Christina slumping forlornly beside the empty cradle and felt mean—selfish.

"Oh Anna Christina, thank you, thank you"

"I'll miss him."

"I know! I'm so sorry about—about everything—your baby, Peter being gone—and now this!" Charlotta's eyes filled with tears.

Anna Christina tried to smile and change the subject. "You look—very fancy."

Charlotta had forgotten the city clothes, and she shrank inside them, embarrassed. "I'll be be back in homespun tomorrow!"

"About tomorrow—" Anna Christina touched her full breasts, "may I feed him as long as I have milk?"

"I would be grateful. I have none to give him!"

"Good-night, then."

Charlotta found her sisters waiting in her room. They had heard the wagon and hurried to dress. They both talked at once.

"They burned haystacks—"

"Herded all the men into the basement of the church—"

"—women and children into the hospital—"

"—drunk and shooting off guns—"

"We were so afraid—thank God for Mr. Mauk!"

"My, look at you!" Sabina finally said.

Charlotta handed the baby to Anna-Maja and pulled off the dress that had caused so much comment. "Do you want it, Sabina?"

"If it fits me—I might wear it to town someday. Just once I'd like to go somewhere without having Bishop Hill written all over me!"

"It isn't that wonderful," Charlotta said, "I'm so glad to be home!"

"Are you sure you're all right, Lotta? Anna-Maja asked anxiously.

"*Now* I am, and you've suffered more than I have, I'm sure! I've been living in a hotel—eating fine food—I even saw a play, and—" she stopped, distracted by little John's demanding cry. He was wide awake now, and he was so used to Anna Christina that he took his mother for a stranger. He shrieked when she reached for him, which hurt her deeply.

"Don't take it to heart," Sabina said, "he has a whole lifetime to get acquainted with you again."

"I'll never give him another chance to forget me, I swear it!"

***

The next day was Sunday. Charlotta wore her red linen dress to church to celebrate the end of her exile, and the whole congregation was joyous at the return of the Prophet, the May morning freshness pouring through open windows, and the brilliance of the sunlight slanting from the east.

Erik usually was the first to arrive at the church, greeting his people with nods and smiles as they entered, but today he was late, and they told each other that he was weary from the journey. When the last peal of the bell died away, he still had not come, and they grew uneasy.

At last he entered the church and walked down the aisle with a heavy tread. The people felt his mood and were bewildered by it, exchanging worried looks as he passed each row of pews with unseeing eyes. When he reached the pulpit, he did not step into the shaft of light that bathed the pulpit but stood in the shadow to one side, taking the big Bible in his hands.

"Beloved friends, he said, "my text for this Lord's Day is II Timothy, chapter four, verses six through eight—" The turning of the pages was the only sound in the sanctuary until he began to read, "For already I am being offered, and the time of my departure is come. I have fought the good fight, I have finished the course, I have kept the faith: henceforth there is laid up for me a crown of righteousness, which the Lord, the righteous judge, shall give to me at that day; and not to me only, but to all them that have loved His appearing."

Erik's leaden tone chilled Charlotta, and the text he had chosen frightened her. And it was strange that he did not step up to the pulpit to begin his sermon. Even in the pastures and clearings he had found some elevation.

"Beloved friends, I shall die a martyr to the faith—" he swallowed hard, and the pause was filled with murmurs of stricken disbelief. He raised his hands for silence. "I would that this cup might pass from me, for I have loved this life and the blessings which God has graciously given me. I dreamed of the New Jerusalem, and it rose on the virgin land of Illinois. God has given many souls into my hand, and He has given me the grace to be your shepherd. He has given me dear ones to love—but it comes to me that my end is near—"

"No!" Nils Helbom shouted.

A woman sobbed aloud, setting off an epidemic of weeping. Even the men cried openly. Charlotta was frozen, as cold as she had been when Pappa died, and she was not aware of the accusing glances aimed at her until Erik spoke.

"What will be is ordained of God, and my ward is without fault. Charlotta Lovisa is dear to me, and God in His unsearchable wisdom has used her in a way we do not understand fully. I command you to cherish her when I am gone!"

Charlotta bent forward over her baby in a silent keening. Was she some kind of a Judas to be put to such agonizing use? *Oh God, how can it be?* She felt a hand on her shoulder. Sophia had risen from her seat to come to her. "We must be strong, Lotta," she whispered, "he needs our strength now."

Erik climbed to the pulpit, gripping its sides with both hands. He announced the celebration of the Lord's Supper, and the people regained some measure of control until he quoted from the gospel of Matthew, "I say unto you, I shall not drink henceforth of this fruit of the vine until that day when I drink it new with you in my Father's kingdom." The sanctuary resounded with wails.

Erik thundered, "The Lord commands you to rejoice at His table! The Bible tells us, 'They sang a hymn and went out.' Sing!"

The hymn was a poor, quavering thing, and the congregation filed from the church silently.

The cook house was funereal, and in the dining room the women set down serving dishes with careful hands, making no sound. Only the children's dining room seemed normal. The youngsters marched to the tables in martial formation and waited for an adult to ask the blessing on their food. No one had the heart to pray, and Charlotta finally took it upon herself to tell them to begin, unblessed. Then she returned to the adult dining room.

The first tender rhubarb stalks of the season had been made into the tart sauce Erik loved, and Charlotta carried the bowl to him, but he pushed it aside.

"It was made expecially for you, Erik!" Sophia said gently.

"I seek other sustenance, he said, holding up his Bible, "I am asking God to let His word fall open at the message He has for me."

Charlotta held her breath as he dropped the worn Bible to the table. The Book of Revelation!

Erik read aloud, "And I looked, and behold a pale horse; and his name that sat on him was Death."

Sophia cried out, and Erik held her, saying, "It was for your sake that I asked once more. It is settled. Now I will eat my rhubarb!"

How can he smile? How can he eat with such pleasure? What has changed? As if he had read her mind, Erik turned to look at Charlotta and said, "When they told David his son was dead, he washed and anointed himself and broke his fast. His sorrow was of no avail. Like King David, I accept God's final word."

Charlotta bunched her apron to her mouth and ran from the dining room. *God, I know I'm nothing to You, but I beg You—don't take him from us!*

***

On Monday morning, the colonists stood silently around the red house, neglecting their assigned duties in the brooding hope of catching a glimpse of Erik. Only the milking was done, and that because it would be a cruelty to the beasts to deny them relief.

When Richard Mascall, one of their American neighbors, drove up in his wagon, he was puzzled by the silent crowd. "What's all this about?"

"Why are *you* here?" Jonas Olsson asked with such suspicion that Mascall was taken aback.

"I looked at the docket at the Cambridge courthouse and

saw a whole string of cases about your finances set for today.
I have some business of my own in Cambridge, so I
thought—"

"We might as well be company for each other and spare
one horse," Erik said. He had come from the red house unnoticed while they all concentrated on Mascall. Sophia came after him, one hand out-stretched, and before he climbed to the
seat beside Mascall, Erik turned and kissed her, holding her
for a long moment.

"Don't go!" she cried.

"I must defend our interests." He settled himself and smiled
down at her, then turned to the driver. "Well, Mr. Mascall,
will you stop the bullet for me today?"

Mascall looked blank, then laughed and said, "It takes me
awhile to figure out when you folks are joking."

As the wagon drove away, Charlotta hurried to Sophia and
guided her back into the house. Sophia staggered, bent over
as if she had received a body blow, but Erik's children were
in the kitchen, and at the sight of them, she took possession
of herself.

"Mathilde, the water crock is nearly empty. Will you please
go to the well for me? Erik, your father left word that you
were to join the corn-planting crew."

When they had gone, Sophia beat her fists on the table and
cried, "He has given up his life! I can't bear it!"

Charlotta tried to find words of comfort, but there were
none — especially not from her, the wife of John Root. The
crowd outside the red house had dispersed, and the day was
as quiet as Good Friday. She stared at the calendar on the
wall. Monday, not Friday. Monday, May 13, 1850.

Charlotta stayed with Sophia all day, saying little but offering her presence. At dusk, Richard Mascall stopped his
wagon outside the red house. He seemed to be alone. Turning
his battered hat in his hands, he came to the door and said,

"Mrs. Jansson, how can I tell you?" He pointed mutely toward the wagon.

Sophia brushed past him to run down the path. After she leaned forward to look into the wagon, she stepped back, standing very straight. Charlotta wanted to run and hide, but she forced herself to approach.

"This is what I had so feared." Sophia said, "How did it happen, Mr. Mascall?"

"John Root shot him, Ma'am, shot an unarmed man in cold blood!"

Charlotta was seized by a dizzying blackness and whirled into merciful nothingness.

***

Erik's body, still dressed in the blood-stained coat, was placed on a simple table before the pulpit in the church, and the people filed past in unbelieving sorrow.

The woman who had been Maja-Stina's housemaid in Sweden knelt at the table, holding up the line as she sobbed violently and cried, "He will rise again! After three days he will rise again like Our Lord!"

Others took up the cry, and soon the church echoed with the expectation of Erik Jansson's resurrection. From her place in the long line in the outside aisle, Charlotta could see Erik, and it seemed that his dead face moved slightly, stirring with breath. She blinked her eyes and tightened her hands on the stems of the prairie flowers she had brought in tribute. Andrew Berglund stood close to her, sorrowful but calm, and she asked him, "Could it be true? Will he rise again?"

"In time, we all shall rise."

***

At noon on the third day the sanctuary was filled, but as the sun moved toward the western horizon and the body of Erik Jansson remained motionless, some went away, disillusioned and hopeless. Others remained to watch and pray. When the shadows grew long, Andrew Berglund quietly told Gilliam the carpenter to prepare a coffin.

Charlotta left the church, numb with grief. She hadn't really expected Erik to rise from the dead, but she had allowed herself to hope that it might be. He had performed other miracles, hadn't he?

Little John was fretful. Young as he was, he was disturbed by the heavy grief around him. She went back to her room in Big Brick and rocked him, crying above his head until no more tears would come. Then she opened the drawer where she kept the Mexican shawl John Root had given her and methodically cut it to bits. She broke the chain of the tiny gold cross as she tore it from her neck, but she couldn't bring herself to destroy the cross itself. "Oh my Lord Jesus," she moaned, "how can I live?"

Lying in his simple, wooden coffin, Erik seemed to be at peace. Had the women so deft at laying out the dead achieved that expression, or had he really defied the violence that took his life with a slight smile?

Every pew in the church was filled, and people stood in the aisles. The American neighbors were there — also strangers who were merely curious about the man murdered at the courthouse. One of the strangers sat in the pew where John Root had awaited his wedding vows. He had come early to get a good seat and looked to be a miserable specimen, but Charlotta gave vent to the bitter thought that she would have done better to marry that man than to twine her life with John Root's.

Her heart ached for young Erik, who tried to be manly in his grief and do what he could to comfort Sophia and his sister. Erik had left a written order that his son was to take his place as soon as he reached his maturity. Until then, their leader would be a guardian appointed by Sophia.

After the eulogies by colonists and Americans, Andrew Berglund preached the funeral sermon. Charlotta scarcely heard what he said, and she only knew that he had finished when Sophia stepped forward to place her hand on Berglund's bowed head, naming him young Erik's guardian.

The final hymn was sung by subdued voices, Berglund offered prayer and the coffin was closed. Six colony men carried it from the church to the waiting funeral wagon to be drawn by horses with pine branches twined in their bridles.

As Charlotta followed the slow procession to the cemetery on the eastern hill, she kept her eyes on the garlands of pine that made the horses flick their ears. The pine spoke of death. At last she believed this. She was Erik's Little Pine Tree, and her bridal crown of pine pointed to his death. She bent forward, biting her lips to stifle a moan, and little John wailed dismally in her arms.

The grave diggers had done their work, leaving a mound of rich, Illinois soil to cover the coffin which the men lowered on ropes without the slightest jar. When Sophia dropped the first moist clod on the wooden lid, Charlotta shuddered at the sound which she dreaded above all others, and then Sophia said, "Peace to his dust!"

For a long moment, the people stood motionless. No one wanted to be the first to go. At length, Berglund raised his hands in benediction and dismissal, but Charlotta stayed, staring at the mound of earth and the simple cross. Sunlight had a special sadness at three o'clock in the afternoon. It said that morning was gone and night was coming. She whispered the words of Arndt, "There is nothing which we should distrust so consistently as love." Erik had condemned Arndt, but the man's words held a somber truth. Holding the baby away from her body to spare him a jolt, she fell to her knees in despair. *If God is love and we must distrust love, then we have nothing!*

Little John grasped a wisp of her hair torn from its braid on the windy hill. He tugged with incredible baby strength, and Charlotta gasped with pain. *In love there is pain—God so loved the world—.* Illumined, she rose slowly. *God moves a baby's hand to speak to me!*

"Good-bye, Erik," she murmured and went to her mother's grave to lay a loving hand on the sun-warmed earth. "I'm free, Mamma, free to listen to God in my own way! Now there is no one in between!"

As she walked down the hill to the village, she felt so close to her father that she spoke to him, too, "Pappa, in less than a week, your *flicka* will be twenty-six years high—ready to take her life in both hands! Oh Pappa, I will think and feel and believe what my own heart tells me is right, God helping me! And I can make this child into a man because I remember you!"

When she reached Big Brick, the sun had lowered slightly and its light seemed less sad. The colors of sunset would soon appear, then stars and a new dawn.

Philadelphia, June, 1850—

Robert Baird moved about the bedroom in a strange kind of dance, trying to keep out of Fermine's way while she packed for their journey to New York. She even smoothed and folded garments with elegance, and he loved to watch, but he knew that he was a hindrance.

"I'll check the post while you finish here." he said.

Fermine gave him a grateful smile and blew a kiss. "Just don't start answering letters, or we'll never get away!"

Henry Martyn's graduation from the University of the City of New York was the reason for their journey, and Fermine was as excited about it as a young girl. She had a new gown and bonnet to wear to the exercises, and Baird had told her she looked far too fetching in them to be the mother of a college graduate. He himself had a new cravat and waistcoat so that Henry need not be ashamed of his father. How proud they were of him! Henry had done well in his studies, and while he had not indicated what his life work would be, they were content to let him pray and ponder until he was sure.

The packet of mail was slender, which would please Fermine. Baird carried it to the hall table for sorting and was glad to find nothing that would require his attention until their return. After all, it was summer. Then he discovered that two envelopes were stuck together with melted sealing wax, and the hidden letter was from Ithamar Pillsbury.

"My dear Robert, Knowing your interest in the Swedish colony at Bishop Hill, I feel obliged to give you shocking news. I was in Cambridge attending to some business matters in the county courthouse on May 13th, and I witnessed the murder of Erik Jansson, the leader of the Swedish community."

"Fermine!" Baird shouted.

She came quickly, alarmed by his tone. "What is it, Robert?"

"Jansson of Bishop Hill has been killed—murdered—" he reached out to take her hand, releasing the unthinking pressure when she winced at the bite of the gold ring, "Sorry, my love—I'm distressed—and thoughtless. Ithamar writes, 'The court had just recessed before the noon meal, and since my lawyer also handles the legal affairs of the colony, I was waiting outside the courtroom to speak with him when he had finished his business with Jansson. We were on the second floor, and Jansson and the lawyer were talking beside an open win-

dow when a man's voice shouted, 'Will you give me my wife?'
Jansson leaned out of the window and said, 'I will give you a
sow! That is a wife good enough for you!' Then he returned
to his conversation with the lawyer.

"The next thing I knew, a dark-haired man who was clearly
furious (and with reason, I'd say), took the stairs three at a
time and shouted Jansson's name. Jansson turned, and there
was a shot. I heard the gun before I saw it.

"Jansson fell with the first shot, but his assailant fired
again and stood over him for the five minutes it took him to
die. When anyone tried to approach to help, he threatened
them with the gun, and he was smiling the whole time. I have
never seen such a smile before, thank God! When he was sure
Jansson was dead, he kicked the body and threw down the
gun. By this time, the sheriff and his men were on the scene,
and they took him without a struggle.

"The killer, I have learned, is a man named John Root, the
Swedish-born husband of Jansson's ward. He wanted his wife
to live with him outside of Bishop Hill, and Jansson would
not give her up to him. They had had trouble about this
before, apparently.

"It was so strange, Robert. Jansson turned to face that
gun as if he expected it, desired it. I believe he deliberately
provoked the man."

"Come, Robert," Fermine said gently, "let me make you
some tea."

He allowed himself to be led to the kitchen, shaking his
head. The words of the Westminster Confession came to him:
God is incomprehensible, Almighty, Most Wise, Most Holy,
Most Free, Most Absolute, working all things according to
the counsel of His own immutable and most righteous will,
for His own glory—most terrible and just in His judgements.

"Fermine, who but Jansson could have brought so many
Swedes to America? He burned books, he glorified himself, he

made slaves of his people—but God used him mightily, and now his job is done."

"Yes, Robert, I know you've always said that it's impossible to kill someone who has not finished the work God requires."

The teakettle whistled, and at the same time the doorbell rang. Fermine attended to the kettle while Baird answered the door.

It was a telegram, and Baird took the communication, awed by the new invention that swallowed distance and more than a little apprehensive about the reason for its use.

"Can't wait to tell you—stop—have decided on ministry—stop—Love, Henry."

Bursting with wordless prayer, Baird wept with joy, not troubling to hide his emotion from the waiting messenger. *Immutable, Immense, Eternal, Incomprehensible, Almighty God!*

The University of Uppsala, August, 1850—

The professor unfolded his first copy of the New York Tribune with eager interest. The paper had been recommended to him because of its attention to literature, and while he could not read English perfectly, he could get the gist of things. After great difficulty, he had succeeded in arranging for a subscription. The news would be out of date, of course, but the book reviews were of perennial interest.

As he started to turn to the book notices, his attention was caught by a black-bordered box. On July 19, a ship had sunk off Fire Island, wherever that was, and among the victims were a writer named Margaret Fuller, her Italian husband and their infant son. The name seemed vaguely familiar. Ah yes! This must be the Margaret Fuller who said in the presence of Thomas Carlyle, "I accept the universe." Carlyle snorted, "Gad! She'd better!" He knew little more about her, but he pushed his glasses low on his nose and stared off into space, saddened by her death.

His sudden mood alarmed him because when he was lonely, he succumbed to sadness easily and remained morose for days. How quiet his rooms were in this dead late summer when all his friends were at the shore. Why hadn't he gone away to Lake Mälaren as always? His course work for the autumn was in hand, and there was nothing to keep him here. He sighed and returned to the newspaper, only to be interrupted by a knock at the door.

The caller was a young man who looked apologetic and determined at the same time. He was a handsome fellow, a perfect Swedish type, blond and blue-eyed with both strength and grace.

"Herr Professor?"

"Yes?"

"I know I should not bother you in holiday time, but I felt I had to come to you. I have a call to preach, and if I am to come to the University, I must arrange my life—I have a farm, and if you find me worthy, I will sell it and come to study here—" the words sounded well-rehearsed.

"Come in, come in! What is your name?"

"Anders Salin, Sir."

"Sit down, Anders, and tell me the nature of your call to preach."

"Well, Sir, I once worked for Erik Jansson as a hired man—do you know of him?"

"I have heard of him. He has gone to America, has he not?"

"Yes, Sir."

"Why didn't you go with him?"

"For two reasons. I loved his cousin, but he would not have that, and I'm sure he lied to her about me!"

"That is the most important reason?"

"No, Sir, but it is the reason why I got away from him while I could still think for myself. Those who were with him all the time came to believe every word he said—"

The professor smiled. "In daily existence and social intercourse, a man cannot help believing as his fellows do. It is only in philosophy that one can live with doubts."

"That's too learned for me, Sir!"

"And for me, perhaps. I was quoting David Hume. But I interrupted you, Anders. What is the second reason?"

"I thought Erik Jansson was right about some things—like the Swedish Church being an empty barrel—so I started to read my Bible and puzzle out why—"

"Did you find an answer?"

"No, Sir, just that there is one—or some. *I'm* like an empty bucket, Sir, teach me!"

Oh glorious plea! Lord, Thou art kind to thy servant Jakob! Aloud he said, "Go and sell your farm, Anders Salin, then come to me as soon as possible and I will prepare you to begin. I will tutor you! By the way, how does it happen that a man of your age owns a farm?"

"When Erik Jansson took the people to North America, they sold land cheap. I'll have to do the same now, I suppose. I can't wait for a fair price any more than they could!"

"Then go to it, and God bless you!"

When Salin had gone out, radiant with gratitude and excitement, the professor hugged himself for sheer joy. He took out his violin and played a bit of Handel in a style the composer would never allow, then he snatched up his hat and set off to do what he should have done in the first place.

The cathedral was deserted, and he sat alone but not at all lonely to contemplate the carved triptych screen of the high altar. The silver casket behind the altar held the bones of St. Erik, whose very existence had been questioned. Some believed in him and some did not. It depended upon their need to claim that ancient royalty descended from the gods. The tombs of Gustavus Vasa and his three consorts represented real lives to all, and the professor found irony in the construction of Vasa's tomb. Four obelisks rose like bedposts from the sarcophagus of the king who gave Sweden an independent church, and did the Bible not say, "The Lord Thy God hateth an obelisk"?

Most meaningful to him was the tomb of Archbishop Jakob Ulfsson, founder of the University, a man both learned and holy. *It's harder to be both now, but one can try.* The appearance of Anders Salin had rescued him from aridity. He had Erik Jansson to thank for that, strangely enough. *Wherever you are, old fellow, I do thank you!* The lowering sun shot through a window and winked in the silver casket behind the high altar.

The professor said softly, "I would seek unto God, and unto God would I commit my cause: Which doeth great things and unsearchable; marvellous things without number! Amen."

—the end—